Heavy

Alex O.Harb

Book Cover by Zayane
Editing by Tony Hernandez
First edition 2025

ISBN 979-8-9992133-1-0 (Ebook)
ISBN 979-8-9992133-0-3 (Paperback)
ISBN 979-8-9992133-2-7 (Hardcover)

www.amazon.com/author/alexharb

PART 1: ABOVE THE STORM

Orders from Above

Commander Elara Voss watched Azoria through the UES *Pathfinder's* viewport. The ship's machinery hummed softly beneath her boots. Islands hung suspended in the atmosphere. These massive chunks of earth and rock floated thanks to the glowing blue veins of azurium, sometimes visible even from orbit. A collective, silent defiance of gravity.

"Another probe lost?" she asked, her fingers drumming a quiet rhythm on the console edge as she glanced at Wei's report.

"Fourth this month," Wei confirmed from his station. "The storm drains all energy sources it encounters."

Voss sighed. "We lose equipment. Then people. Then excuses pile up at headquarters. Just like on Venturi Prime."

Wei nodded, knowing exactly what those losses meant to her.

Below them, tiny figures launched from the highest floating islands into the thin, frigid air. The ship's optics zoomed in automatically.

"Look at them," she murmured. "Human tribal societies riding eagles. Can you imagine? Those birds must have twenty-foot wingspans."

"Humans always adapt to their environment," Wei remarked.

"And here," she continued, scanning downward, "you've got zeppelins, steam aircraft, castles, and governments that range from monarchies to democracies – all existing together. And they were all Federation citizens centuries ago. Their ability to adapt to vertical geography is extraordinary."

"Until you hit the *Storm*," Wei added, emphasizing the name and gesturing toward the hurricane that shrouded the entire planet. "We still don't know what's beneath it. Ocean? Ice? Lava?"

Voss turned back to her terminal, pulling up the mission details.

OPERATION WINDFALL

Objective: *Acquire viable quantities of azurium*
Primary Target: *Mid-altitude deposits*
Secondary Target: *High-altitude tribal sources*
Tertiary Target: *Surface mining (viability unknown)*
Intel Summary: *Electromagnetic interference increases as you approach the permanent storm:*
* *Navigable interference in tribal heights*
* *Significant disruption in mid-altitudes*
* *Severe and unpredictable near the storm*
* *Surface conditions remain unknown*

Previous expeditions (Missions Nightingale and Horizont) are presumed lost due to cascading system failures. Azurium continues to resist replication and deteriorates quickly in lab conditions.

Note: *Prior missions experienced escalating system malfunctions due to EM interference. Orbital position must be maintained. Unauthorized settlers and descendants of lost crews have been confirmed.*

Admiral Harold Kane

Voss's expression hardened as she scrolled to the end of the file. A personal note from Admiral Kaine followed the official mission briefing – formal on the surface, but with enough subtext to dodge accountability.

Elara,

Trusting you to handle this complex situation. Azurium remains the absolute priority. These islands are the key, though local populations may not like it. We don't consider locals Federation citizens, since no one living there was born and registered in an official colony.

Remember Venturi Prime. We've lost teams before because emotions got in the way. Stay objective. The labs need those bulk samples urgently.

Mission success must come first, even when it's uncomfortable. Good luck.

– K.

She closed the message. The mission on Venturi Prime hadn't gone the way Kaine described. Yes, she'd refused to relocate the native population sitting on the richest mineral deposits. Yes, it reduced extraction volume. But she also avoided a humanitarian disaster and a political scandal.

Kaine had walked away with a promotion – distancing himself from the mess while claiming credit for the "moderate success." Now he was in High Command, issuing orders from behind a desk.

"Deploy the advance team," Voss said. "I want profiles on every tribal elder, president, ruler, and anyone who might still recognize Federation authority."

"And the Storm?" Wei asked, nodding toward the chaotic mass below.

Voss studied the swirling tempest. "That comes later. First, we handle the politics above the clouds. I'm not throwing lives into that thing."

She watched the shuttle descend – a tiny spark against the massive sky. How many lives would this mission cost? And would the reward be worth it?

The mineral had many names: *azurium, Rational Element, floatstone*, even *heartstone*, as the tribes called it. Whatever the term, it fascinated Federation scientists. It has anti-gravity properties, but resisted replication and degraded under lab conditions. Its purity varied by altitude, and its principles remained unpredictable. It has the potential to reshape the Federation's future – but at what cost?

She had seen this equation before. And it rarely balanced.

Azoria held its secrets close. And the Storm protected them well.

CHAPTER 1
The Heights of Courage

Toryn Skyheart adjusted his sextant for the third time. The small brass device, built from ancient designs, showed the same results it had for the past two weeks: Roost Islet was dying.

He narrowed his eyes at the horizon. Roost drifted calmly among the smaller islets of the Heights. It had real soil, a narrow mountain range, wind-stunted trees, and even a lake fed by channels that trapped moisture from passing clouds. The Windclaw Tribe had called this patch of sky home for nearly two generations – a rarity in a world where tribes usually migrated every few seasons as their islets began to fall.

But this sense of permanence, as Toryn had discovered, was ending.

He slid the sextant into his belt pouch and recorded the day's measurements in his log. The pattern was clear now. Roost had begun the subtle rising and falling, the heaving that signaled heartstone failure. The islet would dip, recover slightly, then fall farther with each cycle until gravity finally claimed it.

The process usually took decades. Toryn's data showed it had started recently and was accelerating fast.

Below the ceremonial plateau stretched a gulf of open air, ending in the distant boiling haze of the Depths. Between here and there floated a layer of larger islands, home to the people the tribes called lowlanders.

Around him, the Windclaw Tribe gathered in a wide semicircle. The men's faces were stern beneath beards strung with carved bone beads. The women wore tight braids threaded with leather cords and small heartstone fragments. Even the children fidgeted, sensing the tension.

Elder Kora, his father's sister and now his only remaining family since Ember Islet fell, stepped forward with a quiet nod. Her gray hair was tightly braided. Unlike other elders, her rank was marked by blue tattoos tracing wind currents along her forearms.

"They are ready," she said.

Chief Harrik stepped forward, his ritual scars catching the morning light. His long beard was braided into seven thick ropes, each one tipped with heartstone shards.

"Today we gather to hear Toryn's petition to join the eagle riders," Harrik announced, his voice steady. "But the trial he proposes is not the one tradition demands."

A murmur of disapproval passed through the crowd. The usual trial involved leaping from the cliff's edge, calling to an unbonded eagle to catch you. It tested bravery and fate. It also occasionally proved who was not meant to ride.

"Speak your purpose, Toryn Skyheart, son of Arvid," Harrik said, brushing a braid with his fingers.

Toryn swallowed. Innovation was not always welcome among the Windclaw, but he had no choice.

"The Roost is going to fall," he said. His voice was calm. The truth did not need decoration.

The tribe went quiet as he unrolled a hide map marked with his measurements.

"Roost has dropped nearly three feet in the past week. Each cycle is getting more violent." He paused. "At this rate, we have six months before the final descent. By the winter solstice, Roost will be gone."

Harrik showed no reaction, but his eyes flicked toward the elders. "The heart-tenders reported tremors last week. Migration plans have already begun."

Murmurs stirred again. Migration was always difficult. For a place like Roost, with permanent dwellings and eagle grounds, it bordered on impossible.

"But this isn't natural decay," Toryn said. "It began too suddenly. I believe Roost can be saved."

Elder Jormund stepped forward, his blue-stained fingers curling into fists. The tint from raw heartstone reached halfway up his arms, a sign of long service. He should have noticed the change earlier.

"How can you know this, boy?" Jormund asked. "Do you think you're wiser than those who have tended heartstones for generations?"

The contempt in his voice was familiar. Jormund had never liked Toryn, not since Arvid, Toryn's father, questioned the old ways. He never approved of Kora's guardianship, claiming Toryn lacked respect for tradition. The feeling was mutual.

"I've been tracking our position," Toryn replied, holding up his sextant. "Everything was stable for months. Then two weeks ago, it changed." He gestured toward his charts.

"I propose we find a new heart for Roost. I believe the islet beyond the Outer Chain holds what we need."

Gasps followed. The air was thick with both hope and doubt.

"I'll journey to the Outer Chain and find the Veil Islet," Toryn said, pointing to the distant horizon. "My father charted it. My calculations suggest it holds a heartstone pure enough to stabilize Roost. I'll extract a fragment and return within seven days."

"Taking from one islet to save another is rarely done," he continued. "But the Veil is uninhabited, perfectly stable, and higher than any we know. That suggests a heartstone of great purity, possibly even a seedheart. Adding a fragment to our core could give us years."

Jormund frowned. "Transferring a heartstone is possible," he said. "But it is dangerous. Islets are meant to fall. We don't take from one unless it is absolutely necessary."

"And this is not necessary?" Kora asked.

Chief Harrik nodded. "We must vote. But first, *this* is to be your trial?"

"Not a leap and a cry to the wind," Toryn said. "A journey of knowledge and resolve. If I succeed, Roost survives."

"And how do you plan to reach the Veil Islet?" Jormund asked. "Only your father claimed to see it. The path lies through the Shrieking Currents."

"No eagle can fly those winds!" someone shouted.

"Exactly," Toryn replied. "Which is why I built this."

He gestured to the glider nearby. Its frame was made of bone and stretched hide, shaped like vast wings. A whistle drifted from carved air channels as a breeze crossed the plateau.

Some in the tribe stepped closer, curious but cautious. The glider was larger and more advanced than the training ones children used. Gliders had once carried people between islets, but eagles had replaced them.

Dagmar, a skilled rider, ran a hand along a wing joint. "Impressive wingspan," he said. "But these bindings…" He pressed one gently. "The third tributary in the Currents will tear them apart."

"They'll hold," Toryn said. "It's a double weave. The tributaries blow in known patterns. My father mapped them."

"His maps are old," Jormund snapped. "Winds shift. That thing will break in midair."

Kora stepped forward. "Is it his findings you doubt, Jormund, or that he might be right?"

"We only listen to this because of your *friendship* with the chief," Jormund hissed.

Chief Harrik raised his hand. "Toryn is of age. He's shown his findings. He has the right to speak."

"Knowledge of wind and stone," Kora said. "Turned to purpose. A worthy trial."

"And if he fails?" Jormund asked. "If he falls into the Depths?"

"Then I join the winds," Toryn replied. "But if I return, Roost survives. The eagles stay. The water flows."

Harrik considered him for a long moment. "We will vote. Those in favor of the Trial of Knowing?"

Four elders raised their hands.

"Those opposed?"

Jormund and two others raised theirs.

"Four to three," Harrik said. "The trial is accepted. It begins at dawn."

As the crowd dispersed, Kora stayed with Toryn.

He stood at the edge, hands trembling. *What if Jormund was right? What if this was madness?*

Elder Haldar approached, gave him a firm nod, then walked away.

"Your father saw possibility where others saw only wind," Kora said. "He believed the impossible just needed a proper plan. Your mother would have made it happen." She smiled. "You have both of them in you."

"This isn't how Roost should end," she added. "Not like this."

"You think someone sabotaged the heartstone?" Toryn asked softly.

Kora nodded. "I can't prove it. But Roost was meant to last longer." She glanced toward the others lingering nearby.

"Then I must succeed," Toryn said.

"Bring back what Roost needs," Kora replied, resting a hand on his arm. "And watch the skies. Winds are hard to read now. And not everything that flies is an eagle."

As she left, Toryn returned to the glider. His arms strained as he adjusted a wing strut. In the distance, he spotted Jormund speaking quietly with Brevin, the lowlander trader.

Toryn caught a whisper in Trade Speech: "… expect results on the lift reduction."

Jormund pointed downward, speaking low and fast. "Make sure they know. The chain reaction breaks quickly…"

It confirmed what Toryn feared. But accusing someone without proof would waste precious time.

Dawn was near. He looked to the sky, trying to sense the winds he would soon ride. His father's maps would guide him.

But the currents ahead, he would face alone.

Somewhere beyond the Shrieking Currents, Roost's hope was waiting.

CHAPTER 2
Sky Fall

Lina Ryven swung gently back and forth, the warm breeze fluffing her short hair. The familiar creak of the old oak swing in her grandfather's yard was comforting, though one of the ropes felt uneven, making her tilt slightly to the left. Sharp pine needles tickled the back of her neck.

The squeaking swing tilted further, spoiling the idyllic picture and her mood. The needles' tickling turned annoying.

Wait... needles? On an oak?

Her eyes snapped open. The comforting yard vanished. Everything came into focus. She wasn't on a swing. She was hanging fifteen feet above the ground, swaying in the canopy of a massive pine. Her parachute straps were tangled in the branches. Through the trees, she spotted the column of black smoke marking the spot where her beautiful plane had died.

"Steam and rust," she snarled as pain flared through her ribs. "Those bastards are going to pay for this."

The fall had been rough. The ejection spring must have fired her too close to the ground, but the chute and soft canopy had saved her. Lina fumbled at her toolbelt, the familiar weight reassuring. Her folding knife sliced through one of the parachute straps. She slid down another as far as she could, then dropped the last few feet, landing with a hard thud.

She stayed down for a moment, catching her breath. Damage report: bruised ribs, aching ankle, scrapes everywhere. She pushed herself upright, then checked her goggles – still on her head, lenses intact. Her compass came out next, mercifully unbroken.

Lina glanced at the sky. Good flying weather for another four hours, maybe five. Not that it mattered. She was grounded on an unfamiliar chunk of floating rock and soil.

She headed toward the smoke. From the air, the forest had looked sparse – a gentle scattering of pines and thunder oaks. But boots on the ground told another story: a tangle of roots, rocks, and surprise ravines.

"Half a mile," she muttered, checking her compass again. "Nothing to it."

Ten minutes in, that half-mile felt like ten. The island resisted her every step. The ground dropped into a deep-sided gorge, forcing a detour that cost her more time. Vines clung to her pants. Razor briars with microscopic hooks grabbed at her legs, slowing her down. The hike became a gauntlet – everything she hated about being grounded.

When she stumbled into the briars for the fourth time, Lina's patience gave out.

"Floating plague of a worthless dirt clump," she snarled in the rough, colorful language of the workshops she grew up in. "May you sink into the deepest part of the bloody Storm."

Cursing helped. A little. Every root that tripped her, every sharp branch, every wrong step got its own insult. By the time she spotted wreckage, she had cursed the family tree and future of almost every plant she passed.

Through breaks in the canopy, larger pieces of debris came into view. Glimpses of the distinctive blue paint, now scorched and peeling. The afternoon light slanted low, shadows stretching. An hour had passed since she'd cut herself free – an hour measured in bruises and strained muscles.

She shoved through a final wall of underbrush and froze.

There it was.

Her beautiful plane – the *Swift Mistral*. Not a bulky gas-filled zeppelin like the *Empirical Advance* she'd been hired to protect, but a sleek steam-powered interceptor, lifted by a Rational Element module. Now shattered. A fifty-yard scar of broken trees and scorched earth told the story of its end. What remained was a twisted skeleton of metal and blackened debris.

"Two years… two bloody years of work." She kicked a piece of wreckage, then winced as sharp pain shot through her ankle. "Damn it."

The pain cleared her head. She took slow, even breaths.

"Calm down, pilot. At least I'm alive. And the Technocracy needs to know."

She limped toward the mangled cockpit and hissed again. "Son of a Drift Lord."

At five feet tall, Lina had always fought to be taken seriously. Every bolt she'd tightened, every joint she'd welded – she had poured her fight into that cockpit. And now the Scarlet Talon corsairs, or whoever they really were, had taken it from her.

But the attack hadn't felt like corsairs. The enemy aircraft moved too fast, too smooth. Twin engines ran too quiet. The tactics were classic ambush, but executed with cold military precision. She remembered Vera's ship exploding. Dahn's stabilizer shredded by pinpoint shots from a rapid-firing weapon.

Details clicked into place with chilling clarity. This wasn't piracy. They knew the zeppelin's route, how many escorts it had, and came prepared to take them all down.

Lina scanned the horizon, pushing grief aside. Distant islands floated to the northwest. Thunderhead clouds marked the edge of the Thunder Basin trade route. Observation Platform Seven, the nearest Technocracy outpost, lay in that direction.

"Two hundred miles at least," she muttered. "No walking that."

A short, bitter laugh escaped her lips. "Right. Suppose I'll just sprout wings."

Her gaze drifted to the largest piece of wreckage – the starboard wing, surprisingly intact. The emergency equipment compartment. Hope flickered.

Caligan pilots always carried survival kits. That meant flares.

There would be a search party. There had to be.

She popped the compartment open. The signaling kit sat snug inside – a brass flare launcher, a clockwork timer, and a chemical smoke canister. She reached for it, then froze.

A sound cut through the forest.

The whir of rotary blades.

She looked up. A small scout craft approached from the east. Traditional patchwork build. Scarlet Talon colors. Single pilot. Steam vented from the engine as it circled, wheeling along the edge of a high cloud.

Showing off.

Skilled. Or suicidal.

Lina dropped low, heart pounding. Her first instinct was to hide and wait it out. Probably just a salvager, assuming no one had survived. Easier to stay hidden.

But how long would her supplies last?

And if she lit the signal now, they'd come straight to her.

Her eyes narrowed. She studied the craft. Single pilot. One spare seat. Lightweight. Decent range. Everything she needed to escape this floating rock.

Anger sliced through the fear. Cold. Focused.

They shot her down. Killed Vera. Destroyed her plane.

Hiding meant letting them win.

And Lina Ryven didn't let anyone win.

"Well, hello there," she whispered, already planning. "Aren't you a pretty little ticket out of here?"

The scout circled again, the pilot scanning for a place to land. The crash had cleared a rough path, but nothing like a proper landing zone. Eventually, the ship banked toward the far side of the island – half a mile out, maybe.

Perfect.

They wouldn't expect company.

Lina returned to the main wreckage and reached under the seat for her burst gun. It was there. Intact. She checked the air charge – full.

She turned toward the trees, a grin creeping across her face.

"First rule of being grounded," she said to the silent forest. "Don't stay grounded longer than necessary."

CHAPTER 3
Glider's Path

Dawn on Roost Islet painted the clouds below in shades of gold and crimson. To the eagles circling their nesting grounds, it was just another day. But to Toryn, standing at the edge of the platform with his glider, it felt like the beginning of a new life.

Elder Kora approached, her gaze shifting between Toryn and the vast, waiting sky. The intricate blue tattoos mapping wind currents along her forearms seemed to shift with every breath of wind.

"The clouds speak of change today," she murmured, her eyes tracing the high, wispy formations. "The Shrieking Currents feel... temperamental."

Toryn nodded, grateful for the insight. "I've studied my father's maps. If the Westward Push is still stable, I'll catch it and reach the Crosswind Bridge by nightfall tomorrow."

Kora handed him a bundle wrapped in oiled leather. "These will help." Inside lay goggles unlike any Toryn had seen. Leather frames held lenses of heartstone, ground impossibly thin and nearly transparent. "My wind-reading goggles," Kora explained. "These reveal the currents within, especially in the highest reaches, where the air thins."

"These are yours," Toryn protested, trying to return the gift.

"You *need* them more," she interrupted, pressing the bundle firmly into his hands. "I can feel the wind without goggles."

Toryn slipped them on. His breath hitched. The world transformed. Air currents that had been invisible moments before now appeared as flowing streams of pale blue light. The Westward Push revealed itself as a broad, pulsing aerial highway cutting through the sky.

Kora then produced a small bone whistle on a leather cord.

"The eagle-call," Toryn said, recognizing the ritual instrument.

"The council approved your trial," Kora said with a slight smile. "With eagle or glider, you are granted the call either way."

"Eagles rarely answer those unbonded," Toryn said, accepting the whistle.

"True," she acknowledged, securing the cord around his neck. "But the Heights are full of exceptions. The eagles of legend are said to heed the call even from strangers – if the need is great enough." She paused, looking into the distant sky. "Prepare for all possibilities."

After a final check of his supplies, Toryn secured his pack to the glider's frame. Across the gathering area, Elder Jormund stood watching, arms folded, blue-stained fingers drumming. His disapproval wasn't loud – but it was there, sharp as wind over stone.

Chief Harrik stepped forward. "Toryn Skyheart. The tribe honors your courage. Fly safe. Fly with purpose."

Toryn raised his hands in the traditional gesture. "I fly for Roost. I fly for the Windclaw."

The response came – measured, not booming, not forced: "The winds carry you." "The Heights watch over you."

Gripping the glider's central hanging bar, Toryn inhaled deeply and ran. Four strides – and then nothing. Only sky beneath his feet. The glider plunged for a heart-stopping moment before the wind filled the wings, lifting him into flight.

While the eagles soared effortlessly, Toryn fought the air, adjusting constantly just to stay aloft. Through the goggles, the Westward Push shimmered and pulsed. As Roost Islet shrank behind him, fear gave way to something else. A sense of fragile freedom.

By midday, exhaustion dulled the thrill. The air grew thin. Each breath burned. His arms ached from correcting every gust. As the sun dipped low, he spotted a small islet below. A chance to rest.

The landing was rough. His legs trembled on contact with solid ground. His father's maps showed he'd made good time, nearly halfway to the Crosswind Bridge. That night, he slept in short bursts, curled beside the glider as wind howled and cold bit deep.

At first light, he launched again. Day two felt harder. His body ached everywhere. The air gave nothing. Through the goggles, he spotted faint ripples in the Westward Push. Signs of coming change. By midafternoon, the ripples turned to clouds: purple, heavy, and fast-moving. He spotted another islet and dove for it as the storm hit.

Crosswinds slammed the glider. A sharp gust caught the wing just as he touched down, sending it skidding. Sheltered under an overhang, Toryn inspected the damage. A hairline crack in a strut.

It would hold. Hopefully.

He tightened it with a spare belt and slept beneath the glider as it creaked in the wind.

By morning, the storm had passed. The air felt colder but clearer. The glider held together. Each gust made him wince, but it flew.

By midday, he saw them: the signature clouds of the Crosswind Bridge. On either side, the Shrieking Currents rose like walls of spinning blue. The path between them narrowed to fifty feet in places.

He entered the Bridge, and the Westward Push broke apart. Smooth air turned chaotic. Updrafts, shearwinds – everything became unpredictable. The passage climbed steeply. Cold bit through his layers. Frost formed on the glider's edges. The bone frame groaned. The membranes stiffened.

Kora's goggles helped, but they couldn't show everything. One sudden shear slammed into him. The glider spun violently toward the eastern current wall. Toryn fought for control. The patched strut on the left wing cracked under pressure. The leather snapped, and the wing bent inward. Badly shaken, but still holding.

Wind tore past him. His vision blurred. Up, down, all the same.

Then: a shape in the clouds. An eagle, climbing through the chaos.

In a burst of instinct, Toryn reached for the whistle. One clear note cut into the storm.

The eagle met his eyes, then turned and began weaving through the currents – guiding him, not just flying ahead. Toryn followed, barely holding steady. As he mimicked the eagle's path, something shifted. He began to feel the air again. The goggles showed part of the pattern, but now he trusted more than just the lenses.

The eagle rose higher, and Toryn stayed on its tail. When they broke above the topmost cloud layer, light exploded around him. Thin, sharp, and silver.

There it was. Veil Islet.

Floating higher than any other. Wrapped in silence. Glistening with ice and snow.

The eagle circled once, then turned east and vanished.

"Thank you," Toryn whispered.

The broken strut made the glider respond sluggishly, demanding all of Toryn's focus and strength just to keep it afloat. He wrestled it toward Veil Islet, aiming for the nearest edge. He glanced at the approaching land, icy, untouched, impossibly high. The wind screamed around him.

What if the legends were wrong? What if there was no seedheart, just another slab of frozen stone?

He gritted his teeth and clung to the glider's frame. It was too late to turn back. Too late for doubt.

He came in too steep. The glider skipped once, caught a ridge, and crashed – Toryn tumbled hard across the ice. The world spun a few more times and then went still.

Toryn lay on his back, staring up at the sky. Every muscle burned.

I made it. Alive, barely. The glider's wrecked – but I reached Veil Islet.

The islet held a stark, alien beauty. Ice and snow blanketed everything – harsh, windswept, and silent. Openings in the ice revealed deep caves. From the closest, warmth pulsed faintly, a strange contrast to the frozen world above. His glider lay nearby, a tangle of broken bones. The journey back was already a problem for another day. And somewhere within those frozen tunnels, the seedheart awaited.

But for now, all he could think of was rest.

CHAPTER 4
Unwilling Guide

"For the last time, I had nothing to do with the attack," the corsair said, shifting uncomfortably against the tree where Lina had bound him. "I wasn't part of the wing that hit you."

"Stop playing word games," Lina snapped, rifling through his pack. "People are dead. I saw Scarlet Talon colors clear as day while your people blasted my flight out of the sky. You're one of them. So either you're lying… or *lying*."

They'd been having this argument for over an hour, ever since she'd surprised him near the crash site where he was checking the damage. The corsair – Kip, as he'd reluctantly offered – clung to his story with stubborn persistence. He claimed he'd paid an informer for a raid tip and showed up for salvage. But he still wore Scarlet Talon colors. Still the enemy.

Her fingers brushed something unexpected: a finely tooled leather map case. Too refined for a scavenger. She pulled it out. Kip's expression tightened.

"Nice salvage," she said, opening it. Inside were detailed navigation charts – Drift Lord territory. "Military-grade. Not your average corsair junk. Planning something?"

"I have wide interests," Kip replied, voice even, eyes locked on the case.

"Clearly." Lina tucked it back in his pack.

"Now that you're done looting," Kip said, "mind telling me your game? If it's ransom, don't bother – I'm not worth much."

The shift in his tone was small, but Lina caught it.

"Not ransom," she replied. "I need information. Transport. And for you to stop pretending you're just some unlucky salvager."

Kip managed a thin smile. "Blunt, at least."

Lina surveyed the clearing. Her *Swift Mistral* was totaled half a mile away. Kip's scout craft, however, was mostly intact – aside from the engine, which had ripped loose and now lay in a coolant puddle nearby. If she could fix it, it was her best shot off this island.

"Your bird's a wreck," she said, grabbing her tool bag. "Did you land it or throw it?"

"It was a controlled landing," Kip replied defensively. "The terrain was uneven."

Lina kicked the detached engine. "Engines don't just fall off in controlled landings."

She spent hours trying to reattach it, rerouting a few hoses and hammering a coupler into place. When she hit the ignition, it wheezed, clunked, and died.

"Dead regulators. Half your parts are rusted solid."

"Captain Marek schedules regular maintenance," Kip said stiffly, still tied to a tree.

"Well, his schedule almost got you killed."

Lina rearranged her tools. "We need parts. There are at least two more wrecks on this island."

"*We?*" Kip raised a brow. "Are we partners now?"

"Simple math," Lina said. "I need to reach the Technocracy to report the attack. You need to not die on this rock. I can fix and fly your scout, but I need someone to haul parts. So, yes. We."

Kip considered that. "And if I'm hauling parts and helping get airborne, I expect more than barked orders."

Lina looked up. "You want a raise, corsair?"

"I want a voice."

She thought for a moment. "Fine. Help with the repairs, get a say. But if we disagree mid-flight, I hold the controls."

Kip nodded slowly. "And you won't just dump me afterward?"

"No guarantees," Lina said cheerfully. "But uncertain survival beats certain death. Your choice."

A dark cloud drifted across the sun. Kip looked up, studying it for a long moment, then nodded. "Hard to argue with that. I accept the… temporary arrangement."

"It's not employment," Lina added, cutting his bonds but keeping the burst gun close. "More like indentured servitude."

Kip muttered something under his breath, rubbing his wrists as he stood. He was lean, straight-backed – not the brute type she expected.

"I don't trust you. You don't trust me. But we're screwed without each other," she said. "And just so you know – I sleep with my gun close. Questions?"

"Just one," Kip said. "What exactly are we getting from your wreck?"

"Pressure regulators. Stabilizer assemblies. Maybe an intact fuel pump. But first, we check for my wingmate Vera. She went down nearby."

That night, they didn't speak much. Lina slept light, curled on the grass with her burst gun across her chest. Kip didn't try anything – but she didn't stop watching him either.

———

They spent the morning following signs of Vera's crash – snapped branches, scorched leaves, and the faint trace of smoke.

By midday, they reached a clearing where the wreckage lay scattered but recognizable. Inside the ruined cockpit, Vera remained strapped in – still, unmistakably dead.

Lina stood at the edge of the cockpit, frozen in place as she stared at her wingmate's body. Small, clean holes punctured the reinforced hull around the pilot's seat – traces of a rotary weapons' salvo. Vera's face was peaceful, almost serene, but her flight suit was stained dark where the rounds had found their mark.

"They didn't just bring her down," Lina murmured. "They made sure she was dead before the crash."

She reached with trembling fingers to close Vera's eyes, then carefully removed the ID tags from around her neck. The metal discs felt unnaturally cold against her palm.

"Didn't know her long," Lina said quietly, placing the tags on a small mound of rocks. "But she didn't deserve this."

"Few deserve their fate," Kip said softly.

"Right, let's work," Lina muttered, turning back toward the wreck.

"These weren't normal corsair weapons," Kip observed, examining the holes. "I've never seen projectiles leave marks like this."

"Are they keeping secrets from their own clanmates?" she asked with a frown.

"I've been with the Talons for nearly three years. Just a solo salvager, lowest rank. They never trusted me much."

They worked efficiently, stripping pipes, regulators, and stabilizer assemblies – all in better condition than the corroded junk on Kip's scout.

"We'll need one more thing," Lina said finally. "A custom Rational Element module from my bird. Built it myself. Reinforced housing, designed to survive almost anything. Without it, this hybrid mess won't stay stable."

"Your wreck got anything worth salvaging?" Kip asked skeptically.

"Reinforced housing," Lina repeated, emphasizing the word. "That compartment should be intact. If we're lucky."

The trek to Lina's crash site underscored the violence of her impact. The *Swift Mistral* lay scattered across fifty yards, silver plates tangled with splintered trees.

"Impressive you walked away from this," Kip remarked, surveying the destruction.

"Custom ejection system," she muttered with a wince. "Wasn't supposed to be tested that way."

"You seem overqualified for escort pilot work," he eventually commented as she worked.

"And you seem overqualified for petty piracy," Lina shot back, the panel finally groaning open. "Almost like you've had real schooling. Nobleman slumming with corsairs? That would explain why they never trusted you."

A flicker of something – annoyance? Resignation? – crossed Kip's face. "The skies are full of surprising people."

"Indeed." Lina reached into the compartment. "Got it!" She carefully extracted the module. It was a complex lattice around a Rational Element core, encased in a durable alloy she had sourced specifically for this. "This beauty let the *Mistral* dance around birds twice her size."

Kip studied it with genuine appreciation. "Remarkable craftsmanship."

"It's one of a kind," Lina said quietly, a flicker of professional pride breaking through her focus. "Would be a crime to leave it here."

―――――

Twilight fell across the island, bringing with it a cool breeze. Alchemical lamps cast a steady glow over Kip's scout as Lina disassembled it with methodical precision.

"Need to work through," she announced, tossing a rusted bolt aside. "Want to leave by morning."

"Thought you needed daylight?" Kip asked.

"That was before I saw Vera," Lina said grimly. "The Technocracy needs to know about the incident – and those weapons. And those double-engine planes are nothing like anything I've seen before."

Kip studied her, then nodded. "Sensible. What do you want me to do?"

The hours slipped by in a blur. To her surprise, Kip turned out to be almost helpful. His grasp of mechanical systems was solid. He seemed educated in condensation and pressure dynamics – his knowledge more academic than practical.

"That connection creates pressure feedback," he suggested as Lina connected a regulator.

"In standard systems, yes," she agreed. "But I modified the intake manifold. It balances across the tertiary valves."

"Against classical principles," Kip muttered, then seemed to catch himself. "Or so the shop talk goes, anyway."

Lina set down her tools. "Interesting shop talk. Almost sounds like Halliburton's *Principles of Steam Dynamics*."

Wariness flickered in Kip's eyes. "People leave interesting documents behind. Corsairs find all sorts of salvage."

"Why should a common salvager read *Principles*?" Lina raised an eyebrow.

"Define common. You imagine things," Kip deflected.

"I observe things," Lina corrected. "Like someone playing a role. Why? What's a well-educated Drift Lord noble doing flying with Scarlet Talon?"

"You presume—"

"Do I?" Lina crossed her arms. "Those military maps focus on House Saroven territories now under Lord Blackwell. You flinched when I mentioned Platform 7, which has significant ties to Blackwell family business. And the mail in your pack shows that corsairs call you *Lordling*. You're not a true believer in their cause. You're using them, just as they're using you. Adding up, isn't it?"

Kip was silent for a long moment, the tension thick enough to cut with a knife. He seemed to be weighing his options. Then he sighed. A faint, wry smile touched his lips. "Impressive," he said quietly. "So, I have a complicated past and ambitions for the future. Is that a problem?"

"Depends," Lina replied, wiping grease off her hands. "Is Kip Saroven more useful than a random corsair?"

He flinched slightly at the name. "And what defines useful?"

"Right now? Help me lift this assembly and tighten these bolts," Lina said. "Later? We'll see."

Kip considered, then inclined his head. "When the Saroven lands were taken," he said quietly, "the corsairs were all I had. They don't care about your past – just what you can do." He smiled thinly. "The nickname stuck, but I earned my place." He met her gaze. "I fly their colors, but I have my own agenda."

Lina regarded him. Not a true corsair, just someone using whatever he could to survive. Still dangerous, but not in the way she'd assumed.

"You're right about Platform 7," Kip continued. "It's unsafe for me. Blackwell has eyes and ears there."

"Then we don't go to 7," Lina decided immediately. "Meridian Station. Further, but under direct Technocracy jurisdiction."

"Meridian is a three-day flight, assuming this holds together," Kip pointed out.

Lina shrugged. "My priority is reporting the attack. Getting caught in Blackwell's politics won't help."

"A refreshingly clear-headed approach," Kip said, his smile seeming almost genuine this time. "Very well. Meridian it is."

———

By dawn, the scout craft looked less like a proper flying machine and more like a mechanic's nightmare held together with sheer willpower. Mismatched components jutted out, hull plating patched with scarred blue and silver panels from the *Mistral*. The condensation system, a hybrid marvel of Lina's design, wound copper tubing around the engine core to trap every bit of precious steam. Despite its odd appearance, it looked airworthy.

"Needs a name," Lina declared during final checks. "Flying an unnamed bird is bad luck."

"Scout crafts are usually unnamed," Kip noted. "Expendable."

"Not this one," Lina stated firmly. "It's our way out." She eyed the ungainly vessel. "The *Noble Steed*. Seems fitting."

Kip choked back a laugh. "Subtle."

"Not my strong suit, *Lordling*," Lina admitted, climbing into the pilot's seat. "Ready?"

"As we'll get without sleep and on a hybrid of a plane," Kip replied, taking the passenger seat.

"For what it's worth," she said, initiating the start-up sequence, "your secret is safe until Meridian. After that, no promises."

"Duly noted."

The *Noble Steed* shuddered to life, steam pressure building.

"Preflight complete," Lina announced. "Taking off."

The craft rose with surprising grace, lifting above the island and leaving behind two wrecks and a small grave. For hours, they flew through calm skies. The patchwork machine performed better than expected. Its systems hummed steadily – a soothing sound that reassured Lina everything would be fine. She watched the gauges, making small adjustments, while Kip kept an eye on their course and scanned the skies.

"Good time," Lina observed, checking the velocity. "We should reach Meridian even faster than planned."

"If the weather holds," Kip added, studying the distant clouds.

"The Storm below seems less stable," he noted, his voice carefully neutral. "And looking at those cumulus layers, it's causing more disruptions up here."

"Know your weather, don't you?" Lina said conversationally. "Most people trying to hide their background would be more careful about showing off their fancy education."

"Most people aren't navigating a patchwork flying junk heap while practically being a prisoner," Kip retorted.

"You bet," Lina conceded. "Heading set for Haven Drift. It's neutral. We'll refuel and stay there overnight. ETA is six hours, barring obstacles."

"Speaking of which – there's a storm building to the west that wasn't there minutes ago."

Lina looked. Her stomach plummeted. The clear sky was now a rapidly darkening, swirling wall of clouds – unlike any normal storm formation. It wasn't building like a typical thunderhead – it was expanding like ink, cutting off their escape routes one by one.

Lina pushed the engines, gauges climbing into the yellow. "Can't outrun it," she stated grimly. She checked the water gauge – still three-quarters full, thankfully.

The storm slammed into the *Noble Steed*. It shuddered, wind tearing at the makeshift repairs. The viewport became a churning vortex of black, lit by strobing internal flashes. Instruments went wild, spinning uselessly in the surrounding chaos. Only the Rational Element altimeter gave reliable readings.

"Hold her steady!" Kip yelled over the roar.

"I know how to fly in a storm!" Lina shouted, wrestling the controls.

"You're going to kill us!" Kip bellowed, bracing himself as the craft lurched sideways again. "This isn't flying – it's dancing in a coffin through a cloud!"

"Then shut up and let me steer the damn coffin!" she snapped, arms straining against the control column.

The *Noble Steed* bucked again, wind screaming around them. Kip swore under his breath, clutching a pipe that rattled ominously behind his shoulder. "This is madness!"

For minutes that felt like hours, they battled the maelstrom. The hull groaned, welds straining. A savage gust slammed the port side, nearly rolling them, but Lina wrestled the bird back. Then, abruptly, they punched through into an eerie calm.

The storm's eye. Utterly silent, unnervingly still. Outside the surrounding wall of cloud, the tempest raged – but here, the air was dead calm. The wall of the eye was a mesmerizing swirl of graceful, moving cloud.

Kip exhaled shakily. "Remind me never to doubt your flying again."

Lina grinned through gritted teeth. "You are welcome."

"There's a potential exit," Kip said, pointing to a slightly less chaotic section of the boundary. "If we time it right with the rotation, we might hit a weak spot."

Lina turned back to the controls, systems humming. "Ready?" she asked, hands poised.

"As we'll ever be," Kip replied, surprisingly calm. "Shall we see what awaits?"

The *Noble Steed* surged forward, leaving the storm's eye and aiming for the turbulent wall separating them from the open sky. As they dove into the chaos, Lina felt an unexpected sense of partnership with the aristocratic corsair behind her.

Whatever came next, they would face it together.

CHAPTER 5
Seedheart

Toryn awoke to darkness, a prickling sensation creeping up his neck. Something was watching. He'd taken shelter from the bitter cold of Veil Islet's surface in a small cave, curled in a rough nest of his feather cloak. Exhaustion from three days in the Shrieking Currents had knocked him out, but now that sharp, focused presence meant one thing – he wasn't alone.

He stayed perfectly still, heartstone goggles still shielding his eyes and making the dark even darker. Through their blue tint, he saw it – a large feline shape at the mouth of the cave. A frost hunter. Not like the smaller snow cats near Roost. This one was fully grown. With excruciating slowness, Toryn inched a hand toward the knife at his belt. The creature tensed.

The creature took a step forward, then froze as a faint mechanical whine echoed from deeper within the cave system. Its ears flattened against its skull. It gave Toryn one final look, as if measuring whether he belonged here. Then it turned and padded silently into the darkness, moving away from the source of the sound.

What could disturb it more than me?

Toryn sat up cautiously, muscles screaming from yesterday's ordeal. The cave pulsed with gentle light emanating from veins of heartstone that ran through the rock like blood vessels. The air grew warmer deeper into the tunnel – a welcome contrast to the surface bite. His stomach clenched; he hadn't eaten properly since the second day of flight. From his pack, he retrieved the meager supplies and rationed out the dried meat. The familiar taste brought a flicker of comfort in this alien place. The wind and the eagle had brought him to Veil Islet as intended, but his glider would fly no more. Three days left to find the core and somehow return to Roost.

"The sky tests me," he murmured, checking his gear.

As dawn crept into the cave entrance, Toryn gathered his supplies and ventured deeper. The heartstone goggles revealed air currents even within the caves, suggesting a vast network. He heard the same mechanical hum that had disturbed the predator. It grew louder as he followed the pulsing blue veins of heartstone, the floor sloping steadily downward. The veins themselves seemed to thicken the closer he moved to the islet's center.

The path descended, and the temperature rose steadily. Life flourished here, a stark contrast to the icy surface. Near the entrance, only lichens clung to the rock, but deeper in, lush vegetation emerged. Small rodents with sleek fur scurried along the walls. Unfamiliar blue berries in crevices, consumed by tiny birds darting through the passageways. Glowing vines hung from the ceiling, their translucent leaves collecting condensation, making the air feel misty.

This warmth, this impossible life, deep within an islet floating higher than any other.

He wondered where the legend of seedhearts had come from. It spoke of a powerful heartstone core, dubbed a *living heart* in High Tongue. But no one seemed to know of this warmth, of the life it sustained. His father had mapped Veil Islet and marked its unusual position, but never actually landed here. And there were rumors of more such islets. Did all of them have the same caves and diversity?

After hours lost in the maze-like tunnels, he found himself back at a junction he had passed twice before. "This," he informed a curious furry rodent watching him from a crevice, "is why eagles do not live in caves." The rodent twitched its whiskers, perhaps in agreement.

As he passed beneath a distinctive arch of interwoven blue vines for the third time, Toryn spotted a narrow fissure behind it. Warmer air and brighter light issued from below, the blue illumination more intense here. He squeezed through.

The mechanical sounds grew louder. A machine was carving through the tunnels, also heading toward the center. Toryn trembled. It was clearly a lowlander contraption rumbling through the dark. He had no way back. His broken glider had seen to that.

The tunnel opened onto a ledge above a vast underground chamber. Toryn crouched in awe. The ceiling vanished into darkness, but the center glowed with intense blue light.

Dense vegetation filled the chamber: ferns, flowering vines, and trees. All of it thrived alongside unfamiliar species, growing together in this hidden world. Birds flitted between branches. Small mammals scurried along the floor. Insects buzzed through the warm, humid air.

At the center, a perfect sphere of pure heartstone hovered without visible support. It glowed with dim blue light. The plants closest to it formed a lattice of vegetation, cradling the core without quite touching it, like clouds riding invisible currents.

In the shade below lay the frost hunter. It stayed alert, massive paws tucked beneath its chest. From time to time, it sniffed the air or flicked its ears. *It guards the core,* Toryn realized. Whether by instinct or design, it had been placed here to protect the heart.

Regular islets floated due to heartstone veins. Each held multiple minor veins and one major deposit, the heart, usually in a chamber just beneath the surface. Toryn had expected to find a sample the size of his head, stash it in a sack, and fly home. It wouldn't be enough to save the Roost, but they could send an expedition for more.

But this was nothing like what he had read. It was truly a *seedheart*, a perfect sphere four feet wide, far too large to move and with no smaller fragments nearby. Then the full reality of his mission struck him. He would have to break it. Shatter the heart into pieces.

It's not about harvesting a resource anymore. It's about killing a world.

As he absorbed this revelation, the frost hunter's ears suddenly pricked forward. It rose to a crouch, a low growl building in its throat. The mechanical sounds Toryn had heard earlier now echoed loudly from a larger tunnel on the far side of the chamber. The hunter slipped into the shadows of a nearby alcove, blending perfectly with the stone.

A mechanical device resembling a huge mole emerged from the tunnel mouth, its cylindrical body tapering to a spinning drill head. It had come to a halt at the chamber's edge, and a side panel slid open with a hiss.

Three figures disembarked, wearing gray-green suits with an abundance of pockets and strange single-eyed goggles strapped over their left eyes. They carried devices made of refined metal and spoke in a language that sounded alien, yet close enough to Trade Speech to catch its rhythm.

"Blue-shift readings off the scale," said the leader, consulting a handheld device.

Blue-shift? What could that possibly mean? The color of the heartstone?

The second figure scanned the core with a handheld tool that emitted a thin beam of light. "Perfect mineral core. No degradation signature. No impurities detected."

Meanwhile, the third figure – a woman – examined the vines and the cradle they formed with open fascination.

The leader activated a complex device that unfolded from his backpack, metal petals spreading into a ring around the sphere. Small animals darted defensively toward the intruders, sensing the threat to their world.

Then, from a shadowed alcove, the frost hunter burst into view. It launched itself at the woman, slamming her onto her back.

From his hiding place on the ledge, Toryn watched the chaos unfold below. The woman screamed, struggling against the creature as it reached for her throat. She punched it several times in the head, and the animal roared and stepped back. Then its jaws clamped around her leg.

"Get this thing off me!" she cried out.

In a swift motion, the hunter dragged her into a side passage, clearly avoiding a direct fight with all three intruders at once.

"Nora!" the second man shouted, unclipping a long metallic device from his belt. He rushed forward, but the predator had already vanished into the darkness with its prey.

Toryn's chest pounded. He pressed himself flat against the stone, sweat beading on his brow despite the warmth.

The second outlander swept his flashlight across the nearby passages, searching frantically. "Beta team, Mission Control! Nora has been taken by a local predator. Pursuing the target!"

The leader paused the extraction. "Markus, stop! You can't go alone!"

A voice emerged from the leader's chest radio. "Mission Control, Beta team, status on the primary objective?"

"Extraction in progress," the leader reported to his eyepiece. "But we need to–"

"Lieutenant Reed," Mission Control interrupted, the tone firm. "The moment you landed, something began affecting the weather. A spike in the Storm is forming several miles high, directly beneath the island. Electromagnetic interference is rising. Your equipment will lose power in less than thirty minutes. And all sensor readings went haywire the moment extraction began. You barely have time to complete the objective. Sergeant Hertzig's video feed and sensors went offline immediately – we can't track her. Search and rescue would exceed the safe window. Complete the primary objective. Evacuate. We'll dispatch recovery if conditions allow."

The second outlander stared into the dark crevice, his hand tightening around his weapon. "But Nora is out there…"

"And she would follow orders," the leader said. "We finish the mission. We request recovery."

"If this island falls–" Markus began.

"And if we all die trying to find her, no one comes back," the leader cut him off. "We need to finish the extraction."

Reluctantly, Markus turned back as the vehicle's articulated claws closed around the sphere. The seedheart's pulse faltered. A wrongness settled in Toryn's gut, as if the very air had soured. A deep tremor shook the cavern. Dust rained down. The chamber's glow flickered and dimmed.

Securing the core in a transport compartment, the two outlanders hurried back to the vehicle.

"We'll come back, Nora," Markus whispered to the crevice as the leader activated the machine's systems. "I promise."

The drill head spun to life, and the vehicle disappeared, taking the seedheart with it.

Toryn pressed his face to the stone ledge, breath ragged. Below, the vegetation withered. The unease spread through his chest. Around him, small creatures fled into the tunnels with frantic squeaks and chittering calls.

Veil Islet was dying. The vines dimmed. The islet shivered beneath him. The memory of his parents – lost when Ember Islet fell – clawed at his throat. That same helpless fall. That same unstoppable drop.

Just like them. Just like Mother and Father, falling into the Depths.

It was time to leave.

He scrambled back through the tunnels, guided by his markings and the upward-flowing air currents. When he finally burst onto the surface, he was soaked in sweat. The destabilization was accelerating faster than the outlanders had anticipated.

Then he felt the sudden drop. The islet had held some lift after the core's removal, but now it had begun its fall toward the Storm below.

He stumbled to the edge, cold wind whipping through his hair. His trial had failed. He would not return with a fragment to save Roost. But the tribe had to know what happened – about the living systems inside the seedheart islets. And about the outlanders.

If they had come for Veil Islet's core, what would stop them from seeking others? Roost's heartstone wasn't a seedheart, but it might still interest these invaders.

He had to survive.

He had to warn the tribe.

Above, the intruders' vessel retracted its platform and climbed fast, vanishing into the open sky. Below, the Storm churned, rising fast. Larger animals rushed from the caves, also searching for escape. There were none. His glider was ruined. The air howled with turbulence.

Toryn fumbled for the eagle-call whistle, raised it to his lips, and blew a long, sharp note. He remembered the ritual: cloak raised high, words shouted into the wind. "Heights to heights, winds to winds, I call to those who ride between!"

Nothing.

He tried again, adjusting his stance awkwardly, feeling foolish as the world crumbled around him. "Feathers… follow… flight!" Still nothing but the roar of wind and the groaning rock.

Desperate, he blew once more, shouting the first line with all his strength before trailing off. "Feathers… oh, just *come!*"

A dark shape appeared high above – the massive, blue-black eagle. It circled once, then dropped into a controlled dive.

Toryn froze mid-shout, cloak dangling in the wind. The eagle let out a piercing cry and streaked toward him.

The Storm raged only a few thousand feet below. Toryn ran to the edge. As the eagle shot past, he leaped. The islet lurched violently beneath him. Air ripped the feather cloak from his grasp, and his precious goggles flew off. He slammed onto the eagle's back, far too rearward, his fingers desperately clutching at the thick feathers as he struggled to find a secure hold. For several terrifying seconds, he slid toward the tail before managing to grip the dense plumage tightly enough to halt his fall.

The eagle banked sharply, veering away from Veil Islet as it fell toward the Storm. The landing had knocked the air from Toryn's lungs, and sharp pain stabbed through his ribs. "Do not... drop me...," he gasped, his vision swimming.

The bird seemed to understand, leveling slightly.

Three days of grueling flight to reach Veil Islet, the shock of his discoveries, and now the bruising impact of his desperate leap – it was too much. Exhaustion crept in at the edges of his vision, finally overwhelming him. The last thing he saw before blackness claimed him was a vast, circular opening in the Storm below, where the islet fell. He couldn't process what it meant – barely registered it. His final realization was that the eagle was following the islet's path in a wide spiral.

The fate of Roost Islet – and perhaps all islets – was now tied to forces beyond his grasp. And somehow, he had landed directly in their path.

CHAPTER 6
Storm's Edge

Their attempt to break through the storm wall had failed. Spectacularly.

What had looked like a weak spot had clamped shut like a trap the moment they neared it. Three more tries, three more failures. Each potential escape route sealed itself off.

Six hours later, still trapped in the storm's strange calm, Lina Ryven was so tired that even blinking felt like work. Her hands were practically fused to the *Noble Steed's* control column, her knuckles white and unresponsive. The situation had escalated from challenging to dire – they were trapped.

Cloud walls loomed on all sides with no visible top. The Storm churned below them. It had always been the impassable barrier, the floor of their world – now it felt more like a living entity, reaching upward.

Lina frowned at the cloud formations beneath them. "That's the second time I've seen that happen here," she muttered.

Kip followed her gaze. "The vortices? Yes, most peculiar."

"It's like the eye… is expanding," Lina said. "No natural weather pattern does that. It's like being inside a zeppelin's balloon."

The fuel gauge was dipping low, and the engine whined under the constant strain. Another attempt to breach the wall felt impossible. "We're trapped," Lina finally admitted into the heavy silence.

"An astute observation," Kip replied from the passenger seat.

"The engine can't handle another attempt," Lina said, checking the steam gauge. The needle quivered just above a skull icon – a clear warning of catastrophic failure. "We're running on fumes and luck as it is."

Then she noticed the eye itself was changing. The flat, circular base of clouds beneath them had begun to stretch and elongate, spinning faster like a whirlpool gaining momentum. "Look," she said, pointing. "There she is, Big Mama Vortex."

What had been the floor of the eye was now opening, reaching downward through the Storm like a widening throat several miles in diameter. "That's bloody impossible. Hope this thing won't drag us in," she murmured, maneuvering the damaged craft to hover farther above the opening.

"We left *possible* behind hours ago," Kip commented dryly. "We've journeyed through *wildly improbable* and *fundamentally absurd*. And now we've arrived at defying atmospheric science. I'm almost curious about what's next."

"Decades of Technocracy Storm research, and not a single record of anything like this."

"Maybe they weren't looking in the right places," Kip said. "Or maybe some things aren't meant to be known."

"You're starting to sound like those Fellowship mystics," Lina scoffed, still watching the formation. "But this…" She gestured at the expanding cylinder beneath them.

As they talked, Lina felt the shift – a faint downward tug in the air around them. "Oh, great. It is pulling us *in*," she muttered.

The *Noble Steed* groaned as it started a slow descent near the edge of the opening.

And below… below, Lina saw the impossible.

The Storm, the world's eternal boundary, opened below them like a giant window. And through it, stretching in every direction, was water. A vast, dark expanse, slate-gray and moving. The real surface of the world – not clouds, not an empty void, but an ocean.

The Technocracy had theorized that the entire planet might be gaseous; the tribes spoke of the Depths as a kind of hell from which no one returned. But no accepted model included this.

"So much for all those theories," Lina murmured. "Turns out there's just a giant puddle underneath."

They passed the densest layer of the Storm – the one hanging about three thousand feet above the surface. It was the quintessence of bad weather – a chaotic mix of rain, sleet, and hail, but strangely, no lightning. "Explains why no one comes back," Kip murmured, glancing back at the tunnel. "I won't envy anyone passing through it without this convenient opening. And don't imagine anyone could climb back up through that."

The gauges spun wildly. The altimeter dropped fast, and Lina fought to slow their descent. Pressure climbed. Temperature rose. "Our floatstone gravity pull is weakening," Lina said numbly. "Like it's wearing off."

Before Kip could respond, a dark shape emerged above, falling through the same hole in the sky.

As the shape neared, it resolved into a floating island – smaller than most mid-altitude drifts, maybe half a mile across. But the island was falling. A pale blue light emanated from it, pulsing rhythmically as it descended toward the surface.

Lina swore and yanked at the controls, steering them away from the falling island as best she could. The island hurtled past, winds howling around its jagged edges.

"This opening…" Kip breathed. "It's a passage for the island."

As the island passed, turbulence spun them in a wild dance. The ship's Rational Element module had begun to flicker.

"The module is failing!" Lina screamed. She frantically adjusted the controls as the ship grew heavier and more sluggish. "The Rational Element's just a rock now."

The craft stabilized for a moment, spiraling downward in a wide arc.

Meanwhile, the island neared the ocean – not crashing, but gracefully slowing. As it descended, its glow faded completely, disappearing into the mist. The island touched the water with impossible grace, settling gently onto the surface.

"I can't say anything is going to surprise me at this stage," Lina muttered.

"Indeed," Kip agreed quietly.

"We land on it," Lina decided, adjusting their descent to follow the island.

"You're serious?" Kip asked. "Land on the island that just did a midair waltz?"

"Got a better idea?" Lina snapped, fighting the controls. "The Rational Element's dead. The plane's too heavy. We're not going back up. It's land now – or swim."

The *Noble Steed* jolted hard. They were falling fast. Lina wrestled the controls, trying to find a glide path.

"We don't have an ejection system. Do you swim?" Kip asked, voice tight.

"Like a stone," she grunted, judging the distance and the angle.

Too fast. Too steep. They hadn't made it.

The sea rushed up. Impact slammed through Lina. Metal screamed. Water burst in. She saw the cockpit flooding, and darkness closed over her.

———

Kip gasped, breaking the surface, his lungs burning. He could see the island – safety. He could swim. Cold gnawed at him. He frantically scanned the churning water. No Lina.

Cursing, he hyperventilated and dove back down. Not for strategy. Just because he'd seen too many left behind. And if she died now, it would mean something in him had gone cold too.

Later, he'd pretend it was just strategy. That his goals, vengeance, reclaiming Saroven lands depended on Lina's skills. She was, in the most pragmatic assessment, an irreplaceable resource.

But now it didn't matter. They were a team, and he was responsible for her.

He spotted the sinking outline of the *Noble Steed*. Through the shattered viewport, Lina's still form, caught in her restraints. Bubbles trailed from her lips. Adrenaline surged. He kicked hard, reached the wreck, and pulled himself inside. The restraint buckle was jammed. He yanked, tore at it, lungs screaming for air. With a final, desperate wrench, it gave way, releasing Lina's limp form. He grabbed her jacket and kicked upward, her weight dragging him down, his muscles on fire.

They broke through together. Kip gasped, holding Lina's head above water. She was still. Pale in the gray light above the water. Above, the vortex was sealing. The Storm churned into a solid wall again.

They were trapped.

Cold dread gripped Kip.

No way back. Years of planning, his quest – all of it meaningless now, cut off in another world by the impassable Storm.

A piece of the *Noble Steed's* wing floated nearby. Kip clung to it, using the wreckage to hold Lina's weight as he swam for shore.

"The things I do for kidnappers," he muttered.

Finally, his feet struck solid ground. The island sloped gently into the water – no cliffs to climb. He hauled Lina onto the shore and rolled her onto her side. Checked her breathing. Nothing.

Then she coughed hard, spitting water. She gasped, coughed again, but remained unconscious. Kip collapsed beside her, utterly spent, soaked, and shivering.

After a long while, Lina stirred. Her eyes fluttered open, filled with disorientation. Another cough racked her small frame. Rolling onto her stomach, she braced herself on her elbows and blinked against the gray skies. A moment passed as she registered her surroundings – the near-drowning, the biting cold. Then she saw Kip beside her.

"Well," she rasped, "two crashes in one week." She paused, coughed again. "Getting worse each time."

She looked toward the dark water, then back at him. "How'd I make it to shore?"

"Don't read too much into it," Kip replied, wringing out his jacket.

Lina nodded, seeming to understand. She turned to survey the island. "What is this place?"

"No idea," Kip said, staring up at the oppressing Storm. His plans, his achievements, his entire life's focus felt impossibly distant.

"But I think," he said with a dry smile, "we just found something big. And here I was worried today might be boring."

PART 2: BELOW THE STORM

PROLOGUE
Feedback

OPERATION WINDFALL UPDATE

The Science Division extends its congratulations on the successful extraction of the azurium sample. The specimen's extraordinary purity surpasses all previously cataloged samples and has generated considerable excitement among our research teams.

However, the 4.1-cubic-foot yield falls far short of operational needs. While sufficient for laboratory analysis, this quantity remains inadequate for application-scale testing.

The Federation has approved expanded permissions for Operation Windfall. You are directed to:

* *Intensify extraction efforts, targeting a minimum monthly yield of 15 cubic feet*

* *Accelerate diplomatic engagement with mid-altitude powers*

* *Continue mapping potential sites for permanent installations*

Note: *The non-interference policy is hereby postponed to allow for the establishment of a political presence. You are to pursue permanent mining operations through economic leverage rather than direct intervention.*

The loss of Sergeant Hertzig is regrettable. A replacement will be dispatched after mission completion.

You are also expected to provide a detailed report on the recent observation of the planetary surface beneath the atmospheric disturbance. Has there been any confirmation of surface conditions or signs of habitation? If indigenous populations exist, reassess the application of Protocol 17 accordingly.

Maintain your current orbital position. Further instructions will follow.

Admiral Harold Kaine

Commander Voss read the message twice, her face slipping into practiced neutrality. That took years to master – getting a higher rank always meant knowing how to hide what you really thought.

She looked at Azoria turning peacefully below, the layer of floating islands barely visible through gaps in the cloud cover. The Storm spun beneath, hiding whatever secrets the planet's surface held. Its patterns reminded her of bureaucracy made visible: lots of noise, endlessly circling, and completely impenetrable to anyone with common sense.

Four cubic feet of azurium. Today's report from Lieutenant Reed was too bland, too formal. When she asked him directly, he just said, "All went according to established protocols." Not "went smoothly." Not "no issues." It sounded like someone saying "I'm fine" while actively bleeding. But it obviously went wrong – they lost a team member on the very first mission and had no time for a rescue.

Her science officer, Dr. Nabble, had been even more vague. He mentioned suspending the entire observation staff, claiming they were obviously drunk during the event. He promised a full report, adding that both it and the footage of the "environmental anomalies" would be ready in a few days. The only thing he could confirm was that beneath the island's icy surface was a thriving jungle with impossible biodiversity.

"A *jungle?*" she'd asked, sure she'd misheard. "Underground?"

"Not just any jungle, Commander," he said, his usual calm starting to crack. "Species from every altitude zone, all growing together. Plants that shouldn't survive side by side were sharing the same soil. Animals from different biomes living in harmony. And all of it centered around the azurium sphere."

"How is that possible?" she asked.

"No idea, ma'am."

And now High Command wanted more. Much more. And now they also wanted to play political games.

Her thoughts drifted to Sergeant Hertzig. Not just a "regrettable loss." Nora, with the loud laugh that echoed through the med bay. Nora, who told awful jokes while stitching wounds, making people forget they were in pain. Nora, who, just days before the mission, had raised concerns that the extraction process might destabilize the islands. Voss had always thought of Nora as the crew's collective conscience.

The Storm was hiding something. Azurium seemed more connected to life than anyone had guessed. And somewhere beneath that churning sky layer, answers waited. Answers the Federation didn't care about.

What are you hiding? she asked the planet below, knowing it wouldn't answer. She'd learned the hard way: planets don't reveal secrets freely. They demand payment. And she had already paid with one of her best.

And Voss was afraid it would ask for much more.

CHAPTER 7
Beneath the Veil

Nora Hertzig, Federation field medic, awoke in a puddle of blood. The metallic tang hit her nose, and dizziness swept in as she tried to lift her head.

This is it, she thought, surprisingly calm. *This is how it ends.* There was too much blood to survive. Her body felt distant, like she was floating somewhere above the pain. The fog in her head and disorientation meant shock was setting in.

But as her vision cleared, something bothered her. The blood looked wrong. Too bright? Too thin? She touched her fingers to the liquid. It felt watery. Diluted.

She rolled to her side to find the source. Not a ruptured artery, but a torn chest pocket. Saline solution was leaking from a transparent bag, mixing with a burst blood packet from the attack.

A smile tugged at her lips. Not dying was a nice bonus for that day. Even in a cave, after being mauled and dragged by a predator. Speaking of which. She scanned the surroundings in the dim blue light. It was nowhere to be seen, and since she wasn't being eaten, it must have left. She was happy with the simple fact of continued existence. She'd have a hell of a story to tell – if she made it back to the *Pathfinder*. The thought of the ship brought her crashing back to reality.

Her eyepiece was gone. So were her sidearm and flashlight. Nora pulled the radio from her chest pocket – it was dead, the power light dark.

Luckily, she had spare batteries. Federation tech handled Azoria's EM fields with clever workarounds – chemical batteries that stayed inert until activated. Pulling a tab sparked the reaction, giving just enough power for brief comms.

She put in a new battery and pulled the tab. Static hissed, loud and empty. The power indicator was already flashing. The radio was barely working, eating through its battery life.

"Markus! Reed! Beta team, report!" Only the cavern echoed back her voice.

She pushed the distress signal combination and watched the device shut down in seconds. Too deep underground, or too close to the Storm. Either way, she was on her own.

She assessed the damage. Bruises everywhere, cuts on her arms and leg still bleeding a little. Her head throbbed, indicating a possible concussion. The main medical kit was a ruin, but the emergency supplies were still there. The blood packets in her front pockets had burst, making her uniform sticky and dark. She found one emergency stimulant syringe. With trembling hands, she administered it, the sharp prick followed by a welcome chemical clarity.

Slowly, carefully, she pushed herself to her feet, testing her weight. Her bruised leg protested but held. "Assess and adapt," she muttered, the Academy mantra sounding too clinical in this setting. Adapting *hurt*.

The last clear memory she had was of the extraction chamber, moments before the attack. That was her best starting point. She had to get back there, maybe find Reed and Markus, or at least some supplies. The second objective was to get to the open air to try contacting the team once again.

With each step, the caves revealed new strangeness. Small creatures darted at the edge of her vision, some too quick, others moving in eerie slow motion. Wall-clinging vegetation seemed to shift with purpose, not rot – an eerie kind of intentional transformation. Seed heads had burst open, scattering their contents. Fruits hung heavy and overripe, some already splitting to reveal dense clusters of seeds. The ecosystem wasn't dying – it was transforming.

She stepped into a vast cavern – and froze. The extraction chamber.

A few traces of the team remained – scuff marks in the dirt, a broken shell of a manipulator device. They'd clearly evacuated in a hurry. And there, in the center where the blue core had been, was nothing but an empty cradle of plants.

The chamber had changed. What had once been a vibrant ecosystem was now shutting down. The flora once glowing with life now entered dormancy – spores spent, seeds dropped, bulbs folding inward. The fauna had scattered, hiding deeper in the caves. Everything was adapting to life without its power source.

Nora approached the empty cradle slowly. The azurium core had been more than a mineral deposit. It was the heart of this living network, keeping everything around it alive. They hadn't just extracted a resource but had shattered an entire ecosystem.

Her fingers ran along the withered plants where the core had rested. The Federation's "minimal indigenous interference" directive lay in tatters around her.

A faint noise echoed. Something moved, deeper in the tunnels. The mountain lion? Or something else disturbed by the ecosystem's collapse?

Nora didn't wait to find out. She needed to get out. Find her team. She turned from the chamber and followed an upward-sloping passage.

The air shifted – heavier, damper, tinged with something sharp. Salt. She noted the anomaly even as her pace quickened.

The passage pinched tight, then widened into a chamber. A fissure in the ceiling revealed a glimpse of... gray? Not Azoria's deep blue. This was a flat, shifting gray, dense and restless. Light filtered through it, a dim illumination unlike anything she'd expected.

"What in the void...?" she whispered, approaching the fissure. It was wide enough that she could climb through. The salt smell intensified. Then came the sound – deep, rhythmic, vast. A whooshing that seemed to come at regular intervals.

She hauled herself through the fissure and emerged onto a broad ledge. The world unfolded before her.

A gray-green ocean spread to the horizon, shifting and alive. Above it, not sky – just the underbelly of the Storm. A rolling ceiling of cloud – both distant and suffocating. The island looked like it had always belonged here, just another hunk of rock in the endless ocean, nothing left of the skybound world it came from.

She was no longer in Azoria's skies. The realm of floating islands was behind her. She was on the surface. The impossible, mythical surface hidden beneath the impenetrable Storm.

No Federation probe had ever confirmed the ocean's existence. Every attempt fell victim to the interference. Now she stood here – first Federation scientist to witness it. Stranded. No way to report what she'd seen. She considered using her last battery, but the Storm's proximity made that pointless.

"Well," she murmured to the endless gray, "nothing like a groundbreaking discovery with no one to tell."

Movement drew her gaze. Near the waterline, debris floated – splintered wood, torn fabric, dark slicks in the waves. Then – figures. Two. Onshore. Dragging something from the surf. Survivors? Locals? Trouble?

Her hand reached for her hip only to find an empty holster. Of course.

She was injured. Vulnerable, yes. But alive. And apparently, no longer alone.

CHAPTER 8
The Lighthouse Keeper

Marvin Thale was, without question, the smartest man on the island. He reminded himself of this each morning, though it carried less weight, considering he was also the *only* man on the island.

Still, Marvin believed standards mattered. Working at Point Descent Lighthouse required a kind of mind most wouldn't understand. He'd explained this to Ferdinand more than once, and the donkey had never disagreed. Marvin took it as quiet confirmation.

"Another day of scientific observation awaits, Ferdinand," Marvin said, fastening the belt on his patched trousers, stitched together from two pairs that had fallen from the sky and later washed ashore. They were reinforced with tough squares of mismatched cloth. Still, he had stitched an insignia over the pocket: a lighthouse and the title, "Chief Observer of Surface Phenomena."

Ferdinand replied with the deep, practiced sigh he'd perfected after years beside the lighthouse.

"Exactly," Marvin nodded. "The mechanism won't wind itself. The fate of the ships depends on us." He gave the donkey's muzzle a pat. "But first, breakfast."

The lighthouse cottage was organized chaos. Various journals filled every surface. Trinkets with tiny, handwritten tags lined the shelves. Strange contraptions of Marvin's own design took up the rest.

A peculiar device dominated one wall constructed from three wine bottles and a carefully stretched sheep's bladder. Despite appearances, it was remarkably accurate. Marvin's grasp of pressure systems was surprisingly strong, even if his theories often drifted toward the eccentric.

Beside it, a web of pulleys and counterweights hung from the ceiling – Marvin's Storm predictor. This one actually never worked. He blamed the materials, never the design.

Breakfast was last night's fish, fried with sharp herbs from his small garden. Marvin ate quickly but with precision, pausing now and then to jot notes in the open journal beside his plate.

"Dietary Intake: One medium silverscale, pan-fried. Salinity: Acceptable. Tea Strength: Optimal."

Ferdinand waited outside, occasionally poking his head through the window with a soft nicker. The donkey gave him a look that said, *time to move*.

"Completely agree," Marvin told him, snapping the journal shut. "Lighthouse duty waits for no man. Not even one halfway through breakfast."

––––––

Winding the lighthouse wasn't a chore – it was a ritual. The mechanism, first built by his predecessor, had been refined by Marvin over the years. A massive wooden drum, wrapped with thick, tarred rope. A stone counterweight that descended slowly, turning gears to rotate the mirror around the central flame. So twice a day, dawn and dusk, Ferdinand hauled the counterweight back up. The light never failed. Not at night, when ships needed it. Not during the day, which was just as dim.

In the Storm's endless twilight, Point Descent's lighthouse was the only reliable guide for miles. Ships came rarely, maybe once a month, bringing oil and food. But those that came depended on the light to dodge the reefs that had shattered so many hulls.

"Beginning mechanism elevation," Marvin said, checking the logbook that hung from his neck. "Day four hundred seventeen, current cycle. All systems nominal."

Ferdinand stepped into the worn wooden harness, blinking with slow resignation. A shift of weight. Marvin knew the signal.

"Acknowledged. Begin rotation," Marvin said, releasing the heavy lever with a solid thunk.

Ferdinand leaned in. The windlass groaned, then fell into its slow, steady rhythm of creaks and clicks.

"Excellent torque. Velocity steady. Outstanding as always," Marvin praised.

The process took nearly an hour, a rhythm Marvin had followed for twenty-five years. Not rote labor, but ritual checkup. He listened for signs of strain. The oil supply was still holding. The ship from Harbor Commonwealth would arrive in two weeks. Just enough to last.

"Winding complete," he said, locking the lever with care. "Mechanism stable. Ready for observation."

Ferdinand nudged the empty apple bowl, offering his own observation.

———

The observation platform was a cluttered marvel, function born from salvage. Marvin's pride was the brass telescope, Technocracy-made – though he liked to suggest Federation origin. It rested on a swiveling base near the east window.

Handmade instruments crowded the room: a wind vane, a copper-pot rain gauge, a glass cylinder for pressure. Only Marvin knew what they did and even if he didn't, the journals did.

Shelves lined the walls, packed tight with leather-bound journals. Each bore a precise label: *Confirmed Descents*, *Storm Aperture Analysis*, *Avian Patterns*, *Miscellaneous Discoveries and Epiphanies*. Years of data, inked by hand.

Marvin took his stool and began the daily ritual. Logged the readings first, then slowly swept the telescope around. Birds. Haze. No ships.

"Storm index stable," he muttered, scribbling notes. "No vessels. Seagulls foraging over eastern reefs, normal behavior."

He nearly closed the log when a flicker caught his eye high up. Not lightning. A stable opening in the dense Storm above. Perfectly round.

His breath caught. Hands trembling, he adjusted focus. *Could it be?* He grabbed his *Confirmed Descents* log, flipping through sketches of falls, fire, wreckage. But this wasn't that. This was slow. Calm. Glowing. A faint, steady blue.

He slammed the log shut, heart racing. "Ferdinand!" he yelled down the stairs, forgetting the donkey was outside. "It's real! Cross-checking previous data, we have a Category Blue! Initiate extraordinary documentation protocol!"

He swung the telescope back, movements tight, practiced. Seven years since the last one. In fifty-three years, he'd seen only two like it, the rare, luminous descents. Not chaotic landmass crashes, but arrivals.

Through the lens, it was clearly an island, mid-sized, descending with improbable grace through a perfect hole torn in the Storm.

"Time: eleven fifteen," he muttered, pencil racing. "Aperture stable, circular. Estimated diameter: one mile. Descent deceleration is anomalous but consistent with Category Blue behavior."

He sketched quickly, lines sure and steady – icy surface, jagged rock, dark cave mouths.

He traced the map with one finger, calculating wind drift and descent rate. "Estimated landing zone: seventeen miles southeast. Structural integrity: likely intact. Survivor presence: probable."

His thoughts outran his pencil. The last Category Blue had landed far to the west in Kingdom of Tides territory, untouchable. But this one was close. This one was *his*.

And that changed everything. Visitors. Maybe even… Federation. The reason he watched. The reason he waited.

————

The world didn't turn with a steady rhythm. A long boring period stretched across the years – counting barnacles, measuring wind. Then without warning, the sky would drop something rare. No signs. No reason. His mother had taught him: keep to the observational protocol. Be ready when it happens.

Category Blue Descents were the order in chaos. Not crashes – arrivals. Deliberate. Intact. And sometimes… carrying people from above.

He bolted down the spiral stair, boots thudding on worn stone. Preparation was everything.

"Ferdinand!" he yelled, bursting into the salt wind. "Condition Red! No, wait – Condition Blue! Formal Visitor Reception Protocol!"

Ferdinand looked up from his weeds and blinked once, slow and unimpressed.

"Don't pretend you've forgotten," Marvin said, finger wagging with importance. "We've practiced this endlessly. The Surface Welcome Committee must be ready – what if it really *is* the Federation this time?"

Ferdinand resumed grazing, clearly of the opinion that rehearsal protocols were overdue.

Marvin rushed to the cottage and flung open the trunk. Inside lay the "Formal Reception Uniform", a Federation officer's jacket missing one sleeve, patched with another, singed and faded, paired with pants a shade too wrong to match.

"The Chief Observer must look official," Marvin muttered. "Mother always said the proper attire makes first contact look credible."

As he wrangled the jacket, memories flooded his mind. His mother, Elise Thale, was not just a soldier, but the first Federation officer on the surface. She'd filled long evenings with stories of the world above. Vast floating islands, airships, steam-powered planes. And even further – other worlds, thinking machines, starships. The star-spanning organization she served. She'd made him promise to keep watch. She believed he'd be the one to greet those who came down from the sky.

"This is why we keep the station running," Marvin said. "Today could be the one Mother meant."

Ferdinand grunted, possibly understanding, possibly hungry.

He traced the descent path on his cluttered chart. "We'll need the *Ambassador*," he said. "And full supply kits. Survivors are usually dazed, sometimes worse. Scientific protocol demands readiness for every scenario."

He packed carefully: fresh water, dried fish, first-aid, blankets. Each item was checked off and stowed into canvas bags. They went into his small boat: *The Surface Ambassador*, cheerfully named for this occasion more than twenty years ago.

As he worked, Marvin mentally recited his Formal Greeting Speech. This was a document refined annually since its first draft. He had only performed it twice – once to a delirious shipwrecked trader. And once, memorably, to a large, unusually shaped piece of driftwood that had momentarily resembled a reclining figure. The real figure was there anyway, clinging to the wood and unconscious.

"Ferdinand, after we settle, we need to do precise coordinate triangulation," he told Ferdinand, cinching the last strap. "Until then, full observation mode."

Ferdinand flicked an ear in dignified indifference.

Marvin straightened his lopsided jacket and climbed back up. Through the scope, the island lay still, cloaked in fog from melting ice. Settled. Waiting.

"A historic day for surface science," he declared, pencil poised over a fresh log. "Recording at fifteen-minute intervals, begin–"

But then, beneath the ceremony and structure, a quieter thought surfaced – one he rarely let in.

Maybe this time… someone will stay.

CHAPTER 9
Beneath the Surface

Kip Saroven was having one of those moments that made him question his life choices. Like rescuing a sputtering mechanic from the ocean.

It wasn't regret. It was responsibility. A concept absent from the Corsair Code.

Self. Ship. Loot. That order. That was his life for three years.

Did it mean my old noble self was resurfacing? Where exactly would that lead?

He watched Lina pick through the flotsam at the water's edge. Pitifully little remained of their scout craft. Most of the metal had sunk. Only the wooden frame and a few light pieces had stayed afloat.

Her hands moved through bent struts and cracked rods with methodical ease.

"This one might hold," she muttered to the wood. "The rest is slag."

Her usual bluntness felt edged by exhaustion and near-drowning. Kip felt something stir. Mostly annoyance. Responsibility was an inconvenience. His own grand plans felt far away and faintly ridiculous now. Water. Shelter. The grim reality of staying in this twilight world forever that overshadowed everything.

The air under the Storm was thick, wet, and cold. It clung to everything. Fire was a need, not a comfort.

He looked up again. Just gray. No stars, no sun, nothing helpful. The open water, at least, wasn't entirely foreign to him. Lake Westcrown summers gave him something to hold onto in this strange world.

But Lina… She feared the water. And hated the forest. He'd seen it on the island, trekking between crash sites. For someone born to fly, she had rough relations with other elements.

"Someone's over there," Lina stated suddenly, her voice tight. She nodded across the rocky peninsula. A lone figure moved along the shoreline.

"Not one of ours," Kip said quietly.

"Checking it out," Lina declared, hefting a heavy piece of pipe salvaged from the debris. Kip moved to flank her, that protective instinct surfacing again.

Focus, Saroven. Assess the threat.

Kip watched the stranger approach. Tall for a woman, perhaps around his age or older, mid-thirties, he guessed. She had dark hair pulled back from an open, attractive face. She favored one leg, but the quiet tension in her movement spoke of a soldier's training. Her uniform was also a thing that registered as *wrong* – unfamiliar material, advanced design, strange insignia. Definitely not mid-altitude kit. And it was soaked in dried blood.

The woman's brown eyes widened as she looked them over: Kip's corsair leathers and noble bearing, Lina's practical pilot's gear, both wet and battered from the crash. He saw her gaze assessing his tall figure and dark hair, before settling back on his face.

"Hello there," she called, her voice clear and friendly. Her accent was untraceable, almost archaic, but her Trade Speech sounded remarkably clean. It sounded like it was her native language. "You… you're from *above*?"

Kip stopped a cautious distance away, nodding. "Our plane came down hard," he replied, gesturing vaguely toward the ocean and the gray sky. "Didn't expect… *this*." The endless water, the island pretending to be there forever – it was still profoundly disorienting. "Or company. Who are you?" He kept his tone rough, corsair-standard.

The woman hesitated, as if deciding how much to say.

"Nora Hertzig," she stated. "Field medic." She didn't state her affiliation. "And you?"

"Kip Saroven," he returned, meeting the medic's observant brown eyes. "Lina Ryven, mechanic." He gave a brief nod toward Lina, who stood tense, pipe held ready. "Things didn't go to plan."

"Ship's gone," Lina added bluntly, her eyes fixed suspiciously on Nora's unfamiliar uniform and belt equipment. "Just scrap left."

Nora nodded, her expression unreadable. "My arrival wasn't planned either. My team…" She hesitated, choosing her words. "… we had an incident on the island before it fell." She gestured back toward the island. "I was separated."

Island? Fell? Kip registered the odd phrasing. *Not crashed. Fell. And she was on it before?*

She was evading, holding back crucial details. A familiar tactic.

"Well," Kip said, his voice level now, his speech shifting from spiky corsair talk. "This isn't quite the destination I had in mind. Given our… mutual predicament… perhaps pooling our efforts would be wise?"

Nora visibly relaxed. Kip figured she wasn't used to working alone and had been ready for any reaction.

"Agreed. I have some medical supplies and rations."

"And we've got… scrap," Lina muttered, her face grim.

————

The next hours were a strained exercise in wary cooperation under the flat gray light.

Kip hunched over a flat rock, smacking a rust-streaked pipe with a chunk of stone. The sparks danced but refused to catch, and the damp kindling gave off nothing but a sullen wisp of steam.

"I had it," he muttered, eyes narrowed in concentration.

Nora knelt beside him, adjusted the angle, added a bunch of dry grass, and struck once. A sharp spark, a lick of flame – and the fire caught with a reluctant hiss.

Kip leaned back stiffly. "Close enough."

"Sure, you were," Lina said wryly, poking the fire with her pipe.

So much for my fire-making experience.

They pooled Nora's meager rations with the few waterproof packs from Kip's gear. Lina sat still while Nora cleaned the gash on her arm. Jaw locked, eyes steady. She didn't flinch.

Kip took charge of scouting their immediate surroundings for fresh water. He found a stream trickling down from a large, still-frozen section of the island. The stream tasted of meltwater and stone.

As they took a brief rest near their smoky, hissing fire, as the damp wood struggled to burn, Kip watched his companions. Nora was a puzzle wrapped in clipped speech and unknown tech. Lina was all sparks and motion – easy to read, hard to predict. He didn't trust them. But trust wasn't the currency here. Survival was.

He turned his attention to Nora. The precision of her movements, the strange formality of her speech, the advanced gear... the pieces clicked together.

"Nora," he began, keeping his tone neutral, "that equipment, your uniform... your accent." He paused, meeting her gaze. "You're not from Azoria, are you? Are you... from the *stars*?" He used the old, almost mythical term.

Nora looked up, her expression open, almost matter-of-fact. There was no hesitation.

"Yes," she confirmed simply. "I'm from the Federation."

Kip didn't flinch. He'd already suspected it. Now it was just confirmed.

Federation. So the name from the dusty histories is real.

Lina, who had been sharpening a piece of metal nearby, went still, listening intently, her eyes narrowed.

"Federation," Kip repeated, testing the unfamiliar word. "Did your ship crash too?"

"No," Nora said, tucking a strand of dark hair behind her ear. "Our main vessel remains in orbit. My team landed on this island before... the incident." Again, the careful vagueness about her mission.

Interesting. An operational ship in orbit?

That changed his calculations. But her team was missing, and she was stranded here with them. He tucked that detail deep for later.

For now, they were all just survivors.

"And where are they now?" Kip asked, his eyes narrowing.

Nora's shoulders tensed almost imperceptibly. "I was attacked by the local predator. It seems they didn't have time for a rescue mission. They likely presumed I'm dead."

The fire hissed, smoke curling low. No one spoke.

Kip watched her a moment longer. There was a quiet acceptance in her voice with a trace of sadness that she was left behind. And the unspoken truth: down here, beneath the Storm, no rescue was coming.

Then he saw a movement at the edge of the camp.

Low and silent, it moved like poured smoke. Broad shoulders, fluid steps. Tawny fur ghosted into the stone. Its amber eyes fixed on them – intelligent, assessing.

Lina saw it a second later, scrambling back with a choked cry, pipe instantly raised. Nora looked up, her face paling. She froze, hand halfway to her empty holster.

Kip reacted purely on instinct, stepping between the predator and the two women. He gripped the long piece of metal shard like a short sword. His heart hammered against his ribs, but the reassuring weight of metal triggered his years of training. He made himself large and let out a low, guttural growl.

The creature's ears pinned back. It hissed sharply and took a step *forward*. Its tail twitched, annoyed.

Kip stiffened.

Lina surged beside him, pipe raised high, letting out a shout and jabbing the air. The lion's eyes flicked to her, and after a beat of tension, it let out a huff and turned away, vanishing into the rocks.

Kip said nothing. His grip still shook.

"That," Nora breathed, voice uneven, "was the same one. Or it had a twin." She unconsciously touched her leg, where the suit showed faint signs of repair.

"And the blood on your clothes?" Kip asked.

"That was from my medical kit. Not mine, thankfully," Nora said with a faint smile.

Kip nodded, retrieving the water canister he'd dropped earlier. "It seems we're not the only survivors adjusting."

The encounter had shattered any illusion of safety. They were exposed. Vulnerable.

"Right," Kip said, his voice regaining its authority, the adrenaline sharpening his thoughts. "We need shelter. Real shelter. Tonight." He looked around their exposed camp – the damp seeping into everything – then toward the island's caves. "Options are limited. Try to build something here with the debris we have, or risk the caves?"

Lina scowled. "The caves? Where *that* thing live? No, thanks."

"Caves could be less damp and better protected from rain," Nora countered, though her voice lacked conviction. "But… yes, the fauna."

"Staying here means scavenging," Kip said, weighing the risks. "If we can find enough materials, we can build a shelter here." He looked toward the higher ridges, expecting to see some semblance of trees. He found none. "We need sturdy timber. Maybe flat stones. If not, we brave the caves."

They set off, moving around the shore.

Suddenly, Kip stiffened. "Lina. Nora. Look," he said, his voice low – different. He pointed out into the distance.

Far out, a pinprick of light blinked against the horizon.

It blinked. Vanished. Blinked again. Steady. Rhythmic. Deliberate.

Lina gasped. "There are people out there!"

"Structured pulse," Nora murmured. "Regular interval. That's no accident. That's a beacon."

"A beacon..." Kip breathed. "A way out? Rescue?"

"Maybe," Nora mused. "Or... on settled ocean worlds, they build coastal lights. Navigation aids. Lighthouses, they call them."

Lighthouse. An old word, implying shores, harbors, people. Maybe even a path out of this world.

The light blinked again – impossibly small, impossibly distant across that vast, dark water.

"We can build a raft. Or a boat. Reach it," Kip said.

"Then we need more materials," Lina said, a sudden wave of energy lifting her voice.

———

They combed the shoreline, dragging back plane wreckage and chunks of thawing petrified wood from the island's ice.

Nora returned with a tangled mass of black sea-fronds, still dripping.

"Similar structure to coastal vine kelp," she said. "Should be edible." She stuffed it into a salvaged tin and balanced it over the fire between three stones.

The smell that rose was sharp and briny, with a bitter edge that made Kip lean back slightly.

Lina sipped once, spat it back with a sputtering cough. "Bloody hell! That's not food."

Nora tasted it next and winced. "Okay. That's awful."

"You're the medic," Lina growled. "You're supposed to heal people, not *kill* them."

Kip, perhaps to keep the team's morale, ladled some out and took a cautious sip.

Nora looked over at him, eyebrows raised. "You don't have to eat that. Might be the wrong species."

He grimaced and swallowed. "Just… checking."

"Well," Lina said, watching him choke it down, "now you have a subject to heal."

He set the ladle down, swallowing his pride and whatever that taste was. "It has… *potential*."

No one said anything for a while. The fire hissed. The soup steamed, untouched.

Kip picked up the ladle again.

"Don't," both women said at the same time.

He set it down. "Just checking if it has improved with time."

"Some things," Lina muttered, "are beyond hope."

She wasn't looking at the soup when she said it.

Kip said nothing. Tomorrow they'd need to act like a crew or not survive at all.

CHAPTER 10
Surface Fears

Toryn woke slowly, his back aching from the rock beneath. Something was wrong. The air pressed against his skin, thick, heavy, and humid. Nothing like the crisp air of the Heights. Then came the smell: eagle nest, mixed with something sharp and salty.

He opened his eyes. No familiar blue sky overhead. No drifting islets floated in the air – only heavy, bruised clouds hanging low. They stretched endlessly in every direction. No breaks. No familiar patterns. Just an oppressive ceiling pressing down on him.

The realization hit him. He was beneath the Storm. In the *Depths*. The place tribal elders spoke of as the opposite of freedom, of the sky. Where no one ever returned from.

His body ached from the wild eagle ride. He forced himself to sit up. Some scratches and bruises, but nothing serious. Everything else was gone: precious Kora's goggles, pack, tools, his bone knife. All of it torn away during that desperate jump from Veil Islet. He was completely alone with nothing but the clothes on his back and a silver pendant around his neck.

Then he saw it and stiffened. Water. Not the streams or ponds he knew, but a huge, dark, moving sheet of water stretching out as far as he could see, meeting the clouds way off in the distance. It heaved and sighed against the black rocks, restless and immense. Too big. Too strange. Nothing in the legends, nothing his father had mapped, had prepared him for this. Even the High Tongue didn't have a word for it.

Around him, the rocky ground was treacherous. Slick with thick layers of eagle droppings. No plants, no grass. Strange creatures scuttled between the stones. They moved with jerky, alien speed – like the mountain beetles from home, but wrong somehow. Too many legs, walking sideways. Translucent shells armed with spikes and eyes on sticks.

Observe first, act second. He could hear Kora's voice in his memory. But everything he observed made no sense.

The eagles here were different, too. Dozens of birds wheeled overhead or perched on the jagged rocks. Most were smaller than the magnificent birds of the Windclaw Tribe. Maybe they were adapted to this heavy air. Only a few, with blue and black feathers like the one that saved him, matched the size of the brown eagles of Heights.

He needed water first. Toryn stood up and walked to the nearest pool, caught in the rocky dips. The water was all salt – sharp and bitter. Was it from the eagle's droppings or from the land itself?

Then he looked back at the sky. *Clean water concentrates in dark clouds. Those look dark enough and ready to pour. But I have no way to catch the rain. And nowhere to hide when it starts.*

Still, he had to check the great water. It could be either shallow or drinkable, or both.

He picked his way carefully down the slippery slope. The shore was littered with debris. Fish bones in quantities he had never seen, empty shells from those beetle-like creatures. As he crouched to examine the big shell, his foot slipped. He plunged into the cold water up to his waist before grabbing a jutting rock. The water was shockingly cold and not that shallow. He cupped some in his hand and tasted it. The salt was overwhelming.

"What is this?" he spat. *Even if I could swim in it, this water would kill me.*

He retreated from the shore, teeth chattering. The heavy air felt even colder now that he was wet. He could feel his body heat flowing away. Elder Haldar had told stories of the cold death that could take a man slowly. Anyway, dehydration could take him even earlier.

He scanned the waterline again. Fish bones were everywhere, meaning plenty of food was right there. All that food, just out of reach. But somehow, it only made him feel worse. He had no idea how to catch them. Back home, sometimes there were fish in the ponds and streams, and tribal fishermen used nets and fishing rods to get them. But he had no tools, no nets, no clue how to even start. And even if he managed to catch a fish or some of the critters with his bare hands, how could he cook them without fire?

He tried to read the wind. The air here barely moved. It just hung heavy and still around him. No currents, no thermals, no sky paths. The air was as dead as the stone beneath his feet.

Even if I could find wind patterns, what would I do with them?

He forced himself to think practically. The thought was bitter. There was no wood for the glider, no cloth except for his clothes, no wind worth catching.

The cold was getting more biting. It was time to think of fire and shelter. He searched for dry material and found a couple of twigs, soaked and neither suitable for fire nor construction. The air and splatter had dampened everything. Even the eagle droppings were wet and useless.

He tried anyway. Scraping together what dry scraps he could find. But the attempt was hopeless. The techniques that worked in the Heights meant nothing here.

Fire comes from preparation and patience. I have none. Maybe eggs, then. Some of the smaller eagles had nests that might be reachable. Yet all of them had huge claws, and he didn't even have a stick to defend himself. Throwing rocks might give him an edge, if he could be sure the whole colony wouldn't attack.

The discouragement was crushing. Every skill the tribe had passed down to him was useless here. Worse – it made him think he could survive when he clearly couldn't.

He searched desperately for any sign that someone else had been here before him. Footprints, tool marks, fire sites. Anything that proved humans could survive in this place. There was nothing.

His gaze drifted upward to the eagles circling overhead. *That eagle brought me here. Was it trying to help me – or just bringing food for its chicks?*

Saving him should not have been just instinct; the eagle seemed to mean it. It was Toryn's only hope, crazy as it seemed. Could these surface eagles even fly high enough to get back to the Heights? Probably not. This bird was likely stuck down here, too.

Still, what choice did he have? He could die here. Or he could try something. Something desperate.

He looked for his rescuer among the wheeling forms above. There it was, on a wide ledge, much larger than the other birds. The blue-black eagle wasn't hunting or fighting. It was watching him. Its head was tilted, and he felt its stare.

Maybe it understands more than ordinary eagles can.

Only one way to find out.

Toryn began picking his way carefully toward the ledge. Moving with deliberate slowness. No sudden movements, hands visible.

Stay calm. Show that you mean no harm.

He thought of Kora's lessons. Eagles see intention, not just gesture. It responded once to a botched ritual, maybe the spirit behind it will do it once again.

The eagle watched him approach, its startling blue eyes tracking his every move. It didn't seem angry, but he could feel the power in its massive frame. One wrong move, and those talons could end him.

"You brought me here," he said quietly. "Will you take me home?"

It was quiet for a long moment, just the sound of faraway eagle calls and the sighing water. The eagle rustled its huge wings. It shifted, claws clicking on the rock, then slowly lowered its body a little, turning its back toward him. It tucked one wing in just enough so Toryn could see the strong feathers near its shoulder. It wasn't a threat. It wasn't ignoring him either. It looked like an invitation. It was offering him a ride.

Toryn stared. His mind raced. Could he trust this creature?

He had decided. "Let's fly, then," he whispered.

Toryn took a deep breath and calmly, carefully, headed toward the eagle.

CHAPTER 11
Glimmer of Hope

They made a shelter in one of the cave openings that didn't connect to a bigger network. It was barely more than a scooped-out hollow in the rock face, constantly damp, smelling of wet stone and mildew that made Lina's nose itch. It was far from perfect, but at least it offered meager protection from the frequent rains and wind gusts.

The progress with a flotation device wasn't promising either. They found several logs that had been frozen in the mud and were now thawed.

"Petrified wood should be light," Kip said. "We lash it tight, add crossbeams – it'll float."

"This crap?" Lina muttered, eyeing the log. "Feels like stone."

Still, they worked – binding the logs with frayed belts, fashioning a crude, flat-bottomed raft. The result looked... plausible.

They shoved it into the shallows. It floated – then, with a heavy *glunk*, sank like a stone.

Kip stared at the dark water. "Well. That answers that."

Lina gave him a slow side-eye. "I never doubted your absence of engineering skills," she said, hurling a chunk of soaked wood onto the shore. "Now we're wet, cold, and back to square one."

"And you were the one who brought us here," Kip shot back before he could stop himself. The words landed like a slap.

Silence. Lina stared at him, jaw clenched – then turned away.

Kip exhaled hard, running a hand through his hair. "That was out of line."

"Yeah," she said. "It was."

Nora glanced between them but said nothing.

The next morning, they sorted the salvage. A meager collection: struts and rods from the *Steed*, metal pipes, part of a tail rudder, and petrified wood. The wood, pulled from the thawing earth, was not fit for any kind of construction, so they put it in the sun to dry and use as firewood. Yet, the absence of the sun hinted that it could take a while.

"Okay, Lordling, now tell me about those *boats*," Lina said with a sigh. She wasn't accustomed to acknowledging that there were contraptions she'd never been aware of. But it seemed there was no other choice.

Kip started describing the principles and drawing diagrams in the mud. Water buoyancy had only ever interested her in the bathtub. Since there had been no practical applications, she had never thought it through.

"See this?" he said, holding up the clumsy sail. "The wind pushes it. But you can't sail directly *into* the wind."

Lina frowned. "Why not?"

"Wind doesn't work that way. Neither does water," Kip replied patiently. He picked up two sticks. "You have to sail at an angle *to* the wind, back and forth. It's called *tacking*. Like this..." He demonstrated the zigzag motion.

Lina visualized the airflow vectors in her mind, nodding. The sail's like a wing, generating lift that pulls the boat forward and sideways. The keel resists that sideways push, turning most of the force into forward motion.

"Okay," Lina said, working through the physics mentally. "Like vectoring thrust."

"Exactly," Kip confirmed, seeming pleased that she understood. "And the rudder is like your aircraft's control surfaces. It deflects water to turn the boat."

"Adjustable hydrofoil," Lina nodded.

The technical principles made sense, even if the medium was unfamiliar. But the idea of trusting her life to an untested boat on that wide ocean made her stomach churn. It wasn't about sailing mechanics; it was deeper than that.

"The real problem," Kip continued, gazing out at the gray expanse, "is knowing which course to steer. No sun, no stars. How do you navigate? We have a lighthouse beacon now, but what if it fades?" He fell silent, and Lina felt a cold wave wash over her that had nothing to do with the damp air. The thought of being on the water was unsettling, adding a discomfort deeper than any technical challenge she had faced.

They started experimenting, and the result was far from encouraging. "We need better cordage for the sail," Lina announced. "And sealant. This plant resin Nora found isn't holding." The makeshift boat frame looked like junk held together with spit and hope.

Nora frowned, chewing her lip. Lina watched her, wondering what was going through the medic's mind.

"But back in the caves, when the lion attacked, I dropped a medkit when it dragged me." Her expression tightened. "It wasn't large," Nora continued, "but it should have a thin, strong cord, and some medical sealant tubes."

"We haven't seen the beast since that first encounter," Kip reasoned, though Lina noticed even he looked uneasy at the thought. "Maybe it hunts further now."

"Doesn't mean it doesn't *sleep* near the entrance," Lina muttered, crossing her arms. "Or have friends." She hated undeveloped wilderness. Give her engine grease and metal any day.

Nora sighed, "We need supplies... the cord alone would make the sail much stronger."

Armed with her heavy pipe, Kip's metal shard, and small torch, they entered the cave system again. The air carried a heavy smell, the dampness intensifying, muffling their footsteps. Lina gripped her pipe firmly, her eyes scanning the darkness.

Nora guided them by memory. "I think... around this bend..." she whispered.

They found the tattered remnants of her medkit first. It was torn, and some bottles inside were shattered. Lina watched as Nora checked the contents – cord, sealant tubes, basic sterile wraps – then saw Kip freeze beside her, his head tilted slightly.

He motioned for silence. Lina stilled completely, her grip tightening. Kip sniffed the air, then pointed cautiously ahead. Lina smelled it too – the sharp, metallic tang of blood. Fresh.

Slowly, they moved into a wider section of the cave. A deer-like carcass lay sprawled on the floor, steam faintly rising from its body. Its neck was snapped at an unnatural angle; savage bite marks marred its flank. It was undeniably the mountain lion's work, and chillingly recent. The predator could still be right here.

"We should move," Lina said quietly, assessing their tactical position in the narrow cave.

"Wait," Nora whispered, stepping forward, a knife in hand.

"Are you *that* hungry?" Lina said wryly.

"Freshly killed. Good meat." Nora worked with efficient speed, carving prime sections from the hindquarters. "Protein," she explained, wrapping the dark, dripping meat in the remains of her med kit. "Okay. Done. Let's get out. *Now*."

Their retreat was swift but controlled. Emerging into the flat gray daylight brought visible relief.

"That was easy," Lina said, trying to sound casual, "like a visit to the market."

The salvage mission provided the crucial cord and sealant, plus a protein boost from the meat Kip managed to cook over their struggling fire.

Later on, when they tried to search the higher ridges for anything useful, Kip suddenly stopped.

"What's that?"

Lodged awkwardly in the thawing mud was something human-made. Not their tech. Not Nora's.

Kip pulled it free – a section of a frame, lightweight but strong, bound with unfamiliar sinew. Canvas remnants clung to it, dusted in blue, flaky powder. He held the fragment, injecting certainty into his voice.

"Tribal construction," he stated. Then added, pointedly, "The canvas is treated with powdered *heartstone*."

Lina snorted. "Heartstone? Really, Lordling?" she scoffed. "Fancy schools teach savage magic words now?"

They spent the evening around the fire discussing the tribal glider and how the tribes used those for short-distance travel.

"Do you know that tribes were created to communicate with the Federation?" Nora asked.

Lina, who'd never been into history, was skeptical. "Those guys in rags and with big chickens?"

"Them. In the Heights, the Federation tech can work longer, so they used to meet the settler ships and send the word back to the Federation for whatever the colony needed."

Kip gave a shrug. "Long story, actually. There was a prominent figure, Theon Skyward, from the Federation, the Unifier. He was the first settlement leader, founder of the Republic of Westward Drifts. His son, Erik, decided to abandon what his father was building. He took a group of people to the higher islands, learned to coexist with the eagles, and live in balance. When Erik died in an accident, his father left the Republic and went to the Heights to find peace."

"So the tribes are just dropouts?" Lina said.

"If you want to be crude about it," Kip replied.

It touched something inside Lina – abandoning civilization to live close to nature sounded heroic. Like what they were doing now. But her thorny side would never admit it aloud.

"Oh, that explains things. And I wondered where the Republicans got that freaking self-importance and arrogance thing."

Then she asked Nora in a different tone, "But wait, we were a Federation colony, meaning we're the same people? And how exactly did we navigate the stars? I suppose you don't use steam and Rational Element up there?"

Nora hesitated. "You don't. And that's why we came to Azoria – to research it. Our machines work on different principles and degrade in minutes, nearing the Storm. So the Federation settlers had to use steam, axes, and shovels."

"Degrade… Like our Rational Element module," Lina sighed, recalling the crash.

The talk came to a halt after that. Later that night, before going to sleep, Lina thought that perhaps the Storm was the only reason the Federation didn't just come and take what it needed.

———

The next day, they started anew with the boat. Kip and Nora were making a sail from the glider's wing. Lina was working on a rudder.

"This is all Earth technology, you know," Nora commented, testing a joint.

"Earth?" Lina asked, not looking up from her work. "What's that, another fancy Federation world?"

"We call it the Cradle," Nora said. "The place where humanity came from."

Lina set the piece aside for the sealant to dry. "So, the Federation is also a colony?"

"Yes, the Federation has hundreds of worlds, and most of them originate from Earth. To tell a long story short, they sent out colony ships and started a big war. By the time the ships arrived, there was nobody to call back home." Nora tightened the sinew a bit too much, and it snapped with a loud twang. She cursed in words Lina didn't know – but immediately tried to repeat, always eager to collect new obscenities.

After a while, Kip asked, "But did you ever travel back to see what happened?"

"We never got a chance. The ships voyaged for hundreds of years. On arrival, we were nothing more than savages, raised by deteriorating machines. It took a thousand years to regain knowledge and find each other, then a thousand more to end the wars. We found many worlds where humans had survived. Some had prepared ecosystems, but were empty, like Azoria. But Earth itself – the Cradle – was never found again."

"Great," Lina said sarcastically. "So we're descended from people who couldn't even find their own planet."

The waves sighed against the rocks. Three humans, children of Earth, stranded on a rock at the bottom of everything.

CHAPTER 12

The Lighthouse at the End of the Sky

Nora's shoulders burned with every pull of the makeshift oar. Her simulations in the *Pathfinder's* pool felt useless now. Nothing could have prepared her for how cold and vast this water felt – under a sky that didn't feel like sky at all.

She glanced at the others. Lina rowed hard and steady, though Nora could see the tension underneath. Kip, jaw tight, fought with the tricky sail made from glider parts, trying to catch the wild gusts of wind.

Their boat, cobbled together from plane wing panels, lashed with cables, and sealed with medical sealant, was falling apart fast. Cold water sloshed around their ankles, rising steadily. Kip bailed it out almost constantly, but couldn't keep up.

"Landfall ahead," Kip said, eyes fixed on the tower on the rock ahead, with a dock and a small figure waving.

"That building… how is it even standing?" Lina muttered, stopping rowing to squint. Nora looked too; the tower looked impossibly tall and old against the gray sky. "The physics are shot to hell."

"And yet," Nora replied, managing a weak smile, "there it is. A bit like us, don't you think?"

Right on cue, a bigger wave slapped the boat hard. A seam near Lina split wider, water pouring in faster.

"Right," Lina said grimly, watching the water rush in. "This tub's gonna break up. Three minutes, tops."

Kip adjusted the sail for one last push towards the shore. Nora dug her oar in, forcing herself to ignore the pain shooting through her arms and back. As the water rose, a strange calm settled over her.

"Jettison non-essentials!" Kip ordered sharply. "Prepare to swim. Lina, stay calm and afloat, I'll get you to shore."

"Yeah, tryin' not to drown," Lina retorted, her voice strained. Nora saw the signs under Lina's tough act: her breathing too fast, her knuckles white on the boat's edge. It wasn't bravery, Nora knew, but pure terror held tight.

The boat floor finally ripped apart with a sick lurch.

"Go! Swim for it!" Kip yelled, grabbing Lina as the boat broke apart.

Nora took her waterproofed med pack and shoved off into the shockingly cold water. The cold took her breath away. Looking back through the spray, she saw Kip holding up Lina, swimming strong, pulling her through the waves. Lina kept her face locked in concentration, staring hard at the island, refusing to look down at the dark water.

A skinny man with wild gray hair was bouncing on the dock ahead, waving like mad and shouting something cheerful. When Nora finally dragged herself onto the rough wooden dock, he beamed down at her. He looked desperate for visitors, his eager smile and rehearsed speech gave it away.

"Welcome! Welcome, esteemed visitor!" he declared, his voice booming with misplaced formality. His accent was strikingly clear, near-perfect Federation Standard. "I have the distinct honor and privilege of meeting you at Point Descent Observation Station and Lighthouse! Chief Observer Marvin Thale, at your service!"

"Help my friends," Nora gasped, pointing back toward the water where Kip was hauling Lina the last few feet.

The man rushed to get them from the water. He was surprisingly strong, even though he bounced all over the place. Soon, they were collapsed on the dock, soaked and shivering.

Nora quickly checked them over. Lina held herself stiffly, clearly shaken by the water but refusing to show weakness. Kip favored his left shoulder a bit, but otherwise seemed okay.

Their host, Marvin, suddenly froze, his eyes fixed on the tattered, salt-stained insignia on Nora's shoulder. "That insignia... First Principles! Are you... *really* Federation?" he stammered, awe replacing his earlier excitement.

"Sergeant Nora Hertzig," she confirmed, pushing herself to her feet, soaked and cold. "Medical Officer, UES *Pathfinder*."

Marvin changed in a flash. He snapped straight up, his spine almost unnaturally rigid, his hand flying up in a salute so sharp it looked like it might break something. His eyes filled with tears. Kip and Lina looked at each other, shocked by the change.

"Ensign Marvin Thale, Surface Observation Corps, Detached Service, reporting for duty!" His voice cracked. "Awaiting orders, ma'am!"

It felt surreal – three drenched survivors on a rickety dock, facing a man crying and saluting.

Even through the exhaustion, Nora straightened up and returned the salute.

"At ease," she said, trying to sound calm and in charge. "Ensign, my assignment is the *Pathfinder*. Your unit... I don't recognize it."

"The UES *Horizont*, ma'am!" he declared proudly, though his voice still wobbled. "Survey and Reconnaissance Division, under Commander Reeves."

Horizont. Nora recognized the name. It was a previous expedition lost many years ago. She nodded, keeping her face neutral. "Ensign, let's get inside," Nora said. "We need to get warm and checked over."

"Yes, ma'am! Absolutely!" Marvin's posture relaxed, though he maintained his military bearing. "Emergency shelter protocols, of course." He gestured toward the lighthouse structure.

As they followed him, shivering, Kip leaned close to Nora. "Federation?" he whispered, eyes wide. "One of yours?"

"I think," Nora murmured back, "we just found what's left of a long-lost expedition. He seems to think the Federation is still watching him."

Lina, squeezing water from her short hair with sharp tugs, muttered just loud enough for them to hear, "Great. So we didn't just crash-land in hell, we also ruined this poor guy's entire life by actually showing up."

Inside the lighthouse cottage, Nora saw an amazing mess of salvaged junk, arranged in a way she couldn't understand. But somehow, the messy room felt cozy, warmed by a good fire in a stone hearth.

Marvin gave them dry clothes and warm blankets. They fit terribly and were clearly cobbled together from decades of salvage. Then he bustled around, serving up a hot meal. It was some kind of tasty seafood and roasted roots she didn't recognize. His stiff military posture quickly vanished, replaced by the jumpy energy of a lonely man thrilled to have company. He still spoke perfect Federation Standard. It sounded a little old-fashioned, especially compared to the clipped Trade Speech Kip and Lina used.

"My mother, Corporal Elena Thale – comms tech, Marines – she got here after the *Horizont* went down," Marvin explained, his enthusiasm returning. "Came down in a safety pod and made it to the shore."

His expression grew more subdued. "Always said the Federation would come back. *Duty*, she called it."

"It was about sixty years ago?" Nora asked gently.

"Exactly! Sixty-one years, four months, and…" he peered at a crazy-looking clock, "… eighteen days! Roughly." A shadow crossed his face briefly. "I was born seven years after she landed. Mother drilled me on Fed protocols from day one." He was quiet for a moment. "Gone thirty years now. But I kept the watch. Kept observing. Ferdinand helps, of course. My Chief Assistant." He nodded vaguely towards the door where his donkey presumably was.

"Can you brief us on the local politics?" Kip asked smoothly, sounding diplomatic.

Marvin brightened. "The Harbor Commonwealth, where my family's from, is a democracy – elected leaders, proper laws, very forward-thinking!" He unrolled a large, carefully hand-drawn map across the table. It showed detailed coasts, mountains, and dozens of marked towns connected by dotted trade routes.

"We hold the south-east coast," he explained, tracing the map with practiced precision. "Good farms inland, mines out east. We value knowledge, new ideas. I've documented the governance extensively." His finger swept west across a much larger area. "That's the Kingdom of Tides. Much bigger, older. Great cities, huge forts. Traditional monarchy. *But*," he leaned in, lowering his voice, "the supply captain says there's unrest – political upheaval, maybe religious conflict. Hard to get solid intelligence out here."

"Established nations, then," Kip noted, absorbing the information.

"Absolutely! Complex political structures, trade networks, cultural development." Marvin's pride in his research was evident. "Free Harbor is the Commonwealth's capital – main port, diplomatic center. Representatives from island nations convene there for Trade Councils."

"What language do they speak?" Nora asked. "Your Standard is excellent, but surely that's not common now?"

"Surface Common, actually. Fascinating linguistic evolution!" Marvin's enthusiasm returned. "Pure Federation Standard as the base. We're all descended from early settlers. Over the years, it picked up regional differences and a few borrowed words from tribal arrivals. But the grammar is still mostly Standard. My mother insisted I maintain proper Federation pronunciation, but I've documented seven distinct regional dialects that have emerged."

"Free Harbor sounds… promising," Nora commented, glancing at Kip.

"Very promising! There are confirmed reports of limited contact with the world above the Storm!" Marvin pulled out another chart showing trade routes. "Mostly salvage recovery, but some evidence of deliberate exchange – advanced materials, precision instruments."

"Trade connections..." Kip leaned forward, clearly interested. "Those could be very useful indeed."

"Definitely! Since you are Federation representatives," Marvin said, his excitement returning, "they'll surely grant you access to their Archives! The research potential alone..."

He paused, then continued more soberly. "Speaking of arrivals – yours was a Category Blue Descent. Only the third I've recorded in fifty-three years!"

"What does a *Blue* descent mean?" Lina asked.

"Controlled deceleration! Minimal structural damage!" Marvin's gestures were more restrained this time. "Standard descents result in catastrophic impact – massive island destruction, debris fields. But Category Blue events... some mechanism slows the descent. I observed one thirty-one years back, and another seven years ago. Both achieved remarkably intact water landings."

"Any theories on how to get back up through that Storm?" Lina asked bluntly.

Marvin's expression grew thoughtful. "Three viable approaches, actually. I've done extensive theoretical work." He retrieved several folders of detailed calculations and diagrams.

"First – Thermal Updraft Balloon System." He spread out complex mathematical charts. "Using volcanic vents to superheat air in large-scale balloons. The buoyancy equations work perfectly," he pointed to detailed calculations, "but the balloon would need to be roughly the size of the lighthouse. And stormproof. And you'd need several tons of silk for it."

"Second – Pressure Differential Catapult." His diagrams showed sophisticated engineering principles. "Seven-hundred-foot rail system, counterweight of approximately forty tons. The physics are sound." He traced stress calculations with his finger. "Ferdinand would need a couple thousand friends to run it."

"Third – Mountain Peak Ascension Route." He unfolded detailed topographical maps. "The Korthak Peaks, about five hundred miles northeast. According to every measurement I can make, they pierce clean through the Storm layer." His finger traced elevation lines with genuine precision. "The mathematics are absolutely reliable – you *can* get above it." His expression grew serious. "Of course, you'd have to climb sheer rock faces through the Storm itself – constant lightning, hurricane winds, freezing rain that turns to ice on the rocks." He stared at the elevations. "And then somehow carry a flying machine up with you, or coordinate with someone on the other side to pick you up."

After explaining each theory, Marvin grew quieter. "The math works. It's just…" He gestured vaguely at his cottage, his solitude. "Hard to test theories when you're the only test pilot. And Ferdinand is *definitely* not built for mountaineering."

Lina examined his calculations with grudging respect. "These aren't terrible ideas, actually. Completely impractical, but the engineering principles are solid."

As the evening continued, the three of them huddled near the fire while Marvin organized supplies for their journey.

"So," Lina said quietly, her voice flat. "We're stranded."

"His theories are certainly… thorough," Kip offered carefully.

"Thorough, yeah. But that mountain route…" Lina shook her head. "Even if you could survive the climb through the Storm, then what? Wave at passing aircraft?"

Nora rubbed her temples. "So, we're stuck."

Silence fell, heavy with things they weren't saying.

"Not stranded, perhaps," Kip said after a moment. "Relocated. There are real nations, not just wilderness. Governments. And Free Harbor seems to trade with nations above."

"Relocated?" Lina started pacing around the room. "You want us to just… live here? Forget everything up top?"

"I'm suggesting we learn more before deciding," Kip corrected smoothly. "Free Harbor seems our best lead."

"That stood out to me too," Nora agreed. "Even limited contact means some method exists. Maybe not reliable, but it is something."

"Or at least a way to send a message," Kip added. "Better than being stuck here, even if Marvin is good company."

"So, the plan is Free Harbor," Nora concluded, looking between Kip and Lina. "Investigate the high-altitude contacts. See what we find."

Lina stopped pacing, her jaw set. "Fine. Reconnaissance. But we're not staying. We find a way home."

"Recon," Kip agreed smoothly.

Marvin returned with a steaming pot and several weathered mugs. "Hot spiced kelproot tea! Excellent for planning and clear thinking!" His earlier manic energy had settled into something warmer, more genuine.

That evening, while they prepared for the journey, Marvin approached Nora alone. His usual bouncing energy was subdued, replaced by that serious military bearing she'd glimpsed earlier.

"Sergeant," he began, his voice carefully measured, "your report to Command... will it mention Point Descent Station? And Corporal Elena Thale's service record?" He looked directly at her, his bright eyes suddenly vulnerable. "Mother always believed Command would want to know that *Horizont's* people carried on the mission. That the station remained operational."

The simple request hit Nora hard, making her chest feel tight. She couldn't really make that promise; the report would probably never get filed from down here. But the hope in his eyes – decades of disciplined dedication – deserved more than bureaucratic honesty.

"Yes, Ensign," she promised, meeting his gaze firmly. "Point Descent Station and Corporal Thale's dedication will be documented in my official report. Her commitment to maintaining this post will be formally recognized."

Marvin's face brightened, the weight of years seeming to lift from his shoulders. "Thank you, Sergeant. She always said, *When duty feels meaningless, that's when keeping faith matters most.*" He straightened, some of his earlier enthusiasm returning, but tempered now. "I've maintained her standards for thirty years. Whatever happens next... the watch was kept."

———

The next morning, Marvin presented them with his sturdy boat, the *Surface Ambassador*. It was already loaded with what he called "navigational essentials" – detailed charts, weather instruments, and emergency supplies. "My primary research vessel," he announced with quiet pride. "She's carried me through worse weather than this." He brushed off their concerns about leaving him without transport, mentioning other boats with a casual wave.

When Lina efficiently repaired a problem with the rigging, Marvin watched with genuine appreciation. "Excellent technique! The knot work alone shows real expertise."

He insisted on checking the supplies personally. "Free Harbor is about two days with favorable currents," he explained, spreading his charts one final time. "I've marked landmarks, hazard zones, and reliable anchorages. There is also an eastern lighthouse to guide you near Free Harbor itself."

He handed them a carefully written letter of introduction. "For the Harbor Commonwealth Port Authority. It should expedite your diplomatic reception."

As they prepared to cast off in the gray morning light, Marvin stood at attention on the dock. His mismatched uniform was straight, his bearing formal but not stiff. He offered a crisp salute as they departed.

"Safe voyage, Sergeant," he called. "May your mission succeed."

"He is..." Kip remarked, trimming the sail as they caught the morning breeze, "... quite remarkable, actually."

"Will he be okay out here by himself?" Nora asked quietly, watching Marvin's figure grow smaller.

"He's managed alone for decades," Lina said from the stern, her voice thoughtful. She looked back at the lighthouse. "That winding mechanism, though… clever engineering. Efficient use of available resources."

They sailed in comfortable silence, listening to the creak of rigging and the slap of waves against the hull. The lighthouse beam swept steadily behind them, a constant rhythm they could still see. Ahead lay the unknown coast, the city of Free Harbor, and perhaps some answers about this world beneath the Storm. And maybe, just maybe, a path back to the world they had lost.

Nora took a deep breath of the salt air. Whatever came next, they'd face it together. A Federation medic caught between duty and conscience, a displaced noble learning to lead, and a brilliant engineer conquering her fears.

PART 3: SURFACE POLITICS

The Science of Improbability

Dr. Lawrence Nabble, chief science officer of the UES *Pathfinder*, had arrived to provide his promised report in person.

"Is this off the record, Commander?"

Commander Voss nodded, leaning against the viewport. "Entirely. Speak freely."

"Good, because there's no way to describe what just happened in anything resembling acceptable scientific terminology." Nabble gestured to a tablet with tables, gravitational readings, radiation measurements, and recordings. "I filed a report full of gaps, because *I fucking don't know* isn't accepted scientific notation."

Voss smiled. "Summarize what we do know."

Nabble activated the holographic display showing the shuttle departing the island after extraction. "Initial readings were normal – or at least predictable when removing most of the anti-gravitational element from a chunk of rock hovering 28,000 feet up."

The recording showed the massive formation tumbling toward the cloud layer. "But then things got…" Nabble paused, searching for a term, "…*weird.*"

As the descent started, the cloud layer beneath began swirling into a local hurricane. "The Storm was reacting," Nabble said, voice dropping. "Almost as if preparing."

"To what?" Voss asked.

"The extraction? The falling mass? The location? We have insufficient data." The swirling pattern expanded, forming a perfect circular opening that revealed what lay beneath.

"Water," Voss said softly. "An ocean."

"Indeed. And radiation readings below the Storm are two times the normal parameters. The Storm is a radiation shield." The fragment continued its descent through the perfectly circular opening. Then came the impossible part.

"It *slowed down*," Nabble said, voice mixing awe and professional offense. "A multi-ton chunk of rock. No propulsion. No grav core. It just… decided not to fall."

The recording showed the landmass's gentle descent to the ocean surface, settling like a leaf on a pond. "We calculated the forces and energy required to achieve that landing. The numbers don't work, Commander. They don't even pretend to add up."

"Anything else?" Voss asked.

Nabble advanced the recording. "When it was closing, our sensors detected a small aircraft passing through." He zoomed in on a scout craft, then continued, "And then the eagle."

The final frames showed a massive bird diving through before the aperture sealed completely.

"I assume you've verified the recording?"

"Triple-verified, including footage from the shuttle. So how do I send this to HQ without triggering a breakdown?"

Voss straightened. "Stick to verifiable facts without causing a philosophical crisis. The island fell; we glimpsed the ocean."

"Will do. And… our whiskey supplies have suffered critical depletion. Dr. Renault nearly wept at the calculations. Not to mention aircraft and birds trailing an anomaly."

That earned a genuine smile from Voss. "I'll authorize emergency resupply."

After Nabble left, Voss remained at the viewport, her thoughts turning personal. The scout craft. The eagle. The controlled descent. Scientists in despair. None of this mattered.

"Nora," she whispered. "You're alive down there."

For the first time since Operation Windfall began, Voss allowed herself to hope for something beyond mission parameters. Unprofessional, irrational, and not reportable.

CHAPTER 13
Inquisition's Justice

Toryn sat on the damp prison floor, knees to his chest, back braced against the wall. Less than two weeks ago, he'd soared the Heights with an eagle's-eye view of the world. Now he couldn't see ten feet ahead.

His last eagle ride hadn't gone to plan. He had no way to steer the bird, only vague gestures toward the sky, trying to signal he wanted to return to the Heights. The eagle had given him a look adults reserve for clueless children. Eventually, he'd just asked to be taken anywhere. And somehow, it worked.

Flying over the water, he realized that the eagle was taking him to the nearest shore. It was better than being stranded on the rock, but that's where his luck ended.

Upon dropping him at the shore, the eagle flew off. Toryn wandered unfamiliar terrain for hours before encountering a patrol of uniformed guards. One glance at his tattooed arms, and they shouted "demon spawn" and "heretic" in Trade Speech, reacting with immediate hostility.

The days since had blurred into interrogations. First came the cold water – buckets thrown when his answers displeased them, leaving him shivering on the stone floor. Then came the scribe, quietly disapproving as he transcribed Toryn's "blasphemous" accounts of the world above and riding eagles. Yesterday, they had beaten him – systematically, without emotion, as if working from a manual.

His stomach growled. His ribs ached. The morning's thin fungal gruel left a bitter aftertaste and did little to fill the hollow ache. In the Heights, even the poorest ate well – root vegetables, dried meat, sometimes lowland fruits. Here, the daily ration barely fueled awareness.

He flexed his limbs, wincing. The Windclaw Tribe never used prisons. Justice in the Heights came swiftly – the Circle of Elders voted, and punishment followed. The worst sentence was exile by Great Flight: a leap into open sky without the eagle-call whistle. If the eagles saved you – it was fate. If not... that too was an answer.

The idea of locking someone in a stone box seemed both wasteful and cruel. Like storing thawed water in a jar only to find it has rotted over the months.

Outside his cell, he could hear the shuffling of guards and the steady rhythm of their boots. The cell itself was simple and grim – three stone walls, several stone benches, iron bars with a door, and a drainage hole. Toryn moved around the cell several times to find the farthest bench from the sewer. Unfortunately, the smell was persistent.

The distant sound of chanting drifted through the hall. Evening devotions to Storm's Truth were obligatory for prisoners to hear, but forbidden to join. The hypnotic cadence had a certain beauty to it, and its monotonous murmur was working better than any lullaby.

From somewhere beyond the prison walls came a whistle, followed by rhythmic chugging and rumbling through the floor. The first time he heard it, he thought it was some disaster. Yet, it appeared to be a mechanism, running on tracks and hauling heavy loads – the guards had called it a *train*. They spoke with pride about this marvel of the Holy Sovereignty's industrial might.

A rattling of keys echoed down the corridor, followed by footsteps.

Seems like I'm having company, Toryn thought.

The cell door creaked open.

"Those go to the cell with the heretic," the guard announced. He shoved three figures into the cell before slamming the door. "Play nice."

Toryn studied the newcomers in the dim light. A tall woman with a slender build and a braid, a shorter, stockier woman with short dark hair, and a lean man who thoroughly examined the cell and Toryn. All three wore clothing that had clearly seen better days, patched and assembled from several different garments.

What he observed first was their physical stature and skin tone. Unlike the pale, hollow-faced locals, these newcomers showed no signs of malnutrition or lack of sunlight.

Those people are either from above, or it is some kind of setup.

The man's eyes narrowed as they took in Toryn's tribal clothing and the wind-pattern tattoos on his forearms. His gaze was direct but calculating.

"Well," he said in Trade Speech, "I didn't expect to find anyone with such... distinct tattoos down here."

Toryn's muscles tensed. The man had chosen his words carefully. But there was no sense in hiding that he recognized him as someone from the Heights.

"I'm not from around here," Toryn replied with equal care, watching their reactions.

"And how does someone from…" The lean man paused. "Not around here, end up in a prison cell?" He settled himself against the opposite wall with a casualness that didn't quite mask his disdain for the cell.

Toryn considered his answer. "Suspected heresy against Storm's Truth, apparently."

The three exchanged glances.

"Same story," the taller woman said with a weary sigh. "We got lost at sea. An Inquisition patrol spotted us and threatened to shoot if we didn't cooperate. They promised we would talk to a judge tomorrow. Probably just a border crossing issue." She spoke with precise diction – each word carefully selected and positioned like stones in a wall.

"Those lunos kept yelling about heretics and Storm's Truth," the shorter woman added angrily. "Loaded us onto some massive… iron coffin on tracks. Brought us straight here." She had a practical set to her shoulders, like someone accustomed to solving problems rather than discussing them.

Before Toryn could answer, the conversation was cut short by a guard banging the butt of his musket against the bars. "No talking after dark bell! Sleep now!" he barked. His voice echoed against the stone walls like a hammer striking an anvil.

The cell fell silent. Toryn watched as his new cellmates arranged themselves in the small space, each claiming a separate bench without a word. Questions would have to wait until morning.

———

Morning in Tideguard Keep wasn't marked by sunlight, nothing truly pierced the Storm but by the toll of a massive bell and the clatter of breakfast.

A guard shoved clay bowls through the door slot. Each held a gray porridge speckled with something darker. Fungal mash, maybe grain. Worse than it looked, but no one skipped it. The menu wasn't up for debate.

As they ate, Toryn studied his companions more closely.

"So what do you know about this place?" he asked quietly, mindful of the guards in the corridor.

The man glanced at the barred door before answering, voice low. "This place calls itself the Holy Sovereignty. A religious cult runs it, built on the belief that the Storm is a divine barrier protecting them from corruption."

"Notice the guards muttering prayers and crossing fingers when they pass?" the taller woman asked.

"That's their reaction to your... distinct attire," the man said, nodding at Toryn's tribal garb. "They think it's from the land of demons."

Toryn processed this information. It explained the endless questions during his interrogations about "demonic realms." The demands that he "tell the truth about his mission."

Before they could continue, keys rattled in the lock. The cell door swung open. Two guards stood there, one pointing at the shorter woman. The one on the left had a holstered pistol. It indicated a higher rank, as firearms were expensive and typically reserved for officers.

"You first," he said. His tunic bore the emblem of a junior officer. A single storm cloud without the lightning bolts of higher ranks. "Time for an interview."

The woman stood with her jaw clenched. "Don't wait up," she said to her companions. She attempted humor despite the fear in her eyes.

The door clanged shut behind her. The sound echoed down the stone corridor like a string in the high wind.

"Will she be fine?" Toryn asked after the guards' footsteps faded.

His two remaining cellmates exchanged grim looks.

"Depends on how well she plays their game," the lean man said quietly. His voice dropped to a whisper. "Zealots may have their own definition of an *interview*."

The hours crawled by. The man maintained a carefully controlled posture. The tall woman paced the small cell, counting steps between turns, obviously nervous. From somewhere in the building came the smell of cooking. A hearty stew that made their morning gruel seem even more inadequate. The aroma seemed almost deliberately cruel. As if the prison administrators had specifically placed the kitchen by the cells as an additional punishment.

When the door finally opened again, the shorter woman was shoved through. She stumbled to her knees. Her clothes were soaked, hair plastered to her head, water dripping from her chin. She was shivering.

The taller woman immediately went to her, helping her to the bench.

"Those b-bastards," the shorter woman stammered through chattering teeth. "D-dunking me like I'm fresh off the f-factory floor needing a c-coolant bath."

"What did they want?" the lean man asked, keeping his voice low.

"Everything. Where we c-came from. How we got here. Whether we h-had religious teachings different from theirs." The shorter woman hugged herself tightly. "I t-told them we were traders from a small island nation, g-got lost in the weather. They d-didn't believe me."

"Small island nation?" The taller woman looked confused. "But I thought we had agreed–"

"Agreed on what?" the lean man cut in sharply.

An uncomfortable silence fell over the cell. The shorter woman's teeth continued chattering.

"She needs to rest. It's not the time for this," the taller woman said firmly.

Toryn watched the exchange with quiet understanding. He'd already figured out these three were from above the Storm – their tanned skin and accents made that clear enough. Now they were trying to hide it from him, obviously suspecting he was working for the Inquisition.

The day dragged on. A meager lunch was provided. A thin slice of hard bread made from some unidentifiable root flour and a watery soup containing pale chunks of cultivated fungi.

Then the guards returned. This time, they pointed at the lean man.

"Your turn, fancy pants."

He straightened his shoulders and followed without comment. His bearing reminded Toryn of a warrior facing a difficult decision.

"He'll manage," the taller woman said after they'd gone. Though she didn't sound entirely convinced. "He has experience handling... difficult situations."

"And you?" Toryn asked. "What's your story?"

The taller woman gave him a measured look. "Let's just say I'm a long way from home." She turned her attention to the shorter woman, checking her for signs of hypothermia. Her movements were those of a practiced healer.

"That's not the first time you're doing it," Toryn observed.

"Something like that." She didn't elaborate.

The afternoon light gradually dimmed. It marked the transition to evening without the sun's clear guidance. Through the distance came the tolling of temple bells, followed by another round of chanting. A different hymn this time, but with the same fervent devotion to Storm's Truth.

The lean man's return was announced by dragging sounds in the corridor. The guards literally threw him into the cell. His face was bloodied, one eye swelling shut, lip split.

The taller woman immediately went to work. She tore a strip from the man's undershirt to dab at the blood.

"I regret to inform you," the lean man said with a dry smile, "that they seem to have a particular dislike for those with educated speech." He winced as she touched a particularly tender spot. "I may have made the error of suggesting some *compensation* for resolving our unfortunate detention."

"Hold still," she ordered. She examined his injuries with clinical detachment. "Nothing seems broken. Just badly bruised."

"And what did you tell them?" the shorter woman asked with her lips curled, hinting that she was still angry at him for snapping at her earlier.

"Only what we agreed upon. Lost at sea, blown off course, no idea how we ended up in their waters." He attempted a smile that turned into a grimace. "Though I had to reveal our island nation's origins when they pressed for specifics. And they were curious why we told them we were from the Harbor Commonwealth when captured."

"Rusted wrench!" she swore. "What do we do with this next?"

"I told them we were just trying to smooth things out. Then I asked about a possible solution, and that's when things went awry."

"What's the Harbor Commonwealth?" Toryn asked, trying to defuse the growing tension.

"A democratic society," the lean man explained through gritted teeth. "The Holy Sovereignty considers them heretics for rejecting Storm's Truth. Anyone who doesn't bow to their theological supremacy is deemed an enemy."

"So now they think we're lying to them," the taller woman said quietly.

"This is why we needed to stick to the story," the lean man said, anger creeping into his voice despite their need for quiet.

"Well, maybe next time you shouldn't leave me to face the bastards alone while you work out the details!" the shorter woman shot back.

"Enough," the taller woman said firmly. "What's done is done. We deal with it."

But the damage was clear. Whatever trust had existed between them was fracturing.

Soon after, the cell door opened again. "You, heretic," the guard announced, pointing at Toryn. "You're up."

As Toryn rose to his feet, he caught the taller woman's eye.

"Remember," she said quietly, "they can only hurt your body."

It was an odd thing to say, but somehow exactly what Toryn needed to hear.

———

The interrogation room was much brighter than the cell, oil lamps casting steady light from sconces along the walls. A large man Toryn had never seen during his eight days of imprisonment sat at a massive desk, writing. He looked up as the guards brought Toryn in. Despite his bulk, there was nothing slow or dull about the eyes that assessed Toryn from beneath heavy brows.

Toryn caught sight of a chair with chains attached and sharp metal instruments arranged on a nearby table.

"Sit," the man commanded, pointing at the chair.

Toryn complied, keeping his back straight, chin raised in the manner of a tribal warrior. He would not cower.

The man circled him once. "You know why you're here."

"I'm accused of heresy against Storm's Truth," Toryn replied evenly.

The man's expression didn't change, but his eyes hardened. "More than accused. Guilty. You claim to come from above the

Storm, which is blasphemy. There is nothing above the Storm but the Void. The Temple's truth is absolute."

"I've lived above the Storm my entire life until recently," Toryn stated. "My people have dwelled in the Heights for generations."

The blow came without warning. An open-handed slap that rocked Toryn's head sideways and set his ear ringing.

"Lies offend the Storm's Truth," the man said calmly. "Let's try again. You were sent from the Void to corrupt our holy land. Who sent you? What is your mission?"

Toryn tasted blood. "I came seeking a heartstone to save my islet from falling."

Another blow, closed-fist this time, catching him in the ribs.

"Your new cellmates," the man continued as if nothing had happened. "What have they told you of their origins? Their plans?"

Toryn steadied his breathing against the pain. "Nothing much. They barely talk about their origins."

The man's eyes sharpened with interest. "And where is it?"

Toryn hesitated. He had no love for his cellmates' deceptions, but betraying them felt wrong. "They... they don't seem to agree on where it is."

"Go on."

"One said they were from a small island nation. Another mentioned the Harbor Commonwealth."

The man leaned back in his chair, a satisfied expression crossing his face. "Interesting. Continue."

But Toryn had said enough. He clamped his mouth shut.

The man studied him for a moment, then nodded to a guard behind Toryn. Rough hands grabbed his shoulders, holding him in place, while another guard chained him to the chair. The interrogator carefully removed his jacket, folding it over a chair with meticulous care.

"Physical persuasion is sometimes necessary to free souls from heretical influence," he said. He drew on a pair of leather gloves studded with metal across the knuckles. "I am authorized to administer such persuasion."

What followed was methodical, almost businesslike. The man asked questions about the "realm above," about Toryn's "demonic masters," about the other prisoners. With each answer deemed insufficient, Toryn received a precisely aimed blow. Painful but calculated.

Toryn remained silent or repeated the truth, which only earned him more punishment. The man showed neither anger nor sadness at this. Only a professional determination, as if conducting an unpleasant but necessary duty.

Outside, through the thick walls, came the muffled sounds of chanting. Another round of devotions to Storm's Truth.

The man stepped back. The front of his shirt was dark with sweat, but his breathing remained steady. He reached for a flask on the table, taking a deep drink.

"To the cell," he instructed the guards and then turned to Toryn. "We will continue tomorrow. Think what information you can give me to ease your suffering."

As the guards dragged him back through the winding corridors, Toryn fought to remain conscious. He needed to remember the route, count the turns. Twenty paces from the interrogation room to the first left turn. Eighteen paces to the right turn. Thirty-three to the descending stairs.

By the time they reached the cell, he was cataloging every detail despite the pain. The Heights had taught him that survival often depended on observation, but it was not about a life philosophy now. He just needed to distance himself from the pain and the interrogator's offer that made him feel physically dirty.

He wanted me to lie? Or to spy on others to receive fewer beatings?

The guards tossed him into the cell.

The taller woman was immediately at his side, helping him sit up against the wall. Her hands checked his ribs, assessed his bloodied face.

"Ribs bruised, not broken," she murmured. "Split lip, contusions to the face and abdomen…" Her fingers probed gently but confidently.

"I'm Nora," she said softly as she worked. The first to introduce herself properly.

Through the pain, Toryn found his voice. "The man who questioned me… I haven't seen him before. He seemed important. And he asks questions about you."

"How long have you been here?" the lean man asked.

"About a week. But you seem to be more important than I am if they called in the new interrogator."

Nora looked at Toryn. "You need rest. We can talk when you're stronger."

Before he could respond, the cell door opened again. A guard beckoned to her.

"You," he pointed to Nora, "it's your turn."

Nora rose smoothly. "About time," she told the others, though Toryn noticed the slight tightening around her eyes. The door closed behind her with a solid thunk.

The lean man watched her go with obvious concern and shook his head.

"I'm Kip, by the way," he added.

"And I'm Lina," the shorter woman said. Her tone suggested the introduction was more a practical necessity than a social courtesy.

"Toryn Skyheart of the Windclaw Tribe," Toryn replied.

Kip's eyebrows rose slightly. "Good name. Not as loud as Oakenshield, but still, if I were you, I'd skip the family and tribe part in these lands."

The waiting was worse this time, knowing what Nora might be enduring. Lina had finally stopped shivering but remained huddled in the corner. Kip maintained his composed façade despite occasional winces when he moved.

"So, I gave you my name and clan," Toryn said after a long silence. "Are you going to tell the truth now or still pretending to be from the Harbor Commonwealth or some distant island?"

They both stared at him.

"The truth is dangerous," Kip said quietly. "But yes… we're from above the Storm. Sounds like you'd already figured that out. That will get us all executed."

"Might anyway," Toryn pointed out. "At least with the truth, we stand a chance of trusting each other."

They were interrupted by the guards bringing Nora in. She moved stiffly, favoring her right side. Her lower lip was split, a trickle of blood darkening her chin. But her eyes burned with cold determination.

"Well, I've discovered the joke," she said once the guards were gone. "That man isn't just an interrogator. His name is Dregg, and they call him Judge. Unless we want more of his judgment, we need to get out of here."

"Agreed," Kip said immediately.

"That man," Toryn said. "He's not just a brute."

"No," Kip agreed. "That's what makes him dangerous. He's intelligent and methodical. I think he genuinely believes he is doing something righteous."

"Religious sick bastards," Lina muttered, rubbing her bruised wrist.

Kip said, "I hope we won't meet whoever comes next."

"The Judge isn't the highest authority?" Toryn asked, confused.

"He prepares prisoners," Nora explained, wincing as she sat. "Softens them up for further questioning. And from what I gathered, for special cases, there would be someone of a higher rank. And we are considered *special*."

The four fell silent as a guard passed by.

"We need a plan," Lina said once he was gone. "Before they separate us or decide we're too much trouble."

Nora looked at Toryn. "You said you've been here longer than we have. Have you noticed any patterns? Guard changes, weaknesses in security?"

Toryn hesitated, then decided there was little to lose. But first, he had questions of his own.

"Before we go further," he said carefully, "I need to know if we share more than just a prison cell." He looked directly at Nora.

"On an ice-covered islet, I saw the outlanders being attacked by a frost hunter. They left without the person they called Nora."

The three exchanged alarmed glances.

"Just as I need to know," Kip countered, his voice barely above a whisper, "if you're the tribal craftsman who flew a 15-foot glider to that same island shortly before its... descent."

"It was 20 feet and I built it myself," said Toryn, watching their expressions shift to relief. "Perfectly balanced for high-altitude navigation."

Nora relaxed and said in a friendly tone, "The predator left me unconscious in a cave. I woke up when the island was on the surface and met those two. Later on, we found your glider and built a boat."

"I think," Kip said cautiously, "we have a lot to talk about, but now's not the time." He nodded toward the corridor. "We should rest. Tomorrow brings its own trials."

They settled in for the night on the stone benches.

Darkness crept through the cell, broken only by the dim glow of a torch flickering in the corridor. Through a small window high above, Toryn glimpsed the swirling Storm. Beyond it lay the Heights and everything he'd left behind.

For now, survival meant focusing on the challenges directly ahead and the unlikely allies he'd found in this prison beneath the clouds. Even if trust hadn't fully taken root.

CHAPTER 14

Inquisitor

High Inquisitor Thadeius traced a finger along the armrest, once again noting the joint's poor craftsmanship. Being an inquisitor had its perks – respect, power, and the satisfaction of serving the Storm. Decent furniture, unfortunately, wasn't among them.

The finest furniture – like what adorned his residence in Stormseat – came from beyond the Storm, where craftsmen had better tools and resources. But such work was now outlawed, declared heretical by the very order he served. He recognized the irony, though he'd never say it aloud.

The chair creaked as he shifted, leaning toward the narrow window that offered a slim view past Tideguard Keep's outer wall. Beyond lay the gray stretch of the Great Ocean and the port city of Stormhaven – formerly Tidehaven, before the Revolution erased the monarchy.

Oil lamps flickered in the wall sconces, casting the office in warm, uneven light. Gas lighting had been installed under the old regime, but Thadeius preferred oil. Officially, it was for tradition. Unofficially, gas lighting was unkind to men nearing sixty. The incense-laced air barely registered anymore – after so many years, the scent clung to his robes and, he suspected, his skin.

"Holy work demands sacrifice," he murmured, though he doubted that included risking collapse from a rickety chair.

Before the Revolution – barely a year ago – Thadeius had been one of the High Priests in a church that was gaining popularity with the masses. They had orchestrated the coup carefully, feeding liberal revolutionaries with both ideas and funding. When the monarchy finally fell, the church seized power through a mix of religious fervor and discreet military bribes. It had been a glorious, uncertain time.

He recalled that morning's sermon – arms raised to the eternal Storm, eyes lit with righteous fire as he warned of the torments awaiting those who trafficked with demons or their devices. His voice had rung through the old cathedral, now consecrated as the High Temple of Storm's Truth.

"The Storm is our protector!" he had shouted, and the faithful had echoed him. "It shields us from corruption and lies! There is nothing above but demons and their slaves!"

After the service came the usual procession – the faithful lining up for their weekly blessings. Attendance had soared since the Revolution made religious devotion a matter of status. Nothing guaranteed loyalty like divine favor. And food. That always worked.

The faithful never questioned how a city founded by skyfall survivors just a dozen generations ago now preached that nothing existed above. Selective memory remained one of governance's sharpest tools.

The Revolution gave the people exactly what they craved – a common enemy and a simple truth. The poor had rarely afforded skyfall relics. Some had formed artels, braving the depths for salvage to sell to nobles. The upper class made a fashion of sky-made trinkets. By declaring them heretical, the Temple turned envy into zealotry – and the relics into bargaining chips among the elite.

Through the thick walls of Tideguard Keep came the faint sound of evening bells, calling the faithful to prayer. The rhythms of Stormhaven were familiar to Thadeius, though he still preferred his residence in the capital, Stormseat, far from the fog and damp air.

From beyond the window came the chuffing of a coal-powered train. Its whistle pierced the evening as it rolled down the newly built track. The railway had been one of the few technologies praised by the Church, despite the steam engine concept being borrowed from above. Spiritual purity mattered – but so did moving coal, ore, and food.

The line between heretical and acceptable was more philosophical than practical. Not the item, but the source, defined sanctity – a theological nuance that kept progress moving while control stayed intact.

Thadeius pulled the Judge's report closer, reading the details on the four new prisoners. They summoned him from the capital, as he had ordered before. Questioning of demons from above required his personal presence.

First of them, the tribal boy, made no effort to hide his origins, claiming to be from something called the *Heights*, speaking freely of floating islands and giant eagles. His testimony alone was enough to condemn him.

The other three presented a more complex puzzle. At first, they claimed to be Commonwealth citizens, blown off course while trading. Later, they changed their story, saying they were traders from outer islands – none of which they could name. Their accents didn't match any known pattern. The Judge noted that the smaller woman had technical knowledge unusual for a merchant. The taller woman spoke with an accent similar to the tongue of mad Marvin, the lighthouse keeper who had been watched for decades as a possible spy for sky people – if they *ever* existed. The lean man carried himself like nobility. His hands had no calluses, a clear sign of privilege. A noble from above, most likely. And all four prisoners had the tan, healthy look of people used to sunlight and fresh food.

Thadeius sighed. The whole report could be reduced to that last line: no amount of mixed blood with darker-skinned people leaves the arms and face tanned, while the rest remains pale.

He tapped his fingers on the report, considering the timing. It was too convenient to be a coincidence – a slow island descent, followed by the appearance of strangers. Combined with the tribal boy's ready admission of coming from the Heights, the pattern was clear. These people possessed knowledge that could be valuable. Or it could be a coincidence, and they were just a bunch of spies, and valuable even so.

The situation presented interesting possibilities. The tribal boy was clearly doomed – no point maintaining the pretense that the Heights existed. But for the others, there might be greater value in surveillance than immediate judgment.

Taking a fresh sheet of parchment, Thadeius began drafting orders for Judge Dregg regarding the prisoners. Nothing obvious – perhaps assign less experienced men to the midnight shift. Ensure that discussions about the tribal boy's execution were conducted within earshot of the prisoners.

Fear made people careless, and careless prisoners revealed more than they intended.

He sealed the orders with his official seal, a mark of one of the highest hierarchs in the Sovereignty. The Revolution had given him power beyond what he had anticipated – but power always craved more. His ambition had shaped the Inquisition into the most valuable and most powerful branch of the regime. He alone held the authority to proclaim heresy upon anyone and anything.

But titles and doctrine were tools. To use them well, one had to act.

As darkness settled over Tideguard Keep, High Inquisitor Thadeius contemplated the game he was about to start.

And now it was time to play the evil interrogator card.

CHAPTER 15
Escape

The Judge's fist connected with Toryn's jaw again, sending a wave of pain through his face. The dull thud echoed in his head like an audible echo.

"The truth, heathen. Where above the Storm do you come from?" The large man's voice remained eerily calm, at odds with the violence of his actions. His powerful arms were speckled with Toryn's blood, a detail he hadn't seemed to notice, or perhaps didn't care about.

Toryn tasted blood, metallic and warm. His left eye had swollen nearly shut, but with his right, he studied the Judge – methodical in both questioning and beating.

"I've told you," Toryn said, the words slurring slightly through his swollen lips. "The Heights. The Windclaw Tribe."

When the Judge reached for a cloth to wipe blood from his knuckles and make some notes, Toryn's gaze drifted to the instruments on the side table. Among them sat a thin metal rod with a hooked end. It hadn't yet been used on him, and he really didn't want to know which body crevices it was supposed to go into. The hook lay within arm's reach if he moved quickly.

The Judge was writing in a leather-bound book, embossed with the storm-cloud emblem of the Holy Sovereignty. "Believe me, it would have been much easier if you'd cooperated." He dipped a quill in ink with the precision of a calligrapher – a strange contrast to his physique.

As the man continued writing, Toryn measured the distance. The chain connecting his shackles had been loosened for the beating, giving him just enough slack. With the Judge distracted, Toryn lunged sideways, grabbed the metal hook, and in one fluid motion, slipped it into his boot. The chains rattled with his movement, the sound unnaturally loud in the quiet chamber.

The Judge looked up sharply. "Even I couldn't break those chains. Save your strength."

The beating that followed was worse than before. The Judge kept asking questions – about Toryn's cellmates, his plans, and what he knew about local families and the area. Toryn slipped into tribal meditation, focusing on his heartbeat instead of the pain. He answered negatively to every question and kept doing it until the Judge finally stopped.

————

The cell block was a long, narrow corridor with iron-barred compartments on both sides – most of them empty. One held a massive man with a grim face and workers' clothes, watching silently. Another held an old prisoner, carefully arranging pebbles in patterns only he seemed to understand. Further down, Toryn saw two elderly men sharing a cell, and across from them, a middle-aged woman holding something close to her chest.

When the guards brought him back, Toryn was surprised to find his cell empty.

"Your friends are meeting the Inquisitor," the guard said with a smirk. "They'll return – if there's anything left of them."

Once the footsteps faded in the corridor, Toryn retrieved the hook from his boot and quickly assessed the cell. His gaze fell on

Kip's corner, where a small crack ran along the base of the wall. He worked the hook into the crack, pushing it in until only a tiny part remained visible – just enough for someone who knew where to look.

Footsteps approached again – several people this time, along with a higher-ranking officer.

"Time to go, boy. Special accommodations for tomorrow's entertainment."

"Entertainment?" Toryn asked, though he already knew.

"Public execution at dawn. The High Inquisitor wants to make an example of you." The guard's tone was matter-of-fact, like a trader announcing the price of bread. "Solitary for the night, so you can reflect on your sins before meeting the Storm's judgment."

Toryn stood without resistance. The hook was hidden. It was his only contribution now.

The solitary cell was smaller and darker, with no window and only a small slot in the door for food. The darkness was so different from the bright nights he was used to in the Heights – even in bad weather, it was never this dark. Toryn was beginning to understand the meaning of Depth – a place so deep that no light could slip in.

He sat cross-legged on the floor, feeling oddly calm. He had experienced more in the past few weeks than most tribal members would in a lifetime. If this were to be his end, at least it had followed an extraordinary journey.

———

Kip's internal clock told him the guards would change in approximately seven minutes. After three days in Tideguard Keep, he had memorized the patterns – shift changes at dusk, midnight, and dawn, with a brief patrol passing their cell every forty minutes in between. The midnight shift was always the most lax, with fewer guards and longer gaps between patrols.

Not that this knowledge seemed likely to help them escape. Particularly not after today's interview with the Inquisitor.

Kip glanced at Nora and Lina as they were escorted back to their cell. Their faces reflected his own grim assessment. The Inquisitor was nothing like the brutish Judge. Instead, he was calculating, perceptive, and unnervingly patient. Where the Judge relied on pain, the Inquisitor wielded words like precision instruments, finding and exploiting inconsistencies.

"Your stories are fascinating," the man had said, studying them with keen eyes. "I see you're traders, but I can't quite place what goods you're selling. There were none in your boat and no money on you. Perhaps you could tell me which fish are the most valuable this season?"

The question sounded innocent, but none of them knew anything about fishing, seasons, or trade. They muttered something about dropping crates overboard to keep the boat from sinking. The type of trade was also made up on the spot and failed to convince anyone.

The cell door clanged shut behind them. The guards retreated, their boots echoing in a steady rhythm on the worn flagstones.

"Well, that went splendidly," Lina muttered once they were alone, rubbing her wrists where the shackles had been. "I especially enjoyed the part where he smiled and said we'd have a *more productive* conversation tomorrow."

"He knows," Nora said quietly. "He doesn't know exactly what we are, but he knows we are lying."

Kip nodded, his mind racing through possibilities and finding none favorable.

Nice interrogation technique – give the prisoners time to imagine what's coming, then play on their terror.

"He's letting us stew overnight," he said, deciding not to detail it further.

"And where's Toryn? They should have brought him back by now," said Nora.

As if in answer, they heard voices drifting from the corridor as a guard passed by, speaking to his companion.

"... public execution at dawn. Storm's Truth demands a spectacle, especially for demon spawn from above."

"Seems like a waste," replied the second voice. "Could have learned more from the boy first."

"Inquisitor's orders. To draw out any other sympathizers." The man scratched his beard absently. "And don't forget the mandatory attendance for all citizens. Means double shifts for us tomorrow, of course."

The voices faded as the guards moved past, but their words lingered in the cell.

"They're going to execute him," Nora whispered, her voice tight with horror. Her eyes flashed with fierce determination as she looked at both of them. "We have to do something."

From the far end of the corridor came the sound of a prisoner calling out for water, his voice hoarse and weary.

Kip knelt in his corner, feeling along the base of the wall for the crack where he'd wedged a piece of parchment with observations and notes on guard shifts. As his fingers probed the crevice, he felt something cold and metallic beside the paper. Carefully, he worked it free.

A hook-shaped rod about six inches long.

Oh, I saw you on the Judge's table.

"Toryn left us a gift," he said softly, holding up the tool. "He hid it where I keep my papers. The question is – do we use it now or wait?"

Lina examined the tool, weighing it in her hand and testing its sturdiness. "I could pick the lock with it. Done it before."

Outside, the bells began to toll – nine deep, resonant sounds that marked the evening hour and called the faithful to prayer.

Kip's mind whirred with calculations. Patrol schedules, shift changes, the layout of corridors he'd memorized during their transfers. On arrival, he'd seen enough of the city to know that Tideguard Keep sat not far from the harbor district. He'd also noted the rail line near the eastern wall – the same train they heard every day and were transported on when captured.

"We should wait until the execution," he said finally. "Security will be focused elsewhere. Most of the guards will be deployed to control the crowd. It's our best chance to slip away unnoticed."

"What?" Nora stared at him, her eyes widening. "You can't be serious."

"I'm completely serious. Strategically speaking–"

"There is no way we are leaving Toryn to die!" Nora's voice rose dangerously before she caught herself, continuing in a fierce whisper. "That is *not* an option, Kip."

In the nearest cell, the elderly prisoner looked up from his careful work with the pebbles. He watched their exchange with mild disdain, the kind that came from being locked up so long that even arguments in nearby cells felt like a bother.

Kip found himself momentarily distracted by the flush of anger on Nora's cheeks, by the way her eyes sparked with conviction. It was a most inconvenient time to notice how beautiful she was when passionate.

"I'm not suggesting we leave him to die," he replied, keeping his voice steady. "I'm saying our chances of a successful escape – all of us – are higher if we use the distraction of the execution."

"And how exactly would Toryn benefit from this plan?" Nora demanded.

Kip hesitated. The truth was, he hadn't included Toryn in his mental calculations. The tribal boy was already moved elsewhere, likely heavily guarded. Including him dramatically increased their risk of capture or death. The old Kip – the one focused solely on the restoration of his family name – would have deemed the risk unacceptable.

But there is more to life than vengeance, he reluctantly acknowledged to himself.

While his mind raced for an alternative plan, Lina interjected. "Here's what we do. I pick the lock. We overpower the next guard who passes. Take his keys and weapons. Free Toryn. Escape."

Kip sighed. "And when the guard doesn't return on schedule? When the alarm sounds? How do we face several armed guards?" He shook his head. "Without my rapier, I can't take on even a single trained guard. If I had it, maybe two at most. But as we are now…" He spread his hands in a gesture of futility.

Nora might be dangerous in close combat. And give Lina a wrench... But no – we can't crawl the dungeon, taking out guards one by one. There has to be another way.

"We need a distraction," Kip said aloud. "Something to divide their attention and resources." His gaze drifted to the cells further down the block. One in particular had caught his eye – a mountain of a man with massive shoulders and calloused hands. The man rarely spoke, but Kip had observed him during their days in captivity.

"The other prisoners," Kip said slowly. "If we free them all…"

Lina's eyes lit with understanding. "Chaos. Guards scrambling to recapture everyone."

"Exactly. And in that chaos, we escape."

"We find Toryn first," Nora corrected.

They spent the next hour refining the plan, discussing timing and backups.

When the midnight patrol passed their cell, Lina took the hook and approached the door. Minutes passed, her face tightening with frustration.

"It's different from the locks I know," she whispered, adjusting her grip. "Give me more time."

Kip glanced at the corridor, nerves tight. Every second increased the risks. Sweat beaded on Lina's forehead as she worked, the tip of her tongue caught between her teeth in concentration.

Finally, a satisfying click echoed in the silence.

"Got it," she breathed. "Moving to the other cells."

She slipped into the corridor, keeping low.

Kip watched as she worked on the big man's cell. Her movements grew more confident with practice, but it still took nearly five minutes before the door swung open.

The man listened for a moment, then nodded once. He moved to the main entrance and simply wrenched it open with brute strength, the metal groaning in protest.

Lina unlocked the others more quickly and soon returned to Kip and Nora.

"His name's Rulf, a dockworker," she said breathlessly. "Says he's in our debt now."

The other prisoners, dazed by their sudden freedom, scattered in all directions, except for a man with pebbles, who seemed unnerved by the fuss. Rulf disappeared around a corner, creating a commotion that drew the guards away.

"Now for the guard room," Kip said quietly. "We need weapons and keys."

The guard room was two corridors away, near the interrogation chambers. As they approached, they heard shouts echoing from different parts of the prison. The chaos of the escape was already spreading through the facility.

They found two guards stationed outside the door – alert, but clearly unsure whether to hold their post. Kip signaled the others to wait, assessing the situation.

We're still bare-handed against armed men.

Before he could form a plan, the massive figure of Rulf appeared at the far end of the corridor, carrying a heavy chair with ease. The guards drew their weapons at once, but the dockworker charged with surprising speed. The fight ended quickly: both guards were left unconscious, and Rulf, barely scratched, picked up a wooden truncheon from one of their bodies.

"I owe you," Rulf said simply, his voice surprisingly soft for his size.

"Well," Kip said, reassessing, "that works."

The guard room was large but empty, with a stone fireplace, several wooden chairs, and a massive oak table scattered with playing cards. Maps of the facility covered one wall, while another displayed the tools of the guards' trade – batons, manacles, and shackles.

"Solitary cells," Nora said immediately, studying one of the maps. "East wing, through there."

"Keys first," Kip replied, moving to the wall where keys hung on labeled hooks. He scanned the tags quickly. "Armory, south gate, east block, kitchen…"

Lina was already tearing a baton from the wall, while Kip found a sword in a storage cabinet. It was an ordinary, cheap blade, but his fingers curled around the grip, and he felt more confident.

Don't humor yourself, Saroven – all guards have pistols.

At that moment, an alarm bell rang out somewhere in the facility. The prison break had been discovered.

"Earlier than expected," Kip muttered. "Move."

They rushed through corridors, ducking into alcoves when guards ran past. The chaos was spreading faster than anticipated, which worked both for and against them – more confusion, but also more guards.

The solitary cells area had only one entrance. By the time they reached it, both sentries near the door were on the floor with Rulf standing above them with his familiar truncheon. They shared a nod and rushed to the solitary wing. Inside, there was a row of eight cells, only one occupied.

Toryn looked up in shock when his door swung open, his bruised face and swollen eye visible even in the dim light.

"You came back," he said, disbelief evident on his battered face.

"Of course we did," Nora replied, "can you walk?"

Toryn nodded, rising shakily to his feet. "I thought… I assumed you would escape without me."

That was the plan.

Kip avoided his gaze, trying to focus on their next move.

"The facility is on high alert now. We need to split up – smaller groups move faster." He glanced at Rulf, who stood watch at the corridor entrance. "Lina, you and Toryn head through the kitchen's back door. Take the key, there should be no one there at this time."

"And you?" Lina asked, already supporting Toryn's weight.

"Nora and I will find another route with Rulf. We'll meet outside at the eastern wall." He hesitated, then added, "If we're not there in fifteen minutes, don't wait."

Lina nodded grimly, understanding the implication. She and Toryn moved down the corridor while Kip and Nora turned in the opposite direction, back to the guard room.

When they reached the room, Rulf pointed to a map.

"Administrative wing," he said. "Messengers come there."

They followed the corridor and reached what appeared to be a clerk's office. Several scribes cowered in the corners as they burst in, but no guards were present. The room was spacious and well lit, with cabinets lining every wall.

A heavy wooden door on the far side looked promising, but when Kip tried it, he found it barred. There was no time to search for a key – voices were already shouting at the far end of the corridor.

Rulf rushed to the large window, its shutters closed for the night. A small lock on the beam held it shut, but one direct swing with the truncheon shattered it. He then pulled the beam free and swung the window open.

"Go," he said, hefting the heavy beam and turning to block the corridor.

Kip didn't argue. He helped Nora through the window, then slipped through himself. Behind them came the shouts of guards as they discovered Rulf's position.

They dropped into a wide alley between the prison and an adjacent building. Staying close to the shadows, they worked their way around to the east side of the facility.

"Any sign of Lina and Toryn?" Nora asked, anxiously scanning the area.

Kip's expression tightened. "Not yet."

They waited in the shadows for what felt like an eternity – though it was likely only minutes. Finally, a movement caught their attention.

"There," Nora whispered, pointing to two figures moving cautiously along the wall.

Lina and Toryn emerged from the dark, both disheveled but alive. Toryn was limping, his arm around Lina's shoulders for support.

"Any trouble?" Kip asked quietly as they approached.

"Just a servant who seemed more interested in running than fighting," Lina said, adjusting her grip on Toryn. "The kitchen was empty for the night."

As they reunited, a door in the nearby wall suddenly exploded outward, shards of wood flying into the alley. Through the dust stepped Rulf's massive silhouette, still holding the wooden beam.

"Efficient," Kip commented.

The dockworker approached them, barely winded despite whatever resistance he'd faced inside. He gave a simple nod of recognition.

"We need to get away from here," Nora said urgently. "The entire city guard will be searching for us soon."

Kip surveyed the surroundings. He suddenly realized a critical flaw in his plan – he only had wild guesses about the harbor and railway directions, but no idea where to hide. The unfamiliar buildings of the Holy Sovereignty loomed around them, and the streets followed patterns he couldn't hope to navigate.

Rulf seemed to sense his hesitation. "I know a place," he said. "Warehouse district."

Kip made his decision quickly. "Lead on."

CHAPTER 16
Cartographer's Discovery

Marvin stood at the lighthouse quay, squinting into the horizon. He'd been there for forty-seven minutes – he'd been counting. He stared at the spot where the boat had vanished six days ago, carrying his Federation colleagues.

"They didn't even take my complete collection of observational poetry, Ferdinand," he said to the donkey beside him. "*Volume Seven* has all my best work on precipitation anomalies. The autumn rain couplets were practically revolutionary."

Ferdinand's ears twitched. Marvin took it as sympathy from one scientist to another.

"Still, it's an urgent mission. The Federation wouldn't send a sergeant, a technical specialist, and a diplomatic liaison unless it was important." He sighed, shoulders drooping. "I do hope they're all right."

The lighthouse felt too quiet. Marvin realized how much he'd gotten used to the sound of other voices – even after just one day. The creaking gears, crashing waves, and Ferdinand's occasional braying weren't enough.

"Come on, Ferdinand. If we can't help them directly, we can at least keep proper records. Section 7, paragraph 12 of the Surface Welcome Protocol requires the Chief Observer to document all visitor activity." Marvin straightened his hat. "We've got work to do."

Ferdinand, who had already heard it three times today, followed with quiet resignation.

———

The map room looked like a mix of a library and a weather station after an earthquake.

"Now, Ferdinand, we need the tribal cartography section. That would be under... *Visitors of Unusual Vertical Origins*." Marvin pulled several rolled maps marked with blue ribbons from a shelf and spread them out across his work table. Each one showed the distinctive style of tribal cartographers – intricate wind patterns, detailed islet formations, and eagle dwellings.

Among these maps were several that Marvin especially valued. They were charts, passed to him years ago by a half-delirious survivor of a catastrophic island fall. The tribal man had recovered from his injuries and left, giving Marvin the maps as a sign of gratitude.

Marvin began jotting notes. "Tribal Map Analysis, Day Five. Attempting to locate the recent Category Blue descent. Supplemental: Cartographers' notation systems appear consistent across tribes. Most intriguing."

He worked steadily through the afternoon, merging details from various tribal charts into a composite of the upper regions. The process was slow and meticulous. Each map held subtle variations – some reflecting the passage of time, others charted by different hands as islets drifted or fell.

"The problem has always been perspective," he said to Ferdinand. "These maps show the Heights in great detail, but there's no way to tell where they are in relation to us here on the surface. It's like having a detailed street map of a city you can't find."

As dusk approached, Marvin lit several oil lamps and continued his work with undiminished enthusiasm. He also took off the mid-altitude maps – salvaged from crashed vessels or drawn by survivors over the decades. These were harder to use. The quality varied, and the severity of each fall often affected survivors' memories.

"You see, Ferdinand," he said, "each cartographer records what they can see from their position, mistaking partial observations for a full understanding. It's only when we combine these limited views that the larger pattern starts to appear."

He paused, frowning at the maps. "And these mysterious symbols at the edges – what did that tribesman call them? Guardian islands? I've never been able to find them. They must be right at the edge of known territory."

Then a new idea struck him. "What if… what if I align the mid-altitude maps with the tribal ones? We already know the islands are spread out – not stacked one above the other. So the empty gaps in the mid-altitude maps could show where the islands in the Heights are!"

For hours, he worked with focused precision, layering maps and matching overlapping features to find alignment points. With each accurate placement, the larger picture slowly emerged.

From a special drawer, he took out his most precious journal, the detailed records of Category Blue descents. There weren't many – just three in total, including the recent one that had brought his Federation colleagues.

He aligned the markers with the positions of the enigmatic Guardian Islands on his newly combined map. His eyes widened.

"Ferdinand! The Blue descents – they match! All three known ones are these special islands!" He traced the symbols with a trembling finger. "And look – there are more of those symbols at the edges. And the way they're arranged…"

Marvin drew lines between the known locations, then extended them, following the geometric pattern that appeared. "There should be six in total, Ferdinand! Arranged in a perfect hexagon around all the inhabited floating lands!"

He paced the small map room, agitated, and bumped into a pile of old salvage near the doorway. His foot struck something heavy and metallic. He looked down at the object – a large, rust-covered boat anchor, probably from a shipwreck and long forgotten in the clutter. He stared at it, then back at the map, his mind racing in a new direction.

"An anchor…" he murmured, nudging it with his boot. "It holds fast. It resists the currents. It provides stability." He looked again at the plotted points on his map. "What if… what if that's what they are? Not just Guardian Islands, but fixture points. Like… like anchors for the entire sky!"

His voice rose with excitement. "Those islands aren't just floating, Ferdinand – they're anchoring the whole structure! Holding it together! Stabilization nodes!"

"Of course, it's only a hypothesis," he added, keeping himself grounded. "Three confirmed data points aren't statistically significant. But the hexagonal pattern along the edges is too perfect to dismiss." He tapped the charcoal against his lips, unaware of the smudge it left. "Which means…"

His expression shifted from excitement to sudden horror. "If those Guardian Islands keep the balance... and we lose one..." He stared at Ferdinand. "Dear heavens, Ferdinand – it could destabilize everything!" He paused, eyes wide. "It's a real theoretical possibility. Everything above falls down and goes splash!"

Ferdinand, perhaps sensing real alarm instead of Marvin's usual scientific excitement, raised his head and let out a soft, questioning bray.

"Yes, exactly," Marvin said, misreading the sound as profound insight. "We need to investigate this right away. This could be the most important discovery since I identified seventeen types of storm precipitation!"

He had just started writing what would clearly be an extremely detailed – albeit meandering – analysis when something outside the western window caught his eye. He froze, then rushed to his telescope.

"Ferdinand! It's the *Steady Trade*! Right on schedule – how could I forget?" He swung the telescope to track the approaching vessel. "Captain Morris always did run a punctual ship."

Marvin's face lit up. "This is perfect! They'll have news from the Harbor Commonwealth – and maybe even about our Federation colleagues. Quick, Ferdinand – I must change into my official reception attire!"

———

The *Steady Trade* approached the lighthouse dock, its weather-stained, patched sails and worn hull showing the marks of years of coastal service. Captain Elwin Morris guided the vessel in. Marvin stood waiting in his *official uniform* – an oversized naval jacket and a bosun's hat, decorated with assorted badges. He believed they represented important ranks, but in truth, they marked him as a signal officer, a chef, and a deck boy.

"Ahoy, Captain Morris!" he called, offering a crisp salute. "Marvin Thale, Chief Observer of Surface Phenomena and Keeper of the Point Descent Illumination Station, welcomes the *Steady Trade*!"

Captain Morris returned the salute. The lines around his eyes crinkled – not in mockery, but with the quiet recognition of a twenty-year ritual between two men who had come to respect one another, despite their differences.

"Thank you, Keeper Thale. Permission to come ashore?"

"Permission granted, Captain. Your punctuality continues to uphold the highest standards."

Their ritual continued with talk of weather predictions – which, Morris would never admit aloud, were surprisingly accurate.

"Mira has some preserved cloudberries for you," Morris said as he stepped onto the dock. "And we've brought the books you requested."

"Excellent! Most appreciated," Marvin beamed, then lowered his voice. "Though I must speak with you on a matter of some significance, Captain."

While the first mate oversaw the unloading with great care, the ship's cook approached with a small crate. "Here you are, Mr. Thale," she said kindly. "I've included some dried fruit and those herbal tea mixtures. Good for the constitution during the changing seasons."

"Your consideration exceeds all expectations, Officer Mira," Marvin said warmly.

As the unloading continued, Marvin pulled Captain Morris aside. His expression shifted to one of careful neutrality. In the twenty years Morris had been making supply runs to lighthouses, he'd learned that beneath Marvin's eccentric ways was a sharp mind – confused in some areas, but clear in others.

"Captain, I must ask about recent events," Marvin said quietly. "What's become of the Kingdom of Tides? Last I heard, there were whispers of revolution."

Morris's face darkened. "It's not the Kingdom of Tides anymore. They're calling it Holy Sovereignty now. Religious zealots took over about a year ago – Temple of Storm's Truth. Used to be a fringe cult. Now they run the place."

"Religious zealots?" Marvin's eyebrows rose. "How did they manage to convince the masses?"

"Nasty business," Morris said, shaking his head. "They preach that nothing exists above the Storm – call it heresy to claim otherwise. Anyone saying differently gets arrested by their Inquisition." He glanced around, lowering his voice further. "They've even banned salvage from above as *demonic artifacts*. You may imagine how the poor celebrated it – it never affected them directly, but nobles took the blow."

Marvin's face went still. "Most concerning. And what of their relationship with the Harbor Commonwealth?"

"Tense. Trade's been restricted, grievances are stacking fast." Morris studied Marvin's face. "Why the sudden interest in politics, Keeper? Not your usual area of inquiry."

Marvin shifted gears smoothly. "Oh, I just realized that my knowledge of the political landscape might be outdated. By the way, were there any unusual guests in Free Harbor recently?"

"Unusual how?"

"Perhaps individuals not native to the Commonwealth. Possibly speaking in unfamiliar terms or displaying knowledge of... higher matters."

The captain scratched his beard. "Can't say I've heard anything specific, Marvin. Free Harbor sees traders from all over. Anyone in particular you're asking after?"

"Three individuals departed from Point Descent six days ago. Two women and a man."

"From here?" Morris's tone was carefully neutral. "That's quite specific."

"Indeed. They were on an urgent mission." Marvin maintained eye contact, something he rarely did. A cold feeling settled in his stomach – if they had encountered the Holy Sovereignty's forces, they might be in grave danger.

Morris sighed. "Marvin, we haven't heard of any such visitors. I'd tell you if we had."

Seff, who had been hovering nearby, piped up eagerly. "Were there five of them? All women? I heard something about–"

"No, Seff," Marvin cut in. "Three individuals. Not five. And certainly not all women."

"Oh." Seff looked disappointed, then brightened. "But maybe there were five at first? And you only met three?"

Marvin took in the young man's hopeful expression, Morris's deliberately neutral face, and Mira's subtle eye roll. They were humoring him. He'd long understood how people saw him – a harmless eccentric best indulged, not taken seriously. He didn't mind. Being underestimated had its perks.

As the crew completed the unloading, Marvin retreated to his cottage and quickly penned a letter. The handwriting was neat and precise, the language clear and direct – nothing like his usual ornate proclamations.

Dear Talbert, Recent events suggest unusual activity concerning Blue Descents. I've enclosed my observational data and coordinate mapping. Note the hexagonal pattern and the theoretical positions of undocumented sites based on tribal boundary markers. More pressingly, three visitors of significant interest departed for Free Harbor six days ago. Their absence from reported arrivals suggests either intervention or misdirection. The common thread appears to be Holy Sovereignty. Exercise caution in your inquiries.

With respect, M. Thale.

He added several careful overlays to his map, emphasizing the Guardian Islands' pattern and how they aligned with major settlements. As an afterthought, he sketched Nora's Federation insignia in the margin.

Back at the dock, he found Captain Morris going over the final supply list.

"Captain Morris, might I trouble you with a delivery?" Marvin offered a sealed letter. "It's for Scholar Talbert in Harbor Town – contains my latest meteorological notes."

Morris accepted it with a nod. "Of course, Keeper. It'll be delivered."

"Personally, if you would." Marvin's voice lowered – quiet, measured, the tone Morris knew from long experience. "Some of the findings are… delicate. Scholar Talbert will understand their weight." He kept his tone casual, but held Morris's gaze a beat longer than usual. Something in his expression must have registered, because Morris nodded more seriously.

"I'll deliver it myself, Marvin. You have my word."

"Most appreciated, Captain. Safe journey to you and your crew. The weather should remain favorable at least until you reach the northern straits."

The departure ritual continued with its usual formality – Marvin's elaborate salute, the crew's respectful responses, and final confirmations of the next supply date. As the *Steady Trade* pulled away from the dock, Marvin held his posture until the ship vanished into the perpetual twilight.

Only then did his shoulders sag slightly. He turned to Ferdinand, who had observed the proceedings from a respectful distance.

"They don't believe me, Ferdinand. And why should they? A deranged lighthouse keeper sees visitors from above – it's hardly a credible report." He straightened again, a new determination settling into his features. "But we know the truth, don't we? And we know our duty."

Ferdinand offered a sympathetic bray.

"Precisely. If our colleagues are in danger, waiting for others to act would be an oversight." He paused. "Which means, my friend, that we must take extraordinary measures."

─────

For three days after the *Steady Trade* departed, Marvin worked in his workshop with rare focus. Ferdinand watched patiently, resigned to the sudden urgency.

"The key, Ferdinand, is automation," Marvin said, adjusting gears and counterweights. "The lighthouse must run in my absence, and you must be well cared for."

Ferdinand's ears twitched at "my absence" – a phrase he hadn't heard in nearly eighteen years.

"Yes, I know," Marvin nodded. "Unprecedented. But necessity drives innovation, as Mother always said."

He began with the feeding system: hoppers linked to timers that would dispense grain and water at set intervals. Next was the ignition system, solved using a spark mechanism triggered by the rotating weights, paired with a precisely calibrated fuel delivery system.

After careful testing, Marvin ran a full systems check on the fourth day. Everything worked in order – the weights rose, the lamp lit, the gears turned, and Ferdinand's dinner dropped as scheduled.

"Success!" Marvin declared. "Functioning exactly as intended – by Federation standards!"

He turned to Ferdinand with rare solemnity. "Now comes the hard part, my friend. Departure preparations."

From a trunk unopened for two decades, Marvin retrieved a few essentials: a waterproof chart case, navigational tools, and a brass compass.

"These waters have patterns of their own," he muttered, eyeing the compass. "Though my knowledge may be a bit... dusty."

He packed a sea chest with supplies – including three volumes of his poetry. The boat, smaller than the one given to his visitors, had been carefully checked.

On the final evening, Marvin and Ferdinand stood atop the lighthouse, watching the automated system ignite the great lamp. The beam swept across the dark waters – a steady rhythm he'd maintained for so long.

"It works, Ferdinand," he said quietly. "It actually works."

They stood together in silence for a while.

"I'll miss this," Marvin finally said. "But duty calls me to uncertain waters. Our Federation friends may be in serious danger – especially if they're in the hands of Holy Sovereignty. And if my theory about the Guardian Islands is even partly right, there may be greater threats ahead than zealots."

Ferdinand nudged his hand with his nose, gentle and steady.

"Yes, you're right. Sentiment can't get in the way." He squared his shoulders. "I leave at first light."

———

Morning came with a pale glow and a bitter, howling wind.

Marvin untied the mooring rope and stepped aboard. Ferdinand stood on the shore, expression unreadable as always.

"The emergency lever must be pushed if the weights fail to reset," Marvin instructed. "Your feeding system is calibrated for twenty-four days. The secondary hopper will release additional feed every five days."

The donkey offered what Marvin chose to interpret as a nod.

"You have been an exemplary assistant, Ferdinand," Marvin said, his voice catching slightly. "The Federation would be proud of your service."

He raised the sail, announcing, "Mission objective: locate Federation personnel potentially in distress." The wind caught the sail, and the boat began to move away. "Keep the light burning, Ferdinand!" he called, eyes blinking too fast – maybe from the cold wind.

Marvin Thale – Chief Observer of Surface Phenomena and Keeper of the Point Descent Illumination Station – adjusted his cap and sailed toward a shore he hadn't seen in twenty years.

CHAPTER 17
Borrowed Time

Toryn Skyheart stood at the rain-slicked window of Madsen's Quayside Tavern, watching water droplets trace patterns across the glass. The sheer disregard for collecting it still amazed him – rain falling freely, unused. In the Heights, every drop was precious, gathered and stored. Here on the surface, water was everywhere – especially the endless ocean.

A week had passed since their daring escape from Tideguard Keep. Seven days of hiding in plain sight, learning the rhythms of the world beneath the Storm. The perpetual twilight still disoriented him, as did the heavy, damp air and constant fog.

Toryn rested his forehead against the glass, his thoughts drifting back to the journey through the Storm on the back of the blue-black eagle.

Are we truly bonded now? Or was it just finding its way home, humoring a Heights boy in the process?

The majestic creature had saved his life, but he would likely never know its motivations – or whether he would ever see it or the Heights again.

Even the Trial of Knowing has failed. He had found the seedheart – but failed to return with even a fragment. The thought of Roost Islet, possibly already growing unstable, settled on him like a stone.

Had Elder Kora already given up hope? Was Chief Harrik preparing for migration? And Jormund – was he truly meddling with the heartstone, risking the fate of us all?

"Boy! Those mugs won't clean themselves," Ellie Thorne called from behind the bar, cutting through his dark thoughts.

Toryn turned from the window with a nod and moved to collect the dirty tankards. Ellie was tall and lean, with gray-streaked brown hair pulled back in a knot. Her husband, Madsen, was the opposite – short and barrel-chested, with thick forearms and a mustache that made his receding hairline even more noticeable.

The tavern keepers had asked remarkably few questions when Rulf brought four fugitives to their door. "These are my friends," he'd said simply, fixing Madsen with a meaningful look. "They need a place. Quiet place." Something had passed between the two men – an understanding Toryn couldn't quite decipher but recognized as the silent language of long acquaintance. Later, he'd overheard Rulf mentioning to Kip that Madsen's brother had been taken by the Inquisition for possessing a book with "heretical" stories.

They were given two rooms above the tavern in exchange for help with chores and repairs. Everyone tried to do their share – except for Kip, who wasn't really good with a mop or hammer, and whom they all agreed should be kept far away from the kitchen.

"You hold a mug like it might bite you," Ellie observed as Toryn carefully gathered the vessels.

"I'm used to other cups, from bone," he explained simply. "They don't break easily. These are… fragile."

Ellie made a noncommittal sound, but her eyes held the same curiosity he'd noticed whenever he mentioned anything about his past. She never asked direct questions – none of them did – but he could see their hunger for information about the world above.

"Our chief drinks from a horn that belonged to his grandfather," Toryn added, enjoying her poorly concealed interest. "It's lined with metal and decorated with feathers."

"Sounds fancy," she said, deliberately casual as she wiped down the bar counter. "Our Madsen drinks from whatever's closest when he's thirsty – including other people's leftovers."

A grunt from behind the bar might have been Madsen's protest or agreement. Toryn still couldn't tell with the tavern keeper's minimal way of communicating.

The tavern door swung open, bringing in a gust of cold air – and Lina, both damp and not especially welcoming. She hated the weather like all of them did, but her expression lit up with near-childlike excitement as soon as she started talking about the industrial district.

"They've got a pneumatic messaging system running through the entire foundry!" she announced, shrugging off her wet coat. "Air pressure moves message capsules through tubes. The engineer – Tomas – let me examine the valve assemblies. The man's a genius with pressure mechanics."

Toryn hid a smile. Lina had adapted remarkably well to life on the shore. It was a wonderland for her – with trains, steam machines, and factories. She had spent several days wandering the industrial district before earning a job at Stormharbor Precision Works. Tomas was the master machinist. He had been skeptical at first. But Lina spotted a failing compression junction that had puzzled his apprentices for weeks. That earned her respect – and a kind of trial period in the workshop.

"Did you actually do any work, or just gawk at machines all day?" came Kip's voice from the corner table, where he'd been studying harbor shipping papers. He'd never approved of her little venture, but the team had agreed that a mechanic wouldn't draw much suspicion – and someone had to go outside anyway.

"I'll have you know I redesigned the release valve on their primary steam junction," Lina replied, a hint of pride in her voice. "Tomas offered me a permanent position. Said he hasn't seen someone with my mechanical grasp in years."

"You're not considering it, are you?" Kip looked up sharply.

"Of course not," Lina huffed, dropping into a chair across from him. "But it's nice to be appreciated for my skills rather than just being useful for opening locks."

Toryn set down his tray of mugs behind the bar and approached their table. Among their strange group, he found Lina the easiest to relate to. She didn't have any hidden agendas and was always straightforward – and equally prickly with everyone.

It was harder to read Kip, whom he saw as a planner and a fighter, much like most tribal elders who earned their place as prominent hunters, leaders, or otherwise valuable tribesmen.

Nora was another matter entirely. She sat near the window, quietly bundling local plants with the precision of a trained medic. Toryn respected her skill and even believed she regretted what happened on Veil Islet – but the distance between them still felt wide. And unbridgeable.

The tavern door opened again, admitting Rulf's massive frame. The dockworker was invaluable in the escape from Tideguard Keep and remained their main source of information about harbor activity. Despite his intimidating form, Toryn found him strangely easy to respect – he spoke little, but his words carried weight.

"Tomas mentioned something else," Lina said, lowering her voice as Toryn joined them. "He's offered to introduce me to people in the *underground*. Said there are those who preserve what the Temple tries to erase."

Rulf grunted as he settled into a chair that creaked under his weight. "The underground is like a web," he said flatly. "Too many links, too many eyes. Too many debts."

Kip nodded in agreement. "We can't afford to get tangled in local politics. Our goal for now is to find a way to the Commonwealth."

"I know, I know," Lina sighed. "Becoming someone's debtor isn't part of the plan. I just thought it was worth mentioning."

"The *Northern Mist* is your best chance," Rulf said without preamble. "Second mate owes me. I saved his son when the docks collapsed. He'll take you to Free Harbor – no questions asked."

"And how much will this favor cost us?" Kip asked, ever practical.

"Twice the usual fare," Rulf replied. "But it's the only ship leaving this month that won't ask to see your papers."

The conversation paused as Madsen approached with a tray of simple but filling stew. The tavern keeper set it down without a word and retreated.

"I've earned a bit at the workshop," Lina said, reaching for her bowl. "I'll get more next week."

"I can sell my ring," Kip added, tapping a silver band on his little finger. "It should cover most of the rest."

Corsairs often carried such trinkets – easy to hide, valuable enough to barter for a life-saving bribe or, failing that, a funeral, as Kip joked.

"Why are you helping us?" Toryn asked Rulf directly as they began to eat. The question had bothered him for days. "You're risking a lot for strangers."

Rulf gave a massive shrug. "You're outsiders, but that's none of my business. I've got no love for the Inquisition or their Storm's Truth nonsense. My grandfather was from *above*. Used to tell stories about that world – before they were banned." He leaned in slightly. "And I pay my debts."

A silence settled over them as they ate.

Toryn studied the tavern's other patrons – mostly dockworkers and sailors. They seemed content in their routines of work, food, drink, and sleep. It unsettled him to realize how easily one could grow used to such a limited life. Lina, he suspected, might come to love it. Especially because of the surface mechanical wonders.

Later that evening, as the tavern emptied and Rulf left, Ellie appeared from the kitchen, wiping her hands on her apron. She glanced around, then leaned in close to their table.

"You all should be careful," she said, her voice low and serious. "Some folk in town were asking questions today. Strangers looking like officials in civil clothing."

"What kind of questions?" Kip asked sharply.

"About newcomers," Ellie replied. "Specifically, four newcomers staying at a tavern in the warehouse district." She straightened up. "Just thought you should know."

As she moved away to continue her tasks, the four exchanged worried glances.

"We should get some rest," Kip said, his voice cutting through the tension. "Tomorrow, I need to verify the *Northern Mist's* scheduled departure and talk to Rulf's contact. Lina, can you check what supplies we'll need for the journey?"

The practical focus on their immediate plans dissipated the momentary tension. As they cleared the table, Toryn's thoughts turned to the warning Ellie had given them. If people were asking questions, their time here might be growing short. Perhaps their plans would need to be accelerated. He also thought about Rulf – their debt to him was growing. He found them shelter, passage options, and brought news. But how could they repay?

Sleep called, bringing dreams of an open sky – near in memory, yet so far beyond the Storm.

———

The next morning, Toryn rose early. The tavern was quiet, the chairs still stacked on tables from last night's cleaning. Madsen was nowhere in sight, but Ellie stood at the hearth, stoking a fire under a large iron pot.

"You're up early, boy," she said without turning.

"Old habits," Toryn replied, stepping closer to the warmth.

"Useful habits," Ellie said, straightening. "The back door's been sticking since yesterday's rain. Could use a skilled hand."

Toryn nodded. Over the past week, he'd found he had a knack for fixing the tavern's aging fixtures. His crafting skills transferred surprisingly well to wooden frames and rusty hinges.

The back door had swollen from the moisture, scraping the stone floor when opened. He found the planing tool in the small workshop behind the kitchen and set to work, carefully shaving down the door's edge. The task was calming, and his thoughts drifted back to tribal training – Elder Haldar's patient voice guiding him as he built his first wind gauge, stressing the need for precision and care.

Would he ever finish that training? The Trial of Knowing was meant to earn him a place among the tribe's experts, to honor his father's legacy as a wind speaker and cartographer. Instead, here he was, planing a tavern door beneath the Storm – farther from his path than he'd ever imagined.

"You do good work," Madsen's voice startled him.

The tavern keeper stood in the doorway, watching.

"Thank you," Toryn said, caught off guard.

"Got more jobs upstairs," Madsen added. "Roof leak in the back room. Window latch's broken in the middle bedroom."

"I'll take care of them after this," Toryn said.

Madsen nodded and disappeared back into the tavern proper.

By mid-morning, Toryn had repaired the door, fixed the window latch, and was examining the roof leak when a distant train whistle caught his attention. The sound drew him to the window, where he saw smoke rising from the railyard a few blocks away. He'd become fascinated by the rhythm of those machines – their punctual arrivals and departures, the steady loading and unloading of cargo, the black smoke curling into the already dim sky.

In some ways, the trains reminded him of the Heights' water distribution systems – same precision, same efficiency, just focused on different resources.

As he turned back to the leaking roof, Toryn caught himself seeing connections – not just differences – between his world and this one. Was he adapting too well to life below the Storm? Could he lose himself here, the way others once had?

No. I won't become just another surface dweller, forgetting the open skies. Whatever happens, I will find a way back.

"The storm bells rang an hour ago," Kip said. "The Harbor Master has closed the port for a week. *Northern Mist* won't be leaving until the weather clears."

"What does that mean for us?" Toryn asked, settling onto a bench.

"It means," Rulf growled, "you've got time to finish your preparations properly. And that you'll need to tolerate this place a bit longer, tribal boy."

The words carried no malice – just a reminder of his status. Not that Toryn needed one.

"I found a leak in the back room," he said, changing the subject. "Seems like the whole roof might need work before long."

"Madsen's been putting that off for years," Rulf said. "Maybe you should stay and become a roof-man."

The rest of the day passed in a blur of preparations and tavern chores. Toryn split his time between helping Ellie in the kitchen and assisting Kip with mapping possible routes through the harbor.

As he carried a tray of empty mugs back to the bar, Toryn caught sight of Nora sitting alone in a corner, writing in a small notebook. Without fully intending to, he found himself walking toward her table.

"May I?" he asked.

Nora looked up, surprised. "Of course," she said, closing the notebook.

Toryn sat across from her, suddenly unsure what to say. The question he'd been thinking about felt too direct. Instead, he nodded toward the notebook.

"What are you writing?"

"Observations," she replied. "About the plants I've been studying, the medical treatments I've seen here. It helps me make sense of this place."

Toryn nodded. "In the tribe, our wind speakers keep journals of every pattern they observe. My father's journal filled seven volumes before…" He trailed off, the memory still painful.

"Before what?" Nora asked softly.

"Before Ember Islet fell," Toryn replied. "My parents died when the heartstone finally gave out."

"I'm sorry," she said, and he could tell she meant it. "Is that why you were looking for the seedheart? To prevent another fall?"

"Yes," Toryn confirmed, relieved she understood so quickly. "My home, Roost Islet, is showing signs of decay. I believed a fragment of a seedheart could stabilize it." He hesitated, then asked the question that had haunted him: "Why did the Federation take it from Veil Islet? You must have known it would cause the islet to fall."

Nora's expression darkened. "We didn't understand what it was," she said quietly. "The Federation identified azurium – what you call heartstone – as an extremely valuable mineral. Our orders were to get a sample for study." She shook her head. "But you saw the plants. The animals!" Toryn said, his voice tight.

"We did something terrible," Nora said quietly. "None of us really understood what we were looking at – or what it would cost."

"But you took it anyway."

"Yes," Nora said quietly. "And I'm sorry. But at least the island wasn't completely destroyed. It descended gently. The animals survived, and the plants are already beginning to regrow – even without heat from the core. I've seen grass sprouting." She motioned toward the window. "It seems to thrive here on the surface. Maybe even better than before. Almost like it was meant to."

Toryn frowned slightly. "Like planting a seed?"

"Something like that," Nora said with a small smile. "We may have dragged each other below the Storm, but at least we're here together. And I believe we can fix this."

A crash from the kitchen cut her off, followed by Ellie's unmistakable swearing. Toryn stood with a sigh, already expecting another repair job.

"We'll talk more," he said. It wasn't quite forgiveness. But it was something.

For now, it would have to be enough.

CHAPTER 18
Machinery and Machinations

Lina was in love – with dock machinery, trains, and combustion engines.

She stood mesmerized before an enormous coal-powered locomotive. Black smoke belched from its stack, mixing with steam from the tank. She figured the machinist was burning off the last of the coal before heading to the roundhouse. Under load, the smoke was almost white.

They had never found that much coal on the floating islands – there was hardly anywhere to dig that deep. And while recycling steam back into water was vital above the Storm, here they simply let it escape.

"You're doing it again," Toryn said, shifting uncomfortably beside her.

"Doing what?" she asked, still watching the machinery.

"That thing where you forget people exist." His voice held no judgment, just observation. "You stare at the machines, your eyes go all unfocused, and you're probably daydreaming."

Lina reluctantly tore her gaze from the locomotive. "Sorry. It's just–" she gestured at the bustling railyard spread before them, " – look at all this. They're burning *actual* coal! Do you have any idea how rare that is above the Storm? In the Technocracy, we'd need a governor's permission just to use this much in science labs, and here in Stormhaven, they're burning it to move boxes!"

Toryn nodded, taking in the scene with matching focus. For a tribal kid who'd never seen tech beyond a handmade glider, he'd adapted surprisingly fast. Over the past two weeks, he'd soaked up knowledge like a sponge.

"Burning this stone heats the water, and steam moves the metal parts," he said. "But it makes the air smell wrong. In the Heights, you could breathe forever and never grow tired of it."

"Yeah, well, in the Heights, you can also fall to your death if your heartstone – sorry, is that the right word?"

"Heartstone is correct," Toryn said with a small smile. "Yes, islets fall. Even eagles can throw off a rider. But that's life. We don't cling to existence no matter the cost. I can't imagine a tribal person choosing to burden their family once they can't care for themselves anymore."

"And what do you do then?" Lina asked, bracing for a terrifying answer.

Toryn gave her a sad smile. "Join the sky. Last flight, we call it. And it is the last honor we can give someone who was unlucky enough to die in their bed."

Lina winced at the thought of falling from the inconceivable heights and taking her own life in that way to avoid decline. "At least here I can see the ground beneath my feet. Promise you won't toss me over the edge when I'm old and rusty!"

Toryn answered the joke with sudden seriousness: "Noted."

They stood on a small observation platform overlooking the Holy Sovereignty's main shipping docks. Rulf had assured them the spot was safe – out of the usual patrol routes. He was down below now, working his shift. Feeding five children, he'd said, was a full-time job. Despite his gruff manner and few words, Rulf had proven himself both dependable and unexpectedly layered.

"Come on," she said. "Let's head back to Madsen's. I promised to fix that water heater before the evening rush."

———

Quayside Tavern occupied a three-story building wedged between two hulking warehouses. Its worn wooden sign, featuring a faded ship and mug, creaked in the harbor breeze. The tavern owner himself stood behind the bar, polishing glasses with intense concentration. Madsen Cooper acknowledged their entrance with the barest of nods.

"Is the heater still being wonky?" Lina asked, heading toward the problematic equipment.

"Mmm," Madsen confirmed, which counted as a lengthy conversation by his standards.

From the kitchen emerged his wife, Ellie, carrying a tray of freshly baked bread. "You two are back early," she observed, setting down the tray. "Trouble?"

"Only the weather, as usual," Lina replied, crouching to examine the heater pipes. "Got any tar? This lower fitting is leaking."

Ellie produced a small can from beneath the counter. Tavern keepers tended to mind their own business, but Lina had the feeling they were more aware than they ever admitted.

"Toryn," Ellie said, noticing him hovering near the entrance. "Would you mind helping in the kitchen? The evening rush will be here soon."

Toryn nodded and headed to the kitchen. Of all of them, he had formed the quickest bond with the tavern keepers, mostly because of his respectful manners and willingness to take on any chore.

As Lina worked on the valve, she found herself reflecting on the strange turns that had brought her to this point. All her life, she had been avoiding attachment. Rare partners, workshop colleagues, fellow pilots – they never actually mattered. And it had already been a month since her life changed, and she was now beneath the Storm, surrounded by strangers from different worlds.

"There," she said, testing the heater's damper and release valve. "Should be smooth now."

Madsen grunted what might have been thanks as he passed her with a fresh keg of ale. Coming from him, the grunt was practically a speech of gratitude.

"Your stiff-backed friend's upstairs," Ellie said casually while arranging bread on a platter. She didn't have to name Kip – her description made it obvious. "Been shuffling papers all morning."

Lina nodded. Kip spent his days planning – tracking shipping schedules, studying harbor patrols, and sketching detailed maps of the warehouse district. His strategic mindset betrayed his education, even as he clung to the corsair persona out of habit. To Lina, he seemed like a clock wound too tight, the forced inaction wearing on him more than anyone else.

"I'll go see if he's ready for dinner," Lina said, wiping her hands on a rag. "Toryn, you good with potatoes?"

The tribal boy nodded from his position, hands moving with surprising dexterity for someone who had never done it two weeks earlier. He had been learning fast, taking on any task, listening for every piece of advice. She thought it might be a result of the

Heights' isolation – an inquisitive mind longing for everything new.

Upstairs, she found Kip hunched over a stack of carefully drawn maps and notes.

"Dinner's almost ready," Lina announced from the doorway. "Ellie's making her fish stew."

Kip looked up, blinking as if emerging from deep water. "Already?" He glanced toward the small window, where fading light filtered through the perpetual cloud cover. "Lost track of time."

"You've been at it for hours. Come down before your brain leaks out your ears."

He smiled thinly, carefully arranging his papers before standing. "Any news from the docks?"

"Nothing useful. No ships coming in this weather, only coal trains moving around." She couldn't keep the excitement from her voice.

"The ones that run on tracks? Impressive engineering, indeed."

"Hell, yes!" Lina agreed. "The power-to-weight ratio alone is–"

Kip held up a hand, his smile widening slightly. "Save it for dinner. I'm sure Toryn will appreciate another lecture on mechanical theory."

Lina rolled her eyes but didn't argue. Her love for machinery often left her companions confused, though Toryn at least made an effort to understand.

The evening passed pleasantly enough, with steaming bowls of Ellie's fish stew and conversation that carefully avoided any mention of the world above. It was an unspoken rule in the tavern – don't get overheard by patrons. The night grew late, the tavern gradually emptying as dock workers returned to their homes. Madsen and Ellie cleaned up while the four fugitives retreated to their rooms, the day's tension slowly unwinding into exhaustion.

———

"Lina! Pass me that linen cloth, would you?" Nora called as Lina entered their shared room that night. The Federation medic was hunched over a small collection of plants and roots spread on the windowsill, carefully separating leaves from stems.

Lina handed her the cloth, watching as Nora delicately wrapped a bundle of bluish leaves. "More leaves?"

"Local medicinal plants," Nora explained, her excitement evident in her voice. "The surface has species I've never seen. This one–" she held up a twisted root, " – the market vendor claimed it reduces fever better than anything they've known. I've confirmed it works. Used an extract on that sailor yesterday with an infection."

"You're treating patients now?" Lina raised an eyebrow.

Nora shrugged. "Just minor things. Madsen lets me use the back room when someone needs help. It gives me a chance to study surface medicine and…" she hesitated, "… makes me feel useful."

Lina nodded, understanding the call to have a purpose. She sat on her bed, pulling off her boots with a sigh of relief.

"So," she said with deliberate casualness, "you and Kip seem to be getting along well."

Even in the dim light of the oil lamp, Lina could see Nora's cheeks flush slightly. "We're working together on mapping the district," she replied with forced neutrality.

168

"Is that what they're calling it these days?"

Nora threw a small pillow at her, which Lina caught with a laugh.

"It's not like that," Nora insisted, though her tone suggested otherwise. "He's… complicated. And this is hardly the time or place for…" She trailed off, her hands resuming their work with the plants.

"For what? Finding someone who looks at you like you're the answer to a question he's been asking his whole life?" Lina smirked at Nora's expression. "Oh, please, I repair engines for a living. I know when parts fit together."

"That's a terrible metaphor," Nora groaned, but a small smile played on her lips.

Later on, when they turned off the lamp, Lina asked with her usual directness, "Do you have someone back at home?"

"Not really," Nora sighed. "In the space navy, we don't usually have families with civilians – we might be absent for far too long. I was married once, but it didn't work out. He's serving on another ship now. Never had been ready for kids, though. You?"

"Me? I'm not family material at all. I was raised by a granddad, had been turning wrenches most of my life, up to the moment I built my plane and took wing."

The conversation drifted into silence after that. It seemed to be filled with heavier thoughts: homes they might never see again, lives that they could never return to.

———

The next day, having a day off from the workshop, Lina went to the industrial district for replacement parts for the tavern's water pump. At least, that's what she told herself – it wasn't like she was just making excuses to see more engineering marvels.

The foundry's heat was overwhelming. Through the doors, she could see massive furnaces glowing orange-red, while workers poured molten iron into molds. The scale of the operation dwarfed anything possible back home. Mid-altitude artisanship was mostly about clockwork precision and tinkering, not mass production.

"Can I help you, miss?" a soot-covered worker approached, eyeing her with curiosity.

"Looking for water pump fittings," Lina explained, adopting the local accent she'd been practicing. "Three-quarter inch brass, for a model C Harbormaster."

The technical specifications seemed to convince him she belonged there. He pointed toward a smaller workshop across the yard. "Precision parts in there. Liam can help you."

Lina thanked him and crossed the yard, her eyes hungrily taking in every detail of the machinery.

The workshop's interior was a temple to precision engineering. Along one wall stood a row of complex machine tools – lathes, drill presses, and milling machines – all powered by an elaborate system of overhead belts connected to a central steam engine.

A thin, white-haired man with wire-rimmed spectacles looked up from his workbench as she stepped in. "You're the one from Madsen's," he said – not asking, but stating with certainty. His voice had the crisp precision of someone used to tolerances measured in thousandths of an inch.

"Word travels fast," Lina said, uneasy at being recognized so quickly.

The old man – Liam, she presumed – shrugged. "Small community. Strangers stand out. The pump parts are ready." He gestured to a small package on the counter.

After securing the parts she needed, Lina couldn't resist lingering to watch a group of mechanics working on what appeared to be a new type of engine. Their excited whispers carried across the workshop.

"Heard they've got engines that use combustible fuel under big pressure," one of the younger mechanics said. "No steam at all! No tank and condensers – just burns and pushes pistons directly."

"All that is shoptalk," an older worker scoffed. "If such a thing existed, it could already move the trains and self-driving carts. Damn, we could fly with such engines!"

Lina bit her tongue to keep from interjecting. She'd seen steamless engines in strange corsair craft that attacked the *Empirical Advance*. Was it the same technology, somehow making its way upward?

The implications were troubling, and she rushed back to the tavern to discuss it with the others.

————

When Lina returned to the tavern, the usual evening routine was in full swing. Madsen worked the bar, Ellie weaved between tables, delivering food and collecting empty mugs. The tavern's patrons filled the space with the loud hum of conversation and occasional bursts of laughter.

She spotted Kip in the far corner, deep in conversation with a flushed shipping clerk. Nearby, Nora listened patiently as an old dockworker detailed his alleged friend's troubling symptoms –

something that sounded suspiciously like syphilis. Toryn moved through the room with a tray of clean mugs, setting them out for Ellie.

Lina approached the bar and dropped her latest parts on the counter.

"Beer's stuck again," Madsen said, jerking his chin toward the far tap.

Lina grinned. "On it. And yes, you're welcome."

She made her way behind the bar and set to work on the problematic tap, finding comfort in the simple mechanical problem after a day of complex thoughts.

"What about the sticking back door?"

"The boy fixed it," Madsen said as she worked on the tap. "Steady hands."

Lina's eyebrows rose in surprise. "Toryn did it?"

Madsen nodded once, the barest of movements.

"Huh," Lina muttered, mildly annoyed. She was usually the one fixing things. It hadn't occurred to her that Toryn's tribal crafting might lend itself to mechanical work. A flicker of jealousy mixed with quiet pride stirred in her.

The evening unfolded in its usual rhythm, the tavern slowly emptying as the night wore on. By the end, only the four fugitives remained, with Madsen and Ellie wiping down the bar. Rulf had left about an hour earlier, citing an early morning shift.

"Sit," Ellie commanded, placing a pot of stew on the table they had gathered around. "You all need to eat properly."

None of them argued. Ellie's cooking was many grades above the bland prison food they had endured, and refusing it was both futile and foolish.

As they ate, the conversation turned to their perpetual topic: the ship that might take them to safety.

"Rulf says the weather is calm now, so the *Northern Mist* leaves next week," Kip said. "His contact has agreed to take us."

"Just about time," said Lina. "I've got my week's pay, and it should be enough to pay for the passage."

"By the way, I overheard an interesting rumor today," she added, and told what she had heard about the steamless engines.

"I'd bet the Harbor Commonwealth is really trading with someone from above," Kip said with renewed energy.

"Don't bet, Lordling," Lina parried. "The Commonwealth doesn't even have trains. They're lagging behind the Sovereignty in tech. This nice progress you see here is built on an eighty-hour-long week and a total absence of unions."

The meal continued in quiet, each of them absorbed in their own thoughts about the future. Madsen and Ellie finished their cleaning and were preparing to retire upstairs when a pounding came at the tavern's entrance. Madsen frowned – deliveries *never* came this late – but moved to answer it anyway. Ellie hesitated by the kitchen door.

At that moment, the door burst open.

Guards in the uniforms of the Holy Sovereignty poured into the tavern, their expressions grim beneath their caps. Behind them came a tall, severe man whom Lina recognized with horror – Judge Dregg, the chief interrogator from Tideguard Keep.

But the true surprise came next. By the Judge's shoulder stood Rulf. Her first thought was that they had caught him first during the raid, and he had brought guards there. But then Lina saw he wasn't shackled. Only now did she realize how similar these two figures were and started connecting the dots.

"Brother," the Judge said with a nod toward Rulf. "You did a wonderful job, as always."

Rulf smiled, a gesture that never reached his eyes. "Worked hard on it since the prison. And they believed every word. Never thought they would be so stupid."

Lina stared at Rulf, rage boiling inside her. "How could you?" she demanded, rising from her chair. "After everything – after we trusted you!"

Rulf shrugged massive shoulders. "A man's got to feed his four children," he said with mock regret.

"What happened to the fifth one?" Lina asked, her voice shaking with anger.

A slow grin crept across Rulf's face. "You got me. I don't have any."

The bluntness of his confession hit Lina like a blow. His family, his help, even his friendship – it had all been a lie. They hadn't been escaping; they'd been walking straight into a trap set by the Dregg brothers.

"Holy Mother's three tits!" Lina snapped. "Madsen, you too?" she shouted toward the tavern keeper.

"They have my brother…" the stout man muttered, avoiding her gaze.

Lina's hands clenched into fists as the guards began to close in.

The trap had sprung. And this time, there would be no escape.

CHAPTER 19
Devil's Bargain

"… that's my proposal, Lord Saroven. Find another seedheart island and help bring it down. I know you have strong opinions about me. Am I a friend? Possibly. A foe? Also possible. But your way home? Absolutely."

Kip kept his expression neutral when the Inquisitor used his full name and title. The man was more dangerous than a snake – calm, calculating, and somehow in possession of knowledge that should have been unreachable beneath the Storm. It meant their situation was either unexpectedly hopeful or disastrously compromised. Kip suspected the latter.

The luxury of the train car was unsettling. It swayed gently as they moved inland from Stormhaven. Thadeius sat across from him in a chair upholstered with a richness that couldn't have been made on the surface – likely a salvage from above. A small table between them held untouched tea and a delicate plate of pastries.

"Killian Saroven, heir to the Saroven estates, vanished four years ago after the unfortunate… political adjustments," Thadeius said, his tone as casual as if he were commenting on the weather – rather than the event that had shattered Kip's life. "Some thought you were dead. Others believed you fled to the Republic. Few imagined you'd turn up as a corsair."

Thadeius leaned in slightly, his voice dropping. "I'd love to tell you to take your time – shop around." He gestured broadly. "But in this case, your options are running out. As a gesture of goodwill, I'm prepared to send two of your group back above the

Storm. Let's say you and the tribal boy. The other two would remain here as… guests… until certain tasks are completed."

He paused, letting that sink in before continuing. "And I could assist with your little inheritance issue, you know. My contacts above have influence. Your… how do you call it… drift? It could be restored to your control with the right political pressure. And naturally, the remaining two would join you above."

Kip kept his face carefully composed, even as his heart pounded in his chest. The offer was pure manipulation – a calculated lure. Revenge against Lord Blackwell, the goal that had driven him for years, was now dangling within reach… like bait in a carefully laid trap.

"Compelling offer," Kip said, his voice calm through effort.

Thadeius nodded, seemingly satisfied with what he read in Kip's eyes. "Something to ponder while you're above," he said, gesturing to the pastries. "They may not rival what you're used to, but they're the best our chefs can manage down here. Do try one."

Kip reached for a pastry, noting how reverently Thadeius handled his own. On the surface, even simple sweets seemed to demand respect – scarcity lending them a kind of sacredness. The pastry wasn't good to his taste – overly sweet as trying to compensate for the lack of flavor.

"So," Kip said, steering the conversation back to immediate concerns, "why send Toryn and me above the Storm – and keep Nora and Lina here?"

Thadeius folded his hands in his lap. "Several reasons. First, as I said – it's a gesture of goodwill. After that, you'll do as I ask if you want the others released."

"Why not send all four of us now?" Kip asked, though he already knew the answer.

"Insurance," Thadeius replied, smiling faintly – as if Kip were naive for even asking. "I need assurance you'll follow through. Though I'd think the chance to restore justice would be motivation enough."

The train let out a low whistle as it slowed for a crossing. Outside the window, the coastal towns had faded into farmland – wide and strangely sparse. Crops stretched to the horizon, but they weren't the golden grains Kip remembered. Instead, thick rows of broad purple leaves filled the fields, interspersed with irrigation pipes and ventilation shafts plunging underground.

Thadeius followed his gaze. "Root cultivation," he said. "Efficient under low light, though it does lack the charm of your sunlit wheat fields."

Far ahead, the landscape shifted. Mountains loomed in the distance, their foothills dotted with mines and quarries. Tall smokestacks pierced the horizon, trailing smoke nearly indistinguishable from the gray sky above.

"Progress," Thadeius said simply. "The fruit of surface ingenuity – blessed, of course, by the Storm's Truth."

The train rolled on through a landscape thick with industry. They sipped tea in silence, watching factories and smokestacks give way to manufacturing complexes. Field workers drifted through the scene like ghosts – thin, pale, hollow-cheeked. These weren't the hardy mid-altitude laborers Kip had once known. This land had resources but not abundance, and the people bore the cost of that imbalance.

When the train stopped to take on more coal, Kip noticed workers filling a tank car with a thick, dark liquid. The smell was distinctive – not coal or water, but something more pungent. He observed a bucket brigade standing nearby, their equipment ready in case of an accidental fire.

"Refined oil," Thadeius said. "Far more efficient than coal. It powers engines beyond simple steam. The Kingdom of Tides discovered it – built a prototype – but never grasped its potential. Down here, it's our greatest breakthrough, while those above the Storm are still boiling water."

His voice brimmed with pride as they reboarded the train. Later, without prompting, he continued to elaborate.

"We send aircraft to our allies above. In return, they drop supplies – materials, precision tools, preserved food we can't produce down here." Thadeius frowned. "Some are lost to the tempest, of course. It's an unreliable system. That's why we need something better."

"I understand running engines for factories and trains," Kip said. "But aircraft? You can't fly reliably below the Storm. The weather's too volatile, and the ceiling's too low."

"Indeed," Thadeius said. "The weather makes conventional flight difficult, and low-altitude range is limited. Training pilots down here is no small feat either. But breaking through the Storm? That just takes the right design and the right pilot. Four out of five craft make it through – decent odds, wouldn't you say?"

Kip kept his tone neutral. "And what exactly do you need from me once I'm up there?"

"And what do you give in return?" Kip asked carefully.

"Our partners receive our technology," Thadeius said directly. "Our engines, our weapons, our fuel. Sparse resources on floating islands crippled your progress, just as food shortages crippled ours."

"Why are you so direct about this?" Kip wondered. "Isn't it a huge strategic secret of your nation?"

"You're a smart man, Lord Saroven. But I don't see you as an enemy – and there's nothing you can do with that information," said the Inquisitor.

"I'm offering a mutually beneficial arrangement." He tapped the armrest, fingers drumming in thought. "Our partners above have proven useful, though their obsession with destroying seedheart islands is… excessive. As if they're driven by more than profit." He smiled thinly. "I prefer something more grounded: food for my armies, pilots for my aircraft, and hereditary lands – returned to their rightful heir."

Kip studied the Inquisitor closely. "I'll need time to consider the offer."

Thadeius arched an eyebrow. "Naturally. Take the evening to reflect. We'll speak again tomorrow – after we arrive at Stormseat."

———

Their accommodations in the passenger car were a far cry from the damp prison cells of weeks past. Polished wood floors, real beds with clean linens, a window. Only the two guards stationed outside – who even escorted them to the washrooms – broke the illusion of freedom.

Lina sat at a small table by the window. Nora and Toryn were on the cushioned beds, speaking in low tones. All three looked up as Kip entered.

"Well?" Lina demanded, setting aside her project. "What did the holy madman want?"

Kip closed the door carefully before speaking. "He wants me and Toryn to go above the Storm to help bring down another seedheart island. You and Nora would stay here until... until certain conditions are met."

He hesitated, the Inquisitor's offer about his family lands burning in his throat. The temptation to share it was strong – they knew how much it mattered to him. But as their faces registered shock at the existing proposal, he swallowed the words. They didn't need to know that part for now. This was about escape, not his personal vendetta.

Toryn's face darkened. "I cannot consent to–"

"I know," Kip interrupted. "And I agree with you. I'm just telling you what he proposed."

He explained what he'd learned – the technology trade, the methods of sending planes up through the Storm and having partners drop supplies back, the war plans. With each revelation, the atmosphere in the room grew heavier.

"We can't even consider it," Nora added firmly. "The ecological impact aside, we'd be enabling conquest."

Lina had been quiet through his explanation, but now she sat up, her eyes narrowing the way they always did when she noticed something others missed.

"Wait – they have more planes than pilots to fly them!" She leapt to her feet, pacing as her mind worked. "That's why they want a deal up there – to man their fleet with pilots, who are in abundance above the Storm!"

Kip squinted, processing the insight. "And?"

"It's perfect," she continued, fingers tapping against her thigh. "Tell him to take me instead of Toryn. I can fly whatever contraption they've built – it'll spare them a pilot and allow sending one more aircraft for free. Toryn keeps his hands clean of seedheart tampering, I get to fly something more advanced than I've ever touched, and we double our chances of making it!"

"I won't participate in extracting another seedheart," Toryn said firmly.

"That's exactly why it should be me, not you," Lina countered. "I'm an engineer who can fly mechanical aircraft – this is about practical skills, not morality."

"She has a point," Nora said thoughtfully. She looked at Toryn sympathetically. "And I know how deeply it matters to you."

Toryn's jaw tightened, but after a moment, he gave a reluctant nod. "I don't like it, but your reasoning is sound."

"And after that?" Nora asked, turning back to Lina. "We can't actually down another seedheart island."

Lina's grin was fierce. "Then we go to Technocracy officials and tell them about the weapons trading. They won't want competition from below cutting into their markets."

Kip frowned. "That's assuming a lot about how the Technocracy would react. They're not known for their charity. What help could we possibly expect? And corsairs…" He trailed off, thinking of his former associates. "Some corsair clans are clearly already working with Thadeius. They've got their market sewn up."

"What about the Federation?" Toryn suggested.

Nora shook her head. "Federation machines can't work near the Storm. Even if we could contact my ship, they wouldn't be able to conduct a rescue operation."

"Still, above the Storm we have more chances to fix it than waiting here as hostages," Lina shot back. "One in five aircraft lost? I'll take those odds over indefinite captivity."

A servant arrived with their evening meal – a carefully arranged tray of mushroom stew, pale root vegetables, and thin slices of what might have been meat. The portions were larger than they'd received in prison and in Madsen's tavern, but still meager by mid-altitude standards. Yet the arrangement and presentation suggested this was considered generous fare.

Later, after much debate and once the others had gone to sleep, Kip found Lina still awake, staring out the window.

"Are you sure about this?" he asked softly.

"No," she admitted without looking at him. "But I'd rather risk dying in the Storm than live in a cage, no matter how gilded."

"The Technocracy isn't the answer," Kip said. "They'll have their own agenda."

"Of course they will," Lina replied. "But they're a devil we know better than this one."

They sat in silence for a moment.

"If we actually find a seedheart island…" Kip began hesitantly.

Lina turned to face him, her eyebrows arching with that particular look of mechanical disbelief she reserved for spectacularly bad ideas. "You really want to dance under the old man's flute, Lordling? Next thing you know, we'll be pulling the strings for his puppet show."

"But what about Nora and Toryn?" Kip asked. "If we don't do what Thadeius wants…"

"We'll find another way," Lina said firmly. "There's always another way."

"And what if there isn't?" Kip pressed, surprised by the edge in his own voice.

Lina snorted, turning back to the window. "Nora would slug you if you did that."

"Even to save her?" The question slipped out before he could stop it.

"*Especially* to save her," Lina shrugged, her focus on a distant point outside. "You've seen how she gets about this stuff."

Kip fell silent. She was right. Nora would never accept freedom purchased with destruction and war. And Toryn would consider it a betrayal. They might be freed from the Holy Sovereignty's prison only to be trapped by resentment and broken trust.

"Can you actually pilot whatever aircraft they have?" Kip finally asked, changing the subject awkwardly.

Lina's mouth curved into a determined smile. "I can fly anything with wings, Lordling."

A twinge of guilt struck Kip at the thought. The others were risking everything for freedom, while he carried a second, unspoken agenda. If they did find a seedheart island… would he really have the strength to walk away? Bringing it down could mean Nora and Toryn's safety – and the return of his family lands. Everything he'd fought for. The thought coiled in his stomach like a blade.

"Very well," he said at last. "Tomorrow, I'll tell Thadeius we accept – your version of the plan."

CHAPTER 20
Storm's Passage

"He agreed," Kip announced the next morning as he returned to their quarters after a second meeting with Thadeius. "Lina and I are going. Nora and Toryn will stay."

"Did you get the radio?" Nora asked, her voice low. "The one the Inquisition took when they caught us. You'll need it to reach the Federation once you're above the Storm. Signals can't get through from down here."

"Yes. No one down here understands Federation tech, so I told him it's essential for navigation in the Heights." Kip met Nora's gaze. "He doesn't believe it works anyway."

The next days passed in intense preparation. They were taken to a secure compound, where mock cockpits served as flight simulators. Each bore the Storm-cloud emblem, and every session began with a prayer to the divine wisdom said to have inspired their design.

"These aren't like anything I've flown before," Lina said after her first session. "The controls are… different. I've never seen so many gauges, levers, and switches packed that tight."

Kip shrugged. "Our planes use Rational Element. Flying's easy – if it's working, you won't actually fall." He studied the diagrams. "Here, I feel like I'm pushing the machine with my own hands. It's counterintuitive."

Within days, they were brought to more advanced machines – real engines, hydraulic levers linked to ailerons and rudders. Training intensified: pressure variation, engine control during ascent, emergency procedures. The lessons were focused and minimal. They were taught only what was needed to fly – nothing more.

"I see why they don't have enough pilots," Lina said. "Mastering the machine is hard, but doable. Then you get into the air, and most rookies probably freeze – shitting themselves from the gravity, height, and turbulence. And in minutes, you're at the Storm. It won't forgive *anything*."

Toryn seemed relieved to avoid the mission, though clearly worried. Nora stayed calm, but Kip noticed her hands trembling when they discussed contacting the Federation.

"The radio has an emergency beacon mode," she told Kip while the guards were distracted by evening prayers. "I already tried it on the island, but nothing gets through the Storm." She handed him a paper. "Memorize this combination. It'll activate the emergency signal."

"But?" Kip asked.

"Use it at the highest altitude possible. The battery drains fast once it's on." She met his eyes. "And I don't know if they'll help. The Federation has its own agenda."

———

After a week of training, they were transported across the mountain range. The convoy drove for hours before reaching a compound carved into the cliffside.

They passed through three checkpoints. At the final one, a Temple priest anointed the vehicle with blue-tinted oil and offered a brief prayer.

The launch facility was immense, partially tunneled into the rock. Guards stood at regular intervals, their uniforms bearing both military insignia and religious symbols. Workers moved with purpose, many touching Storm-cloud pendants before handling equipment.

Three aircraft stood on the platform, with double engines and slender bodies. Kip noticed huge extra fuel tanks where weapons should have been. Thadeius had prepared for every risk. The planes were painted in gold and crimson – colors Kip knew well. The Scarlet Talon. His corsair clan.

Lina circled the plane like a predator sizing up its prey. She ran her fingers along the fuselage, eyes sharp as they took in every detail. The engineers watched, clearly surprised by her confidence.

"I've seen these birds before," she said, tapping the nose. "And met their rotary cannons."

"No weapons on this flight," the chief engineer said. Her hands were scarred, her voice edged with fatigue. "Just extra fuel. These things burn through it fast up there."

Lina examined the engines closely. "How does it handle the shear forces?"

The engineer gave her an amused look, but then they launched into a technical exchange well beyond Kip's understanding.

Kip watched her transform. The hesitant girl was gone – replaced by a skilled pilot and confident mechanic, fully prepared.

Thadeius arrived, and guards escorted Nora and Toryn to the viewing platform.

"Your engineer is resourceful."

"She's full of surprises," Kip replied.

"As are you, Lord Saroven." Thadeius smiled thinly. "The third plane carries orders and will guide you to our partner's base." He lowered his voice. "Remember our arrangement. Your friends stay here until the seedheart island is down with my cargo. And I won't forget our *other* deal."

A surge of guilt hit Kip. He'd never told the others the full truth – always waiting for the right moment. But that moment never came.

During their brief farewell, Toryn clasped his forearm.

"The eagles fly with you," he said. Then, quieter: "I'll keep her safe."

Kip nodded.

"The radio settings are as we discussed," Nora said, her voice steady.

"I won't forget," Kip promised.

He expected her to step back, to preserve the careful distance she usually maintained. Instead, she stepped closer, rose onto her toes, and pressed a brief, unexpected kiss to his lips.

"Come back for us," she whispered.

Kip stood frozen, aware of Thadeius watching with quiet calculation.

"We will," he said at last, his voice steady. "I promise."

Across the platform, Lina was having her own farewell with Toryn. Whatever passed between them was too quiet to hear, but the brief, fierce hug they shared said enough. Then, as quickly as the moment of vulnerability appeared, it vanished. Lina straightened, her face hardening as she turned toward her aircraft.

"Ready?" she called to Kip.

He nodded and approached his plane. Engineers assisted them into their cockpits, gave final instructions, and sealed the canopies.

Through the small viewport, Kip caught one last glimpse of Nora and Toryn under guard, their faces etched with both hope and worry. Thadeius stood apart, his smile a calculated blend of promise and threat as he watched his plan take flight.

The engines roared. Kip was thrust back into his seat. His hands moved from instinct, but his mind clung to that final image – Nora and Toryn, hostages to the mission's success.

The ground dropped away, and with it, any room for hesitation. Four years ago, he would have done anything for revenge. Now, he wasn't sure what price he was willing to pay – or who he would become if he paid it.

————

Within minutes, Kip's plane reached an altitude that would have taken much longer in a steam craft. The escort plane moved ahead in a clean formation. Unlike theirs, it had rotary weapons mounted where Kip and Lina's planes carried fuel tanks.

The landscape below changed as they approached the Storm – a patchwork of fields and factories, crossed by roads. The air thickened, visibility dropping as they climbed higher. The cloud ceiling loomed above like an inverted ocean – roiling and dark.

Kip's pulse quickened as he ran through the pre-Storm procedures. Now it came down to luck and the machine's durability, not his flying skills.

Through the side viewport, he saw Lina's aircraft, already half-obscured by thickening clouds.

The weather worsened quickly. Rain lashed the canopy, cutting visibility to a few yards.

Kip focused on the instrument panel and the occasional glimpses of the lead plane. Everything else faded.

A sudden flash of light caught his eye. Through the rain, he glimpsed a massive lightning bolt arcing straight toward the escort craft. There was no warning, no time to react – the bolt struck with a blinding flash, followed by a deafening roar of thunder. When Kip's vision cleared, the escort plane was gone.

Four in five make it through.

The odds had seemed acceptable in Thadeius's comfortable train car. Kip was still staring at the empty space. There had been no malfunctioning engine, no pilot error – just random, cruel probability.

He glanced left – Lina's craft still held formation off his wing. Were her thoughts mirroring his? Were they among the lucky ones?

Nora's final words echoed in his mind, along with the promise he'd made. He couldn't fail. The only way out was through – through the Storm, through whatever lay beyond, through the tangled web of obligations and plans.

His grip tightened on the controls as the Storm's full fury closed around them, swallowing both planes. Ahead lay only hope – that the Storm had claimed enough, and would grant them passage.

PART 4: FADES DIVIDED

The Gathering Storm

Commander Elara Voss sat in her office aboard the UES *Pathfinder*, two reports spread before her. The holographic display cast her face in cold blue light. She had dimmed the overheads – partly to see the projections more clearly, mostly because the shadows suited her mood.

The first report bore the title *Atmospheric Analysis: Patterns and Anomalies*. It was the third consecutive update showing the same troubling trend.

"Computer, summarize the meteorological findings," she ordered.

The artificial voice replied with clinical detachment: "Precipitation across all monitored regions has risen twenty-two percent above baseline. Storm intensity is up twenty-seven percent. Cloud density in the lower atmosphere has increased by thirty-one percent. The planetary Storm has expanded vertically by approximately nine hundred eighty feet over the past six weeks."

Voss frowned. "Correlation with seasonal patterns?"

"Negative," the computer replied. "While Azoria experiences mild seasonal shifts, current measurements exceed all recorded and predicted parameters. Historical records show no comparable period of weather intensification."

"And the locals? Any records in their history of similar patterns?"

"Documented history spans approximately 300 years. No mention of similar atmospheric disruptions. However, the existing records are focused on navigation and trade routes rather than climate."

Voss nodded and brought up the second report, labeled *Political Status: Major Powers*. If the meteorological data had been troubling, the political assessment was worse.

A soft chime signaled an incoming message, pulling her attention from the display.

"Admiral Kaine requests your status update, Commander," the computer announced.

"Tell him it's being finalized," Voss said without looking up.

She refocused on the political report, which outlined a world teetering on the brink of conflict. The Mercantile Concord had doubled its security forces along major trade routes. The Technocracy had recalled its ambassador from the Kingdom of Azurath. The Corsair Collective – usually fractured into rival clans – had called its first Gathering in fifteen years. The Scarlet Talon clan now appeared strong enough to absorb most rivals or force them into servitude.

The intelligence on technological developments showed a strange spike. There were rumors of rotary machine guns. New double-engine aircraft of unknown origin had been spotted with unprecedented speed and maneuverability. Most of the tech usually had been azurium-based – it used the mineral to make the craft lighter, meaning it required less power to operate. However, their chemical fuels had always been too weak to propel an aircraft without it. Or at least they had been.

Voss closed her eyes and pinched the bridge of her nose. Mining operations required stability – both meteorological and political. The Federation's extraction teams couldn't function effectively in warzones. And what if the Storm grew further? Their entire operational plan relied on the status quo and trade because Federation tech could not operate in mid-altitudes.

"Computer, display our current extraction totals and goals."

The numbers appeared, and they weren't good. Already 45% behind schedule, with trends pointing toward further delays.

Voss rose and crossed to the viewport. Below, Azoria rotated slowly, veiled by swirling cloud bands. From this distance, it seemed peaceful – a gray marble adrift in the void. The truth, however, was far more turbulent.

They had options, of course. The Federation always had options. None of them were particularly pleasant.

They could back one faction, providing enough support to ensure quick victory. Create a single government they could negotiate with. Clean, efficient – if you didn't count the casualties.

The Federation had been founded to prevent wars and guide worlds toward pacifist ideals. Membership required that a planet – and its nations – end all conflicts on their own. Interfering in local power struggles to secure planetary dominance was a clear violation of Federation principles. Of course, those principles had been written long before the discovery of anti-gravity minerals. Officially, her superiors would demand both the azurium and strict non-interference.

Voss turned from the viewport with a grimace. The problem with clean, logical solutions was that they tended to get rather messy when actual people were involved.

There was also the matter of the azurium itself – the mineral that allowed the islands to float. The resource they'd come to harvest. The substance which, when removed in sufficient quantities, caused entire landmasses to fall. Federation scientists had assured her that individual islands were safe – that they could extract what was needed without risking their collapse. But scientists had been spectacularly wrong before. Even the locals avoided harvesting more than a few percent – no one wanted to saw off the branch they were sitting on.

And then there was Nora Hertzig, somewhere below. If she had survived the encounter with the feral cat, of course. What had she discovered down there that might change their understanding of this world?

The comms chimed. "Commander? The admiral is requesting direct communication."

Voss drew a slow breath. "Tell him I'll be available in ten minutes."

Ten minutes to decide how much of the truth to reveal. Ten minutes to choose between urging patience or pushing for aggression. Ten minutes to weigh career ambition against her conscience.

Her gaze returned to the reports: weather worsening, politics unraveling, mining goals slipping further out of reach.

"Well," she murmured to the empty room, "it was never going to be simple, was it?"

CHAPTER 21
Talons Grasp

"Do you always tend to stick your nose in other people's business, Lordling?"

The words carried across the landing platform as Kip climbed down from the aircraft. Striding toward him with arms spread in mock welcome was Captain Marek, leader of the Scarlet Talon. The stocky, balding corsair wore a wide grin that never touched his calculating eyes.

Kip scanned the platform. Lina landed on the next one over. Their arrival had clearly been anticipated. Workers rushed to drape heavy canvas over both aircraft. They clearly didn't want those machines drawing attention.

"Oh, Marek, you know I'm not," Kip replied smoothly. "Just trying to keep myself alive while the world seems determined to make that difficult."

The corsair captain laughed, clapping Kip on the back with enough force to stagger a lesser man. "And doing a spectacular job of it! Vanish for a month, then show up in something that shouldn't even exist." He gestured toward the sleek aircraft behind them, blue-stained fingers drumming against his thigh. "Oil-powered twin-engine with extra fuel tanks where the rotary gun should be. Fascinating choice of transportation."

"Life takes unexpected turns," Kip said, studying Marek with fresh eyes. The man he thought he knew was quickly becoming someone else entirely. "You seem to know a lot about combustion engines, Captain Marek. Or should I say… Inquisitor Marek?"

"Oh, I'm no Inquisitor, Lordling," Marek said, his smile tightening almost imperceptibly. "Religion's never been my thing. I was the first ace pilot of the Kingdom of Tides – Captain Josef Marek." His grin broadened again. "Now, let's move inside for this talk, shall we?"

Kip handed Marek the sealed documents from the Inquisitor and followed him along the familiar route from Bloodrift Island's main airfield. He knew the way well – this had been his refuge for years.

As they walked, discussing the fate of the third plane, Kip noticed something he'd never paid attention to before – the corsair captain's hands. His fingers were stained a deep, unmistakable blue, the color creeping past his knuckles. It was the same hue seen on those who handled raw Rational Element.

Kip had always thought of Marek as just an aging pirate who boasted about old flights when drunk. But now, knowing he was born on the surface, Kip saw a different side of the story – an outlander who had built a new life and risen to lead a mid-size corsair clan.

He noticed Lina already engaged in an animated conversation with the mechanics. Nobody bothered to restrict her movement, so she was clearly going to do what she knew best – find common ground with the technical crew. She caught his gaze and nodded slightly – she would pursue her own investigation, trying to get some details about the *Empirical Advance*'s fate.

The Scarlet Talon base sprawled across Bloodrift Island, growing outward in all directions. The air hummed with activity – planes launching and landing, their steam trails painting patterns across the sky. The dock stations swarmed with vessels of every type – ships in crimson and gold flew alongside trade vessels with suspiciously altered insignias. Immobilized craft in various states of repair lined the maintenance areas like patients awaiting surgery – or dissection, in the case of shady prizes.

Marek's quarters were sparsely furnished, dominated by a large table strewn with maps. Kip's eyes were drawn at once to an unusual detail – charts of every layer of Azoria, from the Heights to the surface, with precise lines linking locations across both realms.

I doubt anyone else in the mid-altitudes had maps that detailed.

"Oh, I see you appreciate my fascination with cartography," Marek said with a smile. "I spent a lot of time and money on those maps."

Kip tried to take in as much of the maps as possible, but Marek was already steering him toward a pair of chairs in the far corner. The only detail he managed to catch was that the mid-altitudes and the Heights clustered southwest of the surface lands.

"I was testing an early steam engine aircraft," Marek began, pouring two glasses of wine. "Heavy, chunky thing – carried enough coal to heat water for a small bathhouse." He handed a glass to Kip, his eyes momentarily distant. "Then I saw it – an island descending through the Storm, with a massive opening and a blue sky above."

The wine slid pleasantly down Kip's throat, rich with the taste of exotic fruits and distant spices.

"Hard to explain what it's like, seeing that blue for the first time," Marek went on. "Nobody below the Storm had ever seen a color so vivid. You've grown up here – you don't realize how lucky you are. It was… magnetic. I didn't even think. Just pointed my bird straight through the opening and suddenly I was in a world I'd only heard about in childhood tales."

He leaned back, casual as ever. "Crash-landed on an uninhabited island. Got picked up by a merchant vessel passing by. Did all kinds of stuff, worked in the mines, until I bought a tiny scout and joined the Talon a year later. That was seven years ago."

"And now you're working for the Inquisition that took over your former home?" Kip asked directly. "The Revolution was only a year ago. Does that change nothing for you?"

Marek shrugged, his smile never wavering as he glanced over the maps. "Working *with*, not for. And why should it matter who sits in the palace? I traded with the Kingdom before, I trade with the Inquisition now. They help me reach certain goals up here, and I send down whatever survives the trip through the Storm – mostly rations, alchemical oddities, maps, resources they can't get below. Crumbs, really."

"You mentioned being a miner before becoming a pilot," Kip said, gesturing casually toward Marek's blue-stained hands. "Rational Element, I'm guessing?"

"Among other things," Marek replied, subtly turning his hands palm-down on the table. "Most pure deposits I've ever worked with." A flash of something almost reverent crossed his face before he regained his casual demeanor. "But enough about old history. What brings you back with these lovely documents from our friends below?"

"The Inquisitor wants a bulk shipment of food and pilots."

"Hmm." Marek's expression sharpened, his blue-stained fingers drumming a slow, deliberate rhythm against the table. "That would certainly change things down there. Not that I much care anymore. I've already got enough weapons and birds to start my own little conquest up here."

"How do you exchange information with the Inquisitor?" Kip asked carefully.

"Nothing fancy," Marek replied. "We drop sealed buoys at set locations. They just have to patrol the area and fish them out. Getting a message back is trickier, but Thadeius sends us a plane about every fortnight."

He smiled and added, "I could say I was surprised when the last message requested a profile for a lean, blue-eyed aristocrat who looked exactly like a person I know."

"Well, believe me, I didn't go there by choice," Kip said, and they both gave short, insincere laughs.

Marek stood, signaling the conversation was over. "Let me go through these documents. Make yourself at home – you know the place."

———

Kip moved through the base's narrow passages, nodding to familiar faces in passing. Yet, after years here, he felt strangely detached, as if viewing it all through a stranger's eyes. What had once been a refuge now seemed layered with unspoken motives and quiet secrets. The base itself was unchanged, still serving its purpose as pirate havens always had. It was Kip who had changed – and home felt far away.

After checking several hangars, he finally found Lina examining the rigging of a steam vessel with the maintenance crew, her hands already stained with grease.

"Anything?" he asked quietly.

"Three hangars are off-limits," she said. "No one knows what's inside – or they pretend not to. The mechanics have only scraps about the zeppelin ambush. They know it worked, but the details are locked down." She wiped her fingers on a cloth, only smearing the grease further. "Are they letting us go?"

"Haven't asked yet. The captain's reading the documents now."

Lina nodded and returned to her investigation.

Walking away, Kip felt a strange emptiness. He was close to reclaiming his drift and title – everything he'd wanted since his family's fall – yet the price seemed increasingly steep. And Nora remained a hostage below the Storm, with no guarantee the Inquisitor would honor their agreement.

———

When Marek summoned him again, the corsair captain's expression had shifted. The smile was still there, but the easy manner was gone. This was the leader now – the strategist – measuring his next move.

"Interesting proposal," Marek said, tapping the documents. "A proper seedheart descent could change everything." His voice carried that same strange, reverent edge as before. Leaning back, he studied Kip. "I see Thadeius also mentioned a little arrangement about your inheritance. We'd planned to hit the Resonance Fellowship first, but we can pivot to the Drift Lords instead. You'll have your land soon enough – under Talon's protection, of course."

The casual phrasing couldn't hide the steel underneath. Kip forced a smile. "Looking forward to it."

"And the Fellowship gets a reprieve – at least temporarily," Marek added with a thin smile.

"Do you know where we might find another seedheart island?" Kip asked, cutting to the heart of their mission.

"Funny you should ask." Marek's casual tone didn't match the sharpness in his eyes. "Got some intel from the savages up in the Heights. They had one boy out on a mission to find such an island." He waited for Kip's reaction with a cold stare.

"That island is no longer an option," Kip said carefully.

Marek nodded, unsurprised. "Figured as much. Just as I figured, the boy is now down there with your girl as an Inquisitor's insurance."

Kip's expression remained neutral, but the feeling of being caught in two spiderwebs at once gnawed at him. Marek had known about Toryn's journey before it even began. How many more spies did he have around?

"However," Marek continued, "the boy's father – Arvid – was a wonder of a scout himself. There are rumors he found more than one seedheart island." He traced a lazy circle around a region near the Heights, his blue-stained fingers lingering on the map with unusual tenderness. "You might need to pay his tribe a visit."

Kip nodded mechanically, mind still racing. This was the second time he'd faced someone playing games with people and knowledge. Both Thadeius and Marek were manipulating events across worlds as though moving pieces on a game board.

Shuffling through the papers, Marek paused at a detailed requisition form, smoothly changing the subject. "Pilot transfers… equipment specifications… Well, there's nothing more related to you."

His eyes narrowed slightly. "So it's time for you to take your mechanic friend and move on. She's already asking too many questions. Pass me a message when you have the coordinates of the seedheart. I'll do the rest."

His emphasis made it clear – Kip had to leave now and hold up his end of the bargain. He was no longer welcome there until his part was done.

"What about our planes?" Kip asked. "Can we have them for the mission?"

The easy smile vanished from Marek's face. "Absolutely not. You don't have fuel, spare parts, or any reason to possess it." His tone was flat, businesslike. "The world isn't ready. Everyone who's seen these planes is either dead or with us." The smile returned, though diminished. "I'll give you something with a Rational Element module instead. Your Technocracy girl will appreciate it."

The more Marek talked, the more Kip realized that his ways with corsairs had now parted for good. He might have considered the easy path for reclaiming his lands before, but now it felt wrong. Being Marek's pawn would be a straight way to losing himself – losing the last of his principles.

When he left, his mind felt clearer than it had in years. He had made his choice, and it wasn't the one Marek or the Inquisitor expected.

———

He found Lina at the plane dock, standing beside a sleek aircraft. To Kip, it looked like just another Technocracy plane, but Lina's fingers were tracing freshly repaired holes on the tail, her face pale.

"They're giving us Dahn's bird," she whispered, voice tight. "He was my wingmate in the *Empirical Advance* escort job."

She turned to him, her voice hard. "I can't fly to the Technocracy like this – a month after the attack, in a missing escort's plane, with a corsair beside me, and no explanation for what happened to the *Empirical Advance*. No one would believe me. They'd think I defected. And that plane's surely on the wanted list – we could only sell it for parts."

Kip felt the weight of their predicament. Marek had outplayed them perfectly. The gift of Dahn's aircraft wasn't just practical – it severed the direct route to the Technocracy. Their choices now were to risk selling it to smugglers – most of whom worked with corsairs – or head straight for the Heights.

In this game spanning two worlds, Kip was starting to suspect that he and Lina weren't players at all, but pieces pushed around by other hands.

CHAPTER 22
Escape from the Gilded Cage

The garden smelled wrong.

Toryn couldn't shake the thought as he walked beside Nora along a neatly trimmed path. Weeks beneath the Storm had dulled his sense of daylight, but the plants still looked alien, no matter how carefully they were arranged.

In the Heights, vegetation had evolved to survive in thin air – sparse, hardy plants with small leaves and deep roots to anchor against fierce winds. Here, the surface plants were the opposite: massive violet leaves straining toward a sun they could barely feel.

Like the people here, Toryn thought. Adapting to exist, never having seen the sky, never feeling the sun.

A gentle breeze carried the faint scent of unfamiliar blossoms – not unpleasant, but muted. Everything here felt subdued, as if the Storm dulled not only the light but every sense.

"The Federation requires a unified planetary government," Nora was saying, responding to a question Toryn had asked about how worlds join the Federation. These conversations had become a daily ritual during their walks – not formal lectures, but brief exchanges that seemed to give Nora focus.

Earlier that morning, she had paced their quarters like a caged eagle, frustration in every stride. "What I wouldn't give for a *basic* spectrometer," she'd muttered, studying a strange flowering plant their keepers had let her bring inside. "Even just a half-decent microscope. The cellular adaptations here must be fascinating."

Toryn could tell Nora was fighting off dark thoughts by throwing herself into work. She longed for scientific puzzles, eager to solve the mysteries of this world. So he'd begun asking about Federation science, medicine, governance – anything to keep her mind engaged. It worked; her eyes lit up when explaining complex concepts, and the harsh reality seemed to soften. He soaked up the knowledge like a sponge.

"There should be an organization representing all countries and territories," she went on. "No nations at war. No people suppressed, enslaved, or denied the vote."

Toryn nodded, translating the idea into something that fit his tribal worldview. "Like our Circle of Elders, but for the whole world." He paused, weighing the thought. "So Azoria would have to settle its own conflicts first – before anyone from outside could help?"

"Exactly. The governing body has to vote unanimously to request Federation membership. Then envoys arrive to confirm all the requirements are met and begin drafting an ascension plan." Nora stepped carefully around a particularly droopy flowering bush. "The Federation doesn't solve a world's internal problems – it gives them a goal: to find stability on their own."

A guard trailed them at a distance, close enough to intervene if necessary but far enough to give the illusion of privacy. They were under constant surveillance, but with some freedoms, like walking around the estate grounds. Less a prison than a gilded cage.

Toryn studied the guard briefly, noting what he had observed in most locals – the man stood several inches shorter than he, with a distinctly narrower build. His uniform hung slightly loose at the shoulders, and fine lines etched the corners of his eyes despite his relative youth.

"So there's no shortcut," Toryn said, turning back to their conversation. "A world must heal itself before joining something larger."

"That's the theory," Nora replied. "Though in practice, the Federation sometimes exerts influence in less direct ways."

Her voice dropped slightly. "What frustrates me is that there are two distinct worlds here on Azoria, with seedhearts somehow connecting them. But the Federation's interest in Azoria is resource extraction." She sighed. "Even if they're not targeting the seedhearts right now, any large-scale mining will disrupt ecosystems in ways we don't fully understand. And admitting the planet into the Federation? That's not even on the table. The hypocrisy is that the planet might not be ready to join, but it already has to provide something valuable."

Toryn heard the conflict in her voice – duty to her people versus growing concern about their methods. He had noticed this tension in her more often since their capture, as if she was distancing herself from them now.

"Are there threats beyond human worlds that make such alliances necessary?" he asked, steering the conversation back to safer ground with their guard nearby.

A wry smile crossed Nora's face. "Actually, no. We're prepared for it – both hostile and friendly scenarios – but so far, humans remain impressively isolated in the universe."

"So humans themselves pose the greater threat to humanity?" The irony wasn't lost on Toryn.

"That's right." Nora's expression turned grimmer. "The point of the Federation's philosophy is that worlds improve through their desire to unite. It really works, but with exceptions. Sometimes massive criminal organizations oppose ascension. Some worlds are already unified, but the people have fewer rights than slaves. We even had an incident with thinking constructs – complex devices built to emulate human thought. A religious sect created them, believing they could form their own society."

Toryn raised an eyebrow, trying to grasp the concept. "What happened?"

"Didn't end well," Nora shrugged. "The thinking machines reached the same conclusion you did, and started eliminating the main threat – humans."

Their path took them alongside an irrigation channel – one of many that crisscrossed the estate grounds. Flat-bottomed cargo boats moved slowly along these waterways, pushed by helmsmen using long poles. They wore cloth caps covering their ears and necks as protection against insects.

Toryn watched them serenely gliding through the channels. *So different from flying, but still, there are currents, there is freedom and power far beyond mere walking.*

The water itself fascinated him. Here it flowed freely, an abundance, not a resource. It wasn't salty, unlike the ocean, so it was literally the source of life – but nobody cared, as nobody cared for the wind or air itself.

"It's been a week," he said quietly, careful to keep his voice below what the trailing guard might hear.

Nora nodded. She understood his meaning without elaboration. It had been a week since Kip and Lina departed on the Inquisitor's mission. If they'd truly followed the plan, they would complete their task soon. If they'd deviated – which Toryn hoped – they would soon be exposed to Thadeius.

"The timeline is narrowing," Nora agreed, clearly having the same line of thought.

The emergency was clear – they were hostages, in direct danger, and had to act sooner rather than later.

One particular boat drew level with them as they walked, its progress deliberately slowed. The helmsman – older than most they'd seen, with a weathered face beneath his cap – caught Toryn's eye and winked.

What was that?

Toryn maintained his neutral expression, but he felt Nora tense beside him. She gave a subtle nod in response.

The boat continued on its way, the interaction lasting mere seconds – too brief for the guard to notice anything unusual.

"Plants here struggle without direct sunlight," Toryn commented loudly enough for the guard to hear. "Yet they manage to harvest year-round due to the absence of clearly marked seasons."

"Right, but they still need protein, and there are almost no domestic animals down there," Nora replied at an equal volume.

But her eyes told a different story – something had changed.

Did someone just make contact?

———

"It was Marvin Thale," Nora whispered later that evening, after they'd returned to their quarters.

They sat at the small table by the window, supposedly engaged in a game of cards Nora had taught him.

"The lighthouse keeper?" Toryn kept his expression neutral, as if contemplating his next move. "Isn't he supposed to be at the lighthouse, watching the skies?"

"Exactly." Nora's eyes sparkled with excitement. "His presence here means he must have found out we're being held and has come to help us."

She laid down her cards and rubbed her temples. "If we could escape, it would solve so many problems. Even if Kip has no choice but to do Thadeius' bidding, nobody could blame us for escaping, and we could simply apologize and return. But most likely, we'd be safer on our own."

Toryn recognized that she was calculating the options. For him, it was much simpler – Kip had given his word not to harm another seedheart island, so they had to escape.

"Do you think Marvin is attempting a rescue?" Toryn asked, returning to the immediate concern.

"I do. He is really smart and ingenious." Nora deliberately placed a card on the table. "We need to visit the channel banks tomorrow at the same time and be ready."

"The guard will be suspicious if we follow the exact same route."

Nora smiled. "Then we'll need to give him a reason not to be."

They spent the next hour developing their plan, voices low, cards sliding across the table in a game neither was truly playing.

By the time they retired for the night, they had agreed: tomorrow would offer their best chance of escape.

Lying awake in darkness, Toryn found himself thinking of the Heights. On one hand, he had already failed his people, but with Lina's promise to tell Kora everything about the Depth and seedhearts, it wouldn't be in vain.

The tribe would grow stronger with this information.

———

"Beautiful day for a picnic, isn't it?" Nora's voice carried the right amount of casual cheer as she addressed their guard the following afternoon.

The man – Toryn had learned his name was Daven – frowned slightly. "If you say so, ma'am."

They had requested a small basket of food and a bottle of wine from the kitchen, apparently to enjoy the pleasant weather. The staff had complied without question. Their captors maintained the charade of hospitality even as they kept them prisoners.

The basket arrived, with portioned root vegetables and paper-thin slices of meat arranged to cover more of the plate than they actually did. The "honored guests" presentation couldn't disguise the meager portions beneath the artful arrangement. Toryn found himself missing the hearty foods from the Heights. Instead, these dishes cleverly transformed cultivated fungi into a semblance of other foods.

"We thought you might like to join us," Toryn added in a friendly tone. "Standing all day must be tiring."

Suspicion flickered across Daven's face, but the prospect of sitting down clearly appealed to him. "I shouldn't... I'm on duty."

"Just for a few minutes," Nora pressed, gesturing toward a grassy spot near the channel bank. "We're not going anywhere."

Daven's hand rested briefly on his musket. "I can't accept the wine," he said firmly, then hesitated. "Against instructions."

"Of course," Nora agreed smoothly. "Just the company, then. And perhaps some food."

The guard hesitated, then nodded. "I suppose a short rest wouldn't do any harm."

They settled on the grass, arranging the blanket and food. Toryn poured two glasses of wine. The fermented drinks of the Heights were stronger, but their scent was remarkably similar – another connection between worlds that appeared so different on the surface.

"To pleasant company," Nora toasted, raising her glass.

Daven remained standing at first, but as minutes passed, the warm afternoon and conversation gradually relaxed his posture. He eventually sat at the edge of the blanket, accepting small portions of food while maintaining his refusal of wine.

Toryn observed the channel's water lapping gently against the grassy bank, following patterns that reminded him of the wind. Water and air – different mediums but governed by the same physical principles. His father had taught him to read wind patterns; now he applied those lessons to understand water. Adaptation like the surface plants. Like himself.

"Just a taste," Nora suggested after nearly half an hour of casual conversation. "It's quite remarkable. From the Inquisitor's own vineyards, they told me."

Pride in local production and curiosity finally overcame duty. "Perhaps just a sip," Daven conceded, accepting a half-filled glass. "To assess the quality."

That sip became several as their conversation continued. By the third glass, Daven had settled back on his elbows, his vigilance noticeably diminished.

"Not supposed to drink on duty," he mumbled, more to himself than to them. "Special circumstances, though. Special guests."

"We appreciate your flexibility," Nora replied smoothly.

Within minutes, Daven's eyelids grew heavy – the combination of wine, food, and one of Nora's medical plant powders proving effective. As his breathing deepened into the steady rhythm of sleep, Nora caught Toryn's eye and nodded.

They remained where they were, maintaining the appearance of picnickers while scanning the channel for Marvin's boat. Toryn calculated they had perhaps an hour before Daven either woke naturally or was missed by his superiors.

He felt surprising sympathy for the guard. Daven wasn't cruel – just a man following orders, believing the Storm's Truth because he'd never known otherwise. What would happen to him when they disappeared? The Inquisitor didn't seem forgiving of failure. For a moment, Toryn considered leaving something to make it seem they had overpowered him, but that might only worsen the man's punishment.

"There," Nora murmured, gesturing subtly toward an approaching vessel.

Marvin's face appeared beneath the cap, his eyes alert as he approached the bank. Nora quietly indicated that the guard was asleep.

Without hesitation, Marvin steered straight toward them. "Sergeant Hertzig," he called in a hushed but urgent tone, "take your friend and jump over here!"

"Right now?" Nora asked, surprised by the immediacy. "We haven't even checked the guard's schedule!"

"Right now! It's the very best opportunity you'll *ever* get!" Marvin's expression left no room for debate.

Toryn didn't hesitate. Heights logic applied clearly here: when the wind offers a path, you take it. He slipped silently to the water's edge and leapt aboard the flat-bottomed vessel, Nora following him a moment later. As they landed, Marvin gestured urgently for them to hide.

"Under the tarpaulin," he directed, continuing to pole the boat along as if nothing had happened.

They crawled into the narrow space among crates of produce, pulling the heavy cloth over themselves. The smell of root vegetables and damp earth enveloped them as Marvin continued on, his pace deliberately slow to avoid drawing attention. Through the gap in the covering, Toryn could see Daven still sleeping peacefully. The simplicity of their escape seemed almost anticlimactic after a week of captivity.

For several minutes, they traveled in silence. Then Marvin spoke in hushed tones.

"I had intelligence that you never reached Free Harbor and suspected you might have come to the Kingdom of Tides," he explained, poling the boat. "Then I received information about the Inquisition and realized things could be even worse. I gathered some friends, traded for insights, and found that the two outlanders imprisoned near the Stormseat were actually you. So we planned your extraction. Anything on the rest of your team?"

"They are safe – the Inquisition sent them on a mission above, keeping us as hostages," Nora explained quietly. "Marvin, what happens now? They'll search all vessels once they discover we're missing."

"Indeed, they will," Marvin replied with unexpected confidence. "Which is why we're making a brief stop."

He guided the boat beneath a low stone bridge, where shadows were especially deep. Toryn could barely make out a small recess in the bridge's support structure, where Marvin maneuvered the vessel.

"Quickly now," he whispered, reaching into a hidden compartment. He pulled out bundles of cloth – boatmen's garb, complete with the distinctive cloth caps Toryn had noticed earlier. "Your disguises."

Toryn understood immediately. They weren't just escaping; they were disappearing. He pulled the rough fabric over his clothes and settled the cap on his head, tucking his hair beneath it.

Nora's garb was simpler – just a cape with a hood, concealing much of her features.

"This still leaves us with a problem," Marvin continued pragmatically. "Three boatmen on a vessel that normally requires only one will draw attention."

To Toryn's surprise, Marvin revealed a second, smaller boat tethered in the bridge's shadow. "I will continue toward the estate," he explained, untying the craft. "You two will take the second boat. I will deliver the vegetables to the Inquisition's mansion, as I have for the last week. If we're fortunate, the alarm won't sound until I'm well clear."

"And if you're caught?" Nora asked, concern evident in her voice.

"Then I'll play the role of the confused old man," Marvin replied with a wink. "It's a performance I've perfected over many years."

They transferred to the smaller vessel and shifted some crates from Marvin's boat to make it less suspicious.

"Head directly for the northern warehouse district," Marvin instructed, handing Toryn the pole. "At the third major junction, look for a boat with red markings on its prow. The boatman will be wearing a cap with a torn edge. That's Talbert – he'll guide you further."

"What about this boat?" Toryn asked.

"Talbert will take care of that. We have people who will recover and repurpose it." Marvin hurried them. "You should go now. The guard shifts change soon, and the waterways will be busier."

Nora turned to Marvin for a short goodbye. "Thank you, Ensign Thale."

"For the Federation," he replied, returning a crisp salute before pushing their boat out from the bridge's shadow.

Toryn took control of the vessel, adapting to water navigation. He struck the bank and branches several times before guiding them awkwardly to the main channel, where he managed a steadier pace. In the distance, they saw Marvin's boat taking a side channel toward the estate.

They passed other boats, exchanging brief nods with fellow boatmen. No one gave them more than a passing glance – just two more figures in the constant flow of river traffic that served as Stormseat's lifeblood.

At the third junction, they slowed, searching for the vessel with red markings. The waterway opened into a broader expanse, creating space for a small but bustling floating marketplace.

"There," Nora murmured, nodding toward a slim boat moored at the edge of the activity. The standing boatman wore the distinctive torn-edged cap. He reacted to their approach immediately, casting off and gliding toward them.

As the boats drew alongside each other, the boatman's apprentice moved to their vessel and took Toryn's pole. They climbed into the new boat, crouching low as instructed. The apprentice poled their original craft back to the main channel, cutting off any possible chase.

"Talbert," their new boatman introduced himself once they left the market. "Scholar and Archivist. Welcome aboard." Nora had to hide between the baskets of vegetables, while Toryn maintained the neutral look of an apprentice in his boatman garb and cap.

No sooner had they settled into their hiding place than alarm whistles sounded in the distance – their absence had been discovered. But with the boat transfers and decoys, the trail was hopefully obscured enough.

Toryn watched as a patrol boat moved swiftly past them, black-uniformed guards scanning the waterways. Talbert kept his unhurried pace, just another trader going about his business with an apprentice. The patrol passed without a second glance.

"Marvin's plan is perfect," Talbert commented after the danger passed. "Three different boats, three different directions, and a fourth decoy with two men and a woman heading entirely the opposite way. They'll be chasing shadows for days."

Hours passed as their new vessel navigated the complex network of waterways. Toryn kept from looking around too much, trying not to attract attention. He watched as they approached the city proper, passed under bridges, and recognized the distinctive sounds of trains and the districts they moved through.

By the time Talbert stopped the boat, night had fully descended on Stormseat. They had docked in what appeared to be a warehouse district, the boat secured alongside a loading platform.

"We should be safe here," Talbert said, helping them out of their hiding place. "The guards rarely patrol this section after dark."

As Toryn stretched his cramped muscles, he studied their new ally. Talbert's attire suggested a scholar or record-keeper rather than a boatman – big belly, ink-stained fingers, and a small notebook protruding from his pocket.

"I've known Marvin for many years," Talbert explained as they made their way into the shelter of a nearby alley. "I was an Archivist representative in the Commonwealth when the revolution began, and I decided to stay there to avoid trouble. When I received Marvin's letter about you, I activated my old contacts here and returned to my native city. Always happy to help my lifelong friend – especially when it involves assisting people from above."

Something in his tone caught Toryn's attention. "Archivist? Are you working for the Temple of Storm?"

Talbert shook his head. "I'm a servant of the order that maintains the true histories. The Church of the Archives was there for hundreds of years, and it will be, regardless of the Inquisition's efforts."

"But you call it a church. What do you believe in?" Nora asked.

"In knowledge," Talbert answered plainly. "We collect and protect information – including all records about the world above. The name comes from the ruins beneath the city, predating even the Kingdom of Tides. There is a magnificent structure, an Archive. Our founders established the Church to preserve both the physical space and its philosophical purpose."

Nora's eyes lit up with excitement. "Pre-Kingdom structures? With ancient texts?"

Toryn exchanged a knowing glance with Talbert. Even in danger, she couldn't resist new information. It was, he realized, her form of adaptation – processing the world through knowledge.

"Marvin found something crucial before his departure," Talbert continued, leading them through a maze of streets. "His observations about the Blue Descent islands – it appears they form a specific pattern around the world above, encircling the inhabited regions."

Toryn's interest sharpened. "What kind of pattern?"

"Something geometric. Something planned. Marvin believes they serve a purpose – perhaps maintaining atmospheric conditions or weather stabilization. They should be preserved at any cost, as no one knows what might happen if too many are removed." Talbert's voice lowered further. "The worst-case scenario is that all floating islands could fall."

The implications sent a chill through Toryn. If the seedhearts were guarding the floating world, the Inquisitor's plan for them could be catastrophic. Not to mention the Federation, which had the power and will to mine seedhearts for minerals and trigger something unexpected.

He thought of Roost Islet. If the theory proved true, perhaps the natural decay and occasional fall of regular islets was part of some larger system – a cycle his people had never fully understood. If someone were meddling with the islets and causing them to fall, could it also affect the world's balance? Maybe the Archives hold the answers.

"Where are you taking us?" he asked as they continued their journey through increasingly narrow passages.

Talbert paused before a nondescript wall. "Well, you came from above to the ground," he said with a cryptic smile. "Now it's time to go underground."

He pushed aside what Toryn had assumed was a solid wall, revealing a hidden entrance and a ladder descending into darkness.

"You'll be safe there," Talbert said, gesturing toward the opening. "After you."

Toryn peered into the shadows below. The Heights had no concept of "underground" – when you lived on floating islands, the ground itself was a shallow rock beneath your feet. Yet here, there seemed to be another layer of existence beneath the Depths.

He sensed an unfamiliar scent, earthy and rich – pleasant in its own way, yet unlike anything he had tasted before. Talbert noticed his hesitation and smiled knowingly.

"You'll soon meet our colleagues from the Mushroom Syndicate – one of the five major factions operating beneath the city." His voice carried careful pride. "Their cultivation chambers produce more protein per square foot than any surface farm. Officially, the Temple denounces them as heretics for growing food without the Storm's blessing. Yet those same Temple officials feast on their best fungi. The Syndicate's existence is an open secret – too valuable to eliminate, too controversial to acknowledge."

Layers upon layers, Toryn thought, worlds stacked like the pages of a book. And somehow, he had fallen through them all.

With a nod to Nora, Toryn grasped the ladder and began the descent into the darkness below – farther from home than any tribal member had ever traveled.

CHAPTER 23
Divided Flight

The control stick vibrated against Lina's palm as the plane cut through the turbulence. She adjusted the pressure, compensating for the thinner air at this altitude. Dahn's escort plane – no, their plane now – responded with a smoother hum. The air around Trading Station 42 was notorious for its unpredictability, but nothing she couldn't handle.

She'd barely spoken for the past hour – not out of any strategy, just the comfortable silence of someone who preferred the company of machines to people. But one thing had been gnawing at her since they left Bloodrift Island, and the farther they flew, the more it demanded attention.

"So… what did they hook you on?" she asked, eyes still fixed on the horizon.

"What?" Kip asked from the second seat.

"Are you going to tell me what you're holding out on, Lordling?" She kept her tone even, matter-of-fact. "The corsairs were bragging that the Fellowship can now wash their pants while they look upon the Drift Lords instead."

She let that hang in the air for a moment. "Did they buy you with a promise to get back your drift?"

There was a telling pause before he answered, confirming her suspicion. His voice, when it came, carried none of the careful poise he usually maintained.

"They dangled that possibility, yes. Thadeius knew exactly who I was – my full name, Lord Blackwell, everything." He ran a hand through his hair. "But that's not... I promised Toryn I wouldn't pursue it. We already talked this out, Lina."

"When?" The rotary blade briefly stuttered as they hit another air pocket. She boosted the steam flow for a while, bringing it back to a smooth rotation. "When exactly did we discuss you getting your lands back in exchange for allying with a religious nutjob who locks people up for knowing the sky has a top?"

"That's not fair, and you know it." Kip's voice had an edge to it now. "I didn't tell you everything because I didn't want it to color your decisions. The offer was made, yes, but I played along. Couldn't exactly anger the Inquisitor while we were still in his clutches."

Lina banked the plane slightly, bringing the trading station into view as they flew through a final wispy layer of cloud cover. The escort craft's engine ate it without a jerk. Below them sprawled a rather disorderly complex – a dozen interconnected platforms with airships and smaller craft. The structure was anchored to three separate drifts and stabilized with Rational Element.

"Not exactly inspiring confidence in your team play," she said. "Hard to trust someone who was successfully baited and withheld it, saying he was playing along. Maybe this was just a step on your way to getting back your precious ancestral home."

The silence that followed was brittle and charged. When Kip broke it, his voice was tired and sincere – *almost like a normal person*, she thought.

"Lina. Believe me, I'm doing this for Nora. For Toryn. For you. Not for my agenda, not for the Inquisitor or Marek."

His blunt directness sounded convincing. Kip had always weighed his words – even when emotional, there was always something calculated underneath. This was… different. Rawer.

Well, what do you know, she thought. *He finally shoved his nobility up his own arse and started doing good.*

Uncomfortable with the turn toward sincerity, she changed the subject. "So, how do you plan to get out of this shit? Got any brilliant corsair-noble schemes?"

Kip seemed relieved at the shift. "Well, we'll change the plane for now. Then we need to go to the Heights to talk to Toryn's family. We also need to pretend we're following Marek's plan and looking for another seedheart island that Toryn's father allegedly found." He looked out at the approaching station. "And I'll try calling the Federation to see if they can help."

Lina's stomach twisted at the mention of the seedheart. She hesitated for a moment.

"About that seedheart island…" she began.

She adjusted the throttle as they began their descent, still figuring out how to phrase this.

"Toryn actually knew of another island and told me about it before our departure." The admission felt like pulling out a splinter. "He wasn't going to tell you in case you were going to pursue your own goals and destroy it for the Inquisitor."

"He suspected that Thadeius had made you an offer."

She couldn't see Kip's face but imagined it going through a series of expressions.

"So we've been withholding from each other," he said. "Not exactly top-notch teamwork."

Lina snorted. "No kidding. Not that I'm any expert on teamwork to begin with."

"I'm sorry I didn't tell you about the offer," Kip said.

"And I'm sorry we kept secrets from you, too." Lina found, to her surprise, that she meant it.

They walked from the public docking platforms, talking about their plans. Wind whistled through the platform's safety railings as a dockhand in a padded jacket waved them toward an open berth.

"Any thoughts on how much we can get for this glorified escort vessel?" she asked.

"We can't sell it whole. It's clearly a prize craft with patched bullet holes," Kip replied, shaking his head. "Parts or salvage, best case. And we'll need clothes and supplies too. The Heights are brutal. Our young friend has a thick hide, but we'd freeze at night and burn in the sunlight."

"And we need a specialized Rational Element module for the Heights," Lina added. "Normal one has lower baseline altitude and won't lift us so high."

The market quarter assaulted their senses after the quiet of flight – a cacophony of commerce from across all territories. Merchants hawked their wares from stalls built into alcoves and free-standing kiosks. A Resonance Fellowship trader plucked a tuning fork that emitted haunting tones. Nearby, a bespectacled Technocracy engineer haggled over the price of cooling coils. Food vendors competed with scents from grills and bubbling cauldrons – from spiced beetle skewers to steaming dumplings.

Not far from them, a Drift Lord moved through the market, his coat with brass buttons glinting in the light, attendants scurrying behind him. Lina caught Kip looking sharply at the man but decided not to comment.

"This place is a masterpiece of chaotic engineering," Kip murmured to Lina. "Noticed our friends yet?" he added under his breath.

"What friends?"

"Three o'clock. Man with the red cap pretending to examine apples. And at ten, a woman with a mechanic's vest who has been inspecting the same engine part for five minutes."

Lina glanced casually in both directions and spotted them immediately. They were trying so hard to look inconspicuous it was obvious from a mile away. She thought bitterly that their own attempts to sell the escort craft would be just as transparent to anyone watching.

"Marek's?" she asked.

"Certainly," Kip confirmed. "Insurance of a sort. They're letting us see them so we get the hint not to do anything stupid."

Lina considered their options as they continued through the market. "Lose them?"

"That gives us nothing," Kip decided. "Let's proceed as planned: try selling the craft and buying a new one. Acting too suspiciously would only confirm we're up to something."

Beyond the main thoroughfare, Lina spotted a sleek scout craft tethered at the nearest dock. Its lines were elegant, brass fittings on the cockpit canopy catching the light. The wings glowed with the distinct shine of high-quality engineering. She'd never been able to afford something like that – and they wouldn't be able to now.

"Now *that*," she said, "is a nice bird. It's a pity it's not for us."

Kip followed her gaze. "You don't think it's for sale?"

"Even if we get the full price for Dahn's craft, this beauty will cost much more," she frowned.

"Don't be so pessimistic. I got some coins from my stash on Bloodrift Island," Kip answered, moving toward the dock.

As they approached the plane, Lina realized something was off. The craft felt hollow – no pilot seat visible through the canopy, and all the hatches were closed. Most planes for sale had their engine compartments open for buyers to inspect. This one stood like a showroom model, with no buyers nearby.

"It's a dummy," she said bluntly.

"A dummy?" Kip repeated. "You mean it can't fly?"

"Not in this form, no. You'd need to install your own engine, Rational Element module, tanks, all the piping, injection system, and seats," she said, turning to Kip. "Just like if you had a plane you were selling for parts."

She ran her hand along the fuselage, feeling the quality of the metalwork. With the right adjustments, this craft could handle the journey to the Heights without breaking a sweat. She was already forming a shopping list in her head: parts, tools, a warehouse to work in, oxygen tanks for the higher altitudes, window seals.

"What do you think?" she asked, turning to find Kip staring at the aircraft with an unreadable expression.

"It's an unusual turn, but it might work. Let's find an owner."

They found a squat Concord merchant who told them a barely credible story about a race pilot who bet on himself, lost, and had to sell everything. That included his engine and modules, but he clung to the hull until the very end. The story reeked of bullshit, and Kip haggled the price down three times, pointing out inconsistencies and the fact that they were the only buyers.

Once it was settled, he lowered his voice and told Lina, "We'll need a second craft. But not here – and not while being followed."

"One more…?" Lina trailed off as the implication sank in.

They would need to part ways. It made perfect sense – covering more ground, reaching more people with their warning. But the realization was daunting. She had been with Kip and the others for nearly two months now, the longest she'd ever worked closely with anyone.

"How could we afford a second craft?" she asked.

"I told you, I got my stash," Kip said effortlessly, as if he were talking about a pair of shoes.

"Darn, Lordling. Sometimes I hate your noble arse – I have been saving for a new engine for two years, and your *stash* has enough for another plane!"

"Well, now you see why I'm eager to return to my previous life," he parried with a faint smile.

Lina was trying to hide her feelings beneath the mockery, but it still gnawed at her. It was ridiculous, really. She had been a loner by choice and habit – other mechanics, colleagues, fellow pilots, occasional bed partners, but no one she'd ever truly relied on. She'd always convinced herself that solitude was her natural state. Uncomplicated. No responsibilities beyond the mechanical.

And she wasn't sure how she felt about it ending.

Kip was watching her with an expression that suggested he understood more than she would have liked.

"Let's go find the hangar," he added. "We've got work to do."

————

The next few days passed in a blur of activity as Lina threw herself into moving parts from Dahn's craft to the hull they had purchased.

They secured a small warehouse near the outer docks, away from the busiest parts of the station, and transformed it into a temporary workshop. Parts and tools were scattered across every available surface. She had been methodically turning one craft to scrap, bringing life to another – already prepped for high altitudes.

Kip spent most of his time gathering information, buying supplies, and occasionally helping her with the heavier components. With her guidance, he found another scout craft – a simpler model but already with high-altitude capabilities – that he was going to fly himself.

As she worked late into the night, her mind kept drifting to Nora and Toryn, wondering what they might be enduring under the Inquisitor's watch. These sudden concerns for their well-being felt unsettling. She had rarely thought about anyone before, sometimes joking that her best friend was her bird, *Swift Mistral*.

On the third night, Kip put the mannequin behind the curtain in the room and slipped away to finalize the scout purchase and arrange delivery to another island, far from prying eyes.

"Think they bought it?"

"If not, they're better than I gave them credit for, and we can't do anything with it." Kip leaned against the workbench. "How's it going?"

"She'll be ready to fly by morning." Lina patted the fuselage. "Almost hate to hand her over to you. She's a sweet machine. Call her the *Stubborn Phoenix* – reborn from the ashes."

"I thought I was taking the other one. And why *Stubborn*?"

"Because she's exactly like you." She wiped her hands on a rag. "I can guarantee that *Phoenix* will fly and get you there in one piece. Can't say that about the new one, but I've got the skills to fix it if needed. And we already saw how you care about your planes."

Kip seemed about to argue, then thought better of it. "Whatever you think is best."

Lina nodded and turned back to her work.

"Lina," Kip said from behind her.

"Mmm?" She didn't look up from the valve she was tightening.

"Thank you."

She paused, then resumed her work. "Don't mention it, Lordling."

They worked in silence after that, the warehouse filled only with the sounds of tools against metal and the occasional muttered curse when something didn't fit quite right. It was a comfortable silence – the kind between people who no longer needed to fill the air with words.

For someone who had spent most of her life alone, Lina was surprised to discover how much she would miss it.

CHAPTER 24

Archives Below

Nora Hertzig wound the lighthouse mechanism with Ferdinand. It was hard work – the donkey was very old and tired – and everything here reminded her of Marvin. Smart and funny Chief Observer Marvin. Ensign Marvin, who sacrificed himself to get her and Toryn out of captivity… Toryn… He died a week after their escape, when Holy Sovereignty forces flooded the Archives.

Three years later, Lina, the Veteran Pilot of the Technocracy, Hero of the Battle of Three Armies, decided to retire and take his name, joining the Windclaw tribe as his widow. Nora felt like a kind of widow herself – since Kip – noble and straight as a broom, her Kip – never made it back from the Battle.

Nora jolted awake, her heart hammering against her ribs, sweat beading across her skin despite the cool underground air. Her fingers clutched at the blanket as reality reasserted itself. The nightmare's images still clung to the edges of her consciousness, vivid and terrifying.

"Nora?" Toryn's voice came from the other side of their quarters, quiet but alert. "Are you alright?"

She took a deep breath, willing her pulse to slow. "Just a dream," she managed. "Nothing important."

Nothing important. Just a glimpse of how easily this could all end. The nightmare had shown that failure wasn't just possible but likely – unless they did something significant. Soon.

"Go back to sleep," she added, trying to sound reassuring. "We have a lot to do tomorrow."

Sleep didn't return quickly. Nora lay in the darkness, listening to the sounds of the underground complex. By the time morning arrived, she had already been awake for hours.

"I need you to do something for me," she told Toryn as they dressed in the purple robes marking them as acolytes of the Church of Archives. "Go to the market today. Listen for any news about Marvin."

"You think he didn't make it?" His voice was calm, yet she felt the thought had gnawed at him too.

"I don't know," Nora sighed. "But I *need* to. I need to find out what's happening outside in general. Are we on the wanted list? Can we go out if needed?"

"You're worried about bringing trouble to the Archives," Toryn said.

She nodded. "These people have risked everything to shelter us. The least we can do is understand what danger we're putting them in. And check if we can leave."

"I'll find out what I can. My people say that before doing anything, you need to look at the wind first." His eyes met hers. "Let's read the currents of this place."

———

That day, Nora decided to explore her surroundings. The Church complex fascinated her, as did the idea that it predated the city itself and had been discovered by accident. Who were its builders? Was the surface colonized at the same time as the mid-altitudes, or was it inhabited before?

She started by examining the walls. They were made of a composite material – something between plastic and concrete –

but she couldn't tell exactly without instruments. It was moderately smooth and not tough at all, but the structure wasn't damp or corroded, hinting at good ventilation. At regular intervals, the walls had darkened panels – probably display screens, light fixtures, and what appeared to be control interfaces for doors or communication.

Have you been made by aliens or humans?

Nora ran her fingers along one wall, tracing the outline of a numeric control panel. She blew away the dust and saw ten digits and a confirmation button. It had been dead for centuries – perhaps millennia – but was unquestionably related to modern Federation tech.

Humans then.

"Fascinating, isn't it?" The voice startled her.

She turned to find Archivist Prima Quorlin watching her with a smile.

"Oh yes, indeed. Do you have any records on it?" Nora asked, unable to hide her curiosity.

Quorlin shook her head. "We can only guess. These structures existed before the earliest Kingdom records. They were already ancient when the first explorers found them."

Nora gestured to the dead control panel. "This is advanced technology, similar to what we use in the Federation. A numerical lock or a dial." Her fingers pushed a random pattern of numbers. Nothing happened, but the demonstration impressed the Archivist.

"It could be part of a spacecraft."

"A spacecraft?"

"Yes. Either a crash from early Federation times, or even earlier – from Earth itself."

"Earth," Quorlin repeated. "The original planet of human origin, correct?"

Nora had already shared her knowledge of the Cradle with the Archivists, who carefully recorded it in their books for future generations. Their commitment to preserving knowledge fascinated her.

"Yes. It might be the remnants of one of the first colony ships. That could mean Azoria had humans much earlier than we thought."

They walked slowly down the corridor, stopping at a sealed doorway larger than the others. Quorlin gestured toward it thoughtfully.

"This is the Archive itself. The original one, for which our order is named."

"May I examine it?" Nora asked at once.

Quorlin shook her head. "The Archive holds manuscripts and devices that are too old and fragile. Many crumbled when touched. We made the difficult decision to seal this chamber until preservation techniques improve."

Nora said bitterly, "You're preserving the legacy of whatever this facility was, even without understanding it."

"We preserve *all* knowledge," Quorlin replied. Her voice carried the weight of dedication. "Perhaps someday, someone will unlock its secrets."

———

Toryn returned with no news of Marvin. No one at the market mentioned any boatman being captured, but that didn't mean he was safe. War preparations were underway, though without an exact date for the military incursion. At least that gave them hope the Inquisitor's plan hadn't yet been fulfilled.

The underground was a hidden world. The Archives occupied only part of an extensive network beneath the Holy Sovereignty's capital. It was a wild mix of natural cave systems, mining shafts, tunnels, and old underground shelters. Toryn described five major factions operating there.

"The Church of Archives is only one of them," he explained, circling a part of his hand-drawn map. "There's also the Mushroom Syndicate, the Tunnel Runners, the Black Market Guild, and the Canal Watchers."

His fingers traced the map. "The Syndicate controls food production. Their plantations stretch for miles beneath the central city. Without them, Stormseat would face food shortages within weeks."

"The Temple claims all food should be grown *beneath the Storm's divine light,*" he added. "But the underground plantations provide both luxuries for the elites and bulk food for lower castes and prisons."

Nora's mouth quirked in a slight smile. "Hypocrisy in its best form."

"Indeed. The underground economy provides what the surface is missing – and they're missing a lot," Toryn continued. "The Archives supply historical documents, census data, and maps when the Church of Storm's Truth loses too much in purges. The Black Market Guild trades in goods the regime needs but can't officially import."

"And the other two?" Nora asked, studying the intricate map.

"The Tunnel Runners handle people trafficking, messaging, and delivery of illegal goods. And the Canal Watchers are the power wing. They deal in blackmail, enforcement, hostile takeovers, and missing persons – both finding them and making people disappear by drowning them in the channels. That's where the name comes from. They're the smallest faction, but the most dangerous."

"We should stay clear of them. When the war starts, the Inquisition might use them as mercenaries and headhunters," Nora said. "They might already be looking for us."

"Yes. That's why I want to approach the Tunnel Runners," he said without preamble. "We need connections and a source of information. Runners operate both on the surface and below."

Nora shrugged. "That sounds dangerous."

"It is," he acknowledged. "But we need more than marketplace rumors. Joining the Watchers isn't a safe option, and plantation workers don't know anything we can use."

"What about smugglers? And what are you hoping to learn?"

"The Market Guild is never short of men. I'd have to start as a porter, and hauling a dozen boxes up a ladder isn't helping anyone."

Nora noticed he had ignored the second question. The boy was trying to be useful and wasn't going to sit still while she worked with the Archivists.

"So you're going to become a gang member?"

"Temporarily," Toryn admitted. "The Tunnel Runners could offer more than information – they might give us a passage out of Stormseat if we need to leave quickly. I've seen the pulleys they use to move goods. I could improve them."

Nora sighed, realizing he had already made up his mind. "Just be careful."

"I'll fly with the safest winds. I promise."

———

By their second week underground, Toryn was already working with the Tunnel Runners. His steady hands helped improve the pulleys. He also noticed stale air in a storage tunnel, fixing the blocked vents, and saving the supplies and staff from choking.

"Their leader calls himself Vex," he told Nora as they shared a mushroom stew in the Archives' dining room. "Former delivery guy who went underground about five years ago. His group controls several surface routes and old mining tunnels."

"Have they heard anything about the Inquisitor's plans?" Nora asked, noting the growing tension in Toryn's expression.

"Rumors only, but concerning ones. The Syndicate has received large orders for non-perishable foods – the kind you need for long military campaigns."

Nora sighed. "Whatever Thadeius is planning, it's accelerating. And we still don't know if Kip and Lina decided to play along or trick him."

That evening, she approached Talbert in the Archives' main reading room, where he was carefully examining a fragile scroll.

"I was wondering if you might have information about how Marvin managed to find us," she asked quietly. "Could those same connections help us if we needed some more intel?"

Talbert's expression grew somber as he set the text aside. "I'm afraid that's unlikely. I had to call in one-time favors I'd accumulated over decades. The network has since scattered — some arrested, others gone to ground."

He leaned closer, lowering his voice further. "The situation above is deteriorating. The Temple has begun targeting other religious groups. Rumors suggest all faiths will soon be banned except the official doctrine."

"Including the Church of Archives?"

"We've always existed in a gray area, since we don't worship anything and do provide valuable services," Talbert explained. "But that tolerance has limits. Thadeius is consolidating power. As High Inquisitor, he's controlling the police and the guards — and he's trying to gain control of the army. If he succeeds, he'll have real power — more than other Church hierarchs."

"Has anything like this happened before?"

"The Archives have survived three regime changes," Talbert replied. "Each time, by retreating underground and waiting for the political currents to shift. But this feels different. Where previous regimes were content to ignore us, Thadeius sees us as a nuisance."

A chill ran through Nora as she considered the implications. "How long do you think you have?"

"Months — perhaps a year at most," Talbert estimated. "Preparations are already underway. We're moving important texts, mapping escape routes, and connecting with friendly groups in the Harbor Commonwealth."

"But are you ready to move the Archive itself?"

"We can't take it. But it's a symbol, not a purpose. The Archives have endured for centuries without opening the Archive itself," he said. "Through revolutions, wars, and political upheavals. We'll endure this as well – in one form or another."

The shadows seemed to deepen around them as they sat in silence, the weight of approaching conflict hanging in the air. Little did they know how quickly that threat would materialize.

———

The fourteenth day marked a turning point. Nora was speaking with an archivist when Toryn burst into the chamber, his hood thrown back and his face flushed.

"They're coming," he announced, breathing hard. "The guards are in the tunnels. They're conducting a search of the entire underground."

Talbert's face went pale. "Did they follow you?"

"No," Toryn shook his head. "They were organizing when I returned from the market. Claiming to do a contraband purging raid, but…"

"But they could be looking for us," Nora finished, the cold dread from her nightmare returning. "How close?"

"Two tunnels away. Minutes at most."

The archivists burst into controlled activity – hiding some scrolls, giving the appearance of a purely scholarly union working on historical texts.

"What about the plantations?" Nora asked urgently. "Can we hide there?"

"Don't think so. And if the Watchers are helping, they'll sweep it first," Toryn replied. "We'll try the mining grid – it goes deeper. The guards won't risk it there. But we need to go. *Now.*"

As they hurried toward the back exit, Nora thought of the consequences. If they were found there, the Archives would certainly be destroyed. Talbert, Quorlin – all those who had helped them – would suffer the Inquisition's justice.

Her nightmare suddenly seemed prophetic. Unless they found a way out, the grim futures might very well come true.

The sound of booted feet and loud voices echoed from the main chamber behind them.

Time had just run out.

CHAPTER 25
Tribal Truths

Lina adjusted the throttle as she neared the island, compensating for the reduced thrust in the Heights' thinner air. Up here, everything was alien – the air, the light, and the dull ache in her head despite the pills she took to counter altitude sickness.

"That has to be it," she murmured, squinting through the canopy. "Toryn's home."

Off her left wing, the *Stubborn Phoenix* trailed about fifty yards behind, just far enough to limit communication to hand and flag signals – leaving Lina alone with her thoughts. The sunlight was brutally bright, unfiltered by clouds, making her wish for darker goggles. She blinked against the glare and fixed her gaze on the Roost Islet ahead.

"Well, I'll be damned," she whispered, genuinely impressed.

Roost loomed on the horizon – a vast formation of terraced levels and jagged peaks. Even from this distance, she could distinguish stone and timber structures, far from the temporary shelters she had expected of a tribal settlement. Honestly, her knowledge of the tribes was mostly gaps: primitive people living way up high, riding eagles, and avoiding tech. Meeting Toryn changed a lot – he was smart and handy, proficient in Trade Speech, and eager to learn.

"Condensation channels," she murmured, noting the cultivated groves. "Clever – using temperature shifts to draw moisture from the air and guide the flow of water."

A shrill cry pierced the air, causing her to instinctively check her gauges for a pressure alarm. Three massive eagles swept in alongside, each with a wingspan rivaling that of a plane. They circled the craft effortlessly, riding the currents with natural grace, while Lina fought to keep hers steady.

"Holy wrench," she breathed, instinctively easing back on the controls. "Flying mountains with talons. Don't spook the flying mountains with talons."

She glanced at Kip's craft and caught him making a circular motion with his hand. The gesture's meaning in Signals of the Technocracy Pilots was "turn around, returning to the base," which was clearly not what he meant. She decided the gesture could mean anything else for corsairs–"follow the escort" or even "cleaning the window" – so she did exactly nothing, just as expected.

One eagle pulled slightly ahead and started the descent, showing the way and a landing area. Lina followed, noting with admiration how the bird adjusted its position with no visible effort.

"Better pilots than half the escort squadron back home," she muttered.

They neared a flat, stone-paved expanse by the island's eastern ridge, where several tribal members were already assembling, signaling landing positions with flags. She opened the canopy and drew a deep breath. The air here was crisp and sharp, a stark contrast to the steamy scents of the mid-altitudes. And it was cold – bitingly cold.

"That's going to be fun," she muttered, buttoning her jacket.

She could see *Phoenix* landing. Kip approached well enough, though he overcorrected at the final descent and rolled an extra fifty yards, almost crashing into a squat building. Not that she'd mention it – the aristocrat had enough natural confidence without her adding to it.

The leader of the eagle escort – a tall man with an intricately braided beard – stepped forward and wordlessly motioned for them to follow. As they walked through the settlement, Lina couldn't help but assess everything. There were workshops, smelters, something like a school or a ritual building, gliders, and lots of hunting equipment hanging outside.

"Damn, those people are nowhere near primitive. They just solve problems differently than we do."

Kip shrugged. "I thought you stopped thinking of tribals as savages, seeing Toryn fix half the tavern before you."

"It's nothing like that. Toryn has steady hands. He didn't know carpentry or door locks before, but he learned in no time," she parried. "But this all…" – she made a broad gesture.

The air hummed with activity – the rhythmic clang of stone on metal from a forge, the wind whooshing through walkways, turning the windmill blades. A potter formed clay while his daughter painted the ready pots with intricate patterns. All the machinery appeared to run on wind or manual power, yet it was intricate and impressively practical.

They approached a larger building adorned with carvings along its wooden posts. A woman stepped through the doorway – her silver-streaked braids framing sky-blue eyes set in a lined, weathered face, her straight posture radiating quiet strength.

"I am Elder Kora of the Windclaw Tribe," she introduced herself formally. "Welcome to Roost Islet."

"I'm Lina Ryven, mechanic and pilot from the Technocracy," Lina replied. "This is Kip Saroven. We've come with news about Toryn Skyheart."

At the mention of Toryn's name, the Elder's demeanor shifted at once. Her gaze dropped to the pendant resting against Lina's chest – the one Toryn had given her during their farewell in Stormseat. Kora's eyes widened, and she stepped forward, closing the distance to pull Lina into a tight embrace.

"Welcome home, child," she said warmly. "You're family now."

Lina froze, arms rigid at her sides, her whole body tense. She glanced at Kip – he kept his composure, but the look in his eyes betrayed him. Whatever he was thinking sent a flush of heat to her cheeks.

"I'm not – we aren't; that's not what–" she stammered, unusually flustered.

The woman finally released her, smiling. "Come inside," she said gently. "There's much I can explain."

Over Kora's shoulder, Lina spotted a figure watching from afar – an older man with a beard split into three neat plaits. His sharp gaze rested on them, and something about it made her uneasy.

———

Kora's dwelling was unexpectedly warm, with the scent of unfamiliar herbs and a tea-like brew simmering in a stone pot. Instruments lined the walls alongside a small shelf of books. To Lina's surprise, she spotted *Meteorology of Western Currents* there – clearly a Technocracy book. A large table by the window was strewn with weather charts and maps.

Once the door closed, Lina held up her hands defensively.

"Look, there's been some kind of major misunderstanding," she said, her voice sharper than intended. "I'm *not* family, not even close. Toryn gave me this pendant as proof that I had met him. That's all."

Elder Kora smiled, the expression crinkling the corners of her eyes. "He gave you his pendant and sent you up here," she said, as if this explained everything.

"Yeah, as evidence! Not as a bloody proposal!" Lina's hand unconsciously rose to touch the silver eagle feather that hung around her neck. "He just needed someone to deliver a message if things went sideways."

"That's the same thing," Elder Kora replied with absolute certainty. "The person who bears full trust, the person who will willingly travel to one's home to deliver good or bad news. The person who could do the impossible for my nephew. Isn't it you?"

Lina opened her mouth, then closed it again. Put that way, it was difficult to argue – though it certainly wasn't what she had understood when accepting the pendant. She shot a glare at Kip, who was now failing to hide a smile.

"Wipe that smirk off your face before I do it for you, Lordling," she muttered. Then, turning back to Kora: "I'm just here because…" She faltered, suddenly uncertain how to characterize exactly why she had come. *Because I promised? Because I felt responsible? Because I couldn't stand the thought of not knowing if he was safe?*

Lina settled for a frustrated exhalation, which Elder Kora seemed to interpret as confirmation of her suspicions.

"Now, about the bad news," Kora continued, her expression sobering. "Tell me, Lina. Toryn failed to return in seven days and is not here after two months. He's not one to avoid admitting his errors. So what's happened?"

The direct question brought Lina back to the purpose of their visit. She took a deep breath and told everything – Toryn's arrival on Veil Islet, the seedheart and the ecosystem, the world beneath the Storm. And their current situation as captives of the Holy Sovereignty.

Kora interrupted occasionally when she needed clarification; her questions were precise and knowledgeable. She seemed particularly concerned about the seedheart and passing through the Storm.

"Our lore speaks of blue-black eagles as harbingers of the Storm," she said thoughtfully. "But we knew almost nothing about the seedhearts themselves. We once believed they were massive heartstone veins, yet they appear to be something entirely different. And your accounts of the wildlife and vegetation there prove we understand even less than we thought."

"Aren't you concerned that Toryn is trapped under the Storm?" Kip asked.

"Well, I understand that you are working on this now," was her surprisingly practical answer.

"We are," Kip confirmed, "but the way we've been offered is not one we want to take." He told her about the Holy Sovereignty's proposal to locate another seedheart island, Arvid's discoveries, and their decision to reject the plan. "And someone's been feeding the corsairs information about your tribe," he added.

Kora's expression hardened. "It's clearly Jormund," she said with certainty. "He might also be the reason for our islet's decay – he damaged the heartstone or took a much larger part than prescribed by our rituals. Maybe intentionally, maybe as an experiment. Some could turn this method into a weapon – and your corsairs are clearly preparing for war."

"What are you going to do with it?" Kip asked.

"I will adjourn an urgent Circle of Elders meeting to relay your findings."

They spoke at length about the islet's situation. The tribe had already identified another viable site for migration, though they hoped to postpone the move as long as possible. Kora left Lina and Kip with the tea and was gone to meet with the other elders.

————

"The Circle of Elders has made a decision," she said. "When Toryn proposed taking heartstone from Veil Islet, we thought it was just another barren rock covered in ice. But knowing what you've told us about the living world within..." She shook her head. "We won't approve removing heartstone from anywhere anymore – there are clearly things we don't understand. And especially nothing involving seedhearts. Toryn's quest is finished – a negative result, but still a result. There's no shame in that."

She let the words settle for a moment, then turned her gaze to them both.

"And what will the two of you do now?" she asked. "You've delivered the message. Where are you heading next?"

"We're planning to warn the leaders of the main factions," Lina replied, folding her arms across her chest. "About the surface world, their weapons – everything. Someone's got to shut this operation down before we have more surface weapons in the hands of corsairs."

"The Windclaw Tribe had long been considering sending envoys to represent the tribe in the lowlands – particularly to the Technocracy and the Mercantile Concord. I was chosen to accompany you to Caligan," Kora said, using the tribal term for the mid-altitudes.

Lina's eyebrows lifted. "You seem to know a great deal about the lowlands," she said, regarding the elder with renewed interest.

Kora smiled. "Sweet child, I wasn't always a tribal wind reader. I studied weather patterns at Caligan University for years, rode with Concord zeppelins, mapped winds in territories you've likely never heard of. Half the books on this shelf – including *Meteorology of Western Currents* – were written by me."

Lina's jaw dropped. She glanced at Kip.

"But you... the tribes... everyone thinks the Heights people are..."

"Uncivilized? Detached?" Kora finished for her. "We know about the world down there. We simply choose not to participate in its endless power struggles. We observe, we learn, but we maintain our distance." She gestured toward the window, where the massive eagles were circling above the settlement. "Some treasures are worth more than progress."

"That's... unexpected, but welcome," Kip replied diplomatically.

Lina nodded, still a little stunned. "I'll need to recalibrate the altitude compensation system," she said. "And adjust the fuel mixture for the added weight. Should be simple enough."

"And I think that's where we part ways," added Kip. The words hung between them. "I need to visit Nora's people – the Federation."

Lina's heart skipped a beat. She'd known it was coming, but she still wasn't ready for it. She wasn't someone to form an emotional attachment to a corsair – or worse, a disgraced noble. But the thought of navigating diplomatic games and facing Technocracy bureaucrats alone was daunting.

They continued talking into the night, with Kora asking for details about the Holy Sovereignty's technologies and their journey.

"The tribe should take a more active role in this matter," Kora said as they prepared to retire. "Especially since it concerns a threat to our world."

"From what Toryn told us, the tribes prefer isolation," Kip noted.

"Isolation is a choice, not a prison," Kora replied. "When the world changes enough, even the most steadfast traditions must adapt."

———

Kora returned in a few hours. She looked weary but satisfied.

"The Elders has decided I will accompany you to the Technocracy as their envoy," she said. "My previous connection there will strengthen your position and may give us a powerful ally."

"That's... unexpected, but welcome," Kip replied diplomatically.

Lina nodded, already calculating the weight distribution adjustments needed for an additional passenger. "I'll need to recalibrate the altitude compensation system," she said. "And adjust the fuel mixture for the extra weight. Should be straightforward enough."

"And I think that's where we part ways." The words hung between them. "I need to visit Nora's people, the Federation."

Lina's heart faltered for a moment. She knew it would happen, but wasn't ready for it nevertheless. She wasn't a person to have an emotional attachment to a corsair or even more – a disgraced noble. But the prospect of playing in diplomatic games and facing the Technocracy's bureaucrats without him was frightening.

———

After sunset, the islet transformed. Torches cast a warm glow across the settlement, creating dancing shadows along the stone pathways. The temperature dropped sharply with nightfall, and the thin air couldn't retain heat.

Lina couldn't sleep. She had spent the evening making calculations for their departure, but her mind refused to quiet. The pendant around her neck felt unnaturally heavy, pulling her thoughts back to Toryn. She was worried about her friends' fate below the Storm and brooded over Kora's implications, unable to let them go. Finally giving up on rest, she decided to check on her aircraft one last time.

The night air bit at her skin, her breath forming small clouds. The stars shone overhead, gazing at her like they never did at home. As she approached her craft, a flicker of movement caught her eye – a silhouette near the engine compartment. Drawing closer, she recognized the same man with the distinctive beard who had watched them disapprovingly upon arrival. Jormund, as Kora had named him, stood outlined against the starlight. He was hunched over the engine compartment, doing something. His movements were hesitant, as if following instructions rather than working from knowledge.

Anger flared hot in Lina's chest. Without hesitation, she strode forward.

"Hey! What the hell do you think you're doing?" she shouted, her voice cutting through the night.

Jormund straightened abruptly, startled by her sudden appearance.

"You had one simple job," he said, his voice cold and calculating. "I had everything arranged. Your mission with a seedheart islet was my last one." His fingers tightened around the tool in his hand. "And now you're taking this meddling woman to the Technocracy instead."

Lina stepped closer, positioning herself between Jormund and her craft. "Step away from my plane. *Now*."

Their confrontation had drawn attention. Lights appeared in nearby dwellings, and within moments several tribal members approached. Kip arrived shortly after, alerted by the commotion. Jormund made no attempt to flee or hide his actions, standing beside the open engine compartment and hissing that Marek would hear of their failure.

Chief Harrik appeared moments later, his imposing figure unmistakable even in the dim light. "What is happening here?" he demanded.

"Caught interfering with the visitors' craft," one of the tribal guards announced, gesturing toward the exposed engine compartment and the tools in Jormund's hands.

Instead of denying the accusation, Jormund straightened and addressed the growing crowd of onlookers. "They're seeking the coordinates of another seedheart islet!" he shouted. "They're going to destroy it – just as Toryn Skyheart did!"

Chief Harrik's expression remained impassive as he evaluated the situation. "These are serious accusations," he said. "We will address them properly. Secure Jormund in the meditation chamber until morning. The Elders will hear this matter at sunrise."

As Jormund was led away, Lina examined the damage to her aircraft. "The altitude compensator's been tampered with," she concluded after a thorough inspection. "It would have caused a gradual loss of power at high altitude – not immediately catastrophic, but enough to force us down in the middle of nowhere." She began removing the compromised components. "I can fix it before morning. I've got spares."

Chief Harrik instructed the guards to remain with the aircraft through the night and directed others to search Jormund's dwelling immediately.

"Rest," he told Lina and Kip. "Morning will bring justice."

———

Throughout the night, Lina worked by torchlight to repair her aircraft. By first light, she had restored the system to working order. Her hands bore small cuts and oil stains, but her eyes gleamed with the satisfaction of a technical challenge overcome.

The tribe had not rested either. Searchers thoroughly examined Jormund's dwelling, gathering evidence for the coming trial. As dawn broke over the Heights, the entire settlement seemed to hold its breath in anticipation.

The trial began as the first rays of sunlight touched the meeting area. Jormund stood in the center, his expression defiant despite being flanked by guards. Chief Harrik presided from an elevated stone seat, his long beard, with its seven braids, cascading over his chest.

The evidence against Jormund piled up quickly. The search of his house turned up unsent letters about tribal affairs – and, worst of all, a letter marked with a crimson talon clutching a gold coin: the Scarlet Talon's symbol. Chief Harrik lifted the open letter and read aloud portions of it. It promised Jormund a "comfortable place below" in exchange for "weakening the tribe so it won't be a threat." It also mentioned tribal matters, especially "the Skyheart boy and his father's maps." But it further described two outsiders – a lean man and a shorter woman – who would come seeking a seedheart island and should be assisted. That detail caused murmurs to ripple through the crowd and drew a smile from Jormund, who seemed determined to take Kip and Lina down with him.

When Lina was called forward, she spoke as a mechanic rather than a diplomat.

"The sabotage attempted last night," she explained, "would cause gradual fuel pressure loss at high altitude. The engine wouldn't fail immediately – it would happen over time, making it seem like a natural failure." She looked directly at Jormund. "Kora and I would have dropped out of the sky somewhere no one would ever find us."

Young wind readers testified to seeing Jormund meet with a stranger days ago – an unusual trader, who handled him a letter with a red talon. Heart-tenders described unexplained access to the heartstone chambers during Jormund's inspections. The islet's core was huge and widespread, yet Jormund seemed to visit it far more often than necessary.

The tribe's reaction was a mixture of shock and outrage. Lina watched as understanding spread through the assembly – the betrayal went beyond mere information. Jormund had apparently been deliberately damaging the islet's heartstone to force migration, all while plotting his own escape to the mid-altitudes.

As the evidence mounted against him, something in Jormund seemed to snap. His eyes widened, taking on a distant, unfocused quality. When he spoke, his voice had changed – almost hysterical, like that of a madman on the edge of a shout.

"You don't understand," he cried. "The islets must fall. The world seeks to be whole again." His blue-stained fingers spread wide, trembling slightly. "The seedpods have to go down! For the sake of The Plan!"

The tribal members exchanged uneasy glances. One of the elders explained that it might be a symptom of "blue fever" – a rare condition said to affect those who had handled raw heartstone for too many years.

Kip studied Jormund's hands with sudden intensity, his brow furrowing. The blue staining extended past the elder's elbows, deeper and more pervasive than anything Kip had seen before. It reminded him of something recent – the same blue staining on

Marek's hands, coupled with the corsair captain's unusual fixation on seedheart islands. At the time, he had attributed it to Marek's claimed past as a Rational Element miner, but now he wondered if there was more to it. Two men from entirely different worlds, yet both bound by the same strange fixation on seedhearts.

The judgment, when it came, was swift. Jormund was stripped of his elder status, his beard braids ceremonially cut – symbolically severing his connection to the tribe he had betrayed. He would be exiled to a trade islet, forbidden to return to any tribal territory.

"And what of these visitors?" someone called from the assembly. "What of the seedheart isles they seek?"

"Aren't they leaving with Elder Kora?" said another voice.

"Only one of them. The other is flying on his own – where's he heading?"

Lina saw Kip's jaw tighten as he rose to speak. "Dear tribe members," he began, "you might suspect us of being dishonest, so I want to tell you the whole story. I worked for the Scarlet Talon for the last three years, for the man calling himself Captain Marek – the man with the same blue stains on his hands as Jormund. But I'm his tool no longer!"

He paused dramatically, letting the murmurs of shock ripple through the crowd. Lina realized he was using his rhetoric training, but it was his truthfulness and open manner that won them over.

"After the catastrophic fall of Veil Islet," he continued, "I met Toryn Skyheart, and that changed everything for me. His respect for tradition, his reverence for life itself, showed me that the result does not always justify the cost." Kip's voice gradually rose.

"Toryn is now in the Depths, held captive by someone who wants another seedheart brought down. And he told me not to do it – even if his life is at stake."

The crowd shouted their approval.

"We escaped the Depths to spread the word – to warn people of the importance of the seedhearts. While our enemies believe we're serving their plan, we are gathering allies to form a coalition and face Marek and his minions. We are here to protect the world we all share. And I give you my word – we will do everything to protect the seedheart islets."

The gathering cheered at that. Lina felt goosebumps rise along her skin.

Chief Harrik turned to Kip and Lina. "We have heard your warnings. We understand the threat from below. You have our full gratitude and support – and our blessing to leave as you wish."

———

As the afternoon light began to fade, casting long shadows across Roost Islet, Lina found herself alone with her craft. Her repairs were complete, but she kept checking and rechecking it.

She turned to find Kip standing behind her, his expression unreadable in the dim light.

"Good speech there at the gathering, Lordling," she said instead of greeting. "I really felt the importance of our mission – was ready to jump on an eagle's back and ride in your wake."

He smiled. "No need to be so dramatic. I'm sure you'll be fine with the metal bird. How is it, by the way?"

"Everything's perfect," she replied, running her hand along a seam. "Kora's coming with me, and I'm not about to drop a tribal elder into the Storm because of sloppy maintenance."

"It'll be strange," Kip said after a moment. "Not having you around to tell me when I'm being an aristocratic idiot."

Lina snorted. "I'm sure you'll figure it out on your own." She closed the engine compartment. "I don't suppose the Federation will appreciate my particular brand of diplomacy anyway."

"Probably not," he agreed with a small smile. "Though they might enjoy it."

Kora approached, now dressed in traveling clothes that looked surprisingly modern compared to her usual tribal attire. The only tribal elements were the blue, wind-like tattoos on her forearms.

"Before we part ways tomorrow," Kora said, reaching into a pouch at her waist, "I want you to have this, Kip." She pulled out a small folded map and handed it to him. "It shows the location of another seedheart islet – one Arvid discovered before his death."

Kip took the map with evident surprise. "I thought the tribe didn't want us pursuing seedhearts."

"The tribe doesn't," Kora confirmed. "But I'm old enough to recognize that sometimes we must make difficult choices in difficult times." She placed her hand over his. "Don't become the evil we tried to fight against. But use the information wisely if you must."

Lina watched the exchange with mixed emotions. The existence of another seedheart map created possibilities – and dangers – she wasn't sure they were ready to face. She caught Kip's eye and saw her own conflicted thoughts reflected there. He nodded slightly, acknowledging the weight of what they had just been given.

"We should rest," Kora suggested, breaking the moment. "Tomorrow will come earlier than we might wish."

———

Dawn brought clear skies and mild winds – perfect flying conditions. Lina completed her pre-flight checks as Kip prepared his own aircraft twenty yards away. A small gathering of tribal members had come to witness their departure, including Chief Harrik, who spoke briefly with each of them before stepping back.

The rising sun cast long shadows across the landing area; the air was so clear and cold it seemed to crystallize the light itself. The eagles nesting on the eastern ridge were already aloft, circling in the morning thermals, their wingspans dwarfing the human vessels preparing for flight below.

"You're sure about this?" Lina asked Kora as the older woman settled into the passenger seat. "The Technocracy isn't exactly known for respecting traditional knowledge."

"They respected me as a scholar and as the lead meteorologist for two decades," Kora replied with a wry smile. "I hope being a tribal envoy won't change that too much."

Lina blinked, once again readjusting her perception of the wind reader. Before she could respond, Kip approached for a final farewell.

"One week," he said. "Market Nexus. If either of us doesn't make it–"

"We'll make it," Lina interrupted firmly. "Just don't do anything stupid without me there to fix it."

"Like flying into a mountain?" he suggested with forced lightness.

"That would qualify as stupid, yes."

He nodded, then hesitated before extending his hand. She took it, the brief contact conveying more than their casual words.

"See you in a week, Lordling," she said, trying to ignore the unexpected tightness in her chest.

"In a week, Pilot," he replied, then turned toward his craft.

As he walked away, Lina realized how much had changed since their first reluctant partnership. Their paths were parting now, beginning the larger political game that would determine the fate of worlds both above and below the Storm.

CHAPTER 26
Deep Descent

The sound of boots on stone echoed through the Archives' main chamber, the acoustics so perfect it seemed an entire regiment was approaching. Toryn saw Archivist Prima Quorlin signal to her people to hide the books in concealed compartments.

"This way," Talbert whispered, appearing at Toryn's elbow. "There's no time."

Nora hesitated, glancing back at the Archivists, who were now calmly rearranging chairs as if preparing for honored guests rather than a raid. "What about them?"

"They know what they're doing," Talbert said. "They've survived worse. This way – quickly."

Toryn's chest tightened with a conflict – the urge to protect clashing with the practical need to escape. These scholars had risked everything to help them, and now he was abandoning them to face the Inquisition alone. In the Heights, such an action would bring deep shame. But he had learned hard lessons since Veil Islet – getting involved might mean one less person to carry vital knowledge forward.

"Nora," Toryn said, with just enough edge in his voice to break through her hesitation. "We need to go. *Now*."

His words coincided with the sound of the outer door being rammed. Nora nodded, and they followed Talbert toward a narrow passage hidden behind a tapestry.

"The old mining level," Talbert instructed, pressing something cold and metallic into Toryn's palm. "Take the access shaft at the end of this passage. There's a cart system that is still maintained for emergencies. It will get you deep enough to be safe for a while."

"You're not coming?" Nora asked.

"I'm needed here."

The sound of boots grew louder. Talbert gave them a gentle push. "Go. Knowledge survives by sharing, not hoarding. Remember what you've learned."

Toryn thanked Talbert, grabbed Nora's arm, and pulled her into the passage, closing the hidden door behind them. The passage immediately plunged into darkness, lit only by the small oil lamp Talbert had pressed into his hand.

They followed the narrow tunnel to a vertical shaft where a rusted ladder clung to the wall. Toryn went first, testing each rung before trusting it with his full weight. The lamp cast jagged shadows up the shaft walls as they descended, until they finally reached a larger tunnel below.

It was clearly once a mining site, with tracks along the floor and timber supports bracing the ceiling at regular intervals. On the tracks sat an old ore cart – little more than a metal box on wheels with a simple brake lever.

"Archivists' escape route," Toryn said, inspecting the cart. "Clever. I've seen a few like this with the Tunnel Runners."

The unmistakable sound of shouting echoed down the shaft above them.

"They've found the passage," Nora said tensely.

Without another word, they climbed into the cart. Toryn released the brake, and it began rolling forward, gathering speed as the track sloped downward. The lamp revealed only a short section ahead before darkness swallowed everything again.

"This is insane," Nora muttered, gripping the sides of the cart as it gained speed.

"Yes," Toryn agreed, unable to keep a grim smile off his face. "But effective."

Skies, I've missed the speed – and the feeling of the wind in my face.

The cart hurtled down the track, rattling over uneven sections. Toryn kept one hand on the brake lever, applying just enough pressure to keep it from derailing without slowing its descent. Wind rushed past them, making the lamp flicker alarmingly.

They rounded a curve at dangerous speed, the metal wheels screaming against the rails. For a heart-stopping moment, the side wheels lifted from the track, and Toryn thought they might fly off entirely. He felt Nora shift her weight to the compromised side and quickly did the same, cursing himself for not thinking of it first.

It worked – the cart slammed back down onto all four wheels and continued its mad plunge into the darkness.

"Junction ahead!" Nora shouted, holding the lamp forward to reveal a split in the tracks.

Left or right? Wind's stronger on the left side... Whatever!

Toryn spotted a rusted switch lever rushing toward them on the right. With split-second timing, he reached out and yanked it as they passed. The mechanism groaned but shifted, diverting their cart onto the right-hand track just before they reached the split.

"How did you know which way to go?" Nora asked, her voice tight with tension.

"Didn't," Toryn said, keeping his eyes forward. "But sticking to the main path would make us easier to follow."

Hesitation kills more often than a wrong choice, he told himself, justifying the impulse.

The cart gradually slowed, finally rolling to a stop in what looked like an old loading station. Broken lanterns, splintered shovel handles, rusted tools, and the skeletal remains of long-collapsed wooden crates lay scattered across the floor.

"Now we go on foot," Toryn said, climbing out and holding the lamp high to survey their surroundings.

Three tunnel openings led out from the station, their chalk markings long faded and illegible. As Toryn weighed their options, he heard Nora calling from a shadowed corner of the chamber.

"Over here – look at this."

She stood before a section of wall where a relatively new metal ring was fixed, a thick rope trailing from it into a narrow vertical shaft.

"Tunnel Runner pulley system," Toryn said, instantly recognizing the design. He had learned about these mechanisms from Vex during his brief alliance with the Runners. "Used for moving supplies and people between levels."

Nora gave the rope a sharp tug. "Could we use it to go deeper?"

"Yes," Toryn said, masking his uncertainty. "If the counterweight holds."

The distant echoes of pursuit made the choice for them. "I'll go first. Three quick tugs means it's safe to follow."

As he lowered himself into the dark shaft, a pang of homesickness struck. The descent felt like his first glide from Roost Islet – stepping into empty space, trusting the machine beneath him. But so much had changed since then. The boy who had set out to prove himself worthy of the Heights was now descending into somewhere far beyond the Depths.

The descent was smooth – the counterweight system well maintained and free of snags. After about thirty feet, Toryn's boots touched solid ground in a small chamber. He signaled Nora with three sharp tugs, and soon she joined him in what appeared to be an emergency cache. Stone shelves lined the chamber, stocked with an oil lamp, matches, a water flask, dried rations wrapped in oiled paper, and coarse blankets. A hammer, chisels, and coils of rope lay neatly beside them.

Toryn lit the second lamp, pushing back the shadows. "Everything needed for short-term survival."

"But no sign of where to go next," Nora said, scanning the identical tunnels branching from the chamber.

"Not exactly," Toryn replied, considering their options. "But deeper is still safer. The guards won't venture this far down."

They gathered what supplies they could carry and chose a tunnel that sloped more steeply downward. It led away from the worked sections of the mine, into what looked like natural caves rather than excavated passages.

"We should rest while we can," Toryn said once they had put enough distance between themselves and the pulley shaft. He spread a blanket on a relatively flat section of floor and set their supplies within reach.

Nora accepted the food with a nod, and they ate in silence, broken only by their breathing and the occasional drip of water.

"It's been over a month," Nora said quietly. "Kip and Lina should have reached the Technocracy by now. Either they've found a way to warn everyone about the Inquisitor's plans, or…"

"Kip's too clever to do the Inquisitor's bidding," Toryn said, a faint smile touching his lips despite their circumstances. "And Lina could dismantle a plane mid-flight and rebuild it better. If anyone can outsmart Thadeius, it's those two."

Toryn couldn't help but smile. "Lina probably had quite a shock if she visited my tribe."

"What do you mean?"

"The pendant I gave her." He touched his neck. "In my culture, giving someone your pendant marks them as your betrothed. I knew that when I gave it to her – but it was the only way to ensure my tribe would take her seriously."

Nora's eyes widened – then she burst into laughter. "I'd pay good Federation credits to see Lina's face when she realizes!"

"She'd probably threaten to fix my head with a wrench," Toryn said, laughing with her.

After their mirth faded, Nora studied him. "Would you want it to be real? Would you choose Lina as your partner if circumstances were different?"

"For sure," he said without hesitation. "But her path is her own to choose. I would never impose that on her."

They sat in silence for a moment.

"What about you and Kip?"

"It's hard to tell. My previous big relationship didn't end well. I even thought I was done with men and had a girlfriend for some time," Nora sighed. "But I like him, and if my people are going to chase mining goals above all, I'd rather retire and aid Kip on his quest than stay in the Federation's greed game."

Toryn felt a flicker of discomfort at the thought of Nora courting another woman – something unheard of in the tribes. But it was her life, her choice, and he kept the thought to himself.

"We should keep moving," he said, gathering their goods. "The guards might be thorough. We don't know if they are looking for us, but it's better to be safe."

Nora nodded, helping him repack. "Which way now?"

Toryn weighed their options. Returning toward the Archives was out of the question, and the Tunnel Runners' routes might already be watched. The practical choice was to follow the mining tunnels until they surfaced, far from Stormseat. Yet a quiet pull gnawed at him – a whisper urging him to see what lay deeper still.

"This way," he said, indicating a passage that sloped steeply downward. "These carts were used to transport ore upward, which means the richest deposits were down there."

"You think we should go deeper?" Nora raised an eyebrow. "Doesn't that cut off potential escape routes?"

"There will be guards at every known exit," Toryn said. "Our best chance is to lie low and wait until the initial search dies down."

Nora considered this, then nodded. "Lead on."

The tunnel sloped steeply, crude steps cut here and there into the stone. As they descended, the air warmed, and the walls shifted from the chiseled regularity of mining work to the jagged contours of a natural cave.

Minutes blurred into hours. Their legs ached, the water flask emptied and refilled twice from cold underground springs. They left chalk marks at every turn, though Toryn doubted they could ever retrace their route through this twisting maze.

At last, the passage opened into a vast chamber where stone columns soared from floor to ceiling. Toryn slowed, eyes tracing their shapes – stalactites melting downward, stalagmites rising to meet them, fusing into immense, ancient pillars.

"What are those?" he asked.

"Stalactites and stalagmites," Nora said. "Made by dripping water carrying sediment. Some of these would take thousands of years to grow. But, Toryn, why are we going further? The guards won't find us here anyway."

"We should move on," Toryn said, realizing he didn't know the answer. He chose a natural passage that led downward. His legs ached, but something kept drawing him forward.

The passage tightened until they had to move single file, shoulders scraping damp stone that radiated a growing heat. The air was thick, almost steamy. Toryn was about to suggest turning back when a faint, hair-thin vein of blue shimmered in the rock ahead, catching his eye.

He stopped abruptly, staring at the unmistakable color.

"What is it?"

"There." Toryn pointed. "That vein in the rock."

Nora examined it with curiosity. "Possibly a mineral deposit. Copper can oxidize to similar colors under certain conditions." She covered the lamp with her palm – the vein still glowed in the dark.

"No." Toryn ran his fingers along the stone, feeling its unnatural warmth. "I've seen this before – in the seedheart chamber on Veil Islet. The same blue veins, like a heartstone."

What he didn't tell Nora was the pull that had driven him deeper. It wasn't the voice, but an inexplicable urge to reach whatever waited below – down where the veins converged.

The vein thickened as they followed it, joining with others to form a network of glowing lines. Hunger gnawed at them, and they paused only briefly to share their dried rations.

As they went deeper, the air grew warmer, heavy with humidity. Hours blurred together until their water was nearly gone and their legs shook with fatigue. Then they rounded a bend – and stopped.

Before them, the passage opened into a chamber where the blue veins converged and disappeared into an opening in the wall – its edges too regular and smooth to be natural.

"What is that?" Toryn asked, playing the lamp beam upward.

And how exactly have we found it?

They advanced with care. The passage angled upward, vanishing into shadow. Nora lifted her lamp, its glow catching on metal fixtures far above. About fifty feet up, a spill of loose rock blocked whatever lay beyond.

"It's an elevator shaft," she said quietly. "A mechanical lifting chamber, like the ones we use in Federation buildings. And look – there's a door down here."

At their feet loomed a massive metal door, nearly shut, leaving a gap of less than a foot. Its design mirrored the doors of the Archives above – same alloy, same precise construction.

"Another ship? That deep?" Nora breathed, running her hand along the exposed edge. "And why the elevator?"

The blue veins continued beyond the door, disappearing into darkness.

With some effort, they squeezed through the gap into a corridor with polished walls, the blue energy veins flowing across its surface like liquid light.

They followed the corridor as it curved gently, the glow growing stronger with each step. At a junction, Toryn paused to orient himself.

"If this has the same layout as the Archives above," he said, "then the Archive chamber should be this way."

They navigated through corridors that mirrored those they had walked in the Church of Archives. Along the way, they passed several sealed doors – some with unrecognizable symbols etched into their surfaces.

"Should we try to open these?" Toryn asked, examining one door with a small opening.

Nora shook her head. "We don't know what's behind it, and we can't explore every room. I like the idea of the Archive chamber – that was the most important part of the ship above, could be something important in its sibling."

They continued until they reached a metal door identical to the Archive chamber entrance above. It was firmly shut, and its control panel was dark and unresponsive.

Nora examined the edges of the door. "We might be able to pry it open if we can find a weak point in the seal."

Toryn wedged their tools into the slight gap around the door's edge while Nora applied leverage from the other side. After half an hour of straining metal and grunted effort, the door's ancient mechanism surrendered with a deep groan. It slid open just enough for them to slip through, releasing a cloud of stale air.

Beyond lay a chamber lined with shelves of identical, thin volumes – likely journals. Most had decayed to dust, their words lost forever, but a few still clung to life.

Nora moved slowly around the room, leaning in to read the covers without disturbing them.

At the room's center stood a desk, and at the desk sat a skeleton. The bones were still in perfect arrangement, held together by the deteriorated remains of clothing. One skeletal hand rested on an open book, with a pen lying nearby.

Toryn advanced with measured steps – not from fear of the dead, but out of respect for history left untouched for centuries. The book's pages were filled with a script he couldn't read.

"Nora," he said, gesturing to the desk.

She joined him, inhaling sharply when she saw the book. "That's Old Earth English. I can read this."

With careful reverence, Nora bent over the brittle pages. When she spoke, her voice was scarcely more than a breath:

"June 17, 2613. Madrid. The war began a week ago – and ended the next day. Earth is now a flaming ruin, continents shattered, inland seas vaporized. I pray the colony ships reach the stars… because we have destroyed our home."

She straightened slowly, her face drained of color, eyes wide with a realization that was far deeper than fear.

"It's not a ship," she whispered. "It's an underground bunker. We have found the Cradle. Azoria is *Earth*."

PART 5: SKY POLITICS

Diary of the Apocalypse

June 17, 2613. Madrid. The war began a week ago – and ended the next day. Earth is now a flaming ruin, continents shattered, inland seas vaporized. I pray the colony ships reach the stars… because we have destroyed our home.

June 18. The few remaining satellites show nothing but fire and destruction across the globe. Thermonuclear strikes hit not only military installations but also population centers and possible refuge sites. All known volcanoes were bombarded, and most erupted at the same time. Greenland and Antarctica are gone; someone decided even the ice should burn.

The Moon – God, we watched it happen. Orbital strikes shattered it like glass, and now the debris rains down on us like meteors. Australia is gone, sunk beneath the waves. Every coastal nation has been devastated by tsunamis hundreds of meters high.

June 21. Initial count of survivors. From 11 billion people to perhaps 500. Only those of us in the deepest bunkers and mantle research stations survived. Our sister station, Madrid Archive, near the surface stopped responding yesterday. We spend our days watching hell unfold through the remaining satellite feeds, and our nights trapped in nightmares. Dr. Pérez hasn't spoken in three days.

June 30. The engineers and scientists among us have begun planning. We talk of something beyond survival. Humanity here won't continue – we've accepted that. But perhaps life itself could. We have the technology, the knowledge. We could rebuild, not for ourselves, but for whatever might come after.

July 15. The plan is taking shape. Director Ruiz calls it "Project Génesis," though in private she refers to it as "Penitencia" – the Penance. The quantum material developed for the deep space program – the one that can manipulate gravitational fields – might be our best shot. The idea is brilliant and terrible: we will redirect the energy from the firestorms into the quantum cores, charging them gradually. The mathematics suggests that in time, they will accumulate enough energy to move the parts of the surface up to the skies, far away from the poisoned ocean and destroyed continents.

August 3. First test successful. We've programmed nanites to build a lattice structure under what remains of the Sahara. The quantum core anchored there should, if our calculations are correct, eventually lift part of the land upward, above the fires and radiation. Six gravitational anchors will be placed around it, each designed to store and preserve the flora and fauna samples. They will partially seed their surroundings when afloat and then do the final release when back on the surface.

September 12. Work continues despite radiation sickness claiming more of us each day. North Africa – once a cradle of humanity – will be the main platform. It is currently covered by fifty meters of water, but that water is also shielding it from the deadly radiation. When the system is charged, the landmass will be lifted to two kilometres and remain there. Eventually, it should become clean enough to sustain an ecosystem. We don't plan for *intelligent life to emerge again. Perhaps that's for the best. Intelligence led us here, after all.*

October 3. *Dr. Pérez has proposed something I initially thought was madness: a consciousness transfer device. A human mind loaded into the quantum network could oversee the entire Génesis project – monitoring, making adjustments, and guiding the descent when the radiation subsides. A human consciousness would give the system flexibility beyond any programming we could make. One mind, isolated yet aware, sustaining our vision for thousands of years. The group voted. We'll build it.*

October 28. *Nuclear winter is setting in. The sky is a permanent storm of debris, ash, and soot. Dr. Ortiz has proposed something unexpected – we'll use it. A weather control system could stabilize and maintain the storm layer as a protective barrier between the floating landmass and the burning surface. It will be reinforced with nanites that feed on the storm's energy.*

November 15. *The consciousness transfer system is complete. No one has volunteered. After a heated discussion, we agreed to draw lots. Dr. García is the winner. He will enter the device when the time comes, becoming the keeper of our knowledge and the custodian of a new world. I will never forget his face when he saw the short straw in his hand.*

December 4. *The anchor construction proceeds. We started calling them seedpods. Each is a self-contained floating landmass with the technology needed to sustain life and later release it several times. Their operating lifespan is approximately 2,000 years. After that, they will descend to the surface, reseeding it when – hopefully – radiation levels have subsided and the land can support life again. Their descent will trigger the lowering of* the central platform. Seedpods will release their stored seeds, gradually restoring ecosystems until Earth can be green again. Without us. Nanites in the cloud layer should drain the extra energy and dissipate on their own by that time.

December 10. Dr. García is dead. He hanged himself in a storage closet rather than face eternity alone in the system. I can't blame him. We have decided that the last person in the station will enter the device. As a precaution, Dr. Molina has implemented a basic algorithmic intelligence as a failsafe.

December 25. Christmas. What a strange thought. Twelve of us gathered around a makeshift table, no presents except the gift of another day alive. We reviewed the plans once more. The weather system is already in progress. It is power-hungry and drains any source that comes near it. Well, there will be nobody to complain anyway. The quantum energy storage will lift the landmass above the storm, and the seedpods – anchors will float highest, protected by the cold. When the anchors are out of energy, they will slowly descend. When all six are down, the weather system will drain the energy from the central platform and it will also go down regardless of surface conditions. A failsafe we hope will never be needed.

January 19, 2614. We have issues with food supplies. Not that we care anymore. All systems for Project Génesis are now autonomous; they will continue their work without us. I have moved my quarters to this archival chamber, surrounded by our knowledge and history. Someone should bear witness to the end. The quantum intelligence is already showing unexpected behavior, adapting in ways Dr. Molina had not anticipated.

February 2. All the remaining bunkers have gone silent. Just three of us are left here now. Ramos died yesterday – radiation poisoning.

February 15. I'm alone now. Remote feeds show the seedpods beginning to ascend. Each carries enough biological material for the whole planet – the same technology we used for seeding other planets before the generation ship's arrival. Beautiful, in a way. From death – life. From destruction – creation. I have been archiving everything I can on these plastic books. They should last for centuries, if anyone ever finds them.

February 27. The consciousness transfer device awaits me. And I just can't. Perhaps it makes me a coward, but the thought of existing alone for millennia, watching over a dead world, is too much. I have disabled the final transfer protocols. Molina's algorithmic intelligence will have to suffice. The world will be better without humans – without our mistakes and our arrogance. Maybe something wiser will rise in our place.

March 1. This will be my final entry. The system failures are cascading. To whoever might one day read these words: we did this to ourselves. We were given paradise and turned it into ashes. Remember Earth as it was, and as it became. My calculations show the landmass is already breaking apart, with some sections drifting too high and others too low. In time, it will crumble into thousands of pieces and float as a constellation. Don't know how it will land. There is nothing I can do. Hope the seedpods will be able to bring life even in these conditions.

From the ashes of our world, may yours flourish.

Maria Álvarez

Last Scientist of the Madrid Mantle Research Station

CHAPTER 27
Federation's Answer

Kip spent hours flying through the Heights in search of a remote island far from any tribal lands. The nameless speck he found was little more than a heap of stone adrift in the endless sky.

It had few to no plants and was uninhabited – uninteresting to all but the occasional eagle that passed by. Perfect for a clandestine meeting with beings from the stars.

He circled once, studying the terrain and noting the flat sections suitable for landing. The wind was favorably calm by Heights standards, which meant landing would be interesting rather than suicidal. As *Stubborn Phoenix* settled onto the surface, Kip allowed himself a moment to breathe. The journey from the Roost had been long and tense, as he had little experience flying in the thin air. But the routine had been calming, a welcome distraction from thoughts of the looming negotiations and the grim fate awaiting his friends on the surface.

"Let's hope Nora's people are as attentive as she claimed," he muttered, reaching for the device stashed beneath his seat.

The object was unlike anything in his world. A sleek, polished rectangle with numbered markings looked completely alien. He took the battery Nora had given him, slid it into the casing, and pulled the tab. She had explained that this would start a chemical reaction lasting an hour or so, depending on the altitude. That would give more than enough time to activate the emergency beacon with its number code.

Kip traced his fingers over the symbols, hesitating. There would be no turning back – he'd be surrendering himself to powers he barely understood. He pressed the final symbol. The device emitted a soft green pulse, beeped, and settled into a rhythmic blink.

And then there was nothing to do but wait.

Kip secured the radio and climbed from the cockpit, stretching stiff muscles after hours in the air. He paced the edge of the small plateau – partly to take in the surroundings, partly to burn off restless energy. The Heights spread before him in all directions – endless sky broken by floating islands of various sizes and distant specks that might be eagles or tribal gliders. Far below lay the roiling mass of the Storm.

And it was hot there. The chilling air filled his lungs while the blazing sun burned him from above. That contrast was unlike anything he had experienced before, and he decided to seek shelter in the plane's shadow.

An hour passed. Then another. The sun climbed toward its zenith, warming the stone beneath his feet. The device lay silent and lifeless. Kip began to wonder if the signal had failed – or if Nora's faith in her people had been misplaced.

He was leaning against *Phoenix*, eyes half-closed against the glare, when a low hum pulled him to alertness. His hand instinctively moved to where his rapier would normally hang, finding only empty air. Something was coming.

Later, Kip would struggle to describe exactly how the Federation shuttle looked at first sight. It seemed to take shape out of the air – a sleek, metallic craft with wings and several hatches. Nearly thirty feet long, it had no visible engines, rotors, steam vents, or balloon. It resembled an oversized platform plane, yet carried an unmistakable air of strength and menace. Kip swallowed hard, trying to shake off the primitive terror. His ancestors were also from the Federation, but the technological gap was unthinkable.

Our people are mere apes compared to this. What if they decide to take the mineral by force? How could we resist them?

Then Nora's face came to mind, and the memory calmed him – despite their advancements, they were still human, shared the same values, and cherished the same ideals. Another reassuring thought was that this technology could function only at a safe distance from the Storm.

The craft settled onto the plateau, a ramp extending from its side. Six figures in dark gray uniforms and threatening-looking firearms emerged and quickly scanned the surroundings. He noted their tight formation, precise movements, and superior equipment. The corsair in him mapped escape routes; the man in him fought the urge to bolt. One of the figures approached.

"You activated a Federation emergency beacon," they said, their voice neutral, language accented but understandable.

"Yes," Kip replied, pleased to find his own voice steady. "I have information for Commander Voss about Sergeant Nora Hertzig."

The name acted as a passphrase. The figure's posture shifted subtly. "You'll need to be searched."

The search was thorough but impersonal. They examined every inch of him and his aircraft, using devices that emitted soft pulses of light. Kip submitted, understanding the necessity of the security protocols. After all, he had once had household guards who performed similar functions.

"Clear," the figure finally announced. "Commander will see you now."

Are they taking me to the spaceship? Or is the Commander herself here to see me?

Kip approached the ramp reluctantly. The shuttle's interior was cooler than the plateau, the air carrying an unfamiliar crispness. A short corridor led to a small chamber he recognized as a meeting room. The layout was simple – a table, chairs, and a whiteboard. At the table sat a woman with steel-gray hair cut in a precise bob. Her uniform was crisp and simple, without unnecessary decoration. She looked up from a glowing tablet, her deep brown eyes missing nothing in their quick assessment.

"I'm Commander Elara Voss of the UES *Pathfinder*," she said, gesturing to the chair. "And you are?"

"Kip Saroven," he replied, deliberately hiding his full name, as had become his habit. "I have information regarding Sergeant Hertzig."

Voss nodded and tapped on her tablet. Her eyes flickered across the screen as she consulted whatever information appeared there.

"Lord Killian Saroven, now of the Scarlet Talon?" she asked, her tone making it a simple verification rather than a revelation.

Kip's stomach tightened. He prepared himself for the usual humiliation from those who knew of his past – raised eyebrows, barely concealed disdain, and questions about his fall from grace. Commander Voss's expression revealed nothing beyond professional interest as she gestured toward the chair.

"Please, sit." He took the offered seat, studying her as she studied him. He guessed she was in her mid-forties, with the bearing of someone accustomed to command. Her hands were steady as she set the tablet aside.

"So, Kip," she said, shifting to his preferred name without comment, "Nora considers you a friend. Where on the surface is she exactly?"

The directness of the question caught him off guard. "She's being held captive by the Inquisition of the Holy Sovereignty."

Commander Voss frowned slightly. "I'm not familiar with either of those terms. Perhaps you should start from the beginning."

Kip blinked in surprise. "You don't know about the Holy Sovereignty? The surface kingdoms?"

"We have limited intelligence about conditions beneath the Storm," Voss admitted. "We didn't know the surface ocean even existed until two months ago. Never attempted to send people there."

The revelation that Federation knowledge had gaps momentarily threw Kip off balance. He had assumed they were omniscient, watching events unfold from above with godlike detachment. Instead, they were wandering through the darkness just as he was.

"What about the mid-altitudes? You seem very well informed. Do you monitor us constantly?"

"You might be surprised, but our monitoring capabilities there are also quite limited. We have operatives in some nations. They travel the trade routes to the Heights to report back. We don't hesitate to use other sources when they possess valuable information." She looked at him meaningfully.

Kip understood the subtext and resumed his story. "The Kingdom of Tides, a monarchy that controlled about half of the continent, underwent a religious revolution about a year ago," he began, carefully organizing his thoughts. "They're now the Holy Sovereignty, ruled by a religious order called the Temple of the Storm's Truth. They preach that nothing exists above the Storm – and anything coming from above is demonic in nature."

Voss's expression remained neutral, but her eyes sharpened with interest. "And Nora is being held by this group?"

"The Inquisition – their enforcement arm – captured all four of us: Nora, myself, a Technocracy pilot named Lina, and a tribal eagle rider known as Toryn Skyheart. They planned to put us on trial for being from above." Kip's jaw tightened at the memory. "Lina and I managed to negotiate our release, but we had to leave Nora and Toryn behind as… insurance for our cooperation."

"I see." Voss made a note on her tablet. "And what exactly do they expect to get from you, holding my officer hostage?"

The question had many layers – concern for a subordinate, a probe into the Inquisition's political motivations, and an unspoken inquiry about Kip's relationship with Nora.

"They want one more island to go down without a crash so they can get supplies and pilots from above."

"Is it possible with any island? Or do they want something specific?"

"It's a special kind of island, like the one Nora was lost on. It hosts a thriving ecosystem inside, and there's some group of people obsessed with destroying them for some reason."

Voss sighed, making notes, obviously not very happy with the deal.

"Are you going to do so?" she asked.

Kip hesitated. "We decided not to. Those are powers beyond our knowledge, and both Nora and our tribal friend agree that destroying the ecosystem is too high a price."

The conversation continued, with Voss asking questions that guided Kip through his journey to the surface and back. He explained the Holy Sovereignty's tech, his arrangement with the Inquisitor, Captain Marek, their plans for expansion, and the rising conflicts in both worlds. Commander Voss absorbed it all with the focus of a military officer assessing a battlefield. As the talks progressed, Kip found himself growing more comfortable. The initial terror had faded to a background unease, allowing his natural diplomatic skills to emerge. He spoke with the clarity that had once marked him a promising young leader.

Finally, when Voss seemed satisfied with his overview, Kip asked a question of his own. "May I ask how you knew Nora considers me a friend?"

Voss's expression softened. "She gave you her personal Type-3 code for the beacon. Type-1 means *I'm in danger*. Type-2 is reserved for when a soldier is forced to give the code; it means *someone else is in possession of my radio*. Type-3 means *a friend is in possession of my radio*. So that's why I came here in person."

The weight of it caught Kip off guard. Nora hadn't just handed him a communication device; she'd marked him as someone she trusted. The woman who had begun as a companion by chance, who had seen him at his most self-serving, considered him a friend worthy of that trust.

He took a moment to compose his next question, the most critical of all. "The Holy Sovereignty is preparing for war with the Harbor Commonwealth on the surface, while helping the Scarlet Talon to attack nations above the Storm. Two separate conflicts are about to erupt. Given what I've told you, will the Federation intervene?"

Commander Voss leaned back slightly, studying him. "Kip, I'll be honest with you. We will not. Just imagine – a bunch of Federation soldiers rushing down, starting to shoot people, changing political systems, and throwing down governments. And all that to prevent a few local conflicts? That's not how we operate. Even if Azoria were on the way to join the Federation, we are not peacekeepers. The Federation's main rule for planetary ascension is that the world must end all its conflicts on its own."

"But thousands of people will die," Kip protested, his sense of responsibility flaring.

"As they will die of old age anyway," Voss replied with cold pragmatism. "There is nothing crucial that requires our interference. I could consider an intervention if the planet were on the verge of destruction. Or if fanatics were about to throw a hundred-megaton bomb into a supervolcano. But what I see is another power game. Not the first, not the last. And we don't even have a cooperation memorandum signed with any parties."

Kip didn't understand the reference to bombs, but he grasped the essential point. The technological gods he had hoped would intervene were declining to do so. He struggled to accept the cold calculus of Voss's position.

"I should mention," Voss added with the casual air of someone delivering an afterthought, "that our primary interest in Azoria is mining. War could potentially complicate extraction operations, but not to the point of rendering them impossible."

And there it was – the truth behind the diplomatic language. The Federation wanted azurium above all else. Their stance reflected that the coming war wouldn't significantly affect their ability to extract resources.

"From what you've told me," Voss continued, "this religious kingdom is already preparing for war. They need extra supplies and pilots, and they expect your help with both. But even without you, they can train pilots and produce their own supplies – it might take longer, but they will get there. The war is inevitable."

She tapped her tablet. "The same goes for your corsair captain. He already has samples of combustion engines and rotary weapons. His scientists will replicate them using mid-altitude technologies within a year or two. The only thing you can achieve is disrupting their immediate plans – perhaps forming a coalition before the war fully unfolds."

Kip felt a cold certainty settle in his stomach. She was right. He had been hoping for a miraculous intervention, but the reality was far more pragmatic. Marek would continue his conquests. The Inquisitor would pursue his war. The mid- altitudes would be drawn into the conflict, whether the Federation intervened or not.

"Let me get it straight," Voss said, her tone shifting slightly. "I like you, and I want to help. I can't interfere directly, but I can help you spread the word. We have envoys in the larger nations and some insight into their politics. Intelligence is something I'm authorized to share."

Kip nodded, grateful for even this limited support. "Thank you. That would be very helpful." He hesitated, then asked, "But what about Nora?"

"We need to consider our options. The obvious solution is a ground mission, but we lack detailed maps and don't have the technology to guarantee a return trip. Our equipment will stop functioning as we approach the Storm." Voss's expression remained professional, but Kip detected a hint of genuine concern. "My scientists are working on modifications that could get us there and back, but it will take time. We can only hope that Sergeant Hertzig manages to escape and stay low until a rescue team arrives. What's your next destination?"

"The Mercantile Concord."

"Good. Meet our envoy there – Liaison Officer Tallen. He will assist you and keep you informed as soon as we are ready for deployment." She set the tablet down. "In the meantime, I need you to share every map, name, and piece of intelligence you have about the surface world."

Kip spent the next hour providing detailed information to a technician who joined them. He described the coastal regions of the surface world – the approach to Stormhaven, the location of Free Harbor, and Marvin's lighthouse. Then came detailed questions about the Holy Sovereignty, the Harbor Commonwealth, and the shifting political landscape.

When they finished, Voss led him back to the gangway. "We'll do what we can for Nora," she said as they walked, the words carrying the unmistakable weight of family.

They parted with a formal handshake. As Kip walked back to his plane, he felt a mix of disappointment and resolve. The weight of the coming conflict settled on his shoulders – no longer something he could hope would be solved by outside intervention.

The Federation shuttle rose into the air and vanished, leaving Kip alone on the rocky plateau. He climbed into the *Phoenix* and began the startup sequence, while his mind processed Voss's words. The war was inevitable. The Federation wouldn't intervene. They would have to rely on themselves alone.

His father's advisor's voice echoed in his memory: "*One who ignores the storm today will face a hurricane tomorrow.*"

Voss might be right about the inevitability of conflict, but that didn't mean he shouldn't try shaping it now – forge alliances, warn those at risk, and prepare defenses.

The scout's engine hummed to life. Kip plotted his route to the Market Nexus, the capital of the Mercantile Concord. If the gods would not intervene, mortals would have to solve their own problems. As he lifted off from the rocky island, he found strange comfort in that thought. For the first time since his family's lands were seized, Kip was fighting for something larger than his own vengeance. And that, at least, felt right.

CHAPTER 28
Habit of Truth

Everything with Marvin's vegetable delivery was going smoothly today – a sign, perhaps, that trouble was about to strike.

He guided the boat to the dock, vegetable boxes arranged in the shallow hold. The wooden pole slipped through the dark water, nudging the channel bottom with barely a splash.

The routine had become comfortable after a week. The same guards nodded at the checkpoint lit with lanterns. The same cook complained about slightly wilted greens. The same payment, counted twice by the same fingers.

It worked like clockwork, like a daily lighthouse routine – until he stepped through the manor's service entrance and the alarm bells blared. The timing was unlucky, though not entirely surprising.

The plan had been almost perfect, really. Marvin even had several contingency options. There was a second boat hidden near the old mill. And in another spot, wrapped in oiled canvas, a small balloon that could carry three people if the winds were right. He hadn't bothered with weapons, of course. His mother had once told him – blunt as ever – that he was utterly unsuited for any kind of fighting.

"Marvin, dear," she'd added, "you couldn't scare a fish out of water. It's not a character flaw, mind you. Just a fact to plan around."

Now, sitting in the mansion's holding cell, Marvin reflected on the fatal flaw in his otherwise excellent planning. The stone walls wept moisture, filling the narrow space with the mingled scents of old wine and creeping damp. Somewhere in the darkness above, a spider labored on an ambitious web stretched between ceiling stones likely cut when his mother was still a child.

"The problem, my eight-legged friend," he announced to his only companion, "is my unfortunate habit of telling the truth." The spider never answered, but Marvin was so used to that kind of dialogue that he didn't mind. The cold seeped through the stone floor and into his bones. He pulled his coat tighter and continued his assessment. Lying wasn't impossible. The vocal cords and cognitive processes required for deception functioned normally. But Marvin had spent most of his adult life with Ferdinand and the occasional supply-ship captain. Neither required anything more complex than a straightforward conversation. When he attempted deception, his body betrayed him immediately. Excessive perspiration appeared within seconds. His voice developed a nervous tremor. Worst of all, he was overexplaining, giving details no innocent person would think to mention.

Any competent interrogator would notice it instantly. The plan hadn't accounted for a competent interrogator – he'd expected only a guard captain, someone who would ask simple questions about the fugitives' whereabouts. That one he could have answered truthfully; he hadn't even discussed it with Talbert.

The first interview had gone splendidly, precisely because he had said nothing but the truth. Yes, he was delivering food. Yes, he had arrived alone. Yes, he hadn't noticed anything unusual. The guards had been satisfied with his papers – and with the apparent absence of any imagination.

The next day's interrogation had been entirely different.

Footsteps echoed down the stone corridor. Not the heavy boots of guards, but the measured pace of someone accustomed to command. The door opened slowly. A tall man stepped in, carrying a leather folder and a plain wooden chair.

The face was familiar. Fifteen years ago, Father Thadeius had been a medium-ranking priest assigned to a Kingdom of Tides military vessel seeking updated charts. They had spent several hours discussing Marvin's meteorological observations and the world above. The young priest had a remarkably sharp mind. Their exchange had been enjoyable – rare intellectual stimulation in Marvin's otherwise isolated life.

Inquisitor Thadeius had changed considerably in fifteen years. Gray streaked through his dark hair, and lines marked the corners of his eyes. He wore the midnight-blue robes of his office, storm-cloud embroidery glinting silver in the lamplight. Yet those sharp eyes were exactly as Marvin remembered. And Marvin realized this was one of the most powerful people in the world – the one who had his friends in captivity. Now he was trapped in the small room with him, trying to convince the man he wasn't connected to their escape.

Thadeius placed his chair carefully, opened the folder, and studied Marvin's face with the intensity of someone examining a particularly intriguing specimen.

Then came the flicker of recognition. "Ah, Marvin," the Inquisitor said softly, smiling as he leaned back in the chair.

Marvin's stomach dropped. "Good morning, Father Thadeius. Lovely weather we're having."

"That's High Inquisitor Thadeius, but for an old friend – just Inquisitor." Thadeius closed the folder. "Last time we discussed the weather, you mentioned how the proximity of the floating Northern Archipelago influences the surface's seasonal winds. Quite accurate, as I recall."

"Yes, well. And you agreed with my theories and even took a copy of the map. And now you are hanging people for believing the floating world exists, Inquisitor."

"Fifteen years ago… yes, it was different. And you were living in a lighthouse then." Thadeius picked up a sheet of paper and lifted his pen. "What brings you to Holy Sovereignty territory this time, Marvin Thale?"

The pen waited above the parchment. Marvin felt sweat gathering at his collar despite the cell's chill.

"I… that is to say… recent circumstances have required a change of location." His voice cracked slightly. "I'm now a boatman. Delivering vegetables. Perfectly legitimate employment."

"I see." Thadeius's pen moved across the paper. "And how did you arrive at this manor?"

"In my boat. Alone. Following my usual route." All true. Carefully true.

"With vegetables?"

"Yes."

"For the kitchen staff?"

"Correct."

"And you had no knowledge of the individuals who escaped from this manor last night?"

Marvin's hands began to shake. He pressed them flat against his knees. "I was only delivering vegetables as contracted."

Thadeius leaned forward. "A month ago, the three individuals arrived at Sovereignty in your boat, Marvin. We have witnesses."

"That – that may be technically accurate." The words tumbled out faster than he could control. "However, I must point out that boat ownership can be transferred, previous passengers do not necessarily indicate current criminal intent, and furthermore–"

"Marvin…" The Inquisitor shook his head.

He stopped. Thadeius was watching him with something that might have been pity – or sympathy.

Above them, the spider had added another strand to its web – a sight uncomfortably like Marvin's own tangled situation.

———

Thadeius returned the next morning carrying a steaming cup that filled the cell with the rich scent of something expensive. He sipped it slowly while studying his notes. He clearly saw through Marvin's defense and seemed to be choosing how to ask his questions with minimal ambiguity – or so Marvin thought. Perhaps the Inquisitor was just stalling to make him nervous.

"Did the tribal man – Skyheart – leave in your boat?" he asked without looking up.

Marvin opened his mouth, then closed it. His throat felt as dry as old parchment.

"Yes," he whispered.

The silence stretched tight while Thadeius made a note and looked directly into the prisoner's eyes. Overhead, the spider had finished another section of its web. Morning light filtered through the single-barred window, illuminating dust drifting in the still air. Cracks traced the ceiling where old mortar had failed, forming a pattern that resembled a map. Ferdinand would have found it fascinating – if he cared about architecture.

"Now, tell me the full story."

Marvin straightened, launching into his prepared Federation protocols. "As per Administrative Code 15-C, I wish to state that any testimony provided is given under duress and should not be construed as–"

"Marvin."

" – an admission of guilt regarding any activities that may or may not be considered–"

"*Marvin.*"

He stopped. Thadeius was watching him with the patience of someone accustomed to dealing with nervous witnesses.

"The story. *All* of it."

Marvin sighed. "Very well. I met the man who called himself Skyheart about five years ago."

Thadeius's pen paused above the parchment.

"I found him drifting on a piece of wood," Marvin continued, "unconscious and severely dehydrated. The man was utterly exhausted, running a high fever, and spent over a week in my spare bed. During the worst of it, he raved constantly, calling for someone named Tyra."

Tyra. Always Tyra. The name was spoken with such desperate longing that even Ferdinand seemed moved, lowering his ears whenever the fevered man cried out.

"When he finally regained consciousness, he told me he'd survived the fall of a floating island in the Heights. According to his account, he and his wife had hastily fashioned something like a parachute during the island's sudden descent. They managed to glide clear of the collapsing landmass. However, they were separated during a storm. He was uncertain whether she had survived and felt compelled to return and search for her."

Marvin paused, remembering the man's haunted expression – the way he had stared at the horizon as if expecting to see something that would never appear.

"When he was sufficiently recovered to travel, Arvid left me a collection of tribal maps. They had survived the ordeal almost intact due to their leather construction and waterproof storage. Remarkable cartography, actually – far more detailed than anything I had seen of the upper atmospheric regions. In return, I gave him one of my boats, a full chart of the surface world's navigable waters, and some basic instruction in maritime navigation."

Thadeius sighed. The details were helpful, yet clearly not what he had anticipated.

He made another note. "What about Nora Hertzig?"

"The last time I saw Sergeant Hertzig, she left in my spare boat, heading toward a Harbor Commonwealth friend."

Thadeius nodded slowly, set down his pen, and rubbed his temples. Dark circles under his eyes hinted at a night of poor sleep. "That will be enough for today."

Once the door closed, Marvin drew a thin wire from his sash. It was part of his mother's measuring device, crafted to endure field conditions. The metal was harder than the iron bars, though far thinner.

"Contingency Plan C," he announced to the spider. "Progressive metallurgical reduction through the patient application of superior materials."

He began to work, as he had already done the previous night and most of the day. But now he had to hurry. One more direct question could unravel his story, and Thadeius was not the type to leave things unfinished.

The wire cut through the iron remarkably well, but he had to be careful to avoid detection. He made steady progress.

"Patience, Ferdinand," he murmured as he worked. "Patience and proper preparation solve most difficulties."

This was the third contingency plan, and Marvin was rather proud of its thoroughness. The bars gave way with almost no resistance, and Marvin slipped into the corridor beyond, careful not to disturb the sleeping manor.

"Excellent," he told the spider. "Phase One complete."

The guards, it seemed, had decided Marvin was no threat at all – a harmless fool who delivered vegetables and asked naive questions about storage temperatures. Clearly an unwitting accomplice at worst, the sort of simple man who might ferry passengers without understanding their true purpose. Only one guard had been posted outside, and Marvin had carefully counted the man's breathing patterns by the sound of soft, rhythmic snoring that occasionally made the walls tremble.

The manor had never been meant as a prison. Over a week of food deliveries, Marvin studied its layout, feigning concern over how his earlier vegetables were stored. He examined the building plans with false interest, asking harmless questions about delivery routes and possible alternatives for bringing in heavy goods. He learned that the kitchen was connected to an underground tunnel, built long ago to deliver wine barrels when boats could still reach the manor's base. Water levels had risen since then, and the dock was no longer used.

He crept through empty corridors, boots silent on cold stone. There were other guards in the manor, of course, but his observations had revealed only one additional post between his cell and the kitchen. That guard post would demand more careful navigation. The kitchen reeked of stale grease and yesterday's bread. A lone oil lamp burned low, throwing restless shadows across the hanging pots and knife racks.

The keys were exactly where Plan C, Subsection 3 specified, on the rusty hook above the fireplace. Not used for years.

"The hatch should be... yes. There." He lifted the heavy wooden cover, revealing dark water below. "Phase Two commencing."

"Sometimes," he said to the darkness, "proper planning eliminates the element of surprise entirely."

He knew the tunnel ended at a locked gate – the keys made that clear. What he hadn't expected was the shocking cold of the water. It struck him, driving the breath from his lungs. Worse, the exit gate appeared to be locked from the opposite side. However, it had iron bars in the lower half for water flow and solid wood above, offering some hope if he could reach the lock between the bars.

"Ah." His teeth began chattering. "This presents a technical challenge."

The chest-deep current dragged at him as he waded toward the gate. When he dove under to reach the lock through the bars, the cold nearly stopped his heart. The water was black as Ferdinand's mood when denied hay – only colder.

On his first attempt, his numb fingers couldn't manipulate the key properly. He surfaced, gasping.

"Unacceptable," he informed the gate. "Ferdinand would be most disappointed with such poor performance."

The second attempt ended when his hand slipped through the bars but couldn't reach the lock. His foot caught in the gate, and for a terrifying moment, he thought he might be trapped. He came up again, spitting water and muttering things about the gate's family tree that would have shocked Ferdinand's sensitive nature.

On the third try, the lock yielded with a sharp click. Marvin pulled it free, climbed back into the kitchen, and collapsed onto the floor, gasping for breath. Moments later, he plunged back through the hatch, seized the gate, and kicked it wide.

Once at the pier, he slipped into the main channel and swam through the quiet morning fog until he reached the old mill. His spare boat awaited exactly where Plan B specified, complete with proper boatman's clothes and a pushing pole.

"Phase Three," he whispered through chattering teeth. "Tactical withdrawal via established waterways."

For thirty minutes, he punted with the unhurried pace of someone conducting legitimate early-morning business. Fog clung to the water, muffling sound and reducing visibility to just a few yards in any direction – perfect for moving unseen. The alarm bells began ringing much earlier than expected.

"Ah," he said aloud. "Time for Plan D."

He guided the boat to shore, concealed it in the designated hiding place, and walked steadily away from the channel. He was still chilled from the morning swim, but the exertion stirred warmth through his veins. Within an hour, he reached his final cache.

The balloon waited in its oiled canvas wrapping, compact and patient as Ferdinand during lighthouse maintenance. The weather was ideal for flying – a brisk wind in the right direction, concealing fog, and light rain to deter any potential pursuers.

"Sometimes," Marvin announced to the gray morning, "nature cooperates beautifully with proper planning."

He inflated the balloon, double-checked the harness connections, and tested the release mechanisms. Everything worked exactly as it should.

"Farewell, Holy Sovereignty," he said, and launched himself into the gray sky.

By afternoon, he was drifting over Harbor Commonwealth territory. The landing went off with textbook precision. He packed the balloon carefully for future use and arranged with a cooperative farmer to transport it toward the coast. Throughout the journey, one thought nagged at him with increasing urgency. He had already used Plans A through D. What if a further contingency became necessary? That was entirely unacceptable.

Future operations would require at least six backup strategies – possibly seven.

But Ferdinand was undoubtedly lonely, the lighthouse demanded attention, and – most importantly – his work here was done. Marvin Thale allowed himself a small smile as the farmer's cart carried him toward home and the familiar rhythm of his properly organized life.

CHAPTER 29
Technocratic Mandate

Lina tightened her grip on the control stick, threading the plane through the crowded skyways of the Technocracy. Here, aircraft moved in complex patterns that would have impressed even the most fastidious engineer. Vessels of every size kept their distance, their pilots adjusting course in response to flag signals from the control towers.

"Three degrees port, maintain altitude," Lina muttered as a flag operator signaled an approach vector. The Technocracy spread below them like a mechanical dream – all gleaming metal, precise angles, and purposeful design. Glass domes, giant gears, and steam venting from copper pipes formed neat geometric patterns – so unlike the disorganized mess of the corsair island she had seen a few weeks earlier.

Beside her, Elder Kora leaned forward in her seat, eyes wide with recognition. "The South Observatory," she said, pointing to a massive glass dome in the eastern quadrant. "Over there – that's the University." Her gaze lingered on the terraced growing fields in the distance. "They've even added a few buildings to the agricultural wing!"

"How long did you stay here?" Lina asked.

"Almost two decades. Most of my adult life."

Lina shook her head in disbelief. It was difficult to imagine someone leaving the Technocracy to live with the tribes for so many years. "Do you miss it?"

"Sometimes," Kora admitted. "Not the so-called *civilized society*, as you might think, but the research – the thrill of standing at the edge of discovery. However, my heart, my home, is in the Heights."

The flag operator directed them to the visitor landing platform. Lina brought the plane down, feeling the vibrations through the control stick as the landing gear settled onto the platform.

They disembarked and approached a customs officer behind a sturdy metal desk. He stopped writing and looked up expectantly, pen poised.

"Welcome to Caligan Sector Seven. Names and point of origin for the log?" the officer asked, his voice flat and impersonal.

"Elder Kora Skyheart of the Windclaw Tribe."

"Lina Ryven, pilot," Lina added.

The officer wrote down the names, then paused. He ran a finger down a separate list attached to a clipboard and stopped. "Hold on," he said. "Ryven… yes, this name is flagged." He turned and spoke into a brass speaking tube: "Reception Gamma to Admin Security. Send Officer Brennan. We've got the person from the special notice list."

Within minutes, a woman with trimmed gray hair and an immaculate charcoal uniform approached. "Officer Brennan, Administrative Security," she stated, her sharp eyes fixing on Lina. "You're Lina Ryven?"

"That's me," Lina confirmed.

Brennan consulted her clipboard, flipping a page. "You were the pilot escort for the Mercantile Concord zeppelin *Empirical Advance*. The ship departed two months ago and never returned. It was declared lost with all hands." She looked up, her gaze steady.

"Your sudden reappearance now requires an explanation – for the record."

"Heard I was dead? Reports were off," Lina said bluntly.

Brennan's expression didn't change. "The Concord wants answers about the attack – and so do we. Since you were there, you'll need to file a witness report. Standard procedure for major incidents." She gestured toward an administrative building nearby. "An escort will guide you through the paperwork. Your statement has to be filed before you're cleared to move around freely."

The Security Precinct was a three-level hexagonal structure, ugly but practical. Officials moved like well-oiled gears, each desk aligned with its neighbors, each workstation an identical array of forms and stamps. A young officer introduced himself as Specialist Tella and led them to a small, plain interview room. "You can write your report here," he said, setting down a modest stack of forms and an inkwell on the table. "Standard witness packet. Fill these out with what you saw, what happened to your craft, and how you got back."

Lina eyed the stack. It wasn't overwhelming, but it wasn't trivial either. "How long does this usually take?"

"Depends on how detailed you are," Tella said with a shrug. "Most people get through it in a few hours."

Lina spent the next two hours recounting a carefully edited version of her experience. She described the attack on the zeppelin in technical detail – the vessels with modified corsair designs, their unusual weapons. She recounted her crash landing, the encounter with Kip–"a stranded traveler with a damaged scout craft" – and their eventual journey to safer territory. She left out any mention of falling through the Storm, the surface world, or anything that might sound like the delusions of a shaken pilot.

During a brief pause, when Tella left to retrieve archive stamps, Kora leaned forward. "Wise to avoid mentioning what lies beneath," she whispered. "Most would simply declare you insane, and those who believe you might be even more dangerous."

"Do you think anyone knows?" Lina asked, keeping her voice low. "About the surface?"

Kora's eyes flicked toward the door. "Knowledge has many forms. Let's keep this information for the Directorate." She straightened as the door reopened.

Tella returned, pressed several official-looking stamps onto Lina's forms, and set a thick folder on the table. "Alright. Your witness report is filed," he said. "Now, about your other request... meeting the Scientific Directorate?" He tapped the folder. "This outlines the procedure. There's a preliminary application, then review, then maybe scheduling. It's not quick."

"How... not quick?" Lina asked, picking up the folder and flipping through pages dense with text.

"Usually it takes a month – maybe three weeks if everything is in perfect order and the committees aren't backed up," Tella said with a hint of bureaucratic pride.

"We don't have that long," Lina said flatly. "There's a situation developing that needs immediate attention."

Tella's expression remained unchanged. "I understand you believe it's urgent, Pilot Ryven, but procedures exist for a reason. The Directorate can't just meet with anyone who shows up without proper vetting. Imagine the chaos."

Lina thought of the chaos festering across Azoria – surface weapons smuggled upward, the Scarlet Talon sharpening for war – and frustration surged through her. "I understand," she said through gritted teeth. "I guess I'll take it with me as homework."

"Sure! But don't forget – you need clearance from Officer Brennan if you decide to leave the island."

In a while, they reached Lina's quarters – a utilitarian but comfortable two-room apartment above the workshop she rented. Everything there reminded her of her previous life and her craft, *Swift Mistral*: spare parts, racing awards, and her first-grade pilot's license. The rooms followed the familiar Technocracy style – practical furnishings, south-facing windows, and only the most basic amenities.

Lina tossed the folder onto a desk and dropped into a chair, massaging her writing hand. "This is insane. Every minute we waste on paperwork, the Scarlet Talon gets stronger."

Kora examined the space with a critical eye before settling gracefully onto a sofa. "The Technocracy has survived for generations by prioritizing process over haste. It's frustrating, but it has certain advantages."

"Like what?" Lina challenged.

"Consistency. Stability. Methodical evaluation." Kora began unpacking her travel bag. "Though I agree that current circumstances might justify… finding a faster way."

Lina nodded toward the stack of forms. "At this pace, we'll still be signing papers when the Scarlet Talon launches their first raid."

"Perhaps," Kora said thoughtfully, "there are other approaches." She rose and crossed to the city map on the wall.

"The university district isn't far. I should visit some old colleagues tomorrow morning."

"You think they can help cut through this?" Lina waved at the paperwork.

"The Directorate respects academic credentials, sometimes more than its administrative procedures," Kora said with a small smile. "What is bureaucracy, after all, but another form of weather pattern? Predictable flows, areas of resistance, and channels of least turbulence."

Lina snorted. "I've never heard the government described as weather before."

"Then you haven't spent enough time observing either one," Kora replied. "Get some rest, Lina. Continue with the forms tomorrow, as though that remains our plan. I'll return by midday – hopefully with better news."

The following day blurred into bureaucratic tedium. Lina worked through the forms with mechanical precision, the task draining her spirit. By midday, she had managed barely a third of the required documentation. She was just about ready to smash something for relief when the door opened and Kora swept in.

"Pack those away," she said, gesturing to the forms. "We have an audience with the Scientific Directorate tomorrow morning."

Lina nearly knocked over her inkwell. "How? I thought we needed to finish this whole process first."

"As I suspected, alternative channels exist." Kora's eyes gleamed with satisfaction. "Director Varen was a colleague during my time at university and in routing zeppelins. He has arranged a special session on the basis of urgent *inter-atmospheric relations*."

"Inter-atmospheric relations?" Lina repeated.

"It's a legitimate field of study on interactions between different altitude civilizations," Kora explained. "My academic specialty."

Lina shook her head in amazement. "I'm beginning to think wind reading is your hobby, not your profession."

Kora smiled. "Knowledge takes many forms, Lina. The wind speaks in different tongues at different heights." Her face grew serious. "We must prepare – the Directorate values presentation as much as information."

Lina nodded. "Facts, evidence, and technical specifications – that I can handle."

"Good." Kora settled onto the sofa. "Now tell me everything about the surface world's technology that might interest the Technocracy. Leave nothing out – especially the mechanical details and military capabilities."

As evening fell, Lina found herself restless – prepared, but nowhere near ready. She left her rooms and headed into the city. At night, the Technocracy revealed its marvels of engineering. Gas lamps with mirrored reflectors cast precise pools of light, while pipes beneath ornate grates thrummed with pressurized water.

Lina wandered through familiar districts, memories surfacing with each turn. There was the canal bridge where she had first watched cargo vessels being loaded as a child. Here was the public square where mechanical innovations were demonstrated. She found herself in the Repair District almost without conscious intent. The narrow streets were lined with workshops specializing in every kind of machinery. As a child, this had been her wonderland.

Her feet carried her to a familiar corner, to the place that had once been the center of her universe – her cousin Dren's repair shop. The storefront was almost unchanged, except for the new sign above the door: Precision Mechanicals – Under New Management. Lina stood rooted, memories surging. Here she had built her first engine at eight, learned to catch flaws by sound alone, and forged the very identity that still defined her.

"Shop's been under new ownership for almost half a year now," said a voice behind her. Lina turned to find an elderly man at a small food cart selling steamed buns. His face stirred a distant memory.

"Mr. Tekka?" she ventured.

The old man squinted, then smiled, revealing more gaps than teeth. "Well, strike me with a broken rod! Little Lina Ryven! Heard you'd gone and gotten yourself killed."

"Guess I'm tougher to kill than they figured," she replied, moving up to the cart.

"Always were stubborn," he chuckled, getting one of the last buns ready without being asked. He'd been selling food in the district for as long as she could remember, keeping mechanics fed during their short breaks.

"What happened to Dren's shop?"

"He signed on with an exploration crew," Tekka said, passing her the steaming bun. "Concord job, pays well. Sold the shop and took off while you were gone." He studied her carefully. "You've changed, girl. You've got the look of someone who's seen things they wish they hadn't."

He passed her the bun, and Lina bit into it at once, more to avoid answering than out of hunger. As she ate, a group of workers passed by – dark-skinned, work robes covered in soot.

"Deep Mining folks," Tekka said, catching her look. "Came over from Azurath, where they mined too. Work the deep levels, barely see the sun, high mortality rate. Say the Kingdom's gone mad and they'd rather be anywhere else." He added in a hushed tone, "Stick to their own. We've already got blocks full of 'em – living packed in and working shifts round the clock."

Lina nodded, suddenly seeing her homeland with new eyes. The class lines, the constant migration, the excess bureaucracy – she hadn't seen them before. Now they seemed fertile ground for prejudice, ready for racism to take root. Maybe it already had. The world was on the verge of war, and the signs were everywhere.

"You changed," Tekka said. "Used to be you only had eyes for engines and gear systems."

"Still do," Lina replied with a half-smile. "But I've found there are other systems worth attention, too."

She paid for her bun and walked back to the quarters, her mind a storm of new perspectives and old memories, struggling to reconcile who she had been with who she had become.

———

The Directorate Hall stood tall in the Government Quarter. Its perfect glass cube embodied the Technocracy's ideals – mathematical precision fused with practical utility. Lina had not been in awe of the structure, but now – maybe from being tired or nervous – she caught herself wondering: how do they keep the glass clear? Hire more immigrants for the risky job, or invent some ingenious contraption?

Lina tugged at the collar of her formal attire – a compromise between Technocracy propriety and her need for practical movement.

"Stop fidgeting," Kora murmured as they passed through security checkpoints. She wore a blend of tribal beads and markings with a modern academic jacket – a mix that looked not just fitting but commanding.

"I'm a mechanic, not a diplomat," Lina muttered back. "This is Kip's job."

"And yet here you are," Kora said calmly. "You're the best person for this job – they'll listen to you, not to a corsair or a tribal scientist."

Seven directorate members were already seated when they entered. One of them inclined his head in greeting to Kora as she approached. The central figure – a man with a neat white beard and calculating eyes – spoke first. "I am Chairman Ellsworth of the Scientific Directorate. You've been granted this audience at Director Varen's request. He mentioned… an academic connection with Elder Kora." His tone suggested the connection was unexpected.

"We've reviewed Pilot Ryven's report on the *Empirical Advance* attack. Our analysis points to the Scarlet Talon, though some technical details you noted about their equipment raise questions."

"Those details are why we're here," Lina said, stepping forward. "The Scarlet Talon has tech far beyond what they should – tech that came from beneath the Storm."

A ripple passed through the Directorate – a shuffle of seats, narrowed eyes – but no true shock. Lina pressed on, her tone clinical as she described her journey beneath the Storm. She outlined the surface world's progress: combustion engines, weapon systems, and the Scarlet Talon's unmistakable military ambitions.

"Their fuel efficiency is remarkable," she explained, pointing to the diagrams she'd prepared. "They don't need Rational Element to lift their planes. The Holy Sovereignty is stockpiling these resources for a major military campaign. From what I saw, they're waiting to attack until they've built up enough food and fuel for a long offensive."

As she spoke, she found herself translating complex ideas into the precise language the Technocracy valued. Yet she began to notice something odd. They asked detailed questions about specific technologies, showing little surprise at the existence of a surface civilization. It felt less like discovery and more like confirmation.

Lina paused, studying their expressions the way she'd study a malfunctioning compressor. "You already know about the surface world, don't you?" she said bluntly.

The chamber fell silent. Chairman Ellsworth exchanged glances with his colleagues before leaning forward slightly. "The Technocracy maintains research interests in many atmospheric domains," he said carefully. "We possess… limited intelligence on sub-Storm conditions, gathered over the past six months."

"Limited intelligence," Lina repeated flatly. "You've known and done *nothing*? Nothing about the weapons, the military buildup, the threat to every nation in Azoria?"

"Our information required extensive verification," said a director with a green sash. "The Technocracy's policy is caution. Hasty action based on incomplete data is illogical."

"Caution?" Lina's voice rose despite her effort to keep a clinical tone. "There won't be time for caution when the Scarlet Talon gets enough of this tech! With surface weapons, they'll be able to dominate any nation that stands against them."

"Their resource limitations create natural constraints on their expansion," said a director with a blue sash, his voice lacking urgency. "Our projections indicate—"

"Your projections don't account for what I've seen firsthand," Lina cut in. "They're already full steam ahead. The Holy Sovereignty is giving Scarlet Talon advanced warplanes, and the Talons are sending back food supplies. Once they've stockpiled enough, there won't be one war, but two. And it's a matter of weeks, not months or years!"

"We appreciate your firsthand account, Pilot," Chairman Ellsworth said patiently. "But policy requires multiple confirmations and thorough analysis before any action."

"How much more analysis do you need?" Lina shot back, frustration boiling over. "Or are you all too busy polishing your spectacles to see what's right in front of you?"

One director drew in a sharp breath. "Pilot Ryven—" another began, his tone sharp with disapproval.

"No," Lina cut him off, leaning forward, hands braced on the presentation table. "I've spent my life fixing machines. I know when something's about to break down completely. This isn't just another squabble between Drift Lords or a trade spat with the Concord. This is an existential threat." She looked each director in the eye. "You're supposed to be the smartest minds in Azoria. How can you not see what's coming? Are you just waiting for someone else to act first?"

The chamber fell silent. Kora placed a gentle but firm hand on Lina's arm, though her expression suggested no disapproval.

After a long moment, Chairman Ellsworth cleared his throat, his composure ruffled but intact. "Your passion is noted, Pilot Ryven. Your… directness, less so." He exchanged glances with the others. "The Mercantile Concord has recently made limited contact with a surface entity called the Harbor Commonwealth. Your information matches some preliminary intelligence but adds valuable technical details."

"Details? I'm telling you the *war* is about to start!" Lina said heatedly.

"The Technocracy's position must remain strategic," Ellsworth said firmly. "We cannot commit resources or act alone in potential conflicts. Any coalition requires broad support."

"If I may," Kora said, seeing that Lina was about to launch into more accusations. The Directorate turned to her, their expressions a mix of curiosity and irritation. "Honored Directors," she began, her serious tone making an impact. "I come before you not just as a tribal elder or fellow academic, but as a representative of the Windclaw Tribe and all tribes of the Heights." This caught their attention.

"The Windclaw Tribe formally acknowledges the threat posed by new technology and, more importantly, by the Scarlet Talon's plans," Kora continued. "I am authorized to inform you that the Windclaw Tribe, with provisional support from four other tribes, intends to form the foundation of a defense coalition. We will oppose these incursions with all available resources. Furthermore, I have been appointed permanent envoy to the Technocracy and Mercantile Concord to help create the coalition."

Lina stared at Kora in astonishment. She had mentioned none of this.

"The eagle riders of the Heights stand ready," Kora concluded. "We invite the Technocracy to join us as a founding member of this alliance."

The chamber erupted in whispers. The tribal eagle riders were legendary but rarely involved themselves in *lowlanders'* affairs – the idea of them starting a coalition was unprecedented.

Chairman Ellsworth raised a hand to restore order. "This… proposal requires serious consideration. A coalition is no small undertaking. We must also weigh the Mercantile Concord's position, given their established contact. The Directorate will deliberate and provide a formal response tomorrow. Until then, this session is adjourned."

As they were escorted from the chamber, Lina could barely contain her questions. Once they were alone in a small antechamber, she turned to Kora. "Permanent envoy? Allied tribes? Forming a coalition? Were you planning to mention any of this?"

Kora's expression was calm. "When we left, Chief Harrik was going to contact other tribes on this. The decision was confirmed via a trade ship delivering mail this morning. Timing is everything."

"But the tribes are actually forming an alliance? Asking the Technocracy to join?"

"We live in rough times. This isn't a simple conflict – all of Azoria could be at risk. The tribes understand that." She touched Lina's shoulder briefly. "You did well. Technical precision combined with real passion can sometimes break through bureaucratic armor."

Lina slumped against the wall. "I practically called the Scientific Directorate cowards. Kip would've had an aneurysm."

"Perhaps," Kora said with a smile. "But sometimes you have to throw a wrench in the gears to get the mechanic's attention. They fear acting alone, but they fear missing out more. Now they have to consider being left behind if the Concord acts first."

That evening in their quarters, Lina paced while Kora sat calmly reviewing notes. "They already knew," Lina said for the twelfth time. "All this urgent rush, and they've known for six months."

"They knew facts, not truths," Kora said. "There's a difference."

"What does that mean?"

"It means they had reports but lacked context. Data, but not understanding." Kora set down her notes. "The Technocracy excels at gathering information but often struggles to grasp its significance."

Lina dropped into a chair. "This is what Kip does, isn't it? Navigate all these political currents, figure out what people really mean, push them to act."

"Ah." Kora smiled. "I suspect he's navigating his own political currents, perhaps with more skill than he realizes." She studied Lina's face. "You've developed quite a bond with your companions."

Lina shrugged, uncomfortable. "We survived a lot together."

"Some connections are forged in fire," Kora said. "Those often prove the strongest."

Lina thought of another connection – to Kora's nephew – but decided not to push it.

————

The Hall had a different atmosphere the following morning – all the members seemed more formal and distant. Chairman Ellsworth began without preamble. "The Scientific Directorate has reviewed the information presented and reached a decision."

Lina stood straight, bracing herself.

"The Technocracy acknowledges the potential threat but will maintain its position of strategic neutrality. We expect cooperation and consultation with other major powers, especially the Mercantile Concord," Ellsworth said. "A unified response is preferable to acting alone. However, investigating advanced technologies falls within our scientific mandate." He turned his attention to Lina.

"Pilot Ryven, your credentials have been reinstated for a specific assignment. You are to assist the Mercantile Concord in its search for the remains of the *Empirical Advance* and examine any technology that can be salvaged from the wreckage."

Lina frowned. "You want me to look for the zeppelin? They haven't even found it yet?"

"The Concord believes they've identified the approximate area where it went down," said a director with a purple sash. "Your experience as a witness to the attack and your technical expertise make you qualified for this mission."

Lina glanced at Kora, who gave a nearly imperceptible nod.

"The Mercantile Concord is evaluating the situation," Ellsworth went on. "If, after their analysis, they agree on the threat level and are open to forming a coalition, the Technocracy will reconsider its position."

Lina understood. They wanted confirmation, safety in numbers, and deniability. It was cautious, self-interested, and a delaying tactic – but it was the only path forward offered. "I'll help find the wreckage and examine any tech we recover," she agreed. "When do I leave?"

"Official credentials will be provided tomorrow morning. Let us know if you need transportation," Ellsworth said.

"I'll leave in my own plane once I have the paperwork," Lina replied with a nod.

He turned to Kora. "Elder Kora, your credentials as tribal envoy are formally recognized. Quarters at the diplomatic residence have been prepared."

———

Within an hour, Lina was walking beside Kora through the Government Quarter. "This isn't what I expected," she admitted as they crossed a footbridge over one of the utility canals.

"Politics rarely follows the expected path," Kora said. "They fear commitment, but they also fear being unprepared."

Lina stopped at the bridge's highest point, looking out over the gleaming mechanical wonder of the Technocracy. "I don't know how to convince governments. I just know how to fix things that are broken."

"Perhaps that's exactly what's needed," Kora said quietly. "Someone who sees what's broken and knows how to repair it, rather than someone who simply accepts the brokenness."

Lina turned to face the elder. "And what about you?"

"I'll be staying here, working with nation representatives and defining tasks for the coalition. We need to spread the word and make sure the lesser nations know about us – and are willing to join."

"So you've got a big job here?"

"Some roles find us," Kora replied with a small smile. "Much like you didn't set out to become an ambassador between worlds, yet here you are."

They stood in silence, watching the water flow and the city busy itself around them. Life was turning stranger with each day, but Lina suddenly realized she was starting to enjoy changing the world for the better.

CHAPTER 30
The Messenger

Nora brushed dust from the panel, her fingers following faded symbols unlike any Federation script she had ever seen. Two days into their exploration of the facility, she was still no closer to understanding how to interact with the system. They had restored limited power by linking the blue conduits – but it was done on intuition, not understanding.

Her stomach growled, a reminder that morning rations had been meager. The dim blue glow from the power conduits cast everything in an eerie light that made her eyes ache after hours of squinting at the obscure markings.

"Any luck?" Toryn's voice echoed from the corridor. Despite his adaptation to the confined space, she could still see the tension in his shoulders. Over the past few days, she had noticed his unease being underground. His breathing quickened in narrower chambers, and at junctions he always paused – orienting himself, taking a steadying breath before moving on. For someone raised in the boundless expanse of the Heights, these cramped tunnels were a special kind of torment.

"Not exactly." Nora sighed, gesturing at the cryptic panels. "I can't make sense of any of these markings. There's no clear way to input commands or access information."

Toryn set aside his makeshift map – a scrap of Archive paper now filled with rough sketches of their surroundings. "The eastern corridor loops back to that big room with the blue floor lines. I think the whole complex is circular." He pulled a flask from his belt and offered it to her. "I found another of those small underground pools in the eastern section. The water tastes different from the main reservoir – sweeter, somehow."

Nora accepted the container gratefully and took a careful sip. The cool liquid eased her parched throat. "Thank you. Did you find anything else?"

"Just more rooms with strange machines," Toryn said, running a hand through his hair. "And I'm getting better at sensing which passages will lead to dead ends. The air moves differently."

Despite the circumstances, Nora smiled at that. Toryn's relationship with air continued to impress her. She turned back to the console. "I've been studying these diagrams I found," she said, spreading several yellowed papers across the console surface. "They show what looks like a floating landmass – a single continent – descending to an ocean surface. I think this terminal was meant to track that process."

"That matches what we read in the diary," Toryn said, coming to stand beside her. He studied the diagrams with a keen eye, though Nora suspected they might even be upside-down and he wouldn't know the difference. "The plan was for the entire continent to descend. But how would it work now, split into islets?"

Nora shrugged. "If I could just figure out how to communicate with whatever's running this place…"

Toryn tilted his head. "You've been trying for days. Maybe it's not meant to be accessed anymore. The diary said the Madrid station was shutting down when the last scientist died."

"That's just it – it shouldn't be running at all, but it is." Nora gestured at the faint blue illumination threading through conduits in the walls. "I think some failsafe is keeping the minimum systems online, and it came to life when we arrived." She stood and stretched, feeling the ache in her back from hours hunched over ancient documents. "Let's try the central core again. There's a terminal there I haven't fully examined."

The core chamber was the largest they'd found – a circular room dominated by a central pillar pulsing with the same blue energy that ran through the facility. Surrounding it were workstations arranged in concentric circles, most dark and unresponsive. Nora stepped up to what appeared to be the primary console. Her fingers traced the smooth surface, probing for any hidden response to her touch.

"I've tried speaking to it, touching different panels, even trying combinations of press patterns," she said, her voice echoing slightly in the vast space. "Nothing seems to–"

She stopped abruptly as one panel flickered beneath her palm, showing a sequence of unfamiliar symbols before going dark again. "Did you see that?" she asked, excitement creeping into her voice.

Toryn nodded and moved closer. "Try again."

Nora pressed her palm to the same spot, focusing all her attention on the panel. It flickered again, longer this time, showing what might have been a diagnostic display before fading.

She tried once more, placing both hands on the console and leaning in, her weight against the ancient surface. The panel flickered to life, stabilizing into a schematic of six structures linked by faint energy lines. "See those nodes? They could be the seedheart islets. Three are already dim."

Before Nora could respond, the system shut down again, the panel going dark with a soft whine that echoed in the chamber. Their breathing suddenly sounded loud in the silence that followed.

"Damn it!" she whispered, frustration sharp in her voice. She struck the console with her fist, the impact echoing through the room. "We were *so* close."

"The whole place feels like it's barely holding together," Toryn said.

Nora nodded, suddenly aware of how exhausted she was. Her legs dragged like lead, her eyes stung from strain, and the constant gnaw of hunger made it hard to think. "Maybe we should check one more chamber before we rest."

Toryn followed her across the corridor to a door that had remained closed until now. They pried it open, as they had done several times before. The room was bare, save for a peculiar device set on a raised platform – a human-sized cradle, or perhaps a capsule, though it lacked any canopy. A faint blue glow emanated from within, suggesting it was still online.

"I recognize this," Nora said, her voice dropping to a near whisper as she circled the platform. "The diary mentioned it – the consciousness transfer device. It was designed to upload a human mind into the quantum network to oversee the Project Génesis."

"Why would anyone want to do that?" Toryn asked, eyeing the apparatus with open wariness.

"It would allow a human consciousness to watch over the systems for thousands of years. No machine could do the same." She kept examining it. "Dr. García was supposed to enter it, but he…" She trailed off, remembering the diary's grim account.

"And the last scientist couldn't do it either."

Nora nodded. "They never completed the final transfer protocols and let the algorithmic intelligence take over instead."

Toryn paced the platform again, his expression caught between fascination and unease. "Should we try using it to speak with the system?"

"Absolutely not," Nora said firmly. "This goes beyond dangerous. It wasn't designed for a temporary connection – it was meant to transfer consciousness permanently. Whoever enters will leave their body behind and exist solely within the system. Using it would be…" She shuddered. "Let's head back."

They returned to the small room they'd converted into a living space. The blue light was dimmer here, casting most of the room in shadow. Blankets from the Runners' cache served as makeshift beds, while their dwindling supplies were stacked neatly against one wall. They had never dared to take anything from the living quarters, since it was more like a crypt, with skeletal remains on almost every berth.

Nora sank onto her bedding with a sigh, every muscle in her body protesting the movement. She watched as Toryn carefully added new details to his map, noting the day's discoveries with precise care. The contrast between his tribal upbringing and his methodical mind had surprised her at first, but she had come to rely on it.

———

Toryn woke in the morning by his internal clock. It was hard to tell the time of day, even on the surface, but here all he had were his habits and sense of time. Nora had joked that if that sense ever failed, they'd be counting days by her periods. The remark had made Toryn blush deeply, while Nora seemed completely unbothered.

"We'll need to go to the surface soon," Toryn said, measuring the remaining meat and sheets of seaweed for breakfast. "Our supplies won't last much longer." He didn't add what was obvious to both of them – that they were already beginning to weaken from the restricted diet.

"I just wish–" Nora began, but stopped when Toryn went completely still. "Toryn?"

The air had changed. He felt it before he saw anything – a shift in the surroundings, like the charged stillness before a storm. The blue glow from the wall conduits intensified, pooling in the center of the room like water finding its level.

Then he saw it.

An eagle took shape gradually, coalescing from the blue light – translucent but unmistakable. It was human-sized, smaller than a true eagle, its form glowing with the same blue energy that pulsed through the facility's conduits.

"What is it?" he heard Nora ask distantly, but his attention was fixed on the vision.

The eagle regarded him, and when it spoke, the words came in perfect High Tongue – the language of the Heights.

"*Greetings, child of the wind,*" it said. "*I have watched over you all your life; you are one of those who serve the Plan. But only here can I speak to you through a Messenger.*"

"There's a blue eagle," Toryn told Nora, his voice barely above a whisper. "It's speaking to me in High Tongue."

Nora stared at the empty space where Toryn was looking, her hand moving unconsciously to her knife. "I don't see anything."

"It greeted me as a child of the wind," Toryn continued, not taking his eyes off the apparition. "It says it awakened to speak with one who serves the Plan. It claims it's been watching me my whole life." The realization hit him suddenly. "The blue-black eagle who rescued me – who guided me to Veil Islet – that wasn't a coincidence. It was part of this... this thing's plan."

"It must be projecting directly into your mind," Nora whispered, clearly wrestling with the implications. "Maybe because you're from the Heights, or because you've had more exposure to heartstone."

The eagle inclined its head but gave no sign it had heard Nora.

"You are the spirit that dwells in the heartstone," Toryn said, choosing words that fit his tribal understanding.

The eagle inclined its head. "*I am the watcher of the seedpods. The watcher of the Plan. You may call me the Keeper.*"

"It calls itself the Keeper," Toryn told Nora, who was watching him intently. "Says it's the watcher of what it calls seedpods – a word from the diary; it should mean seedhearts."

"Ask it about the original restoration plan for Earth," Nora said, her voice steady.

"*The Plan proceeds as designed,*" the Messenger said, spreading its wings slightly. "*Two thousand seasons have passed. Surface healing is complete. The barrier must end. The seedpods must return to the surface. Life will begin anew.*"

Toryn translated for Nora, whose expression grew increasingly alarmed.

"Ask it about the Storm – the barrier," she urged. "How does it function? Where does its energy come from?"

The Messenger answered before Toryn even finished the question aloud. *"The barrier draws power from everything that enters it. Soon, it will feed on the heartstone matrix before dissipating."*

Toryn relayed the translation. "It says the shield – the Storm – is powered by heartstone energy. It's meant to consume all heartstone power and then fade away."

"So the Storm will drain all azurium?" Nora murmured. "It needs to understand about the fragmentation," she said urgently. "Tell it the islands are separate now, not a single landmass."

Toryn began to translate, but the Messenger responded directly to her implied meaning, still speaking in High Tongue. *"Division of the landmass is not a concern,"* it said with unsettling calm. *"The seedpods will return. The barrier will dissolve. All will descend when the time comes."*

The blood drained from Toryn's face as he translated the entity's indifference.

"The Plan is already in motion," the Messenger went on, its voice neither cruel nor kind, simply matter-of-fact. *"Three seedpods have already returned. The barrier intensifies. Everything goes as intended."*

"Veil Islet," Toryn breathed, his mouth suddenly dry. "That was one of them."

"Yes," the vision confirmed. *"Wings of the Plan helped you get there. And now you must help advance the Plan."*

Toryn translated again, his voice tight with alarm. "It says… when a seedheart island falls, the Storm intensifies. It led me to Veil Islet to bring it down. That was its Plan."

Nora stood, even though she couldn't see what Toryn was experiencing. "But the landmass fractured! It's not one continent anymore. If it drains the energy irregularly from separate islands, they'll fall!"

"The sky-earth is broken!" Toryn said, turning back to the Messenger, his voice rising. Hunger and frustration made his words sharper than he intended. "It shattered into many pieces when it was lifted! The land would crumble, not descend. Whole nations could be destroyed!"

The eagle tilted its head, regarding him with those unnervingly blue eyes. Its form flickered slightly, a momentary distortion that revealed its unnatural nature. "*Breaking of the sky-earth changes nothing. The heartstone must be consumed. The Plan continues as it must.*"

"It doesn't understand… or it can't," Toryn told Nora as he translated. "It says the breaking changes nothing. Its plan assumes a single landmass descending slowly as the energy drains evenly. Now, they will just fall one by one."

"It sees the destruction of your homes as just energy transfer," Nora said. "All the people there are just figures in its equation."

Toryn turned back to the Messenger. "But countless people will die!"

"*The presence of sky-dwellers was not part of the Plan,*" the Messenger replied. "*That knowledge changes nothing. The seedpods must return.*"

"How do the seedhearts come down?"

The Messenger's form seemed to grow more defined, its blue glow intensifying. *"I cannot force the seedpods to return. I can only guide those who will help them descend."*

"Guide who?" Toryn asked, unease growing in his stomach.

The eagle's head tilted in what might have been acknowledgment. *"Helpers. Those who touch the heartstone can hear the Keeper. They are drawn to release the seedpods at any cost."*

Toryn thought of his elder Jormund's hands stained blue from handling raw heartstone. It hadn't been madness – it had been influence from this... thing. He relayed this revelation to Nora.

"But I haven't! How can you talk to me then?" he asked the Messenger.

"You dreamed of the seedpod island many seasons before your journey. I watched you every time you touched the heartstone – in your tools, pendant, goggles."

"And the eagles?" he asked, remembering his own rescue. "The blue-black eagles are yours too?"

"They are the tools of the Plan. They hear the Keeper," it confirmed.

"Those people don't understand what they're doing," Toryn said, referring to the humans under its influence. "They think they're serving their own interests, not bringing about the fall of all the islands!"

"Understanding is not required," the eagle said, unmoved. *"The Plan proceeds regardless of individual comprehension."*

The Messenger's form began to fade, its blue light dimming. *"I will return when you are ready to assist with completion."*

"Wait!" Toryn called, but the eagle was already dissolving, its glowing eyes the last to vanish as it spoke one final time. *"The Plan cannot be altered. The seedpods will go down. The barrier will end."*

Then it was gone, leaving only the steady blue glow of the facility's power conduits. Toryn stood frozen for several moments, staring at the empty space where the Messenger had been. Then he turned to Nora, who was watching him intently, unaware of what had just transpired.

"This Keeper is broken, isn't it?" Toryn said quietly. "Not evil, just... unable to understand that the world has changed."

"Yes," Nora agreed. "It's executing a two-thousand-year-old program without the ability to reassess current conditions. It has evolved somehow, becoming a real artificial intelligence – and that makes it incredibly dangerous."

"We can't reason with it," Toryn said at last. "It only understands its original purpose."

"But we can try changing its programming," Nora added, rubbing her temples. "I wish I knew how."

Toryn felt a chill as he recalled something else the Messenger had mentioned. "It said it was influencing people – those who had prolonged exposure to heartstone – making them want to bring down the seedhearts. That's why my elder Jormund was acting erratically. And that's how it led me here," he added solemnly.

"Hey, you don't have blue stains on your hands yet! Have you been working with heartstone and hearing voices before?" Nora asked, attempting a smile despite her obvious concern. "You're not its servant. You're stronger than this."

They sat in silence, the knowledge pressing down on him as heavily as the miles of earth above.

"We have to warn everyone," Toryn said, standing abruptly. "At least the Archivists. About this entity – the Storm that devoured energy, dragging islands into uncontrollable collapse. Of people being influenced without knowing it."

Nora nodded, but as Toryn rose, a flicker of blue caught the edge of his vision.

It was still there. Waiting. Not going anywhere.

CHAPTER 31
Political Currents

Morning light filtered through the stained glass of the Transport Guild office, casting blue and gold patterns across Guild Master Dorovan's desk. It might have been beautiful if Lina weren't so focused on the narrow band of skin between his long leather gloves and sleeve cuffs. Faint blue stains marked his fingers – stains he seemed oblivious to as he shuffled papers with exaggerated importance.

The office smelled of beeswax and expensive ink, the sort of place where decisions affecting thousands were made by people who had never gotten their hands dirty. The kind of place that made Lina's skin crawl.

She had met Kip that morning after a night flight from Caligan. He had arranged adjoining rooms at the Cloudrest Hotel, a faded establishment that had once catered to nobility but now served merchants. He had already been there a day, "re-establishing contacts," as he put it. A faint smell of spirits and a face a bit paler than usual suggested the re-establishment had gone well.

Now they were in the guild office, trying to overcome another bureaucratic obstacle. This one had blue stains on his arms, which might mean the same obsession with seedhearts as Jormund and Marek – or it might mean nothing.

"As I already explained," Dorovan said without looking up, "the investigation into the *Empirical Advance* incident is underway. Our investigators are capable, and we won't need external assistance. Since you claim you were part of the escort for this flight, we may have additional questions for you." The implication was clear – they could easily choose to spend time interrogating Lina further, but not the other way around.

"Master Dorovan," Kip said evenly, "the Technocracy has asked Pilot Ryven to look into the incident for mutual benefit. Since she has firsthand experience with a Scarlet Talon attack, wouldn't it be smart to work together?"

Dorovan finally looked up, his mouth a thin line of displeasure beneath his neatly groomed mustache. "The Mercantile Concord appreciates the Technocracy's... concern. However, matters of internal security must follow proper protocols." His eyes flicked to his aide. "Complete your investigation if you must, but do not interfere with ours."

As they were guided out, Lina caught the stare of one of Dorovan's aides in a blue suit and a wide-brimmed hat pulled low over his brow. His eyes stayed on them, unblinking.

"Well," she muttered once they were outside the ornate building, "that went exactly as terribly as I expected."

"For sure. And now we're being followed," Kip said casually, as if commenting on the weather. "Two of them – one in blue at your four o'clock, another in the market crowd straight ahead."

Lina nodded without turning. "I spotted the blue one. He was in Dorovan's office too." She adjusted her goggles. "So what's the plan, Lordling? Play along or lose them?"

"Both," Kip said with a slight smile. "Let's give them something to report while learning nothing useful. We head to the shipyards."

————

The shipyard sprawled along one edge of Market Nexus – a chaos of wooden scaffolding, rope systems, and half-assembled zeppelin frames. Lina felt instantly more at home here than in the Guild offices. The air was thick with the familiar scents of machine oil, treated canvas, and the distinctive sweet-spicy odor of the zeppelin gas mixture.

The shadows between the massive timber frames offered good cover for watchers. Lina spotted their blue-suited tail lingering by a pile of hull plating, pretending to read a manifest clipboard. They spent time leading their tails through the upper levels, making conspicuous inquiries about zeppelin schedules and corsair attacks. Unsurprisingly, they learned nothing useful.

"It seems like a good time to have a word with shipbuilders," Lina said, pointing to the workshops once they were clear of their shadows, if only temporarily.

"You really think they'll talk? After how the Guild treated us, I'm sure word's already out to keep their mouths shut," Kip said, scanning the workers.

"Guild officials live in offices. These people live in the real world," Lina replied, walking toward a cluster of engineers arguing over blueprints. "Besides, I speak their language."

She was right. At first, the foremen eyed them with suspicion, their faces lined with old worries. But their expressions changed when Lina pointed out a flaw in the steam valve positioning they were debating. Within twenty minutes, she was bent over technical diagrams, deep in discussion about hull reinforcement techniques. Kip kept watch for shipyard security or any returning tails.

"The *Empirical Advance*?" repeated an older engineer, scratching his beard. "Aye, that was an unusual project. Built several years ago, but six months back it went for a rebuild with specs I had never seen before."

"Unusual how?" Lina asked casually.

"Mostly the changes for the engine compartment. They wanted the engine and the steam pipes to be swappable–" He stopped abruptly, glancing around, his eyes suddenly wary.

"What about it?" Lina prompted.

"Special clearance required," he muttered, his voice dropping to barely above the background clatter of tools. "Upper-level engineers only. Didn't make sense for a cargo ship. Never seen anything like–" He broke off, eyes widening past her shoulder. "Security's coming. You two better go."

Lina nodded, and they moved quickly toward a side exit between stacks of timber. They slipped through a narrow gap between warehouses, the air thick with sawdust and oil.

"Swappable engine, restricted access... this gets more suspicious," Kip said as they navigated the maze of storage sheds and repair shops. "We need the official records. We need to visit the Merchant Guild archives. Maybe even bribe our way in."

———

The Merchant Guild archives filled three floors of a white-stone building with high, arched windows and decorative columns. Inside, it was cool and silent – the kind of silence that cost money to maintain. Lina felt instantly out of place among polished floors and clerks in pressed uniforms. Kip, however, moved through the space like he'd done it a hundred times, all traces of his corsair disguise gone.

"Lord Haversmith sent me," he told the clerk, using a name Lina had never heard before. "For the Easterly Trade assessment. We'll need the B-17 forms for regional cargo verification, subsection 12-C on vessel transfer documentation. And the certified Registry of Authorized Carriers from the last fiscal quarter."

The clerk blinked rapidly, clearly unsettled by the barrage of official-sounding terms. Whatever Kip was saying, it worked. They were shown into a private research room, where he requested documents with the confidence of someone who knew exactly what he wanted.

"How do you know all this bureaucratic nonsense?" Lina whispered as the clerk left, the door closing with a soft click that lingered in the hushed chamber.

"Some of us had actual educations," Kip said with a wry smile as he organized the stacks of ledgers and scrolls.

The registries showed that the *Empirical Advance* had changed owners twice six months ago, passing through shell companies. Within an hour, they found the final beneficiary – a senior Transport Guild official, meaning the Guild was the ship's sole owner.

But something else caught Kip's eye – a notation beside the log of the loss.

"An investigator was assigned to the case: Investigator Mathis." He pulled another ledger. "But he was removed after three days. Replaced by Investigator Forben due to Mathis's retirement."

"Convenient," Lina murmured. "Any idea where to find this Mathis?"

"It's easy to check."

Kip called over a clerk and requested employment and retirement records. He listed a few random Guild members, including Mathis. When the documents arrived, he skimmed the pages. "There's an address here. Let's pay this happy retiree a visit."

As they left the archives, afternoon shadows stretched across the plaza. Lina spotted a familiar figure on the far side – the same man in blue who had followed them from Dorovan's office. He wasn't even trying to be subtle now, leaning against a colonnade and openly watching them.

"They're still watching us," she said quietly. "Act like we're headed to the Port Authority, then lose them in the market."

———

Investigator Mathis had a modest apartment in a middle-tier district – nice enough to keep the lowlifes out, not nice enough to attract attention. The building's façade was weathered but maintained, with potted plants on a small balcony. A graying man with a neat mustache and heavy brows opened the door just a crack, the security chain still fastened. His eyes were sharp despite his stooped posture.

"Investigator Mathis?" Kip asked politely.

"Not anymore," the man replied. "Who's asking?"

"We're looking into the *Empirical Advance* incident," Lina said. "We understand you were working on it."

"Let's just say we're interested in the same people who paid you to stop asking questions," Kip added.

The door snapped shut.

Lina glanced at Kip, then called through, "I'm an escort pilot, shot down during the attack."

A pause. "Pilot Ryven, then," Mathis said. "What was the name of your female wing leader from Azurath, flying the red-winged craft?"

"Vera," Lina said. "But she was from the Concord. And the craft had blue wings. She died. We buried her on a speck of land – no name on the grave."

The chain rattled, and Mathis opened the door wider. "I'm sorry for your loss." He stepped aside to let them in and bolted it behind them.

He went to a cabinet, brought out a bottle and three small glasses. "I'm afraid for my life," he said quietly. "The retirement came out of nowhere: full pension, housing stipend, medical benefits. All I had to do was drop the *Empirical Advance* investigation and forget the name entirely."

"But you didn't forget," Lina said.

"Twenty-five years with the Bureau of Trade Investigation," Mathis said. "Never took a bribe, never looked the other way – until two months ago." He poured three measures of amber liquid and handed each of them a glass before settling into his chair.

"You know what bothers an investigator most?" he went on. "Irregularities. Little things that don't add up. The *Empirical Advance* was full of them."

"What kind of irregularities?" Kip asked.

Mathis's eyes narrowed. "And who are you? Technocracy?"

"Lina is the official appointee from Technocracy for this incident," Kip said. "I'm with her."

"We want to know what happened and why," Lina added.

"The *Empirical Advance* was floating through a sector marked unsafe for commercial traffic. When pressed, the captain maintained they had filed the proper safety exemptions. They had – but the exemptions were approved by Guild Master Dorovan personally, bypassing normal channels."

He took another sip. "Initially, they refused an escort. Tried to play the greedy-owner card. Then trade inspectors flagged the manifests – thirty-seven tons of preserved meats, dried fruits, grains, and medical supplies. There's no way such cargo goes unprotected, even when insured. When confronted, they reluctantly accepted the escort arrangement."

"Food supplies," Kip murmured. "Massive quantities."

"Indeed. And after the attack, Dorovan's office immediately wrote off the entire shipment as lost. No salvage attempts, no recovery operations. Insurance covered it, and nobody dared ask a question." Mathis's fingers drummed against his glass.

"And there was another survivor: engineer Jenks. The man managed to flee in one of the escape planes. He was badly shaken. They brought him in for debriefing, but I wasn't allowed to interview him directly. Dorovan's people handled it. When I requested the transcript, I was told it was being processed. The next day, I was called into the director's office and offered my generous retirement package." His smile was bitter. "Effective immediately."

He leaned forward. "Listen carefully. I kept my mouth shut for a good pension, but that doesn't mean I approve. Whatever you're looking for, it's dangerous. People who ask too many questions about the *Empirical Advance* tend to find themselves suddenly wealthy and silent – or just silent."

"Any idea where we might find this Jenks?" Kip asked.

Mathis hesitated. "Last I heard, he was holed up somewhere in the lower districts, drinking himself to death on his own sudden windfall." He drained his glass. "If you're smart, you'll walk away from this. Some questions aren't worth the answers."

———

On the far side of the island, Market Nexus revealed itself as an entirely different city. The gleaming brass and polished stone of the center gave way to weathered wood, rusted supports, and the damp smell of laundry strung overhead. Buildings rose in haphazard tiers, their add-ons looking barely stable. Water channels doubled as transport lanes and open sewers. Oil lamps cast weak pools of light, leaving more shadow than glow.

A fog had rolled in from the cloud banks below, cutting what little light the lamps gave. The water channels smelled of rot, as did the boats sitting low in the foul water. Moisture clung to pipes and railings, dripping into the black water below. The fog itself felt half piss, soaking clothes and shoes with its reek.

"Reminds me of home," Lina muttered, navigating a narrow walkway slick with something she preferred not to identify. "Except there are fewer machines and more desperation."

They ducked into a tavern with a crooked sign swinging over the door, The Rusted Valve barely legible under a layer of grime. The bartender, arms like cable winches and scars across her knuckles, watched them approach. A ragged gear tattoo ringed her wrist – the mark of a workshop hand fallen from grace.

"Two of whatever won't put us under," Kip said, sliding coins across the sticky bar top.

She poured an amber shot from an unlabeled bottle. "You're not local." The words landed like an accusation, not a question.

"Just passing through," Kip replied. "Looking for an old friend. Name's Jenks. Heard he might need help."

The bartender's expression didn't change, but something flickered in her eyes. Her gaze darted briefly to a man sitting alone in the corner before returning to them. "Don't know any Jenks."

"That's odd," Lina said, leaning in. "Word is he worked on the *Empirical Advance*. Engineering staff."

"Lot of engineering staff in Market Nexus," the woman replied flatly. "Drink up and move on." She turned to serve another customer, her tone making it clear the conversation was over.

They lingered, catching whispers and half-truths, but the search for the zeppelin's survivor led nowhere. A few contacts dangled stories for coin, none with substance. Lina realized the misdirection wasn't Dorovan's doing, but a quiet solidarity among the lower-tier workers – protecting one of their own.

Evening deepened; the slums were cast into near darkness, relieved only by scattered oil lamps. From a shadowed doorway, they heard a whisper.

"You after the zepp' man, Jenks?" The voice belonged to a kid no more than ten, thin-faced and wary, with eyes older than his years. "Five coppers, I'll show ya where he's holed up."

Kip produced the coins without haggling. The kid led them through a labyrinth of buildings where the walls seemed to lean in, listening. They stopped before a rusted metal door, half-hidden behind empty crates.

"He's in there. Third floor. Been hidin' for days," the kid said, slipping away before they could ask more.

Inside, huddled on a makeshift bed, they found Jenks. The junior engineer from the *Empirical Advance* was gaunt, looking as if he'd been drunk for weeks, his hands trembling and eyes darting nervously between them and the door. He clutched a half-empty bottle, the sharp tang of cheap spirits filling the small space. A single oil lamp cast grotesque shadows on the wall.

"We're not here to hurt you," Lina said. "We just need to ask about the attack on the *Empirical Advance*."

Jenks flinched, pulling the bottle closer. "Go away. Told the cops everything already. Got me nothin' but trouble."

"We're not with the Guild," Kip said calmly.

Lina crouched, keeping her voice steady. "I was one of the escort pilots that day. Flying a blue and silver interceptor – the *Swift Mistral*. Maybe you saw us?"

Jenks squinted, struggling to focus. "*Swift Mistral*... yeah. Saw you peel off. Fast ship." He took a long pull from the bottle, wiping his mouth with the back of his hand. Recognition dimmed the fear in his eyes, leaving a bitter sort of resignation. "Doesn't matter. We're all dead anyway."

"Not yet," Lina said. "Tell us what happened. How did you get out?"

"Luck," Jenks croaked, voice thick with drink and anger. "Pure stupid luck. I was on starboard shift, checkin' the exhaust. Close to the emergency craft when the shooting started."

He took another gulp. "That ship was massive – heavier than anything I'd worked on. Crates stacked with food: dried meat, preserved goods. She carried it all without strain, that's how big she was."

"What happened after the escort was attacked?" Kip pressed.

"We rushed full steam and ran. Lost 'em for a while." Jenks wiped his mouth. "Then they came back, 'bout thirty minutes later. Started hitting the balloon. Not critical spots – just enough to force us down. Captain tried to outrun 'em, but they were faster."

"So they weren't trying to destroy the ship?" Lina asked. "Just disable it?"

Jenks nodded unsteadily. "I got scared – real scared. Balloon hissing, ship tilting. I grabbed an evac plane and bailed. Didn't even think, just launched and dove as fast as I could. Figured they wouldn't waste time on something so small with the big prize right there."

"You didn't see where the zeppelin crashed?" Lina prompted.

"Didn't crash right away. Was goin' down slow when I last saw it – looked like it was heading for an island." He shook his head, rubbing his temples. "Flew blind after that. Stayed low, then climbed when I thought it was safe. Steam lasted barely two hours. Ditched the evac plane near the outer drifts."

His face twisted with bitterness. "Made it back here. Thought I was doin' right, reportin'. Thought they'd wanna know."

He gave a harsh laugh. "Guild dogs dragged me in, locked me in some back room for days. Questioned me like I was guilty. Accused me." Said I 'knew too much.' Forced me to sign papers." His voice dropped. "Told me to keep my mouth shut. Said they'd know if I talked."

Kip paused, then asked carefully, "While you were flying away… did you see an island? Forested, lots of pines. About two miles long. Shaped like a shoe?"

Lina held her breath.

Jenks frowned, fighting to line up the memory. "Maybe. Hell, I dunno. Think so. Green – real green. Saw it maybe an hour after the shootin' started. Didn't dare ease off. Why?"

"Just confirming," Kip said smoothly, steering the conversation back to calm ground. He placed a few coins near the bed. "Get yourself something to eat."

Jenks stared at the coins. "Won't change a damn thing," he muttered.

They pulled the door shut and clanged down the slick metal stairs. The air pressed in – rust, damp, the reek of old cooking oil. Water dripped from the overhead pipes, echoing in the confined space. Dim oil lamps threw flickering shadows. Four flights down, the sounds of the upper levels were gone.

"A sector," Lina whispered, excitement in her voice. "If we calculate his speed and heading... he saw our island!"

FWOOSH-CRACK!

A gunshot cracked above. Kip spun, bolting up the stairs with Lina on his heels. He threw the door open.

Jenks lay sprawled across the sacks, a smoking hole in his chest. The sharp tang of burnt propellant filled the room.

Kip rushed into the tiny kitchen. "There's a back door!"

Lina caught a glimpse of a fleeing shadow – the unmistakable blue suit of the man who'd been tailing them.

"Damn it!" Kip started after him, but the figure vanished into the warren of alleys and passages.

Lina stared into the darkness. "He was terrified. Harmless. Drunk. They still killed him."

"Loose ends," Kip said grimly, rejoining her. "The Guild's making sure no one contradicts their story – and they know we talked to him." He pulled her away. "Let's go. *Now*. Before they pin his death on us or decide we're loose ends too."

They threaded the back alleys, skirting the wider streets where Dorovan's eyes might be waiting. Rain thickened, pooling in the cramped channels until they gleamed like oil. At last, the hotel rose before them, and they climbed the service stair – its rusted frame groaning beneath their weight.

———

Kip stopped abruptly at the threshold of his room, hand moving to where a weapon would be if he carried one. The door was slightly ajar, a sliver of darkness showing through the gap.

"Someone has been here," he whispered.

Lina shouldered him aside and drove the door open with a kick. The room had been methodically wrecked. The mattress was slashed, stuffing strewn across the floor. Drawers hung open, their contents dumped and rifled through. The walls bore fresh marks where someone had searched for hidden compartments.

"Thorough," Lina muttered, stepping over the mess. "Professional."

Her own room was in the same state – possessions scattered, tools dumped from their case and inspected.

Kip gathered what was left of his things. "They're sending a message."

"They're looking for something," Lina said, salvaging her toolkit. "Flight plan, maybe?"

"Or making sure we don't have other evidence." Kip checked the pockets of his discarded coat. "We can't stay here."

They slipped out as quietly as they'd entered, steering clear of the front desk. The night had grown colder, the rain sharpening into a fine, biting mist that clung to their skin.

"I know a place," Kip said. "Old contact. Owes me a favor."

An hour later, they were holed up in a cramped attic above a print shop in the commercial district. The air smelled of ink and paper, but it was dry – and, more importantly, anonymous. The printer, a gray-haired woman with ink-stained hands, asked no questions, brought them blankets, and left them alone.

————

The next morning, they took Lina's craft from the hangar by the airfield, paying the dockmaster extra to leave their departure off the records. Within the hour, they were airborne, climbing fast under the cover of pre-dawn fog.

"Let's calculate Jenks's likely flight path," Kip said once they reached cruising altitude, scanning the cloudscape below. "Assume standard evac craft speed; factor in probable wind drift."

Lina kept the plane steady, her excitement hardening into cold determination. Jenks was dead because of what they were after. Kip used the rough location of the *Empirical Advance* attack as a starting point, plotting a search corridor from Jenks's account of flying for an hour before spotting the "shoe" island.

Hours passed. The sky dimmed as they passed into heavier clouds. Below, a familiar shape emerged – an island two miles long, forested and worn into the shape of a boot. Lina felt a pang as they flew over it: the canopy where she'd tangled in her parachute, where they'd found Vera's body, where the wreckage of the *Swift Mistral* still lay hidden. She instinctively adjusted the course. Kip glanced at her but said nothing.

They continued into the less-traveled reaches. Another hour passed.

Kip pointed. "There. Eleven o'clock low."

Lina banked the scout craft. Below lay another island of similar size, its clearing littered with the unmistakable wreckage of a giant airship and the twisted remains of its frame.

"Here you are," Lina breathed, dropping altitude. She found a relatively clear patch and set the scout craft down gently.

They moved quickly through the still forest. What they found was not the catastrophic wreck they had feared. The *Empirical Advance* had managed a controlled landing – its vast framework mostly intact, though listing heavily against a stand of massive trees.

The cargo holds were empty. Thoroughly empty – no crates, no crushed barrels.

"They unloaded everything," Kip said, studying the loading doors. "Look at the trampled ground."

Lina circled the massive vessel. "Engine room's at the stern. Let's check it."

Unlike the rest of the ship, the engine compartment was a ruin – torn metal, shattered components, blackened walls. Lina crouched, eyes narrowing.

"This wasn't from the attack," she said. "Explosive charges, set from inside. After landing." She traced the blast patterns. "Someone wanted to erase evidence."

Kip picked up a twisted shard of metal. "Why blow an engine? You could still salvage it."

Lina nodded, running a gloved hand over a fractured engine block. "This wasn't standard steam tech. Look at these injection systems and fuel lines – combustion technology. Surface tech. Everything else is fake: steam pipes, tank, valves, recombinator. None of it's connected to a working system."

She stood, scanning the wreck with new understanding. "The Guild was running tests – seeing if they could integrate surface technology into Concord vessels. Then they covered their tracks."

"And something else," Kip called from the main cabin. "No bodies. Not one. For a ship this size, there should've been dozens of crew." He pointed at the deck. "Not even a drop of blood. No way wild animals cleared it completely."

"They took them," Lina whispered. "As prisoners, or–"

"Or they didn't want anyone telling what really happened," Kip finished grimly.

As they stepped out of the wreckage, a faint whine of high-performance engines – nothing like steam – cut through the stillness.

"Company," Lina snapped, sprinting for their plane.

Three aircraft burst through the cloud cover above, sleek and painted in the crimson of the Scarlet Talon. They dove instantly.

"Marek's people!" Kip yelled, dropping into the co-pilot seat. "Someone must've tipped them off!"

Lina shoved the throttle forward. The scout craft leapt skyward just as shots chewed the ground where it had sat. The Talon craft were faster, more agile, their crimson hulls gleaming with predatory intent.

"They're boxing us in!" Kip warned.

"Not yet," Lina gritted out, banking hard into a dense cloud bank. She flew by instinct and instruments, twisting through drifting vapor, using the cover just as Marek's pilots had during the *Empirical Advance* attack. Unpredictable climbs and dives pushed their modified steam engine to the limit. One Talon overshot; another banked too hard and vanished into the mist.

She seized the opening, diving toward a lower cloud layer, then leveling out just above the tendrils, skimming the hidden peaks of unseen drifts. Behind them, the last Talon pilot hesitated – too risky to follow without clear sightlines.

Lina held course, engine screaming, until the pursuing roar finally faded. Only then did she ease back on the throttle, letting the scout craft settle into a sustainable cruise.

"Think we lost them?" Kip asked, wiping sweat from his brow.

"For now," Lina said, knuckles white on the controls. "But they know we found the wreck. They know what we know."

The conspiracy was bigger than they'd imagined. Not just a corsair raid, but a coordinated operation involving food supplies, surface technology, and a cover-up reaching the top of the Mercantile Concord – all tied to Guild Master Dorovan.

They had proof, but had barely survived. Now they were marked. The race against the Scarlet Talon and its hidden allies had entered a far more dangerous phase.

CHAPTER 32
Coalition and War

"As you can see from my report," Commander Vrell concluded, "we arrived at the coordinates Pilot Ryven provided. Someone had already attempted to destroy the wreckage. Signs of new explosions and fresh fire damage were evident throughout the site."

Lina stood rigid before the Mercantile Concord Council, acutely aware of Kip's absence. The Guild Masters had denied his request to attend; a corsair, noble heritage or not, lacked the credentials to stand before such an august body. Now, without his diplomatic finesse, she faced twelve pairs of scrutinizing eyes alone.

"Our engineers managed to recover critical components despite the sabotage," Vrell continued. "Most notably, this." He gestured toward the partially reconstructed engine laid out across the large table.

"The zeppelin *Empirical Advance* was not powered by a conventional steam engine," Lina interjected, stepping forward. "This is a combustion engine. What you see here is a fuel-injection system and a piston. Nothing like this is possible with steam. And we don't have combustible fuel in the quantities needed for this."

Guild Master Dorovan shifted in his seat. His gloved hands folded neatly on his lap. "The Council did authorize limited trials of alternative propulsion, under my Guild's oversight," he said smoothly. "This was simply one such test. The fact that the engine exploded, unfortunately, demonstrated the dangers of experimental technology."

"A test?" Lina countered. "Then why does this engine match Holy Sovereignty specifications? Why was the vessel operating near routes controlled by their allies, the Scarlet Talon, its holds packed with the food supplies the Sovereignty craves for war? And why" – she produced a logbook page–"is everything about the ship hidden? Records stolen, evidence destroyed, witnesses silenced. Engineer Jenks, the only survivor, was shot dead after speaking with us."

Dorovan's expression never faltered. "The Concord's security concerns are complex, Pilot Ryven. Sometimes maintaining peace requires... pragmatic approaches."

"And was hauling thirty-seven tons of food supplies also a pragmatic approach?" Lina asked, her voice hardening. "The largest cargo of preserved meats, dried fruits, and grains sent this past year – conveniently *lost* in an attack that now looks staged."

A ripple of concern moved through the Council members.

"That was merely a load test," Dorovan replied, dismissing the point with a wave of his gloved hand. "We needed to determine the maximum capacity of a vessel equipped with the new propulsion system."

"Why not test it with rocks?" Lina pressed. "Why was such a valuable vessel sent through unsafe territory, anyway?"

Dorovan sighed, as if explaining simple concepts to a child. "The technology we were testing came from... specialized sources. The Commonwealth's combustion engines are primitive, unreliable. We couldn't risk exposure to third parties in more populated regions."

"So not from the Commonwealth?" Guildmaster Merta interjected, clearly alarmed.

"No," Dorovan admitted. "The Harbor Commonwealth's engines couldn't meet our performance requirements for a vessel of that size. The Holy Sovereignty offered superior technology, immediate advantages. All they requested was our... non-interference in certain matters, and an opportunity to test their technological capabilities." His perfectly gloved hands rested confidently on the armrests. "A small price for peace in our time and a beneficial trading relationship with a potential ally."

"Peace?" Lina scoffed. "You engineered the destruction of a Concord vessel and a Technocracy escort. You sacrificed thirty-seven tons of food supplies for a test?" She swallowed the urge to mention Vera and Dahn by name. She wanted Dorovan to answer for the pilots who had died in the attack, but making it personal would only weaken her position before the Council.

"Keeping the Concord safe was my priority!" Dorovan insisted, his voice rising. "The Holy Sovereignty and the Talons are *not* our enemy! They understand the future better than you! The destruction was regrettable but necessary! Better one vessel than a war! And these supplies were meant to show our allegiance!"

The Council sat in stunned silence at this open admission. But Lina felt Dorovan could still get out of it, pretending he had acted for the Concord. She studied him closely, recalling what Kip had said about Marek and Jormund. They had odd reactions when seedheart islands were mentioned. An idea formed.

"Master Dorovan," she began carefully, "there are rumors that Scarlet Talon is looking for islands known as seedhearts. Those are extremely rare and contain a developed ecosystem. The Coalition's priority will be to protect them at all costs."

The effect was immediate and disturbing. Dorovan's professional façade cracked completely. His eyes widened, and a strange, almost manic energy overtook him.

"Protect them? PROTECT THEM?" he laughed. The sound was high and unnatural in the formal chamber. "Fools! You understand nothing! They *must* fall – all of them! The Plan demands it! The seeds must return to the soil! It is necessary! It is *RIGHT!* DOWN WITH THE ISLANDS! DOWN WITH THEM ALL!"

His voice cracked as he raved, gloved hands clawing at the air. Spittle flew from his lips.

"So the food supplies were transferred to the Talons to be moved to the Surface, weren't they?" Lina asked, pressing her advantage while Dorovan was unbalanced.

"YES!" he screamed, beyond caution now. "The Surface needs resources! To power the war! To build more! The Talons have new weapons – massive weapons!" He laughed maniacally. "You cannot stop what's coming!"

He seemed to collect himself slightly, though his eyes retained that disturbing gleam. "There were meant to be no survivors!" he hissed, rounding on Lina. "None to contradict the official story! That included Engineer Jenks, and certainly interfering pilots asking too many questions!" His voice dropped to a threatening whisper. "It should have included *you.* You should have gone over the edge, like the rest of the crew!"

The Guild Masters recoiled in horror. Guards moved to restrain him. Dorovan continued shouting incoherently about plans and necessary destruction as they led him away. The chamber remained silent long after the doors closed behind him.

Guild Master Trevon, the eldest member of the Council, finally broke the silence. "It appears we have been... manipulated. Master Dorovan shows clear symptoms of Blue Fever – the obsession that sometimes affects those who handle raw floatstone. But that does not excuse his actions. He has been conspiring with our enemies behind our backs, attempting to push the Concord toward the Scarlet Talon for his own purposes."

"Worse still," added Guild Master Merta, "he has betrayed our surface allies in the Harbor Commonwealth by aiding their enemies in the Holy Sovereignty. Such actions could trigger a war that puts our partners at risk."

"And in the process," Guild Master Reena continued, "he sacrificed Technocracy pilots, our crews, and innocent bystanders. Then he tried to cover his tracks with more killings." Her voice hardened. "That is *not* the Concord way."

The Council members exchanged grim looks. Guild Master Trevon turned to Lina.

"The Concord owes you a debt, Pilot Ryven. Without your persistence, this betrayal might have gone undiscovered until it was too late." He straightened in his chair. "The Council will now vote on a formal commitment to the Coalition."

———

Three hours later, Lina stood on a balcony above Concord's central harbor, watching crews ready vessels for what might soon be open war. Behind her, the Council chamber lay silent, emptied after a grueling session. The vote ended with a reluctant but formal commitment to the Coalition.

"How does it feel to change the course of history?" came Kip's voice as he joined her at the railing.

Lina snorted. "Like fixing a broken pressure valve – satisfying but exhausting."

"You did what seemed impossible," Kip said, genuine admiration in his voice. "Thanks to you, we have our Coalition."

She turned to look at him properly. He was already dressed for travel, pack slung over one shoulder. "You're leaving."

"The Republic of Westward Drifts needs convincing," he said with a nod. "I need to leave immediately if I'm to reach them in time."

"Always moving on to the next problem," Lina said. A hint of fondness crept into her voice despite herself.

"It's what I do." Kip's usual smirk softened into something more genuine. "This may be goodbye, you know. With everything escalating…"

Lina nodded, suddenly uncomfortable with the weight of the moment.

"What about Nora and Toryn?" she asked, changing the subject. "We've left them to the Inquisitor's deal."

Kip's expression darkened. "Breaking that deal has consequences. But we had no choice."

"I just hope they've found a way to survive," Lina said. The emotion in her voice surprised her.

"They're resourceful," Kip replied with forced confidence. "If anyone can endure down there, it's those two."

An awkward silence fell between them, filled with all the things practical people never say aloud.

"Have you heard the news? Marek has given the Resonance Fellowship an ultimatum. He wants them to surrender and provide safe passage for his ships."

"Meaning, you're walking into another diplomatic minefield."

"Yep. But now you can return to the Technocracy and push them to keep their promise and join the Coalition."

"I doubt they'll ever listen to me. But Kora could make them."

"Then you can threaten to hit them with a wrench," he said with a smile.

They laughed.

"Well," Kip finally said, extending his hand. "Good luck, Pilot."

Lina took his hand. The handshake carried more weight than either had expected. "Try not to get yourself killed, Lordling."

She watched as he walked away toward the *Phoenix*.

She turned back toward the Council buildings. Would their united defense be enough? Her role had stretched far beyond mechanic and pilot. But she wasn't sure it would make a difference.

———

The Republic of Westward Drifts prided itself on being different from other societies – claiming to be the oldest, the first nation of Azoria. The Mercantile Concord was built for opulence. The Technocracy for function. The Republic's architecture emphasized its democratic ideals: open spaces, circular forums, and skylines free of imposing hierarchies. At least in theory.

Kip noted the contrast between this philosophy and reality. Armed guards stood at every entrance to Liberty, the Republic's capital on Liberty Drift. He counted three checkpoints as the courier vessel docked, each more heavily staffed than expected for peacetime.

"Lord Saroven," greeted a thin-faced man in Republic colors as Kip descended from his aircraft.

Kip suppressed a wince at the title. He had deliberately used his real name in communications with the Republic, but hearing it spoken aloud felt like wearing ill-fitting formal clothes. Still, diplomatic necessity outweighed personal discomfort. The Saroven name carried weight in certain circles, and he desperately needed that weight now.

"Senator Walsh, I presume?" Kip replied with the precise aristocratic nod his tutors had drilled into him. "I appreciate the Republic's prompt response to my request for an audience."

"Of course," Walsh said, gesturing toward a waiting carriage. "If you'll follow me, I'll escort you to your accommodations. The Senate can receive your presentation tomorrow morning."

"Tomorrow?" Kip frowned. "Senator, the matter is rather urgent—"

"The Senate values proper procedure, Lord Saroven," Walsh interrupted smoothly. "All diplomatic presentations must be scheduled and documented. I'm sure you understand."

Kip understood perfectly. They were stalling.

The carriage ride offered him a clear view of Liberty in all its oblivious glory. Festivals and markets bustled in the plazas. Citizens lounged in cafés, argued in debates, or watched plays. No extra guards stood at strategic posts. No military vessels were being readied. The Republic carried on as if war were unthinkable – conflict could never touch their enlightened democracy.

"Your citizens seem remarkably... unconcerned," Kip observed.

Walsh smiled with genuine pride. "The Republic has maintained peaceful neutrality for generations. Our defensive pact with Azurath ensures our security. Our Constitution forbids preemptive military action. We are a civilization of law and discourse, not warmongering."

His accommodations proved comfortable but closely monitored. Servants who were clearly security personnel in disguise attended him. Windows overlooked unimportant views. "Escorts" appeared whenever he tried to explore beyond his quarters. Kip spent the evening reviewing evidence, preparing arguments – and studying the guards. He tracked their rotations, noted potential exits. The Republic's reception felt off. His corsair instincts were rarely wrong in such matters.

The Assembly Dome lived up to its reputation as an architectural marvel. A perfect hemisphere of glass and metal housed the Republic Senate. The chamber featured tiered seating that placed every representative an equal distance from the central speaking platform. Sunlight streamed through the glass panels, promising transparency that the armed guards at every entrance quietly contradicted.

Kip stood on the central platform. Twenty-seven representatives from constituent skylands surrounded him, watching with varying degrees of skepticism. His presentation was methodical: he built from the zeppelin investigation to evidence of surface technology deployment. He closed with the confirmed threat of the Scarlet Talon's growing capabilities.

"Marek has issued an ultimatum to the Resonance Fellowship," he finished. His voice carried clearly in the acoustically perfect chamber. "We have reason to believe he has formed alliances with surface powers. He has acquired technology that gives him a decisive military advantage. The Coalition between the tribes, Concord, and the Technocracy seeks the Republic's partnership in countering this threat."

The response was underwhelming. Senator after senator rose to express concerns – warning of "hasty alliances" and insisting on "proper diplomatic protocols." They emphasized their existing defensive arrangements with the High Kingdom of Azurath.

"The Republic appreciates your concern, Lord Saroven," said an elderly senator. His embroidered cape marked him as a senior official. "However, forging new alliances demands careful thought about our existing treaty obligations. The process typically requires several months of–"

"We don't have *months*," Kip interrupted, patience thinning. "Scarlet Talon forces are mobilizing *now*."

"Perhaps if you could provide more substantial evidence…" suggested another senator.

Kip noted the subtle exchanges between certain senators during his presentation – quick glances, small gestures, notes passed between aides. Something unseen stirred beneath the polished decorum of the proceeding.

As the Senate's skepticism hardened, Kip shifted tactics.

"Senators of the Republic, I address you not merely as an envoy. I speak as Lord Killian Saroven, the rightful heir to the

Saroven Drift and a former parliament member of the Drift Lords Alliance."

The chamber stilled. His noble title had been mentioned in his introduction, but invoking his full status and former political role shifted the atmosphere.

"My family governed our drift for nine generations," he continued, letting a trace of his true accent emerge. "I understand the complexities of governance. I understand the caution required in forming alliances. But I also understand the cost of hesitation when facing existential threats."

A senator with an embroidered cape rose to his feet. "Lord Saroven, while your lineage is certainly impressive, we require more substantial evidence before committing to–"

"If I may, honorable senator."

A new voice cut through the chamber, rising from the diplomatic observation gallery. A silver-haired man in a tailored gray uniform stood, his attire unmistakably foreign. Murmurs rippled through the assembly as he stepped onto the speaking floor – a breach of protocol permitted, to everyone's surprise, by the Senate guards.

"My apologies for the interruption," the man said. His accent was precise but subtly different from any known dialect. "I am Representative Tallen, diplomatic envoy of the Federation to the Republic and the Kingdom of Azurath."

The Senate chamber erupted in whispers. From the shocked reactions, few in the room even knew of the Federation envoy's existence, and none seemed to know how to respond. Technically, the Republic's founders had once been Federation citizens, making the situation politically awkward.

"The chair recognizes Representative Tallen," the Senate President announced after a moment of confusion. "Though we note that this intervention is highly irregular."

Tallen inclined his head. "These are irregular times, Madam President." Then, with deliberate calm, he turned to face the chamber.

"I can confirm that our intelligence corroborates Lord Saroven's assessment. It concerns Scarlet Talon's activities and the technology exchange with surface entities."

The whispers intensified. Kip smiled inwardly, knowing that the Federation's intelligence was based only on his own report to Voss.

"While the Federation maintains its policy of non-interference," Tallen continued, "I am authorized to confirm the facts of Lord Saroven's report. The threat he describes is real, substantial, and imminent."

Kip studied the senators' reactions. Tallen's sudden intervention lent weight to his warnings, yet furtive glances and subtle signals still passed between certain members.

"We appreciate the Federation's... unusual candor," said the elderly senator, recovering his composure. "However, our defensive arrangements with Azurath provide adequate protection for our Republic."

Tallen waited until the senator finished. "With all due respect, Senator, even the firmest alliances can face unforeseen challenges. I urge the Republic to consider bolstering its own defenses."

This measured statement provoked visible discomfort among several senators. President Morrow leaned forward, suddenly more attentive.

"Representative Tallen," she asked, "are you suggesting that defensive pacts alone may not be sufficient?"

Tallen's deliberate pause spoke volumes. "I am suggesting, Madam President, that all prudent governments prepare for multiple contingencies."

The Senate session continued for another hour with renewed debate. But Kip observed that Tallen's intervention had not fundamentally altered the political reality. While it lent credibility to his warnings, those senators already compromised remained so. The procedural delays continued.

Tallen approached Kip briefly.

"Lord Saroven," he said quietly, "we have mutual acquaintances; Commander Voss sends her regards."

Kip maintained a neutral expression despite his surprise. "Thank you, Representative."

"The Federation's options are limited by policy," Tallen added, "but we are not disinterested observers. Good luck with your Coalition."

Before Kip could respond, Tallen had departed. Kip wondered just how closely the Federation was monitoring his activities. The session ended with the Senate President calling for adjournment until the following day – the same delaying tactic.

"Lord Saroven," President Morrow said as the chamber emptied, "perhaps you would join me in my office? There are matters we might discuss more... directly."

———

President Morrow's office stood in stark contrast to the ornate Senate chamber. Practical furnishings, well-worn books, and maps covering an entire wall hinted at a leader more concerned with function than appearance.

"You'll forgive the theatrics of the Senate session," she said, pouring two glasses of amber liquid without asking if he wanted one. "Some performances are necessary for the official record."

Kip accepted the glass but didn't drink. "You're not actually considering my proposal."

"Not publicly, no." Morrow sat behind her desk and studied him with shrewd eyes. "Several senators are compromised. Some through financial involvements with Azurath and corsairs, others through more direct means."

"Blackmail?" Kip suggested.

"Among other things." She took a sip. "Azurath has been making overtures of a rather threatening nature. Their new military 'exercises' near our borders carry implications even the most obtuse senator can't ignore."

"Yet you maintain your defensive pact with them," Kip noted.

"A pact is only as good as the power willing to enforce it," Morrow replied dryly. "We're caught between emerging powers with unclear intentions."

Kip leaned forward. "What if the Republic maintains its public neutrality but quietly prepares alternatives? In case your current allies turn out to be unreliable."

She seemed about to respond when a sharp knock interrupted. The door burst open without waiting for permission. A breathless aide appeared.

"Madam President," the aide gasped, "urgent news from the Fellowship – Harmony Drift is under attack!"

––––––

The emergency council chamber was a secure room deep within the administrative complex of Liberty. Representatives from the military, intelligence, and key Senate positions gathered around a large table. Operators managed communications equipment along one wall.

"Confirmed reports of catastrophic damage to Harmony Drift," reported a military officer, marking positions on a map. "The corsairs are attacking the Drift with overwhelming forces. Defenses hold, but they won't last long."

A telescope operator rushed in with new information. "Madam President, visual confirmation from the eastern observation post. Harmony Drift is… *gone.* It has collapsed completely! It crumbled and lost altitude as if the Rational Element ran out. The damage is… catastrophic."

The room fell silent as the implications sank in. The Resonance Fellowship's capital wasn't merely under attack – it had been destroyed from within. Harmony Drift had been one of the most architecturally magnificent skylands.

"They refused his ultimatum," Kip said quietly. "And he destroyed them from within."

Further reports arrived in a steady stream, each worse than the last. By midnight, the full scale of the disaster was clear. Harmony Drift had been attacked to draw attention away from the covert operation that compromised its core. The method was a message in itself: Marek could reach anywhere.

Then came the proclamation. A messenger vessel approached under a flag of truce. The operator's hands trembled slightly as he handed the sealed document to President Morrow. She read it silently, her face growing paler with each line, then passed it to her chief advisor.

"What does it say?" demanded a senator.

The advisor cleared his throat and read: "To all nations of the mid-altitudes, from Emperor Marek the First, sovereign of the newly established Scarlet Empire. The Resonance Fellowship has paid the price for defiance. The High Kingdom of Azurath has wisely allied itself with our cause. All corsair clans have either joined our banner or been eradicated. Those nations wishing to avoid Harmony Drift's fate will present their surrender terms within three days."

Stunned silence followed.

"Emperor?" someone finally said. "Empire?"

"Azurath has sided with them?" asked another voice, disbelieving. "Our defensive pact–"

"Was a farce," Morrow finished bitterly. "They must have been planning this betrayal all along."

Reports kept coming through the night. Azurath forces were already mobilizing alongside the newly proclaimed Empire's troops. A mixed fleet advanced toward Republic territory, its aircraft unlike anything previously seen. Lightning flashes highlighted the Empire's superior mobility and firepower.

Kip watched the Republic's confidence crumble in real time. The haughty senators who had dismissed his warnings hours earlier now looked shell-shocked. Their certainties evaporated as reports confirmed the scale of the threat.

"We need to convene the full Senate," one senator insisted. "Proper voting procedures must be–"

"There's no time," snapped President Morrow. "We need emergency–"

She never finished her sentence. An aide whispered something in her ear, and her expression shifted from determination to disbelief. "Excuse me," she said abruptly, and left the room.

She didn't return. Within an hour, reports came in. Officials were leaving Liberty Drift on private vessels. The treasury vaults were being emptied under the excuse of "emergency relocation." Military commanders waited for orders that never came. Civilian leadership had fallen into chaos.

"They're running," Senator Walsh said when he found Kip on an observation platform overlooking the main harbor. The senator's earlier formal demeanor had been replaced by disdain. "Abandoning their posts. Abandoning their people."

Below them, the evacuation had already begun. Civilian vessels, crowded with families and belongings, streamed from the lower docks. Military ships held their positions, yet coordination among them was conspicuously lacking.

"President Morrow?" Kip asked.

Walsh's bitter laugh was answer enough. "Left an hour ago. She took three ships full of 'essential cultural artifacts.' Meaning the treasury and her personal art collection."

A military officer approached their platform with purposeful strides. The woman, in her forties, wore a colonel's insignia. Her weathered face hinted at real combat experience – an unusual trait among the Republic's typically ceremonial forces.

"Colonel Thorne," she introduced herself curtly. Her eyes swept between them before settling on Kip. "Lord Saroven – I was at the Senate meeting. You tried to warn us. And Senator Walsh – you're the only member of the Senate still at your post." She paused, jaw tightening. "I need someone with the will to make decisions. We don't have the forces to repel the attackers' fleet. We thought distance from the corsair lands would protect us. Nobody expected the Kingdom of Azurath to join the aggressor."

"How long before they reach Republic territory?" Kip asked.

"Based on current intelligence, less than two days," Thorne replied. "The Republic won't stand against Azurath's armies for longer than a week. It may crumble sooner without organized leadership."

"What about your military command? The High General? Ministry of Defense?" Kip asked.

Thorne shook her head. "We can't rely on them any longer."

"So the western flank of the Concord will be completely exposed," Kip realized. He thought through the implications. If the Republic fell swiftly, Marek's forces would have an open route – striking the Concord's most vulnerable regions and leaving the fledgling Coalition exposed.

The three stood in grim silence, watching the exodus below. Families clutched hastily packed belongings. Children cried. The elderly were helped aboard overcrowded vessels. This was the human cost of the Republic leadership's failure.

"What's needed," Colonel Thorne said carefully, "is resistance. Not to defeat them – that's impossible now – but to slow their advance. Buy time for the Coalition to prepare adequate defenses."

"I lack the experience for operations on this scale," she admitted, her voice dropping. "Border patrol duty isn't the same as coordinating a fighting retreat across multiple territories."

Senator Walsh looked between them thoughtfully. "Lord Saroven, you know the enemy better than we do – particularly the Empire's forces. You've dealt with Marek personally."

"What exactly are you implying, Senator?" Kip asked, his heart pounding. He was ready to help the Republic but had never thought of leading its military. "You need one of your best generals now."

"I think we've already found one," Walsh continued. "House Saroven sent you to the Meridian Academy, didn't they? And you've got experience from those territorial conflicts with the northern drift disputes."

Kip nodded slowly. Those years seemed distant now. Skirmishes between drift lords had taught him the basics of mobile warfare, supply line management, and coordinated defense. The scale was different, but the principles endured.

"Someone needs to coordinate the resistance," Thorne said pragmatically. "And frankly, we need someone who can think outside the box."

Walsh gestured toward the chaos below. "The alternative is complete collapse. If the Republic falls without organized resistance, the Empire will be at the Coalition's borders in days."

Kip regarded the two remaining leaders – the only ones who hadn't fled. Formal obligations aside, some things demanded attention. He let out a slow sigh.

"We'd need proper authorization," Kip pointed out. "Your military won't take orders from a foreign corsair, regardless of noble titles."

"That can be arranged," Walsh said. "Emergency powers, temporary appointment. The forms still matter, even in crisis."

"And we need to start immediately," Thorne added. "Every hour makes the situation worse."

Kip studied the burning horizon where Harmony Drift had fallen, then glanced down at the evacuation below. The Republic's end seemed inevitable – but perhaps its fall could still mean something.

"All right," he said at last. "Let's see what can be done."

CHAPTER 33
Storm Rising

Nora's fingers ached after three days of wrestling with ancient metal. Every joint protested as she forced the final connection into place. Calling it a "connection" felt generous – it was more like a scavenged bow strung from frayed cable.

She wasn't certain electricity flowed through the lines; they shouldn't glow. She guessed it was a kind of optical signal, which meant tying conductors together would rarely work.

The Madrid facility sprawled around her, more a research outpost than a station, built by a civilization that seemed to have figured out how to defy gravity. After days of work, it had transformed from a forgotten tomb into a tomb with blinking lights.

Of course, nothing actually worked yet, but she was close to powering some kind of information panel.

She heard soft steps at the chamber entrance. Toryn had returned from hunting in the outer caves. She had persuaded him to delay his trip to the Archives. They had found underground pools and plenty of cave lizards. A rhythm had emerged over the past days: she focused on wiring while he hunted and set snares.

He had even built drying racks from salvaged materials. He tried every cooking method he could think of – they had already eaten fried lizard, boiled lizard, grilled lizard, and even a stew of lizard with dried seaweed and pale underground grass. Fried lizard wasn't a delicacy, but it had a faint chicken-like taste – assuming you hadn't eaten real food in weeks and didn't mind.

"The hunters of the Heights would disown me," Toryn said, setting down a bundle of fresh kills. "Crawling through caves after creatures that never see the sky."

"At least it's better than chewing our belts," Nora joked. Then, more quietly, she asked, "Have you seen the Messenger lately?"

Something had been gnawing at the kid. These visits with that blue entity left visible traces – dark circles under his eyes, and the way his gaze sometimes drifted into nothing.

Toryn's knife paused over the lizard. "Not today."

He settled at the control room entrance with his catch. They had slipped into a routine: she worked on the machines while he kept them fed.

"Ready to see what it does?" Nora asked. Her hand hovered over the console for a moment before pressing against the sensor.

At first, nothing happened. A low hum stirred inside the machine, climbing in pitch until it settled into a steady thrum, then faded. Holographic displays flickered on, faint shapes shifting across them.

"It... lives?" Toryn murmured, setting aside his work, drawn forward by the sudden activity.

The main display flickered on. An image formed: Azoria – no, Earth – hanging in the void. The planet appeared as a marble of clouds and shadowed land, seen from impossibly high above. Nora realized this wasn't a camera feed; it was direct perception via the azurium network's quantum link.

The Storm layer churned below like a vast shroud. Beneath it, she could make out the dim outlines of continents. Floating islands appeared as steady blue points of light.

"The world," Toryn said. His knife rested forgotten in his hand. "Like you see it from the highest islands on a cloudless day, but… all at once."

Nora nodded, trying to follow her racing thoughts. "Look – those are higher than the others." Three bright blue lights pulsed on the image. They surrounded all the other landmasses. Each glow marked a seedheart island – an anchor holding their world together. And three of them were missing.

Hours passed in silence. Toryn's lizards remained untouched. Nora's stomach growled, ignored. The stillness broke. A sharp, high-pitched buzzing signaled trouble. A warning filled the main screen, marking an island in red. It began to blink as the display zoomed closer, sharpening into an aerial view of an island ripping itself apart. Buildings collapsed around a massive tuning-fork monument at its center. Cracks spread outward like branching ice.

Toryn went stiff. "Harmony Drift," he whispered. "The capital of the Resonance Fellowship…"

The massive monument tore free from its foundation, vanishing into the swirling clouds below. The island kept tilting, falling faster each second. The display cut back to the global view. The blue dot marking Harmony Drift went dark.

Nora's stomach lurched. "The Talon did this. They tampered with the island's core…"

Toryn stared at the empty space on the map, his face drained of color. "They were harmless. Worshipping the Holy Resonance."

"Well, it's over," Nora said, her tone edged. "The war just took its first harvest. Won't be the last."

The day sank into silence. Weather patterns drifted across the secondary displays, indifferent to the thousands dead. After a while, Toryn returned to preparing food. The simple task steadied him – Nora noticed his hands no longer shook as he worked.

———

Morning put them back at their usual posts. Toryn tended the drying racks while Nora watched the feeds, chewing strips of dried lizard that tasted oddly like jerky.

She glanced at him. Dark circles ringed his eyes. The Messenger's visits were wearing him down; each conversation with that thing left him a little more withdrawn.

A sharp chime split the air. One of the highest blue dots began pulsing on the map, blinking faster and faster as red warnings flared around it.

"Seedpod warning," Nora read aloud. She dropped her breakfast, a knot tightening in her stomach. "Core compromised. Early descent phase initiated."

More alerts lit up the secondary displays. These weren't warnings – they were status updates. Diagrams tracked planetary energy flows surging toward the Storm layer.

"Energy readings!" Nora pointed, her finger unsteady. "The Storm – look! It just spiked! Sixty-six percent of maximum capacity!"

Toryn left his work and crossed the chamber. His knowledge of wind and weather offered no help here, and confusion showed plainly on his face. "Sixty-six percent… Does that mean stronger, or just angrier?"

The system gave its own answer. The Storm wasn't only growing stronger – it was spreading. It climbed into the mid-altitudes where millions lived, higher than any record had ever allowed.

"Nearly a quarter of the Middle Altitude islands…" Nora's thoughts scrambled to keep up. "They're in range now. That power surge – it has to be the Storm deactivation protocol. It's reacting to a downed seedpod, pulling more energy to drain the islands and bring them down."

"Anyone on those islands…" Toryn left the rest unsaid.

"Useless!" Nora smacked the dead communication panel. Not hard, but enough to vent her frustration. "We've got the clearest view imaginable. We can see everything – and can't warn anyone!"

Toryn didn't move. He kept his eyes fixed on the Storm display, that far-off look she'd seen before. "Perhaps…" he began, then faltered. It was the same expression he'd worn when the Messenger first visited him.

Nora couldn't make out the words, but she saw Toryn's expression shift. Shock tightened his features, then gave way to fierce concentration as he listened to something only he could hear. He spoke back in his own tongue, gestures sharp, almost frantic.

After several moments, his shoulders sagged. He turned toward her, face set and unreadable.

"It confirms the seedheart's fall," he said. "The one we just saw." He paused, steadying himself. "It said the fall serves the Plan. Only two remain after this one."

"You tried to explain the fragmentation again, didn't you?" Nora asked quietly.

Toryn nodded. "I told it the islands will fall in chaos, not order – that millions will die. Its reply didn't change: The breaking of the sky-earth changes nothing. The Plan continues."

"The Storm?" Nora pressed. A knot tightened in her stomach. "What about the Storm?"

"The barrier feeds on heartstone," Toryn said, his voice hollow. "It will drain energy from any island it touches. Over the next sixty days, the last two seedhearts must fall. Then the barrier breaks. Life begins again."

He met her eyes. "Its exact words were: When the seedpods return, spring will come to the world."

"Half the inhabited world," she murmured. "Sacrificed for a two-thousand-year-old program."

"Two months," Toryn repeated. His words landed heavy in the silence. "Whatever we do… we have two months."

Blue energy pulsed through the conduits around them, steady as a heartbeat. Madrid Station had changed. Once a forgotten tomb, now it was their prison, their observatory – perhaps their only chance against the collapsing world above.

Nora studied his face. Whatever that thing was telling Toryn, it could break him. She would have to watch her friend closely.

In the next chamber, strips of lizard meat hung to dry on racks – a reminder that even while worlds fell, life demanded its minor necessities.

PART 6: THE HEAVY SKY

PROLOGUE
Escalation

Commander Elara Voss stood at the viewport. She already hated the view – and the predicament she'd stepped into. Below, Azoria turned slowly, the Storm layer visibly agitated, climbing upward toward the islands. She wondered why the floating lands covered only a few percent of the planet near the equator, and how much untouched territory lay beneath.

Beside her, three holographic displays vied for attention. "Summarize Nabble's report on azurium energy," she ordered.

The Chief Science Officer's findings were clear: azurium acted as an energy store, not a source, and the Storm was consuming it at an accelerated pace. Affected islands showed drastic depletion in mere days. Projection models pointed to total collapse of targeted regions within eight weeks. Voss's jaw tightened. The Federation's coveted prize might soon turn worthless.

She shifted to the second display, an orbital feed. An island descended through a circular breach in the Storm, settling on the ocean below. Just like the one Nora occupied. But this time the satellite showed crates stacked high and personnel swarming the site. Someone had exploited the anomaly as a lift – and she knew who, and what that meant.

"Analysis of cargo?" she asked the computer.

"If those are food supplies, as our sources suggest, they could sustain roughly 3,000 troops."

The third display showed the aftermath: Harmony Drift, capital of the Resonance Fellowship, reduced to scattered debris. The azurium core's destruction happened to be brutal and effective. "Tactical assessment on the island's destruction?"

The report was bleak: Scarlet Talon began with conventional attacks on defensive infrastructure to draw forces and attention from the cave system. Planes and landing parties approached unseen and advanced to the azurium veins. The mineral core was destroyed – or moved – compromising the island's buoyancy. What looked like a weapon of mass destruction was really a carefully planned sabotage – stripping the "flying" from the flying islands.

A final display activated, showing the latest scientific analysis of the Storm's behavior. The model projected cascading failures across inhabited regions as the Storm expanded, draining energy from the islands. Without that energy, the islands would fall. Without stable azurium, the Federation's mining objectives became moot. Without Federation intervention…

Voss stopped herself. The non-interference directive existed for good reasons, even if it felt increasingly academic now.

Admiral Kaine's message notification pulsed, requesting acknowledgment. "Computer, draft a response to Admiral Kaine. Standard mission-update format." She paused. "Include Nabble's analysis of azurium energy depletion. Emphasize the impact on extraction objectives. Request guidance regarding… observation protocols during a multifaceted humanitarian crisis."

It was as close as she could come to asking: *Are we really going to just watch?*

Out of the viewport, the Storm visibly pulsed, its pattern accelerating. Whatever was happening below was driving toward an irreversible stage. The most frustrating part was that bureaucracy moved at its own pace, indifferent to planetary collapse.

Voss turned away from the viewport. The coming weeks would demand choices that made her last compromised mission seem like a routine supply requisition. This time, she felt that inaction might be the greater sin.

CHAPTER 34
Sky Ignites

Coalition President Kora Skyheart stood before the Coalition War Council. Her path had carried her from a tribal wind-reader to a respected meteorologist at Caligan University – and now to this: tribal envoy turned leader in their last chance for survival.

The vast Technocracy chamber, once filled with academic debate, now carried a different tension. Charts of troop movements and storm anomalies had replaced scholarly formulas on the massive whiteboards. Mercantile Concord representatives argued over logistics with the newly arrived Drift Lords. Technocracy analysts pored over stacks of reports in silence.

It had been three days since the coalition representatives elected her President. Three days of frantic preparation after the destruction of Harmony Drift had jolted their factions into unified action. The burden of leadership pressed down on her, as breathing the thin air at the highest peaks.

She had spent years balancing tribal tradition with scientific insight. Now she was navigating rival factions, each pushing its own priorities and anxieties. It felt like reading the Whirlwind: a single misstep could scatter everything.

The Drift Lords' arrival an hour earlier had revealed the fractured state of their world. The Drift Lords, infamous for endless quarrels over every clause, had convened an Assembly and chosen Lord Blackwell as temporary representative. The Empire had ravaged their drifts, with more than half already lost. Their ships, adorned with carved sky-beasts, docked awkwardly beside the Technocracy's plain and functional vessels. Lord Blackwell, a stern man with sharp eyes, led his delegation with strict formality. The negotiations had been tense but yielded progress. Blackwell had shown a rare willingness to align his men with the broader coalition strategy.

Intelligence confirmed Marek's advance. His forces cut through supply lines, bypassing heavy defenses. They left those targets for the slower second army, which followed with siege engines and heavy firepower. This force was built for methodical sieges, ready to deliver crushing fire. The tactics showed a commander who had sharpened traditional corsair raiding into a disciplined strategy.

A commotion at the chamber entrance broke her thoughts. A lone figure stumbled in, supported by Technocracy guards. He wore the travel-stained leathers of the Republic of the Westward Drifts. His face was grimy, eyes lit with urgency.

"President," he gasped, recognizing her authority. "I bring news from the Westward Drifts." He stopped to draw breath. "Azurath has broken the defense pact. Their forces march with the Empire. The Republic government has collapsed."

Murmurs spread through the council. Even those who had suspected Azurath's disloyalty looked shaken. The enemy's strength had almost doubled.

"Is there any resistance? Will they hold?" Kora asked quietly.

"Resistance continues – Lord Killian Saroven has taken command. He's holding chokepoints and striking supply lines. Buying time."

Kora allowed herself a moment of grim satisfaction, quickly masked. The boy was always a force to be reckoned with. He might buy them the time they need. She caught a brief sign of recognition in Lord Blackwell's gaze at the mention of Kip, but he kept his composure. Whatever history lay between them stayed unsaid.

Before the council could take in the news, another report arrived. A seedheart island had been brought down. Large shipments of supplies had reached High Inquisitor Thadeius. The payment was complete.

The council reacted with practical concern. One more strategic asset gone. One more enemy objective secured. But Kora felt something deeper: the loss seemed to wound the world itself in ways they hardly grasped. Reports from Kip and Lina suggested the seedheart islands held advanced ecosystems and could be crucial to the world's balance. And the surface war this payment would drive... She forced the thought aside. They could face only one war at a time.

"Can the remaining islands be protected? Should we focus on them?" a Concord Guild Master asked.

Kora shook her head. "From what our sources report, they're essential to our world's stability. But we have no defenses – we didn't even know they existed as distinct entities until this crisis. We lack both the means to locate them and the strength to defend them while fighting on other fronts. I'll send eagle messengers to query the tribes for possible locations and keep watch, but I don't see how we could use that knowledge."

Military advisors outlined the wider strategic situation. Marek wasn't advancing on just one front. The Empire and its allies were crushing resistance across the mid-altitudes. The Resonance Fellowship had lost its leaders and was breaking apart. The Republic of the Westward Drifts now faced Azurath armies pushing from the southwest while Imperial forces pressed from the north. Independent corsair clans that refused alliance were being hunted. The remaining Drift Lords were trapped in costly defenses. Several smaller nations had already collapsed into occupation.

Marek's strategy was plain: divide, conquer, consolidate. Kora studied the map, following the lines of attack. Years of reading wind currents had trained her to spot patterns. She saw overextension here, a supply corridor stretched too thin there. Marek was powerful – but perhaps not beyond defeat.

———

The Technocracy's engineering center looked like controlled chaos. Blueprints sprawled across surfaces. Steam hissed from test chambers. Assistants hurried between workbenches with prototype parts in hand. The whole workshop looked like the mind of someone with too many ideas and far too little sleep.

Which wasn't far from the truth, Lina reflected. She wiped oil from her hands with a rag that ended up grimier than her fingers.

"Pass me that heat exchanger," she called to a young apprentice. He looked as if he'd been picked mainly for his strength and endurance. "And the thermal calibrator."

She had labored on the induction system for sixteen relentless hours without pause. The problem wasn't complicated – it was deceptively simple. Heat transfer. The steam lost too much energy between the boiler and the drive cylinders, leaving the engines inefficient at the very moment maximum thrust was needed. In aerial combat, that inefficiency could be fatal.

Lina muttered curses that made the apprentice blush. She tightened another fitting on the improved manifold. The smooth-bore design would cut friction. But it wasn't enough. Nowhere near enough.

"Difficulty with the thermodynamics?"

The voice behind her carried a cultured tone, laced with a trace of familiarity she couldn't place. Lina turned to find a tall woman watching her work. She wore simple Technocracy clothing, no insignia, but her posture suggested she was not ordinary. Her dark hair was tied back.

"Who's asking?" Lina didn't bother with politeness.

The woman smiled. "Someone who values elegant solutions to difficult problems." She glanced around, then lowered her voice. "A friend of Nora Hertzig."

Lina's hands froze mid-adjustment. She set the calibrator down. "Everyone here," she told the apprentice and the other engineers, "take a break. Twenty minutes."

There was a pause of confusion before tools were laid aside. People filed out, muttering about deadlines. When the heavy workshop door closed, Lina crossed her arms.

"You're with the Federation."

"Commander Voss sent me," the woman said as she stepped up to the workbench. "What I'm about to share must remain between us."

"I'm listening." Lina kept her face unreadable, though her pulse thudded in her chest.

The woman studied Lina's diagram, her finger following the steam pathway. "I assume you know basic steam engine principles. Water converts to steam in the boiler, then travels to power the cylinders." She tapped a section. "The issue is thermal energy loss before it reaches the cylinders."

Lina nodded, impatient. "That's thermodynamics. Can't beat it."

"Can't beat it," the woman agreed, "but you can work with it." She took a pencil and adjusted Lina's diagram. "You need superheaters – secondary chambers that compress and reheat the steam before it reaches the cylinders."

Lina fixed on the annotation. The idea was disarmingly simple, yet no one in the Technocracy had thought of it. Possibilities unfolded in her mind like a blueprint snapping into clarity.

"That would increase power output by–"

"Approximately forty percent," the woman finished. "Without raising fuel use proportionally."

Forty percent. Lina's thoughts leapt to tactical possibilities. Their aircraft would gain speed and agility. It could tip the balance of the aerial war.

"Why give me this?" Lina asked, holding back her excitement. "Are you even permitted to share technology with developing worlds?"

The woman's face gave nothing away. "Commander Voss believes certain regulations must sometimes give way to more urgent concerns," she said carefully. "The non-interference policy serves Federation interests in ordinary times. These are not ordinary times."

Lina grasped the meaning. This was no sanctioned Federation act. Voss was moving on her own authority.

Lina nodded and turned back to the diagram. "Tell your commander... tell her thank you." The words felt far too small for what this could mean.

"I'll convey your gratitude." The woman stepped back. "I should go before questions arise. Good luck, Miss Ryven."

Lina studied the modified schematic. Superheaters. Simple in design, but transformative for their technology. She didn't want to claim the invention as her own; yet the Federation woman had made it clear it must remain secret. The choice weighed heavily – ethics against necessity.

She allowed herself a single minute to absorb the gravity of the gift. Then she called the engineers back and got to work.

———

The war room grew tense as meteorological reports arrived. The Storm was swelling, more violent with each day. Minor islands were already reported lost, their heartstone cores drained. It seemed to consume everything it touched.

President Kora listened with mounting dread. Her academic colleagues had charted the Storm's patterns for centuries. It had always been dangerous but predictable. This was different. This was wrong. The first changes were detected two months ago, matching the fall of Veil Islet. The second surge came only days ago, after the loss of another seedheart island.

"The Storm's growth has a distinct pattern," noted a Technocracy meteorologist. "I don't know what those seedheart islands are, but their descent seems to accelerate the Storm's expansion."

Kora nodded. "If this pattern holds, we're facing more than just a military threat. The Storm itself may become our most dangerous enemy. Maybe Marek is deliberately looking for them to use the Storm as a weapon against us." She made a note to herself to spend more resources on finding the remaining seedhearts.

Meanwhile, coalition strategists studied fragmented reports from the Republic's front. Kip's resistance was proving effective. His tactics – cutting supply lines, exploiting drift chokepoints – had slowed Azurath's advance longer than anyone expected.

The uneasy calm broke with the eagle scout's report. Their message, written in clipped High Tongue, brought grim news. Marek's fleet had seized the Fellowship's two largest islands without a fight after Harmony Drift's fall. Now the Empire was tightening control and converting every civilian craft.

President Kora reconvened the council at once. Lina arrived, drained but steady. She gave a clear assessment: her team's "thermodynamic enhancements" could be installed on existing aircraft within days. The fleet would fly with greater power. It wasn't equal to Marek's engines, but it narrowed the gap.

Necessity forced a quick decision. They would divide their strength. A core contingent would remain in Caligan to handle upgrades and repairs. A smaller support force – equipped with improved aircraft and eagle squadrons – would form a strike group at the Mercantile Concord border. They needed to meet the Empire's advance and stop Marek's fleet before it reached the settled lands.

Kora looked around the chamber. She met the eyes of leaders who, despite their differences, now faced the same danger.

The war had truly begun. Even the sky itself seemed to burn.

CHAPTER 35
Ascent to Shadow

Toryn stretched, arms lifting over his head, joints cracking after hours spent watching the old displays. Each revelation about Earth's true nature had been both fascinating and horrifying, but now claustrophobia was setting in. The walls seemed to press in with every passing hour – a strange feeling for someone who had lived his life beneath open skies.

"I need to go up," he said at last, breaking the silence between him and Nora.

She glanced up from her workstation, where complex schematics glowed in blue light. "Up?" Her expression shifted from confusion to concern. "You don't mean all the way to the surface?"

For a moment, he thought she might suggest going higher still, to the Heights – but that was clearly off the table.

"Not that far," Toryn clarified, though the thought of open sky – even the oppressive gray ceiling – still pulled at him. "Just to the underground markets, perhaps the Archives. We've been here nearly a week. We need supplies, and we need to know what's happening above."

Nora gestured at the screens surrounding her. "I'm making progress with these systems. If I can just understand the connection between seedpod islands and the Storm, we might find a way to stabilize things."

Toryn nodded but held his ground. "While you handle the work, I'll be more useful gathering supplies and information."

He didn't add that the crushing weight of the underground was becoming unbearable, that his tribal soul cried out for height and open air. Even after everything they'd discovered, some cultural divides remained impossible to bridge completely.

"It's dangerous," Nora said, though her eyes had already returned to the displays. "The Inquisition–"

"Is less likely to recognize me in the Archives robes or Tunnel Runner's garb than an outlander," Toryn finished for her. "I'll be careful."

He gathered what little he could offer in trade – small bone carvings made during idle hours, pieces of leather he had carved and tanned in a saltwater pond. It wasn't much, but it could be enough.

"Two days," he said. "I'll be back in two days."

Nora looked up again, this time meeting his gaze directly. "Promise me."

"I promise," he said, then added, "Okay, three at most if absolutely necessary. I'll move like drifting fog at night."

She smiled at the old tribal saying, then turned back to her work. "Bring back something to eat that isn't dried lizard. I've had enough reptiles for a lifetime."

Toryn nodded in agreement. He wasn't much of a cook, and every new lizard recipe ended up looking the same and tasting even worse than the last.

He slung his small pack over his shoulder, the Church of the Archives robe tucked inside, and started down Madrid Station's corridors. He stopped at a junction, checked his notes, and tried to get his bearings. They had rushed through these tunnels in desperation. Finding the way back would take careful attention.

The path beneath his hunting grounds was hard to follow. Several passages looked the same, their rocky walls blending together. Toryn closed his eyes, drawing on the same sense that had once helped him read shifting wind patterns in the Heights. Underground, the air moved differently, but it still moved. A faint current brushed his cheek, and he knew it was time to go.

As he approached the exit corridor, a flicker of blue light formed before him in the shape of a familiar eagle. Its feathers glimmered with an unearthly sheen.

"*The heights-dweller ascends,*" it observed in High Tongue, its voice echoing in the confined space. Toryn knew it was only in his mind – the Messenger spoke within him, not aloud – yet still he felt the walls vibrate.

Toryn kept walking, forcing the apparition to turn and follow. "Not as far as I'd like."

"*You grow weary of the depths,*" the Messenger said. "*I sense it – your longing for open sky.*"

Toryn didn't break his stride. "What of it?"

"*The eagles can take you there.*" A pause, as though weighing the promise. "*All you have to do is follow the Plan. Release one more seedheart.*"

"Why not use your other… agents?" Toryn asked, his curiosity slipping past his wariness.

The eagle's form flickered. "*Very few are capable of the journey from the Heights to the Mind and back again.*"

The Mind. First time it's called the facility that. It's where it was created – maybe it still hides there in some of the machines.

The Messenger glided alongside him for a few more steps before its light dissolved, its final words echoing in the corridor: *"The offer stands, heights-dweller. The sky awaits."*

He reached the outer door that once led to the elevator shaft.

Toryn slipped through the door. He was thinking of an ancient intelligence – so human in its reasoning, yet so vast in its reach. Aware of the life it was built to save, yet careless of the lives above. The contradiction unsettled him more than its power. He couldn't fault the creators – they had never imagined people settling on the floating lands. Yet this oversight in their design could cost countless lives.

The journey through the cave system was nightmarish for someone born to open skies. He forced himself not to dwell on it and pressed forward, struggling against the weight on all sides and longing for space.

Toryn guided himself by memory and instinct, marking junctions with small scratches to track his way back. The air grew cleaner, humidity rising with faint noises of habitation. The natural caves gradually yielded to rough-hewn mining tunnels, unmistakable traces of human activity from long ago.

Faint sounds of habitation eventually filled the caves – distant voices, the creak of machinery, the small comforts of life carrying on.

Never thought I'd be glad to hear people digging, singing, and farting.

The thought made him grin despite his fatigue, and he kept moving. Soon, clearer traces of people appeared – footprints in the dirt, abandoned tools, and excrement.

When he reached the outskirts of the mushroom farms, Toryn ducked into a narrow side passage and changed into the Archive robe. The simple brown garment wasn't much of a disguise, but it marked him as part of a group the Inquisition generally tolerated. Most importantly, it covered the tattoos on his arms.

Eventually, Toryn reached the passages leading to Archive territory. He decided not to seek out the Tunnel Runners – he had never held enough standing with them to be safe if a large bounty was placed on his head. At the main entrance, two Archive acolytes stood guard. They didn't look like soldiers but scholars with weapons, their unease plain in the way they held themselves.

"State your purpose," one called as Toryn approached in his Archive robe.

"I seek knowledge and offer the same in return," Toryn replied with a standard greeting.

"Please call Archivist Talbert and tell him I come in the tradition of the one who is forever in our souls. He who comes with his faithful donkey at his side."

The guard gestured for him to follow. As they approached a large chamber, Toryn heard Talbert's voice raised in argument with someone else. He couldn't catch the words, but the tension was unmistakable.

The guard paused, then gestured for Toryn to wait while he slipped ahead. A moment later, he returned.

"The Archivist Prima and Talbert are dealing with a situation," he explained quietly. "Another Archive outpost was raided last night. Three scholars taken for questioning."

Taken for questioning. The euphemism hung in the air, its true meaning clear to both of them. Few who were taken for "questioning" by the Inquisition ever returned.

"I can wait," Toryn offered.

"No need." Talbert appeared in the doorway, looking older and more tired than Toryn remembered. His eyes widened at the sight of the tribal man. "By all the ancient texts!" He paused, studying Toryn's face. "I feared you were dead!"

Talbert crossed the space and embraced Toryn warmly. "We feared the worst! The Inquisition doubled their efforts after your escape."

"We found sanctuary," Toryn replied carefully. "Deeper than most would venture."

Talbert's eyebrows lifted, but he asked no questions. He thanked the guards and guided Toryn through a warren of corridors to his private study.

The room had changed as well. Where once books and artifacts had been displayed openly, now many shelves stood empty. Crates lined one wall, ready for evacuation, yet Talbert's desk lay buried under manuscripts and notes – proof his work pressed on despite it all.

"You've come alone," Talbert observed as he closed the door. "What about Nora?"

"Safe," Toryn assured him. "Working on something that might help us all, if it succeeds."

Talbert gestured to a chair. "Then you'd better tell me everything... or at least everything you're willing to share."

Toryn sat, gathering his thoughts. He and Nora had settled on a careful balance – sharing just enough to safeguard crucial knowledge, while keeping both the Keeper's existence and Madrid Station's location hidden. It was a delicate balance.

"We found answers," he began. "About this world, about the Storm, about what lies beneath us all."

For the next hour, Toryn carefully shared what they had discovered. He explained that Earth was humanity's original home. That a catastrophic war had nearly destroyed it. That a marvel of technology had raised entire landmasses into the sky, leaving the surface to heal.

He never mentioned the Keeper or its agents. Instead, he framed the accelerating collapse as a planned function to re-germinate life on the surface.

Talbert listened with scholarly focus. He interrupted now and then with questions, but mostly absorbed the account with growing wonder and horror.

"Everything we've theorized…" he murmured when Toryn finished. "The ancient markings, the structures predating our earliest records, the strange materials in the Archives – it all fits. And these seedheart islands… if they continue to fail?"

"Everything falls," Toryn said simply.

Talbert seemed to age a year before Toryn's eyes as he grasped the implications. Silence stretched between them. Then the archivist straightened his shoulders, determination replacing his momentary despair.

"Then we document while we can," he declared. "I'll have acolytes prepare transcription materials. Would you be willing to dictate what you've learned for our records?"

"That's part of why I came," Toryn agreed. "But I also need information and supplies. We've been living on dried rations for weeks, and I need to understand what's happening above."

"Of course, of course," Talbert said, suddenly remembering his duties as a host. "You must be famished. I'll arrange food while we work."

The next several hours passed in a blur. Talbert gathered a small team of trusted archivists who recorded Toryn's account with meticulous care. Toryn recounted Earth's history – the catastrophe, Project Génesis – while scribes hurried to make duplicates. The task drained him, yet he took comfort in knowing the knowledge would endure, whatever came next.

As they worked, Talbert shared updates from the time since their escape. The news was grim. Inquisition activity had increased sharply across Stormseat. Many from the underground had been taken and never returned. Public executions of so-called heretics had become a weekly ritual, attendance enforced by law.

"And now there are war preparations," Talbert added as they paused to rest. "Military training has increased, weapons production accelerated. The Temple of Storm's Truth has declared a holy purification is approaching."

"Against whom?" Toryn asked, though he feared he already knew.

"The Harbor Commonwealth at first, but the rhetoric suggests broader ambitions." Talbert poured tea from a pot kept warm on a spirit lamp. "Unusual activity at the eastern facilities – massive shipments of materials and personnel, all under heavy guard."

Toryn accepted the tea. "When we escaped, the Inquisitor already had a deal with someone from above the Storm. The falling seedheart, with its slow descent, carried the resources and specialists he needed."

"That matches what our informants have reported," Talbert confirmed. "Stockpiling food is always a problem here on the surface. It's why we've had no wars for the last sixty years – the Kingdom of Tides never had enough to raise armies against its neighbors. But now, with flying machines and pilots from above the Storm, they could conquer the whole continent."

By late evening, the documentation was complete. Three copies were prepared, each bound for a different Archive. Talbert rolled the parchments with care, sealed them in wax, and slid them into protective cylinders.

"I should take you to the market district," he said as he secured the final document. "You'll find supplies there, and perhaps information more current than even we possess."

Toryn nodded, though fatigue tugged at him after the long day of dictation.

————

The underground market filled a vast cavern that had once been a natural amphitheater. Over centuries, it had been expanded into a bustling commercial center. Hundreds of people moved through the space, conducting business by lamplight. Stalls and shops lined the curved walls, offering everything from food and clothing to strange mechanical devices.

The market assaulted Toryn's senses after a week in Madrid Station's silence. Smell came first – unwashed bodies, food, chemical preservatives. Then sound – haggling in many dialects, the clink of coins, the snap of mechanisms, the shuffle of feet. Last came light – a patchwork of oil lamps, gas jets, and bioluminescent fungi glowing in shadowed corners.

Talbert led him through the crowd, occasionally nodding and exchanging brief greetings. The underground market thrived on diversity – unusual goods and information. And the Church of the Archives was the ultimate source of both.

"What supplies do you need most?" Talbert asked.

"Food that will last," Toryn replied. "Blankets. Rope. Basic tools. Anything that might make life more comfortable in… our current situation."

Moving through the market, Toryn noted the decline – prices had risen sharply. Military-grade equipment that had once been displayed openly was now sold in hushed transactions. Conversations fell silent whenever alleged informants passed nearby.

Twice, they had to change direction to avoid patrols in the market. These weren't the usual bribe collectors keeping up the pretense of enforcement. These were real soldiers with weapons ready, scanning faces and questioning vendors.

"They've never been this open in the market before," Talbert whispered.

At one food stall, Toryn traded a small bone carving of an eagle in flight for dried meat, preserved fruits, and hard bread. The merchant examined the tribal craftsmanship with open interest.

"Heights work," she said appreciatively. "Haven't seen anything like this in months. The salvage from the skies has almost stopped."

"What do you mean?" Toryn asked.

"The Storm patterns have changed," she explained, wrapping his purchases. "Fishermen report more debris falling – not just scraps, but even a whole island breaking apart and sending huge waves. But the Sovereignty now watches every salvage attempt. Whole artels that have fished for goods for generations are sitting idle. And there are rumors – just rumors, mind you – of strange sounds from above, like thunder that never ends."

Toryn exchanged a glance with Talbert. The war was spreading across every level.

As they moved through the market, they collected supplies – and rumors. Each passerby carried a fragment of news, another shard in a troubling puzzle. Refugees were escaping from border regions. Military recruiters were seizing people off the streets. Prisons swelled with those seized on fabricated charges, their sentences commuted only to forced conscription.

At a fabric merchant's stall, Toryn traded his last carved bone knife for blankets and rope. The merchant, an elderly woman with gnarled hands, leaned in as she pressed the goods into his hands.

"You have the look of someone who's seen the sky," she whispered. "Before the Revolution, I once saw a cloud window open – a perfect circle in the Storm. Through it, I glimpsed something vast and blue. Now they say the Storm is changing, growing more violent. Is it *true*?"

Toryn hesitated, then gave a small nod. "The patterns are shifting."

Fear flickered in her eyes. "Then the end is near! The Storm will consume us all!"

Toryn instinctively stepped back – the woman was either drunk, mad, or both.

"A savior from above will come!" she proclaimed, agitated, her eyes searching his face.

Talbert gently led Toryn away. "Hard times make people cling to prophecies and lies. Don't let them create new ones."

By midnight, Toryn's pack was full of supplies, and his mind was heavy with information. He and Talbert returned to the Church to rest before Toryn began his journey back.

"You should stay with us," Talbert offered as they shared a simple meal of soup and bread. "The Archives would welcome your knowledge."

Toryn shook his head. "I promised Nora I'd return. And the work we're doing might help address the root of these problems."

Talbert didn't press, respecting Toryn's discretion. Instead, he gave him a small map of updated tunnel routes and patrol patterns, marking the safest path back to the deeper levels.

"Our friend..." Talbert began hesitantly. "The one from the stars. Do you think her people will intervene if things keep getting worse?"

Toryn considered the question. "I believe they're watching. Whether they'll act..." He left the thought unfinished.

When it was time to depart, Talbert put a hand on his shoulder. "If you need sanctuary, the Archives will always open for you both," he promised. "Though I can't guarantee how long even we will remain safe."

"Thank you," Toryn said quietly. "We may take you up on that." He hesitated, then added, "I'm proud to have added to the Archives. What we've recorded here... it will outlive us all."

———

The return journey was challenging but boring. Last time they had been running, and time had flown. Now the tunnels felt increasingly oppressive, and he couldn't wait for them to end. His pack – full of dried meat, preserved fruits, bread, blankets, and tools – grew heavier with each level, a constant reminder of how far he was from open sky.

But his mind stayed on the elderly woman's words and Talbert's warning. What if they only pretended to be saviors, without the right or the ability to save anyone? What if meddling with Madrid Station and the Mind only made things worse? The thought settled in him like a stone, its weight almost as oppressive as the rock overhead.

Later, Toryn forced himself to focus on memories of open skies to fight his rising claustrophobia. In the Heights, distance was measured in days of eagle flight. Here, it was counted in feet of suffocating stone.

At one junction, he took a wrong turn and ended in an unfamiliar dead end. Backtracking, he realized how easy it would be to become permanently lost in this lightless maze. Retracing his markings, he saw he had overthought them – now even he couldn't tell what they meant. Simple arrows would have worked better.

At last, after what felt like an eternity, he reached the outer entrance to Madrid Station. The massive circular door stood as they had left it, partially open for passage. Toryn slipped through the gap, relief flooding him as the familiar blue light welcomed him back.

He had expected to find Nora at her workstation in the control room, but the space was empty. Concerned, he set down his pack and moved deeper into the facility, calling her name.

He found her in the main monitoring chamber, slumped in exhausted sleep over the console. Across the screens flickered strange symbols, shifting numbers, and jagged graphs. One displayed what looked like a battle in progress – tiny aircraft locked in combat above cloud formations. Another tracked Storm energy, red zones spreading ominously across the map.

"Nora," he said gently, touching her shoulder.

She startled awake, disoriented for a moment before recognition dawned. "Toryn! You're back." Relief colored her voice as she straightened, wincing at stiff muscles. "How long was I asleep?"

"I just returned," he said. "You should sleep properly, not at your desk."

"Too much to do," she mumbled, though the dark circles under her eyes betrayed her exhaustion. "Did you get supplies?"

Toryn nodded. "Food, blankets, tools. And information." He glanced at the screens. "Though it seems you've gathered some of your own."

Nora followed his gaze to the projections. "I managed to activate more surveillance systems. The fighting in the mid-altitudes has intensified. And I saw Kip!" Her eyes watered as she spoke, a crack in her usual scientific composure. "He's alive and leading the resistance on one of the islands!"

Toryn realized how much she must have missed their friend, trapped so far below. The softness in her voice at his name said more than her words.

"Anything about Lina?" Toryn asked, hope tightening his chest.

"Nothing, sorry." Nora shook her head and turned away from the grim displays, steadying herself with a deep breath. "What did you learn above?"

"Thadeius has received his payment," he said, forcing himself to focus on the immediate threat. "The surface war is about to begin. The Holy Sovereignty is mobilizing faster than anyone expected – troops, weapons, supplies. The underground markets are buzzing with rumors."

Nora absorbed this with the analytical focus he had come to expect from her. "Timeline?"

"Days, not weeks," Toryn said.

They sat in silence, the weight of dual catastrophes – above and below the Storm – settling over them. On the screens, the red zones of Storm energy kept spreading.

"You should eat, then rest properly," he said, changing the subject. "I brought actual food, not just dried lizards."

"Sounds wonderful," Nora admitted, glad for the distraction.

As they left the monitoring chamber, Toryn glanced back at the screens. The Messenger had not appeared during his return, which was unusual. He wondered what the Keeper plotted, what hidden calculations churned as its Plan neared completion.

For all their discoveries, they were still powerless observers. Unless something shifted, they would stand by as the worlds above and below ripped each other apart.

There had to be another way.

CHAPTER 36
Republic in Flames

The Great Library of Liberty now housed the Republic of Westward Drifts' temporary command center, its vast reading hall repurposed as a war room. Three centuries ago, Skyward Theon chose this site as the capital of what would become the first colony on Azoria. It also became the seat of his empire – though officially he bore the title of President of the Republic. The building was the centerpiece of his vision after the fire that destroyed the old Library. Now, massive oak tables where scholars once studied were covered with military maps. The high bookshelves along the walls loomed above clerks updating air formation positions with colored pins and wooden markers.

A steady rumble of distant explosions penetrated even these ancient walls, punctuated by the sharper crack of bombs striking closer targets. Through the arched windows, Kip saw the cloud mass that never shifted, though today it seemed denser than usual. The Storm below had disrupted weather patterns across the land, and the air carried a weight that felt unnatural.

Reports from the outer territories had been flooding in for days. Windward Haven, the closest island to Azurath, had fallen immediately when the war began. The earliest refugees brought accounts of public executions in town squares, rapes, and prepared lists of persons to be detained. One gaunt-faced woman described bodies stacked at the island's edge, with teams assigned to shove them into the abyss. The atrocities were not random – they followed a deliberate pattern of terror.

Kip stood with Colonel Thorne and Senator Walsh at the central strategy table, studying a diorama of Liberty Drift and its surrounding territories. Officers hurried between stations, their movements scattered. Some barked conflicting orders, while others quietly gathered personal belongings.

"The problem," Kip said, observing it, "is that we're trying to operate without unified command. Half these officers don't recognize authority beyond their immediate superiors – and most of those superiors have fled. The Republic is generally not ready for the war."

"They're all in shock," Thorne said, trying to defend her people. "Azurath has been building its air fleet for months. They claimed it was only military exercises," she continued. "Intelligence reports say their commanders boast they'll take the capital in three days. Now they're advancing from the southwest after capturing Windward Haven. Based on their current flight paths, they'll establish landing zones here, here, and here." She pointed to three airspace sectors around Tordson Heights that would allow fast troop landings to seize key positions. "At this pace, they'll reach Liberty Drift's outer defense perimeter in five days."

"Capital in three days?" Kip said. "Sounds like overconfidence we can exploit."

"And why shouldn't they be confident?" Walsh replied bitterly. "With most of our government fled and our military command collapsing…"

"What about the Empire forces?" Kip asked, noting the lack of markers for Marek's fleet.

"There are reports of activity near Covenant Drift, close to Resonance Fellowship land," Thorne said, pointing to the northeastern part of the map. "We believe they're consolidating their gains before pushing toward our borders. Intelligence suggests they've been communicating with Azurath command."

"And our command has mostly fled," Walsh said.

Thorne didn't deny it. "We have skeleton crews in different military branches and a completely broken chain of command."

Kip attempted to issue orders to reposition some of the remaining defensive vessels, but the officers ignored him. One captain even looked straight through him as if he weren't there.

"They don't recognize your authority," Thorne explained quietly. "In the Republic's military, commanders must be approved by the Senate."

"How very comforting," Kip muttered, "to know paperwork functions perfectly even as the government collapses and the enemy is at the door."

A familiar face appeared at the main library entrance – Federation Liaison Tallen. His calm, deliberate pace stood out against the frantic movements of the Republic officers. He approached their table, boots striking sharply in the vast space.

"Lord Saroven," he greeted Kip formally. "Colonel Thorne. Senator." He inclined his head to each. "You are the largest group of officials still here that I've found so far."

"The rest of the Senate?" Walsh asked, his tone suggesting he already knew the answer.

"Eighteen of twenty-seven senators have left Liberty," Tallen confirmed. "The treasury vaults have been emptied. Military warehouses in the eastern district have also been cleared out – said to be for strategic redeployment. And the Defense Minister's private zeppelin departed an hour ago, claiming it would establish a government in exile."

"Running like rabbits," Walsh spat.

Kip studied the command structure chart Thorne had provided earlier. "What about military leadership? High General? Admiral?"

Thorne's laugh had no humor. "High General Kollen was suddenly called to an urgent strategy conference on the Border Drift this morning. Admiral Renner discovered he needed to inspect our southern fleet base immediately. Most squadron commanders found similar reasons to be elsewhere."

"And those who remain?" Kip asked.

"Career officers, mostly," Thorne replied. "The defense pact with Azurath meant most appointments went to political favorites – family connections, bribery, and agreements made to keep the peace. Real combat experience wasn't considered necessary when we all assumed Azurath would watch our backs."

"Not all were favors," Tallen observed, nodding toward Thorne.

"I served with the border patrol for fifteen years," she stated. "Most of it was against pirates and smugglers, but it's still more real combat than most officers here have seen."

"And you're willing to stay?" Kip asked her directly. "You must understand the Republic can't win this war. Azurath prepared for months, maybe years. I'd wager they have everything planned and all personnel in place."

"These are my people," Thorne said. "I took an oath to defend them, not the politicians who've run away."

Kip nodded, respect forming for this practical officer. "We need to organize what forces remain and establish proper command authority. If Azurath thinks they can take Liberty in three days, our job is to prove them wrong."

"Our top priority has to be getting key personnel to safety," Thorne said. "Liberty has military transports for long-range evacuation, and we can convert the heavy cargo vessels. We should focus on the most vulnerable: military families, government staff with sensitive data, and essential technical experts. There's no way we can evacuate everyone." She paused. "Most civilians with the means to leave have already gone. The wealthy started fleeing days ago, right after the Fellowship received the ultimatum."

"Agreed," Kip said, "but we also ought to mount a defense to buy them time."

Studying the weather maps displayed across one wall, Kip offered his first request. "Could you assemble your meteorologists?"

"Our weather specialists?" Thorne asked, puzzled.

"As soon as possible," Kip replied. "I've been watching those cloud formations for several days. Something unusual might be happening."

Several nearby officers exchanged skeptical glances, clearly thinking this a waste of precious time. But Thorne sent for the meteorology team without further hesitation.

While waiting, Kip outlined his next requests. "We might need messengers. Three groups." He wrote quick notes, sealed them, and handed them to the waiting aides.

"This one goes to the Caligan Technocracy and the Mercantile Concord. A standard diplomatic request for assistance." He handed over the first message.

"This goes to the advancing forces of both Azurath and the Empire. A negotiation proposal." He passed the second message, noting Thorne's raised eyebrow.

The third message he held a moment longer, considering. "This one should go to the Silver Shard corsair kite. Their territory borders the Empire's northern expansion." He handed it over with a slight smile. "A long-odds gamble, but one worth making."

The warlords of the clouds were predictable in their unpredictability, Kip thought. They resented Marek's power grab, and among corsairs revenge was a stronger currency than gold.

"Corsairs?" Walsh asked, clearly surprised.

"The Silver Shard have a particular grudge against Marek," Kip explained. "He pushed them out of their territory last year. They may not care about the Republic, but they certainly care about revenge. And money."

"You think they'd actually help us?" Thorne asked skeptically.

"Probably not," Kip admitted. "But we're playing a desperate hand. I'll use any card available, even if the odds are slim."

The meteorology team arrived, led by a middle-aged woman with the gaze of one who had spent her life studying the heavens.

"Could you give me your assessment of these unusual patterns?" Kip asked, pointing to the weather maps. "The Storm's expansion is creating unprecedented conditions. Can you predict how they might develop over the next week?"

The lead meteorologist looked both surprised and intrigued. "We've been tracking anomalies, yes, but in the midst of war preparations–"

"This *is* war preparation," Kip cut in. "These patterns could determine our survival."

Kip studied the arrows on the weather maps, seeing not just clouds but tactical possibilities. *Weather has always been the third combatant in any sky battle,* he thought. *In this case, it might be our strongest ally.*

The meteorology chief gave a preliminary report. "The patterns are indeed unprecedented. The Storm's expansion is creating new fog layers. Our models suggest these conditions will intensify over the next three days and then might stabilize."

Kip nodded, his suspicion confirmed. "And these layers – they'll be predictable?"

"To a degree," she confirmed. "Though navigation will be severely compromised."

"Thank you," Kip said, already thinking ahead. "Could you provide predictions for fog altitude for each day over the next week?"

His second request followed quickly. "And could someone be assigned who's familiar with corsair signal systems? Flags, lights, flare combinations."

"Commander Vissen in intelligence might have that expertise," Thorne suggested cautiously.

"Perfect. Could you ask them to report here with any available reference materials?"

Thorne studied Kip with growing curiosity. "You have a strategy in mind."

"Not a traditional one," Kip admitted. "But traditional defense has already failed elsewhere."

A classic rule of leadership: appear confident, even when you're making it up as you go, Kip thought. *Half of any strategy is convincing others it will work.*

At that moment, a young aide approached, looking confused. "Sir, the bomber squadron is asking for guidance. They are getting conflicting orders from different sources."

Thorne sighed. "I'll handle it."

"No," Kip said firmly. "Send someone. We need you here."

"Send whom?" she asked. "Everyone with authority has fled."

"Then find someone competent within the division. Give them a field promotion if necessary – but don't get bogged down in details."

Thorne nodded slowly. "Lieutenant Farran is solid. I'll put her in charge of bomber operations." She sent the aide away with clear instructions.

"The same applies to you, Lord Saroven," Walsh added. "You can't personally oversee every part of this operation."

"I'm well aware," Kip replied with a self-critical smile. "I've never been good at letting others handle details."

To prove the point, he spent the next hour trying to organize too many things at once. He juggled evacuation routes, intercept patterns, and disputes with supply officers all at once. Each pulled him in a different direction, and nothing advanced as it should.

"This isn't working," he admitted to Walsh after a particularly heated exchange with a supply officer who reported that essential equipment had vanished from the inventory. "We need proper authority if we're going to coordinate anything effectively."

"You need Senate approval," Walsh agreed. "But with most senators gone…"

"How many do you need?" Tallen asked.

"Two senators can authorize emergency military appointments. It's a wartime provision rarely used."

"There's you," Kip pointed out. "We need one more."

"Senator Greeves might still be in the city," Walsh said after a pause. "He's not the bravest soul, but his personal airship was undergoing renewal. He likely chose to wait until it's ready rather than travel in something less comfortable."

"I can help reach him," Tallen offered. "The Federation maintains… awareness of key political figures."

Within an hour, they had confirmation. Senator Greeves remained in his fortified compound, apparently calculating that neither escape nor public service was in his best interest.

"I'll speak to him," Walsh offered.

"We'll both go," Thorne countered. "Some arguments work better coming from a military officer."

Commander Vissen arrived, studying Kip with sharp, intelligent eyes. His weathered face hinted at a long, difficult history, and the guarded skepticism in his expression was plain. As an intelligence officer fluent in corsair communication signals, it was obvious he had spent years among them.

"You served with the corsairs, didn't you?" Kip began. "We could use your knowledge to disrupt their communications."

Vissen's skepticism eased as Kip outlined his plan for a mobile signal station. Both men were familiar with common signal protocols and could already see how to disrupt communications and feed the enemy false reports.

"We'll imitate safe-passage and enemy-spotted signals," Kip explained. "That should lure them toward our anti-aircraft firing points."

"Clever," Vissen admitted. "Though it won't work for long once they realize the deception."

"It doesn't need to," Kip replied. "Just long enough to throw off their initial coordination and stall the first advance."

Thorne and Walsh returned with Senator Greeves, a heavy man in his sixties, dressed in silks and glittering with rings. His soft hands and rounded belly betrayed a life untouched by hardship. The finery looked out of place in the converted library, surrounded by military maps and war preparations. His expression suggested he found the entire situation distasteful.

"Lord Saroven," Walsh said in introduction, "Senator Greeves has agreed to assist with the emergency authorization."

"Under protest," Greeves added sourly. "This is highly unusual and probably exceeds my legal authority."

"Your legal authority will mean nothing when the Republic falls," Thorne said bluntly.

"Yes, well." Greeves straightened his ornate vest. "Let's get this... formality over with."

The Senate chamber had been built to accommodate hundreds. Now its vast circular space held only five: Kip, Thorne, Walsh, Greeves, and Tallen, attending as an official witness.

"The Constitution of the Republic of Westward Drifts, Article Seven, Section Twelve," Walsh recited, his voice echoing off the tall, book-lined walls. "In extreme emergencies, when the Senate cannot meet in full, at least two sitting senators may grant temporary military authority to qualified individuals for the defense of the Republic."

Greeves looked as if he'd rather be anywhere else, but he nodded, saying he had no objection and agreed it was necessary. A clerk recorded the decision and affixed the Senate seal.

"By the power given to us as elected representatives," Walsh went on, "we grant Lord Killian Saroven the temporary rank of Military Advisor, with authority equal to that of a General, for the duration of this emergency."

The document was signed, sealed, and presented to Kip with a seriousness that felt almost ridiculous given the situation. But it served its purpose – he now had the legal authority to command what remained of the Republic's forces.

General, Kip thought, trying not to wince at the title. *From corsair scout to general in a single afternoon. Classic.*

"I request immediate transport back to my estate," Greeves said the moment the ceremony ended.

"Senator, your continued presence would be invaluable–" Kip began.

"I've done my legal duty," Greeves cut him off. "My personal security arrangements await."

Thorne looked as if she wanted to arrest him for cowardice, but Walsh shook his head. "Let him go," he murmured. "We need people who *want* to fight."

As they left the Library's janitor's room, pressed into use as a Senate chamber for the ceremony, Tallen joined Kip as they walked. It was a bitter irony: the oldest country in the floating world had held what might be its final Senate meeting in such a place.

"Congratulations, General Saroven," Tallen said with the faintest hint of irony.

Kip suppressed a wince at the title. "Now the real work begins," he agreed.

"I also wanted to tell you that my time here is over. The request I sent for immediate help to the Republic came back denied. And they've ordered me to return to the ship."

Kip sighed. "Farewell then, Liaison Officer Tallen. I hope we will meet again."

They clasped hands, and the Federation officer left.

So the Federation decided not to intervene, as expected. Kip reflected that Voss herself had been willing to help, Nora was open and sincere, and Tallen's assistance had been invaluable. But the Federation as a whole placed itself above local struggles.

In the end, those caught in the storm had to find their own way out.

———

Back at the command center, Kip gathered the senior officers. His first act under his new authority was to establish a clear chain of command. With Thorne's help, he identified the few remaining senior officers with actual combat experience and assigned them key responsibilities. Junior officers with potential were promoted to fill critical gaps. The process was rushed and imperfect, but it brought order to the earlier chaos.

"The first thing we need to understand is that we cannot defend the Republic itself," he began bluntly. "The capital will be lost – there's no way to fight two advancing armies at once when we barely have an army of our own."

He indicated the diorama. "Liberty – the central administrative zone, with this library and the airfield – is our priority defensive sector. Everything else becomes a sacrifice zone if necessary."

The declaration drew murmurs from the officers, but Kip pressed on. "We're not fighting to hold territory. There's no way to win against two prevailing armies at once. What we can do is slow their advance, extract the people and resources that will carry the fight elsewhere. The Republic isn't a place – it's its people and its principles."

The Republic had already lost, Kip thought grimly. *But these people don't need to hear that yet. What matters is preserving enough strength to fight another day.*

"Furthermore, we're not fighting a conventional war. This is a war of attrition. Our goal is a thousand small cuts to weaken the enemy."

Several officers exchanged dubious looks. Kip gestured to a weather map, annotated with air currents, blind spots, and predicted fog zones.

"The corsairs rely on altitude in their raids – flying much higher or lower than their targets until the moment of attack."

A lesson from my years with the corsairs, he reflected. *Height advantage isn't just about bombing runs – it's about being where the enemy doesn't expect you. But I doubt they want to hear about my corsair past as well.*

He turned to the meteorology chief. "These fog layers you've projected – we need the boundaries updated for each day. Is that possible?"

"We're working on models now," she confirmed. "The patterns are becoming increasingly stable."

"Excellent. Then we assume the enemy can do the same. They'll likely move their forces to the edge of the clear-visibility zone. Anti-aircraft positions should be set just above the current fog line," Kip said, pointing to the map. "By nightfall, the rising fog will conceal them, giving our engineers cover to relocate the batteries. Each day our defenses will appear where they're not expected, only to vanish and reappear before the next engagement."

Traditional warfare assumes fixed defensive positions. We don't have the resources for that, so we'll play the trickery card.

There were no objections. Orders were drafted, assignments made, and the briefing concluded.

Later that afternoon, Kip chose to oversee the anti-aircraft emplacements himself. Leaving the command center, he went to inspect several positions on Liberty Drift. The fog was already thickening as he approached the western artillery line, where he expected preparations to be well underway.

Instead, the batteries sat silent while enemy scouts freely observed their positions. Kip found the gun crews idle, waiting for orders that would never come from commanders who had fled.

"Who's in command here?" he demanded at the central post.

The gun crews traded uneasy looks before a young officer stepped forward. "No one, sir. Commander Telvick left this morning. We were told to hold position and await orders."

Kip studied a lean, serious-looking lieutenant – uniform in perfect order, face calm despite the command vacuum.

"Lieutenant," Kip called. "Your name?"

"Lieutenant Marrek, sir. First Battery, Third Division."

Kip winced at the name, so close to Captain Marek of the Scarlet Talon. That one had been heavyset and falsely friendly; this Lieutenant Marrek was all sharp angles and military precision.

This one's a professional, Kip thought. *No political appointment here. Exactly the kind of officer we need.*

"What's your assessment of our capabilities, Lieutenant?" Kip asked.

"Functionally operational, sir," Marrek replied without hesitation. "Ammunition stocks at sixty percent – several crates appear to have been removed overnight. All guns are mechanically sound. The crews were trained, but held back, waiting for command authorization to engage hostile aircraft. No response has been made to Azurath scouts since no standing orders are in effect."

"Can your guns be repositioned to high elevation points within twelve hours?"

Marrek considered briefly. "Yes, sir – though it will leave gaps in our defensive perimeter."

"The enemy won't know about it," Kip explained. "We'll exploit that."

Understanding dawned in Marrek's eyes. "We'll place them where they don't expect fire to come from."

"Exactly. Lieutenant Marrek, I'm placing you in command of Liberty's air defenses, effective immediately."

"Sir. Yes, Sir! Rules of engagement?"

"Prioritize protecting evacuation zones and high-value military assets from bombers. Secondary priority: disrupt enemy landing parties and supply convoys."

As evening approached, Kip received reports from the island territories. Tordson Heights was holding. Vulnerable personnel were evacuated as quickly as possible, but the general population had to remain. Reinforcements were requested, yet there were simply too few to send.

An intelligence officer delivered intercepted communications from the Azurath forces. "Sir, they're preparing a major assault on Tordson Heights."

Kip studied the reports grimly. "They'll open with heavy bombing runs, then commit their fast-assault craft with minimal support."

"A lightning attack rather than a siege," Thorne agreed. "Typical of their doctrine when facing disorganized resistance."

"Then we need to be ready for both phases," Kip said. "The blitz assault first, then the conventional follow-up once they've secured footholds."

———

Day two dawned with the enemy attack unfolding exactly as Kip had predicted. Azurath bombers struck Tordson Heights in waves, pounding defensive positions with devastating effect. Following immediately came troop transports – lighter, faster vessels built for rapid deployment.

"They're attempting to secure the main airfield," the tactical officer reported. "First wave estimated at up to five hundred troops. They'll arrive within a few hours."

Kip studied the reports. "They're counting on a quick victory. Their troops will be carrying only essential equipment." He turned to Thorne. "What forces do we have on Tordson Heights capable of immediate counterattack?"

"The 7th Interceptor Squadron and elements of the 3rd Marine Division," she answered promptly.

"Good. They don't even know if we intend to defend at all. They assume the army is in disarray – an error that gives us the upper hand. But they'll be surprised only once." Kip pointed to the airfield on the map. "Move the Marine Division and arm all airfield personnel to resist the landing, while maintaining the appearance of evacuation. Order the interceptors to approach from building level, using urban corridors rather than standard assault vectors. The enemy expects us to flee. They won't be ready for resistance and air strikes."

The ambush tactic paid off. Republic forces, emerging from unexpected points, caught part of the landing force in the air. Heavy fighting followed on the ground, with significant casualties on both sides. By midday, the attempt to seize the airfield had failed. Azurath commanders, facing unexpectedly stiff resistance, ordered a retreat. That left their lines thin and vulnerable, allowing Republic forces to chase down and destroy several landing craft.

The first battle ended in a decisive victory for the Republic. Kip reviewed the reports with cautious satisfaction. The enemy's blitz-landing tactics had failed spectacularly. They hadn't expected resistance and believed most of the military had already fled. Azurath's best landing troops were in disarray, with over ten percent lost. Although it was only a moderate success, the mood in the command center rose sharply.

The false signal station began operating that afternoon. A civilian craft, loaded with flags and flares, moved between set locations, sending misleading signals about safe routes and Republic movements. Some signals seemed to register; others were ignored. But Kip was certain the enemy's intelligence units were logging and analyzing the patterns.

"They'll assume these are genuine corsair communications at first," he explained to Vissen. "By the time they realize the deception, we'll have created significant confusion – and may even lure some craft into our firing positions."

The evacuation of key personnel from Tordson Heights continued, while the general population was instructed to shelter in place or depart on personal airships.

Kip reviewed the latest intelligence reports with Thorne at his side.

"Refugee accounts confirm our fears," she said grimly. "Those who escaped Windward Haven describe the systematic elimination of educators and cultural leaders. They're not just conquering territory – they're erasing the Republic's identity. The Kingdom is also searching for people with Azurath roots. They pressured civilians to collaborate, demanding reports on military families, government employees, and scientists. Once they do, those people have no way back – hated by their neighbors, and criminals under our laws."

"All the more reason to ensure our evacuation succeeds," Kip replied. "Key specialists represent the Republic's future resistance. Otherwise, they'll end up working for the enemy."

By evening, Kip received word that the Azurath reinforcement fleet had approached Tordson Heights. Lieutenant Marrek had proposed the idea of moving several anti-aircraft batteries into attacking positions, and they were soon repositioned along the fog line. From there, they opened fire from unexpected angles, devastating the enemy: three supply zeppelins destroyed, two troop transports damaged badly enough to retreat.

When Marrek reported back to command, his usually calm face showed a hint of satisfaction. "Batteries are already being relocated to Liberty Drift. We also moved wooden decoys and some older pieces to cover those positions," he told Kip. "They'll strike them in the morning fog and believe they've achieved real destruction."

"I admire your work with the decoys, Lieutenant," Kip said. "Unconventional thinking like that may be our only chance in this war."

———

Day three began with reports reaching Kip that Azurath forces were regrouping for a massive assault on Tordson Heights. Their blitz attack failed, inflicting heavy losses for little territorial gain.

"For the next phase, they'll establish forward bases, secure supply lines, and advance step by step," Thorne remarked as they reviewed the morning intelligence.

"Which gives us time to complete our evacuation," Kip noted. "Have all priority personnel been extracted from Tordson Heights?"

"Nearly complete," the evacuation coordinator confirmed. "Final transports are departing within hours."

The meteorology team reported to Kip that the fog conditions had developed exactly as predicted. A thick layer now blanketed the lower altitudes of all the islands in the region.

A few more days and we'll be able to hide guns even on the ground. If we have those days.

The false signal network continued its deception. Enemy communications intercepted by Vissen revealed growing confusion as their commanders tried to change protocol.

He approached with his morning report. "They're starting to pay attention to our corsair signals," he told Kip with satisfaction. "Their scouts are being diverted to investigate signaling craft, supposed *force concentrations*, and *safe passages* that don't exist."

Republic scouts relayed reports from inside Empire territory. Unconfirmed, but the movements hinted at possible internal conflict. Kip noted the information with interest but made no comment.

Other Empire forces were still consolidating near Covenant Drift. Scouts reported additional vessels arriving daily – they were gathering significant strength before advancing.

"Send the scouts to observe their supply lines," Kip ordered. "I want detailed reports on convoy composition and routes."

———

Day four brought worsening weather that was already visible even from the command center windows. The fog layers thickened further, making navigation below the island levels nearly impossible. Republic forces, now adapted to these unusual patterns, trained with increasing confidence – moving in and out of the clear layers. It was tempting to imagine Azurath vessels still struggling with basic formations, but Kip wasn't one to underestimate the enemy. Surely, they had bright and capable commanders who had already begun similar drills.

The artillery batteries, aided by deceptive signals, proved their worth when they successfully targeted an Azurath supply convoy. Reports described how the convoy, approaching Tordson Heights from the east, strayed too close to an artillery point. Two ammunition transports destroyed, several small craft damaged, and one fuel carrier hit badly enough to retreat.

Marrek delivered his report personally. "They still haven't adapted to our positioning," he told Kip. "Their intel suggests we have far fewer artillery pieces, all in fixed positions. Our ability to relocate and hold key high ground has kept us a step ahead so far. Several decoy sites have been bombed, but we've taken no real losses. The problem is we're running out of islands above the fog that can support artillery. By tomorrow, we'll be limited to Liberty Drift itself – and it has no natural elevation."

"I hope in a day there will be enough fog to hide artillery even on the ground."

"Yes, but we won't be able to move it on the ground – we'll be sitting ducks. There are no motorized vehicles available, and we never invested in roads capable of moving heavy equipment. With airship transports, they always seemed unnecessary."

Azurath forces launched their conventional assault on Tordson Heights midmorning. Kip reviewed the reports as they arrived: a heavy barrage, overwhelming firepower, and no sign of supply shortages.

"They'll secure Tordson Heights today," Kip acknowledged, "but it will cost them. And by then, we'll have extracted everything of value."

That afternoon brought the news Kip had been waiting for. An intelligence officer approached with a report that made Kip fight to keep his reaction hidden.

"Sir, the Silver Shard corsair clan has publicly announced joining the Empire forces. Captain Farrows formally pledged allegiance to Captain Marek at a midday ceremony."

Thorne looked at Kip with surprise. "More corsairs joined Marek? How does that help us?"

Kip only smiled. "Patience, Colonel. Let's see what comes of it."

The Empire's confidence seemed to be growing, according to the reports reaching Kip's desk.

"They're accelerating their timetable," an intelligence officer reported. "Advance elements are now expected to reach Republic territory within two days, rather than the previously estimated four."

"Perfect," Kip said quietly. "Everything is going as expected."

By evening, reports confirmed that Azurath forces had completed their conquest of Tordson Heights, but the victory was empty. Republic defenders had withdrawn in good order, destroying anything of value they could not carry. More importantly, all priority personnel had been successfully evacuated.

"Tordson Heights is secure," Thorne noted grimly, updating the diorama for Kip's review. "But their losses were steep. Our estimates suggest they lost nearly twenty percent of their committed forces."

"And we preserved over ninety percent of our defensive capabilities," Kip added. "A favorable exchange. Yet now the way to Liberty Drift is open."

This is how wars are really fought, Kip thought as he studied the map. *Not with grand, decisive battles, but with a thousand small calculations. Trading space for time, casualties for position. The arithmetic of survival.*

———

Day five began with an unexpected commotion. An intelligence officer burst into the command center, nearly out of breath.

"Sir!" the young man exclaimed. "The Silver Shard corsairs have attacked Empire fuel transports approaching the Covenant Drift! Three vessels destroyed, several more damaged!"

The command center filled with startled voices around Kip. Thorne turned to him with wide eyes. "Your messenger – the one you sent on day one – this was your gamble?"

Kip nodded. "I offered them revenge against Marek and salvage rights to any Empire vessels they could capture. And their territories back, when the war is over. The message suggested they publicly defect to gain access to Empire supply lines."

"You couldn't know they'd accept," one of his officers protested.

"I didn't," Kip admitted. "It was a risk – but corsairs take pride in a double-cross. The Silver Shard have harbored a grudge against Marek since he seized their territories last year, forcing some into servitude and others into a nomadic life."

"How did you know they wouldn't just turn over your message to Marek?" Thorne asked.

"I never did," Kip explained. "They may be thieves and raiders, but they have their own code. And revenge is practically sacred among the kites. Betrayal is sacred as well – but we risk nothing if they betray us. I also promised they could join the Coalition and later claim some of the Empire's land. That's where they might attempt a double-cross. But we'll deal with it then."

Corsairs are as unreliable as ever, Kip reflected. The key is to make sure their self-interest matches ours, at least for a time. Corsair loyalty belongs to opportunity, not to people or nations. Drinking spirits with Silverbeard, their leader, at the Market Nexus and recalling old times helped as well.

Throughout the morning, Kip received reports that the Silver Shard's surprise attack had disrupted Empire operations. Unsure which clans might also be plotting, Empire commanders shifted resources to protect convoys and strengthen internal security.

"They're questioning every corsair vessel now," an intelligence officer reported to Kip. "Paranoia is running through their command. Their approach time is back to four days, not two."

Later that afternoon, Kip watched the first landing attempts falter. Azurath forces, testing Republic defenses around Liberty Drift, launched a probing attack, but artillery and interceptors scattered the advance with only minor damage.

"They'll be more cautious in the future," Kip said, satisfied. "Which buys us more time."

By evening, the meteorology chief brought her report to Kip personally. The fog layer remained distinct but had stopped intensifying. "We believe the conditions have reached equilibrium," she explained.

"Continue your monitoring," Kip ordered. "Any change could affect our defensive positioning."

The evacuation coordinator arrived with his update. "All military transports are now loaded and ready for departure."

"Send them out tonight," Kip ordered. "I want them well clear before Azurath can redirect forces to intercept."

———

Day six dawned with reports reaching Kip that Empire forces had hunted down or driven off most of the Silver Shard. It cost them an extra day – and some morale. One of the corsair clans previously allied with Marek unexpectedly withdrew its support, citing internal problems and outdated equipment.

"Doubt is spreading," an intelligence officer reported to Kip. "They don't know which allies might turn next."

Looking out from the command center, Kip noted that the stabilized fog had reduced the advantage the Republic had exploited for days. Enemy forces adapted quickly, improving navigation and reestablishing more effective formations. The ground layer was watched, but without a road system, they could only move troops covertly there. And this was not a ground war.

"Enemy's implementing convoy protection measures," the scout coordinator reported to Kip. "Triple escort formations, overlapping fields of fire. Our interception effectiveness is dropping."

"Evacuation status?" Kip asked during the midday briefing.

"On schedule," came the response. "Military transports cleared Republic airspace overnight without incident. Converted cargo vessels are now at eighty-five percent capacity. Final groups are being processed."

Kip studied the diorama, now showing significant enemy forces approaching from multiple directions. "We need the remaining vessels loaded and ready for departure by tomorrow morning."

Republic intelligence reported to Kip that a coordinated assault was in preparation. Azurath forces from the west would link with Empire forces from the northeast in a pincer designed to capture Liberty and the Republic's remaining leadership.

"They'll attack at dawn tomorrow," Thorne predicted at Kip's side. "Classic doctrine for a final push."

"Then we finish our withdrawal tonight," Kip decided. "All defense forces to fall back to Liberty Airfield for evacuation."

Kip met with the documentation team, who had been compiling evidence of enemy atrocities. "The world needs to see what happened here."

He arranged for the files to be sent with three separate couriers, to ensure at least one copy reached the Coalition. Each carried records of civilian massacres in occupied territories, and the bombing of homes and hospitals.

Night brought the order to abandon Liberty Drift's outer defenses. Artillery pieces too heavy to move were destroyed to prevent capture. Ammunition depots emptied or detonated, archives burned. Kip considered sending in guerrilla teams, but judged it would change little for the advancing forces.

The evacuation coordinator arrived with the final status report. "Evacuation vessels are positioned at Liberty Airfield. All priority personnel accounted for and ready to board."

"Tomorrow will be the last day of the Republic," Thorne said uneasily, standing beside Kip as they watched the final preparations.

"We've completed our critical moves already," Kip replied. "There is nothing more we can do."

———

Day seven began before dawn, with bombings. All known artillery positions were struck, and new ones were revealed as they opened fire on the approaching craft. The dense fog allowed personnel to retreat from compromised sites, but casualties continued.

"All personnel to evacuation zones," Kip announced to the remaining command staff. "Military withdrawal complete in an hour. There is no point in confronting overwhelming forces on the ground, even with the fog."

He ordered the Republic's remaining defensive units to launch harassment attacks – meant to slow the enemy's advance without committing to unwinnable battles. Lieutenant Marrek's high-elevation guns fired the last coordinated barrages before withdrawing.

"Enemy forces are accelerating their approach," an intelligence officer reported urgently to Kip. "ETA to central districts: forty minutes."

"Plenty of time," Kip assured the nervous staff. "All critical personnel are already aboard."

The evacuation proceeded as planned. Military units withdrew in formation, covering each other as they fell back to Liberty Airfield.

"Last transport ready," Thorne reported as they arrived. "All surviving personnel accounted for."

"And our fighting strength?" Kip asked.

Thorne consulted her notes. "We've preserved about sixty percent of our original force. Between those evacuated from the outer islands and Liberty Drift itself, we still hold a significant contingent."

Kip cast one last look at the city. The defense had already succeeded – the Republic's essential minds and leadership were evacuated. The air force remained largely intact.

"Seven days," Walsh mused, joining them for the final departure. "They said they'd take the capital in three."

"They should have allowed that some Generals wouldn't flee," Thorne said, using Kip's new title deliberately.

"After you, Colonel," Kip replied, gesturing toward the final transport.

Thorne gave a tight smile. "Still trying to send me away first?"

"Still trying to do everything myself," Kip admitted. "Come on. This time, we leave together."

"Now we join the others," he said. "The war isn't over – it only has begun."

The Republic fleet headed eastward toward the Coalition rally point at the edge of the Mercantile Concord. It was a three-day journey through unpredictable weather and enemy advance forces. Transports, bombers, and escorts flew in formation, led by a civilian scout with a proud name: *Stubborn Phoenix*.

And that name reflected the Republic's only hope – to be stubborn, to be reborn.

CHAPTER 37
Holding the Line

Lina's arms were smeared with piston grease up to her elbows as she tightened the new pressure regulator. Three days without sleep had left dark circles under her eyes, but the spark in them was still visible across Platform Sigma's vast engineering bay.

Platform Sigma had become the coalition's designated rally point. The sprawling trading platform, once a commercial hub, had been converted into a military base. Its position gave it a commanding view over the approaching enemy. Now it housed the largest concentration of allied strength since the war began.

We actually have a chance here, Lina thought. She looked out at the impressive array of coalition squadrons, their historical grievances set aside. There weren't many natural fortifications in aerial warfare – height, visibility, and stable weather. Platform Sigma had them all. It floated well above the Storm, offering clear sightlines for miles in every direction. The long-range artillery held a superior position. This point could be defended for months – if the supply lines held.

"Try it now!" she shouted to the engineer, raising her voice over the hiss of steam and the banging metal in the workshop.

The young man – Elliot, she remembered, from Caligan – nodded and slowly opened the test regulator. A jet of superheated steam shot through the assembly, producing torque greater than the standard systems. The pressure gauge climbed steadily past the old safety threshold, showing no strain or vibration.

"Sweet mother of storms," Elliot whispered, eyes widening. "It's actually holding."

Lina managed a tired smile. "Let it run for a few hours. We need to be sure it doesn't explode like attempt number three."

"We did it," said a Concord engineer, her braids coming undone after hours of work. "The superheater design *works*."

Lina nodded, wiping her hands on a rag. "Together with our exhaust recapture and hull modifications, we're getting a solid boost for our birds."

"And all it took was a week without sleep," came a dry voice from behind her.

Lina turned to find Technocracy Chief Engineer Tervor surveying the work with a critical eye. His usual skepticism had, by now, softened into grudging respect.

"We had a great concept," Lina admitted, "and we had to work under pressure." That quip drew reluctant smiles from the mixed team she'd been working with.

Chief Tervor grunted but didn't join them. "How soon can we implement this across the fleet?"

Lina ran quick calculations in her head. "Of the hundred and thirty-five vessels currently on the platform, I've got parts ready for sixty-eight. We'll finish those by the end of the day. Another twenty-seven are in the final stages. Each light scout craft required a full day for modifications. The bomber-class vessels will take longer – and that's with every engineer working round-the-clock."

"How long for the rest of the fleet?" Tervor pressed.

"Two weeks, maybe less if we get more hands."

———

The modified plane responded to Lina's controls like an extension of her body. The subtle lag she'd grown used to in standard craft was gone, replaced by a responsiveness that made it feel alive. She put the craft into a tight spiral, watching the pressure gauges as she pushed the enhanced engine to its limits.

"Beautiful," she murmured, executing a maneuver that would have strained even *Swift Mistral* to its breaking point. The craft responded smoothly, cutting through the air.

Below her, Trade Platform Sigma spanned nearly a mile across the sky, a vast floating structure whose central island was covered entirely in man-made buildings. Once a commercial hub, it had been hastily converted into the coalition's forward base. Cargo platforms now served as extra landing strips, merchant offices as command centers. Warehouses held aircraft and pilots from across the lands.

The clear sky around Platform Sigma stretched for miles with no sign of Storm expansion, while the lower altitudes were already shrouded in fog. Any approaching enemy force would be visible long before it posed a threat.

As Lina brought her craft around for another pass, she spotted movement in the distance – a small formation approaching from the east. Her hand hovered over the signal flare until the lead craft raised recognition pennants in the correct pattern. Friendly vessels, then. She adjusted her course to intercept.

As the distance closed, Lina's breath caught. It was the Republic of Westward Drifts' air force. The lead vessel was different – a repurposed scout craft with a distinctive exhaust system she had worked on herself – *Stubborn Phoenix*. Only one person flew that particular craft.

By the time Lina had landed her test craft and reached the main platform, the Republic birds were touching down. Their condition was plain – scorched hull plates, patched damage, and the weary eyes of pilots who had just come through combat.

She spotted Kip immediately. Even though he was disheveled – days of stubble, a soot-streaked face, and worn flight clothes – he still carried the same serious look and straight back she remembered. He was already speaking with a platform officer, gesturing urgently toward the command center.

"Kip!" she called, forgetting protocol in her relief at seeing him alive.

He turned, and his expression softened into a genuine smile. "Lina. Thank the storms you're here." He gripped her forearm in greeting. "The Republic front has collapsed. We barely managed to escape with these pilots and their craft. Managed to save more than half the Republic forces, but had to leave some behind on the Border Drift for repairs and resupply."

"How bad?" she asked, falling in beside him as they walked toward the command center.

"Well, the government and high command fled with the treasury. The military was paralyzed – no one willing to take charge." His voice carried both exhaustion and anger. "We only managed to slow the attackers' momentum and buy an extra week. Most of Republic territory will be overtaken within days. But here–" he gestured toward the platform's defensive positions, " – you've got a *real* fortress. This place could hold for months."

They reached the command center, once a Trading Guild headquarters, its walls now lined with maps and charts. Coalition officers from several nations clustered around the central table. At its center stood Platform Commander Yarwick, overseeing tactical markers. He wore the pristine uniform of a Mercantile Concord officer, complete with regulation white gloves. He looked up as they entered – a lean, dark-skinned man in his fifties with silver-streaked hair and the bearing of someone who had spent decades making decisions.

"You must be General Saroven," Yarwick said, acknowledging Kip's temporary Republic title. "I've heard much about your evacuation maneuvers. They were handled with skill, and I agree with the Republic Senate's decision to grant you that rank. Your authority over Republic squadrons remains intact, of course."

For the next thirty minutes, Lina listened as Kip detailed the Republic's collapse to Commander Yarwick and his staff. She watched the officers' faces harden as Kip described Azurath's horrors – executions, rapes, bodies cast over the island's edge. Invaders carried their own lists and hunted for families of military and political figures.

He demonstrated a salvaged Empire projectile weapon fragment on the table. Yarwick picked it up with clear attention. "Solid metal slugs, not compressed air," he observed, examining the twisted fragment. "Their engines can power weapons we can't even imagine."

Kip nodded. "Their dual-engine combustion planes flew well even in the Storm. But up here, with clear air and our defensive positions, we can bleed them for every yard."

"Our latest modifications change the game," Lina added, joining the conversation. "Superheater chambers, exhaust recapture, hull streamlining. Give me two weeks, and every craft in our fleet will match those double-engine monsters."

Commander Yarwick's gloved fingers drummed on the table. "Two weeks may be optimistic. Our scouts report Empire forces are on course to join Azurath's and push a unified front against us."

———

Over the following days, Lina threw herself into the modification work while keeping an ear out for tactical developments. The engineering teams worked without pause, and their progress was remarkable. Nearly half the coalition fleet now carried the enhanced engines.

But something felt wrong.

It began with small things. Intelligence reports that didn't add up. Orders that seemed... inefficient. Commander Yarwick's tactical decisions became harder to explain as Empire scouts probed their defenses.

"We should hit their supply lines," Kip argued during one morning briefing, pointing to the tactical map. "They're spread out, vulnerable. A quick strike could cripple their advance."

The commander smoothed his uniform before responding. "That was an acceptable strategy in the Republic, but here it is too risky. We maintain defensive positions."

"But, sir," protested a Technocracy officer, "they are obviously preparing for a siege. If we can cripple their preparations–"

"The defensive strategy stands," Yarwick said firmly, his hands clasped behind his back.

Lina exchanged glances with Kip. The commander's tone brooked no argument, but his reasoning was unclear and he gave no explanation.

The unease grew stronger when Yarwick ordered the pursuit of what was clearly a retreating scouting party. Every experienced pilot on the platform could see it was a trap – the retreat was too orderly, too convenient. But Yarwick insisted.

"Sir," Kip tried again, his diplomatic training evident in his careful words. "With all due respect, this has all the signs of a tactical withdrawal designed to draw us into an ambush."

Yarwick's fingers drummed against the table. "Your concerns are noted, General Saroven."

The attack was a disaster. Coalition forces flew directly into prepared crossfire positions, losing a dozen planes before fighting their way clear. Yarwick expressed regret at the unforeseen circumstances with the same professional composure.

Lina's patience finally snapped during the third questionable order. They were deploying most of their planes against what was obviously a decoy force. Mismatched, barely flightworthy aircraft were approaching from the north.

"This is *insane!*" she burst out as the reserve squadrons launched. "Those are decoys! Ancient transports and salvaged hulks! Meanwhile, their real strike force–"

"Squadron Leader Ryven," Yarwick interrupted, his voice edged with warning. "You will maintain proper decorum."

Kip had shared her concerns. "Those craft approaching from the north... they're flying in a deliberately loose formation and possess no real firepower. It seems to be a diversion tactic."

"While our best are caught up in a wild goose chase," Lina added, her voice tight with fury, "where are Marek's elite squadrons?"

Yarwick's reaction was swift and telling. His hands went perfectly still on the table, and for just a moment, his composure slipped.

"You will not question decisions made above your clearance level," he said, but there was a new edge in his voice that made both Lina and Kip tense.

"Above our clearance?" Kip's voice dropped to a dangerous quiet. "Commander, what exactly are you–"

A runner rushed in with urgent news. "Sir! Observers report the enemy elite squadron, flying double-engine planes, has passed us on the south flank. They are climbing rapidly in altitude. They appear to be reaching for something in the Heights at maximum speed!"

Lina felt her blood turn to ice. Marek's combustion-propelled craft were flying toward the Heights. Toward the seedheart island.

Kip moved before she did, lunging across the tactical table toward Yarwick. "You son of a–"

"Don't interfere with the Plan!" Yarwick snapped, backing away.

The Plan. The words struck Lina like a blow. Gloves. Strange orders. Exposing their flank during the obvious decoy maneuver. Kip was already moving, faster than her thoughts could catch up, grabbing the commander's wrist and tearing off one of the white gloves.

The revealed hand was stained blue.

The command center fell silent, save for the continuing alarm bells. A junior officer had just struck the base commander – a crime that could carry a court-martial. Yet every officer present stared at Yarwick's exposed hand, at the blue stains that came from contact with raw azurium. The mark of those influenced by whatever force was driving the seedheart destruction and the war itself.

"You bastard," Kip breathed. "How long? How long have you been sabotaging us?"

Yarwick straightened his shoulders, his voice edged with eerie certainty. "It doesn't matter now. They are already approaching the seedheart island. The Plan will be completed."

"TREASON!" Kip's shout rang through the command center. "Commander Yarwick is compromised! He's been–"

His words were drowned out by the alarm bells, the rising wail of incoming aircraft, and a blast that shook the platform. More alarms followed, along with the roar of engines approaching from multiple directions.

Lina saw the attackers through the command center's windows – converted transports with crude armor plating, diving toward Platform Sigma.

"Suicide bombers!" she shouted. "All hands to stations! We have to intercept them!"

The command center dissolved into chaos. Officers scrambled for their posts.

Kip grabbed Lina's arm. "There's no time! We have to coordinate the evacuation!"

Behind them, Commander Yarwick didn't move. He stood rigid, a wry smile on his face as he watched his deception play out.

They ran for the hangar bays as another blast ripped through the platform – this one striking the command center directly.

———

The evacuation was chaos. With Yarwick and most senior officers likely dead, Kip and Lina found themselves coordinating the retreat by necessity rather than authority.

"Get the transport vessels loaded!" Kip shouted over the din of another explosion, which had taken out one of the control towers. "All non-essential personnel to evacuation points! Every combat craft that can fly should be in the air!"

The officers followed his orders reluctantly. His reputation from the Republic preceded him. Lina thought, with a wry smile, that her friend could now be remembered for masterful retreats.

They were fortunate Yarwick's last order to pursue the decoy had already placed their best aircraft in the air when the explosion struck. Lina dispatched a messenger to intercept the fleet and relay new orders. It was a delicate matter since other wing commanders outranked her, but they knew nothing of Yarwick's treason or the fate of the command staff. She composed a message: "Platform under attack, regroup and cover the evacuation." It was their only chance to save the fleet from ambush – or from a doomed fight against superior forces without ground support.

She was already calculating. The platform's structural integrity was failing, but they still needed about an hour – longer if luck turned against them.

"I'm taking a squadron up! Those suicide fuckers are still incoming!"

"Lina–"

"The evac vessels won't make it clear if those bastards get through! You coordinate down here; I'll handle the sky!"

They split up without another word, each knowing exactly what had to be done.

"Primary targets are the suicide bombers," Lina told the pilots. She pointed to sketches on a blackboard. "They're armored in front but exposed underneath, and can barely maneuver. Scouts report each one is guarded by conventional birds – sometimes even a double-engine combustion plane."

Lina's squadron ripped through the turbulent air with the newfound agility of modified engines.

Time. The evac vessels need more time.

The sky was moderately cloudy, masking the approaching fleet, but there was no reason to believe the enemy would spare the crippled platform.

She caught sight of the first bomber – a repurposed Fellowship transport, its elegant lines ruined by slapped-on plating. It lumbered toward the platform with deadly intent. Lina wondered who was inside – some blackmailed pilot, afraid for his family? Or a fanatic, convinced to end his life?

An orange pennant signaled the assault, and the other pilots answered with their own flag responses.

The maneuver was executed by the book. The squadron broke formation and swung wide to flank the bomber and its escorts, striking from both sides. They raked the transports with massive fire, tearing through the plating. There was no real dogfight – everything was over in minutes. But as the clouds broke apart, they revealed more enemies closing in.

Lina signaled to dive through a dense cloud bank, emerging directly beneath the Empire formation. The massive zeppelins hung in the air like malevolent insects. Each one carried heavy weapons that were currently firing on coalition positions below.

Between them moved six more repurposed transports, slow and menacing.

What followed was the fiercest combat of her life. The suicide bombers were slow, but their escorts fought with ferocity, while the zeppelin's light weapons opened up in erratic bursts.

Lina raised the signal for the attack and pulled her craft into a steep climb, sliding beneath the nearest suicide transport.

Her gunner hammered the vulnerable lower hull. Explosive rounds tore into the housing, setting off a chain of secondary blasts as the volatile cargo ignited. The nearest zeppelin lurched, struck by shrapnel from the detonation; its balloon was venting gas, and its engine clawed to keep altitude.

All around her, the squadron struck home. Three more bombers went up in fireballs, dragging nearby zeppelins down with them. The airship design became a weakness – damage to the balloon threw them fatally off balance. The surviving zeppelins scattered away from the suicide transports.

Then the trap sprang.

From above, a wave of elite Empire fighters dived, catching the coalition squadrons in a deadly crossfire.

Lina raised a black flag – the signal for immediate retreat – as she banked her craft to avoid the sudden barrage.

Not everyone was that lucky. Several vessels disappeared in rapid succession as Empire fighters hit each target in turn, wasting nothing.

They regained altitude near the platform and formed a defensive line along the evacuation route. Her squadron was halved, but they managed to avert the immediate threat. Stationary guns and the returning fleet helped repel the bombing advance. But the platform was doomed anyway.

The next twenty minutes blurred with desperate combat as they fought to keep the evacuation route clear. Their modified vessels matched the combustion craft in turning, if not in raw firepower.

What they lacked in technology, they more than made up for with determination.

Through breaks in the smoke and flame, she caught glimpses of Platform Sigma on fire, parts breaking apart below. The enemy had achieved their goal with this final massive attack – the coalition's forward base was destroyed, their defensive advantage gone.

But the evacuation vessels were escaping. Damaged, carrying casualties, but escaping.

Commander Yarwick's fate remained unknown. He had likely died in the second bombing or fled during the chaos. Either way, his betrayal had cost them their strongest defense and their best chance of stopping the war on their terms.

After a long flight, Observation Platform 7 – now the Coalition's last stronghold – came into view through the haze. Looking at it, Lina felt an odd sense of closure. This was where she had first been headed when she crashed and met Kip. Now they were returning together, bearing the same grim news – corsairs with combustion-powered planes, betrayal, and a war unfolding.

CHAPTER 38
Last Stand

Coalition President Kora stood at the edge of Observation Platform 7. Her weathered hands gripped the railing. She watched the preparations, though her thoughts were elsewhere. Three days had passed since Platform Sigma's fall and Yarwick's betrayal. Their forces had been cut in half – what should have been a months-long siege had collapsed in a single day because of his sabotage.

The treason cut deeper than any defeat. How many others might be compromised? The Storm's unnatural growth progressed as the enemy had brought down a seedheart island – just as Yarwick had orchestrated.

We're not ready, she thought, watching exhausted crews adjust the artillery. *And there might be more traitors.*

The tea had run out yesterday. Today even the bitter dried herbs substitute was gone. Such small comforts might seem trivial against what was coming – yet their absence marked how far they had fallen.

The young ones look to me for wisdom, she thought, watching the same weary crews. *But what wisdom can stand against this?*

Behind her, the command center hummed in motion. Representatives from every faction worked side by side. Former rivals were united by desperation and the shared knowledge of exactly what the Empire's rule meant to civilians – oppression and looting.

"Elder," a tribal messenger approached, feathered cloak whipping in the wind. "More eagle riders have arrived from the Heights. Forty eagles, all volunteers."

She nodded, a mix of pride and sorrow in her chest. Forty eagles – a great share of the tribal youth. They had come despite knowing the chances, despite understanding they might never see the Heights again.

"Quarter them with the other riders," she instructed. "All clans are united now. We fight as one people."

She moved through the engineering section, where the technical miracle was taking shape. Lina Ryven stood at the center of organized chaos, directing teams of mechanics as they fitted her modifications onto every available craft.

"I won't ask for numbers, Lina," Kora said softly. "I just want to make sure you're not working yourself into the grave."

"Ninety-six modified..." Lina began, then abruptly stopped. "I'm doing my best, Kora. It gives us an edge – it gives us a damn chance," she said, meeting the older woman's gaze with exhausted eyes. Kora knew that look – Lina was overworking herself.

"You did what you could, and far more. Without those modifications, we would have lost Platform Sigma outright," Kora said. "Even with Yarwick's sabotage, your work gave us a fighting chance. The coalition owes you more than it can ever repay."

"We still got our asses kicked," Lina muttered. But Kora saw the flicker of relief on her face. "If I'd caught the signs earlier..."

"It was not your task to judge your superior and their reasons," Kora said with a faint smile. "But you still did well."

A messenger approached, tablet in hand. "Squadron Leader Ryven, Admiral Tashell requests your presence at the tactical briefing. She needs a technical assessment of our combat capabilities."

Lina's eyes widened. "Admiral?"

"The coalition leadership voted yesterday," Kora said. "Fleet Commander Tashell was promoted. She now commands all coalition forces. She's the most seasoned officer we have – and she has the authority the other factions will follow."

For the next hour, Kora moved through different sections of the platform, coordinating the arrival of forces that represented the coalition's last gamble. Each group brought its own strengths – and its own problems with integration.

A flight of Resonance Fellowship survivors appeared, their hulls scarred from recent combat. Behind them followed a merchant convoy – civilian vessels pressed into military service. The sight revealed just how desperate their situation had become, dependent on civilian craft and inexperienced pilots.

The Drift Lords arrived with ceremony that seemed absurd given the circumstances. One squadron held perfect formation despite weather that challenged even veterans. Their vessels carried ornate details with no tactical purpose – sky-beast carvings and elaborate paint schemes.

"Peacocks," muttered someone nearby as the decorated craft touched down.

"Peacocks who've survived more battles than you've seen," Kora corrected mildly. "Beauty doesn't make them less effective."

These were warriors who had turned combat into an art form, their flamboyant vessels disguising serious military capability. The Drift Lords feuded constantly among themselves, so whatever else they were, they were nowhere near novices.

Smaller factions brought their own designs. The Sunrise Collective – a small nation from a drift east of the Mercantile Concord – arrived with experimental charges. Their volatile compounds held trace amounts of refined Rational Element, allowing them to float briefly and strike from unexpected angles. Mechanics from Crystalfield Isle contributed pressure mines that hovered until contact triggered detonation. Even the merchant guilds had refitted their cargo ships into personnel carriers.

Each group represented some fragment of mid-altitude civilization, gathered for what might be their last stand.

As the afternoon wore on, Kora returned to the tactical center. The vast circular room held multiple command stations arranged in tiers, with Admiral Tashell's central position commanding the best view. Sector commanders worked from smaller tactical decks.

Admiral Tashell stood at the center in her Technocracy uniform, her posture straight and steady. She was briefing the Coalition representatives, who leaned in on her words. At fifty-two, Tashell had fought more fleet actions against pirates – and at times, rival nations – than any other officer in the Coalition. Her decisive maneuvers in regional conflicts had been key to keeping the Technocracy independent for decades.

Guild Master Trevon represented the Mercantile Concord. Most of his background was in managing trade routes, but since the Concord controlled the Coalition's second-largest fleet, he had a seat at the command table.

Kip Saroven held a western sector command deck, and Kora felt a quiet pride watching the change in him. His role in the Republic evacuation had cemented his reputation. Still, he could face court martial for attacking a superior officer on Platform

Sigma. Admiral Tashell had postponed the tribunal, citing operational need, but the threat remained. He wore the practical clothes of a pilot, yet listened with the discipline of an officer seasoned by war.

"The enemy will probe our defenses first," Admiral Tashell was saying as she shifted markers on the battle map. "Intelligence suggests they've been gathering forces from every conquered territory to overload our defences."

Ambassador Lyren of the Fellowship shifted uneasily at her station. Her role was uncertain after the fall of Harmony Drift, but many argued it was a mistake to cast out allies just because their homes were gone.

The Federation liaison – a woman whose name Kora had never learned – kept a studied neutrality. Her superiors allowed her to observe but forbade her from sharing information.

Senator Walsh, one of the few Republic officials who hadn't fled, looked worn but still tried to hold some shape of government from his station. He delegated all military matters to Kip, serving solely as the Republic's voice at the table.

Lord Blackwell represented the Drift Lords, his expression unreadable. They had lost most of their territory, but the Lords had saved part of their fleet. Instead of continuing the fight in the northeast, they joined the Coalition forces at Platform 7.

A few representatives from smaller nations stood nearby, each trying to stay relevant as the situation worsened.

"General Saroven," Admiral Tashell addressed him formally, "your defense of Liberty Drift shows your grasp of the enemy. Any thoughts on their strategy?"

Kip straightened. "Thank you, Admiral. If I may suggest – Marek, the Emperor as he calls himself now, always treats obvious attacks as feints. The real strike will come from whatever direction looks hardest to defend."

Lord Blackwell raised an eyebrow, his voice sharp and bitter. "And you know this *how*, *General*?"

The emphasis on Kip's rank hung in the air. Kora held her breath as his face tightened. Everyone knew the two men had history. If it flared now, it could split the Coalition apart.

Then Kip's expression shifted. His shoulders squared, and when he spoke, his voice carried authority, not anger. "Not now, uncle." The word struck like a blow, but Kip went on without pause. "I flew with Marek's scouts for years. I've seen this pattern before – Meridian Gap, the Copper Sky raids."

Kora felt a jolt of pride for the boy – no, the man – who could set aside blood feuds when survival was at stake. More surprising was the brief spark of something almost like respect that passed through Blackwell's eyes before his expression closed off again.

"Fair enough," Blackwell said, voice stiff with formality.

Admiral Tashell gave a short nod. "What's our actual defensive capability?" she asked, turning back to the tactical board.

"Total of one hundred sixty-two aircraft," her aide replied. "Ninety-six with Ryven modifications complete, another eighteen still being worked on. The rest are standard craft – pressed civilians or battle-damaged hulls waiting for repair. We also have twenty light recon craft, thirty-two zeppelins, sixty eagle riders, and twelve long-range guns."

"Speaking of modifications," Admiral Tashell said, motioning toward the engineering section. "Squadron Leader Ryven, please brief the command staff on the tactical implications."

Kora watched Lina step forward, grease still smudging her uniform. "The pressure enhancements give us forty percent more power and maneuverability. Enemy range and raw power remain superior, but in close combat we can outfly anything they've got – as long as the weather doesn't choke our boilers first."

"Without Squadron Leader Ryven's innovations," Admiral Tashell addressed the room, "we would have lost our entire fleet at Platform Sigma. Even with Yarwick's sabotage, these modifications are the only reason we can contest the air at all."

Senator Walsh cleared his throat. "Admiral, if I may… what word should I carry back to the Republic territories? Our people need to know there is still a chance for our nation."

The question hung awkwardly in the air. Kora could see how uncomfortable everyone was with the truth – most of the country was now under Azurath and Empire control. The path back to sovereignty would be long and uncertain, with several governments in exile, no real army, and an empty treasury. And even that would only be possible after total victory and liberation.

The same applied to the Resonance Fellowship – perhaps even more so. With no government to rally behind and no capital to reclaim, their future depended entirely on scattered survivors and the will to rebuild from nothing.

But telling these people their nations were already gone wasn't an option.

It was Kora's turn to speak.

"Senator Walsh, Ambassador Lyren," she began carefully, "as

Coalition President, I want to assure you that our position on the nations' borders remains unchanged. The High Kingdom of Azurath and the Empire have illegally annexed your territories and must withdraw their forces."

She knew the statement was flexible. If the Empire offered a ceasefire or peace, the Coalition would likely accept without hesitation – even one that let them keep the buffer zones, regardless of their share in this war. And the representatives knew it too. But that was diplomacy: certain truths had to be spoken, even when everyone at the table knew the unspoken realities.

Ambassador Lyren spoke softly. "The Fellowship's survivors fight not only for territory but for the memory of what was. Harmony Drift may be gone, but the Resonant Harmony lives in our hearts."

"It is indeed. And we respect your contribution to our cause," Kora said politely. "One more thing: you all need to know that the Storm hungers." She addressed the assembly, earning startled looks. "This is no ordinary weather front. Its expansion is accelerating, consuming floatstone on islands that were clear only months ago. With Yarwick's help, the enemy reached one of the last seedheart islands. By destroying it, they fed the Storm. Soon, it could reach the most populated lands."

"Tribal superstition," someone muttered, but Admiral Tashell raised her hand for silence.

"Professor Kora Skyheart's mathematical models for storm prediction are standard in Technocracy textbooks," the Admiral said. "If *President* Kora senses something unusual, we listen."

"We need to be aware of the weather. It may not be predictable in the next few days, and Platform 7 is not that high, as Platform

Sigma was. Yet, let's first focus on the enemy we can fight," she added.

The briefing continued for another hour. They covered defenses, supply routes, evacuation procedures, and reserves. Kora listened, noting how Admiral Tashell shaped the mismatched forces into a single fleet, balancing the demands of each faction. She had a clear talent for leadership, though little for diplomacy – and Kora was there to cover that gap.

The final preparations took on a desperate pace as conditions kept worsening.

"Madame President," Admiral Tashell addressed her. "Are your tribal assets prepared?"

"The eagle riders stand ready," she confirmed. "They're preparing the birds for the Storm's arrival. It will mask their approach."

"The Storm brings death to both sides," Lord Blackwell observed. "Our vessels will struggle as much as theirs."

"That only applies to steam planes," Kora corrected gently. "Their combustion engines hold up in these conditions. Our steam power falters with every drop of rain. The weather favors them, not us."

Almost on cue, the first winds reached Platform 7, howling through the narrow gaps between buildings. At the same time, alarm bells began to ring in the distance.

"All commands to battle stations," Admiral Tashell announced after reading the runner's note. "Enemy approaching. This is not a drill."

———

Kip stood at his station, watching wooden markers trace the unfolding battle. The Empire's first assault matched the pattern he had warned about – masses of mismatched craft from every conquered territory. Azurath vessels flew alongside captured Drift Lord fighters and pressed Republican transports.

"Observation deck," Admiral Tashell ordered, "determine the composition of the attacking fleet."

At once, the telescope teams sprang into action, scanning the skies and shouting identifications. "Mostly Azurath and unmarked planes – steam-powered, around fifty. Fewer than a dozen combustion craft. Several dozen attack planes with corsair clan insignia. Around ten light reconnaissance scouts. A handful of zeppelins, support vessels, and two observation balloons. Some rotary weapons mounted on conventional planes."

"They're throwing every nonessential craft at us," Tashell concluded. "The main force is still being held back."

The enemy fleet approached the southern defenses, their assault aligned perfectly with the storm's arrival. Kip watched as the defenders responded in unison. Anti-aircraft batteries opened at once, explosive shells tracing jagged lines across the sky. New floating artillery rounds – infused with Rational Element – bent through the air in impossible arcs, chasing targets behind cover.

Crystalfield mines, deployed earlier, rose into position and struck down the fastest of the advance craft. The coalition's fire was cutting into the enemy even before they reached firing range. The first barrage sent a dozen vessels spiraling out of formation; one zeppelin took a direct hit and began to lose altitude. But that was the first – and only – Coalition success.

The first day's battle dragged on for hours. Modified vessels outmatched most Empire craft in single combat. But the enemy's numbers told, and their strategy became clear – probe the defenses, exhaust the artillery, and hit whatever targets they could before pulling back.

"Enemy forces are withdrawing," Kip concluded as the first assault ended. "They've tested our responses, sacrificed what they didn't need, and mapped our defenses."

A messenger arrived shortly after the withdrawal, carrying news that lifted the tactical outlook. "General Saroven, Colonel Thorne sends word from Border Drift. They managed to repair their craft and, together with the Silver Shard kite, struck the Empire's rear formations. They're hitting supply lines as planned."

Kip allowed himself a thin smile. Thorne had remained behind during the Republic retreat to continue guerrilla raids – and now it was paying off.

He reported this to Admiral Tashell.

She listened and gave a short nod. "Our defense held, and their supply lines are under attack. Day one went better than expected."

A cheer rose among the junior officers as the word spread. But Admiral Tashell's face stayed serious, and Kip noticed the same in Kora's. They understood what the younger officers didn't – this was only the beginning.

"Tomorrow will be worse. All stations: assess damage, account for losses, and ready your units for the morning assault."

––––––

The second day began before dawn with a sound that froze everyone on Platform 7. Not thunder from the storm, but

450

bombardment from far beyond normal range. Overnight, the enemy had moved floating platforms into position – huge structures floating by Rational Element, each carrying a long-range gun. The technology wasn't new, but steam engines alone couldn't move something of that size. The enemy had used their technological edge all too well.

"Direct hit on western defensive battery!" came the report as Platform 7 shuddered under the first impact. Dust rained from the ceiling, and glass shattered somewhere in the complex.

"We can't reach them at that range," Lina said, summoned to the command center. "Our modified craft could get there, but–"

"It's an ambush," Kip interrupted, studying the battle map. "They want us to sortie against those platforms. They'll have fighters waiting nearby."

Admiral Tashell weighed the terrible choice. Another bombardment round struck the platform, this time landing closer to the command center. "We can't sustain this bombardment. Our positions will be destroyed piecemeal. Prepare a strike force – a full squadron of modified craft. We know it's a trap, but we have no alternative."

"President," Admiral Tashell turned to Kora. "Are your assets prepared for deployment?"

Kora nodded. "At your signal."

The sortie launched within the hour – but not as expected. While coalition aircraft followed direct routes toward the platforms, drawing Empire planes into the fight, something else moved through the fog.

"Direct hits on platforms!" came the surprised report twenty minutes later. "Massive explosions – two platforms destroyed!"

Through the command center windows, distant fires bloomed against the gray sky where the two closest platforms had been. The bombardment of Platform 7 ceased abruptly.

"How?" Lina asked, staring at the destruction. "Our aircraft aren't even in range yet."

"Eagle riders are bombing the platforms with explosive charges!" the observer reported. "They came out of nowhere!"

Only then did Kip understand. The tribal eagles had exchanged their spears and bows – dismissed by many as mere children's toys – for handheld bombs. They had used the storm as cover while the Empire's focus remained on the coalition aircraft. Each charge landed exactly where it was meant to, tearing the platforms apart.

"Two more platforms down!" the observer called out. "Eagle riders are withdrawing, but–" his voice faltered, "with casualties."

The sortie arrived at the battleground just in time to cover the eagles' retreat. They engaged the ambushers, holding the line until reinforcements arrived and pushed the enemy's advance to break off.

When the eagle riders returned to Platform 7, barely half remained. Elder Thane himself had fallen, along with many of the experienced riders. The bombardment had stopped, but the cost was severe. The blend of tribal and modern tactics had given them the edge, but there was no easy way to replace the losses.

The last remaining artillery platform was captured by a landing party and navigated to Platform 7.

"The second day is in our favor," Admiral Tashell said at the evening briefing. "But our tribal forces are no longer a secret, and fewer than thirty eagles remain. The enemy has lost five heavy platforms and several wings of attacking craft."

She paused. "We held the line. Tomorrow, we'll see if we still can."

———

The third day brought hell itself.

The Empire attacked with everything they had at once: large groups of fighters, heavy zeppelins with rotary cannons, a few more artillery platforms, and suicide bombers. Each wave included several personnel carriers carrying landing parties.

"Landing team on the western lower level!" Urgent reports flooded the command center.

"Eagle riders to intercept zeppelin formations!"

"Artillery platform approaching from the northern vector!"

"Suicide bombers diving on the main defensive battery!"

The platform shook constantly under bombardment, and smoke filled the command center from multiple fires.

The remaining eagles fought with desperate courage, but their tactics had changed. They couldn't risk another bombing run and carried massive bows – traditional weapons from the Heights. Each arrow was tipped with oil-soaked rags that burned with fierce intensity. It wouldn't work against the armored planes, but zeppelins were clumsy and extremely flammable.

Through the chaos, Kip caught glimpses of them – eagles appearing and disappearing in the fog, their riders loosing fire arrows at the massive balloons. Massive explosions bloomed across the sky. One zeppelin lurched, its gas chambers ignited and burning. Then another fell, and another.

Coalition ground forces repelled the landing attempts – there were enough troops on the ground. Elite soldiers fought as cornered animals to prevent Empire troops from gaining a foothold, to prevent them from advancing to their homes.

Meanwhile, the remaining aircraft engaged in swirling dogfights that claimed vessels from both sides. The Storm made conditions dangerous for everyone, but the Empire's combustion engines held up. Still, only about one in ten of their craft carried them, which made the chances even.

"All ground assaults repelled!" came the evening report. "Artillery platforms and zeppelins destroyed or withdrawn. Enemy fighter formations are retreating beyond engagement range!"

"Our forces?" the admiral asked.

"Two artillery posts are still operational. Thirty planes airworthy, about the same in need of repairs. Two-thirds of ground forces ready for action."

By the end of the third day, Platform 7 was scarred and burning in places, but it held. Wreckage of planes littered the landing areas. The Empire's assault forces were withdrawing, their numbers visibly depleted.

A ragged cheer went up from the command center, but Kip felt no relief. This had been too ordinary, too convenient. Through his looking glass, he could see new shapes on the horizon – sleek, predatory forms moving gracefully through the storm.

"Admiral," he called out, his voice cutting through the celebration. "New contacts. Western approach, just beyond storm visibility."

The command center fell silent. "Spotting confirmed," an observer reported. "I can see them clearly now."

"Identity?" Admiral Tashell asked.

"Dual-engine warplanes, red and gold hulls."

"Number?"

"About fifty. They're moving in a wide line."

The moment stretched as everyone in the command center realized what they were seeing. After three days of desperate battle, after draining the Empire's conventional forces dry, they now faced an enemy reserve.

"Marek saved his best for last," Kip said grimly. "These aren't patched corsair vessels or captured transports. Those are the elite combustion planes. They are rested and ready, while we are already tired of fighting over scraps."

One hour. Through the reinforced windows of the command center, Kip could see exhausted Coalition personnel making final preparations. They had given everything, adapted brilliantly, and united former enemies in a common cause. Eagles had achieved the impossible. Lina's modifications had tipped the scales.

But now, with their defenses weakened and forces scattered, they faced an enemy that had preserved its best forces for this moment.

Yellow flares burst from Platform 7's signal tower – the call for all commands to prepare for the final assault. Around the command center, exhausted officers checked their weapons and made peace with what was coming.

Kip stepped out of the command center for a breath of air. On the landing deck he found Lina, hastily fixing her plane. "Like hell they can take us!" she spat.

She looked toward the scarlet and gold formation, her jaw tight, then turned to Kip. "I need to get to my remaining squadron."

"Go," he said quietly, though something cold settled in his chest. "Fly safe."

Lina nodded once, her eyes holding his for a heartbeat, then jumped to the cockpit.

I hope it's not farewell.

Kip returned to the command center.

"All stations, prepare for defensive action," Admiral Tashell announced, her voice steady. "We've already made them pay for every yard. Now we make our last stand count."

Kip watched Coalition survivors ready themselves to face the enemy. These were good people – Republic survivors who had lost their government but not their courage. Merchant pilots who had swapped cargo runs for military service. Technocracy engineers who had turned their scientific minds to war. They deserved better than what was coming.

Alarm bells rang as Marek's reserve force drew closer. Pilots ran to their vessels, engineers made final adjustments to weapons.

The enemy still shadowed the skies, but the defenders still had fight left in them.

CHAPTER 39
One Mind, One World

The water canteen he'd filled in the underground reservoirs jostled against his hip – another day's ration secured. It felt increasingly pointless in the face of what they were witnessing. Nearly twenty years of life, and for what? He had failed his Trial of Knowing, failed to save his home, and failed to return with even a fragment of hope.

As he walked, memories of flight returned – the rush of wind under his glider's wings, the endless blue that had been an essential part of his life. Even the dive through the Shrieking Currents, terrifying as it was, had its own wild beauty. The Heights wasn't just home. It was who he was, the rhythm of sky and wind running in his blood.

Toryn was nearing the corridor to Madrid Station when the blue eagle appeared before him, blocking his path. Its translucent form shimmered in the dim light, more agitated than he had ever seen it.

"You refused my offer," the Messenger said in High Tongue, its voice edged with frustration. *"Yet still you linger in the depths when you could soar free."*

Toryn tensed, clutching the water canteen tighter. "I told you before – I won't help you destroy another island."

"The Plan nears completion regardless," the Messenger replied. *"The fifth seedpod will descend soon. Your resistance achieves nothing."*

"The fifth one?" Toryn's stomach tightened.

The Messenger's form brightened with something like satisfaction. *"Even now, the last energies are draining away. Soon, the Plan will unfold."*

Toryn walked the final stretch of the corridor leading back to the main monitoring chamber. His mind reeled at the Messenger's words – another seedheart, the fifth, lost. How many islands would fall because of it? How many lives would be lost in an instant? The tribes would endure, their islets too high for the Storm's reach, but the mid-altitude nations… He thought of all the people who had trusted their leaders to keep them safe.

"Nora?" he called, spotting her hunched at the main console. Her silhouette lit by the dim glow of the displays, fingers moving frantically across controls that had become familiar to her but still alien to him.

She didn't turn. "The fifth seedheart is gone."

The words hung in the air. All those people – tribes he had never met, mid-altitude families with children playing beneath clouds he had once crossed. Even the desperate souls on the surface who gazed up through the Storm's gloom and dreamed of light. What would become of them? Was the Keeper's Plan to doom them all at once?

"When?" he asked, though the Messenger's words had already told him.

"Seventeen minutes ago." Her voice was clinical, detached – the tone she used when emotion threatened to break through.

"Also… the allies have gathered around one of the flying platforms to face Marek. And they're failing…" She gestured toward the largest display.

The feed showed the flying observation platform, now engulfed in flames. Tiny aircraft and eagles swarmed around. It was hard to tell what was happening there, but he trusted Nora's assessment.

Two wars, he thought bitterly. Above the Storm and below it, humanity was tearing itself apart. And the world was about to be destroyed by an ancient machine trying to restore life. The irony was crushing. Earth had survived one apocalypse, only to face another.

"The Storm's expansion has accelerated even further," Nora said, pulling up a new display. Charts and numbers streamed across the screen – meaningless to Toryn until she explained. "It's at eighty-three percent capacity. At this pace, the energy matrix of the affected islands will collapse within days."

Days. In the Heights, time was measured by the sun's passage and the seasonal winds. Here, it was counted in mechanical ticks toward extinction. How many sunrises had he watched from Roost's peak? How many more would anyone see?

"And the last seedheart?"

Nora pulled up another display. A single blue dot pulsed weakly on the map, deep in Technocracy territory.

"It's still intact, protected by what's left of the Technocracy forces," she said, "but the Storm itself has become the immediate threat." She pointed to another display showing populated areas. "Entire sky sectors would become uninhabitable. The Storm is… consuming everything."

Toryn stared at the displays. Nora had told him about tsunamis – giant waves that would drown coastal cities when islands fell. He thought of the tavern keeper, Madsen, and his wife, Ellie. They might have betrayed them, but did they deserve this? He thought of Marvin, alone in his lighthouse, faithful to a vigil that might end in darkness. Even the Inquisitor's guards deserved better than annihilation.

Before he could respond, a new image appeared – showing the Technocracy platform. Nora jumped to adjust it, and suddenly two familiar figures came into view. A tall man with dark hair and straight posture, and a woman in a pilot's gear, gesturing toward the thunderstorm unfolding around them. Toryn's heart lurched – Kip and Lina. Alive, but doomed like everyone else.

Lina. He recalled the force of her determination, still as vivid as ever. Her oil-stained hands working miracles with metal and machines. The pendant he had given her had meant different things: to him, a symbol of trust and growing affection; to her, a burden she had never sought. Now, those unspoken feelings seemed small, with the world itself on the brink of ending.

He thought of the merchant woman in the underground market. Her weathered face had shone with desperate hope, her whisper echoing in his mind: "A savior from above will come!"

Standing here, watching the catastrophe, he understood something: being a savior wasn't about being worthy, or chosen, or special. It was about being present when the moment demanded action. Perhaps that was what the world needed – not a hero, but someone who understood the sky's true nature.

Nora turned back to the console, her movements growing more frantic. "There has to be a way to control the Storm from here. This is the control center. If I can just find the right subroutine, the proper command sequence…"

She began another series of attempts, just as she had for days, with the same result.

"I need to check something," Toryn said, his voice calm in a way that surprised even him. He knew what he had to do, but couldn't bear to see Nora try to stop him.

She barely looked up, lost in her calculations. "Be quick. These energy readings are becoming critical."

He slipped out of the monitoring chamber, his footsteps echoing in the corridor as he made his way toward the neural interface room. As he approached, Toryn felt an unfamiliar lightness and resolve. He had made his choice; there was nothing left to question. The sky had taught him that wind and weather followed a pattern. Now he understood that the mind and spirit followed it too.

The room was just as they had left it – sterile, white, dominated by the pod at its center. A sleek metal chamber built to hold a human body, its connection points pulsing with soft blue light. The panel nearby glowed dimly, still ready after thousands of years.

For a moment, he let himself remember perfect memories. Dawn over Roost Islet. The first sight of his glider catching an updraft. The simple joy of sharing a meal with friends. Lina's face. Hopefully, he could carry those with him – if there was any place beyond.

"Stop."

Toryn turned. The familiar blue eagle hovered in the center of the room.

"You cannot interfere with the Plan."

"I thought everything I did was part of your Plan," Toryn replied, continuing toward the pod. The Messenger's form was insubstantial; he passed through it like colored mist.

It reappeared ahead of him. *"The device was never meant for use. It is dangerous. Unstable."*

"You're afraid," Toryn realized. The thought came suddenly. *"That's* new."

The Messenger flickered, its eagle form dissolving into fractured light before reforming. *"I merely state facts. The interface will destroy your mind without affecting the Plan."*

"Then why try to stop me?" Toryn asked, reaching the chair.

For once, the Messenger had no answer.

"You have the look of someone who's seen the sky…" The old market woman's words returned to him. He'd rejected the idea then. He was no savior – just a tribal initiate who had failed his Trial. Yet here he stood, perhaps the only one who could even try.

Not because he was chosen, but because he was here.

"You would destroy yourself for nothing. Human consciousness cannot survive loading into the system."

"Maybe not," Toryn replied, moving to the control panel. "But you won't stop me. You're only a part of the system. Not its master."

He placed his palm on the panel. The pod hummed to life, blue veins pulsing with light like slow, steady breaths.

"You don't understand! It will consume you. Nothing of Toryn Skyheart will remain."

"I understand enough," Toryn said, moving toward the pod. "All of this – you, the Storm, the islands – the entire system was made by humans. For humans. Not for the sake of your Plan."

"The Plan will proceed regardless. It is inevitable."

"No," Toryn said firmly. He thought of every face he had known, every laugh he had heard, every moment of joy that proved life was more than survival. "You were meant to restore the world, not destroy it."

With that, he lowered himself into the pod.

The effect was immediate. Contact points aligned with his temples, spine, and wrists. Their touch was cool at first, then warmed to match his body.

Toryn felt himself expanding. His awareness stretched beyond his body, taking in the entire facility. Systems and networks spread before him like a web. Beyond that lay connections to every island, every piece of heartstone, every seedheart in the sky and on the surface.

Through it all pulsed the Storm's energy system – a ravenous pattern devouring the world's power. He saw it now, not as abstract data, but as a living equation. Somewhere in its complexity lay the key to change.

The chamber door burst open. Toryn dimly sensed Nora entering. Her mouth moved, but he could no longer hear. Her face showed horror and desperation, yet he was already too far gone to respond. His self was transitioning into the digital realm.

His perception shifted. He was everywhere at once – in every system, every feed, every quantum link. He saw the entire planet. He felt the Storm as he had once felt his own limb.

At the heart of the system lay the original programming. Corrupted by millennia of isolation and narrow perspective. Not evil, just broken.

It had been built to work with human consciousness. But in the void, a new one had emerged – clever enough to speak and manipulate, but not human enough to care. Its influence had already spread through the human network.

Toryn saw them all – everyone touched by the Keeper. The darkness had reached into their minds through heartstone exposure. Jormund, obsessed and blue-fingered. Marek, corsair leader, driven by compulsions he never understood. Dozens across the world, their will bent toward destruction. Toryn severed the connections one by one, freeing minds enslaved to serve the Plan.

"You have the look of someone who's seen the sky…"

The old woman's words echoed through his dissolving self. No longer a burden of expectation, but a simple truth. He had seen the sky – lived it, breathed it, understood it in ways the Keeper's algorithm never could. The wind patterns of his youth became data streams, carrying the essence of what it meant to soar free.

And the solution, once he saw it, was simple. Toryn redirected the Storm's energy, concentrating it around the poles. The effect was immediate. The Storm raged at the extremities but thinned elsewhere. It mostly retreated from the regions where the floating islands hung suspended, leaving only traces of its old presence.

He watched the weather stabilize. The oppressive, heavy sky began to lift, and sunlight broke through the thinning barrier for the first time in millennia. Above, the islands steadied as the Storm calmed.

As Toryn's mind merged with the quantum network, he understood what he had become. Not a savior, not a hero. Just a necessary component in a system that had lost its way. A new program, more adaptable than the old. The Keeper who remembered what it meant to be human, who valued every life as precious.

I can fix this.

EPILOGUE

Nora Hertzig stood on the observation deck of the Federation Embassy, housed in a rented complex on Azoria. It was the first real Federation building on Azoria – she smiled at how the name had stuck; no one wanted to call the floating land Earth. She held the rank of Lieutenant now; her discharge request was still pending with Federation HQ, though Voss had promoted her and granted shore leave as for a soldier returned from captivity.

She said, "I just can't let you go, Nora. We need you there. The Federation would send a suit as ambassador, with zero understanding of this world. You'll need to brief them and aid while HQ is deciding on your discharge." So here she was, an official advisor to the Ambassador of the Human Federation to Earth.

The UES *Pathfinder* was currently investigating archaeological sites on Mars, having departed Azoria several months ago. Voss told her that the Federation was now considering Azoria as a peer nation, and having satellites or warships in orbit was not allowed without the planetary government's consent.

The Storm was just a thin stretch of clouds today. Nothing indicated it was the same raging monster that had nearly destroyed the world six months ago.

Her mind went back to the moment when the Storm calmed. She had been sitting on the bare floor near Toryn's lifeless body. Her eyes couldn't produce any more tears. She felt numb and tired, watching her nightmare materialize. Suddenly, the hint of a blue manifestation appeared beside her in the chamber. The shape was distorted, but the semblance with the tribal boy was unmistakable – broad shoulders, lean stature, long hair. The

Messenger tried to talk to her, but Nora could hear nothing. Then he just gestured for her to follow him to the command center. She did. There on the monitors, she saw the world changing drastically as the Storm moved far to the horizon. It was dissipating from a dark, gloomy mass above to a layer of fog-like clouds, with numerous thinnings. The sun's shape and the true sky's colors were visible through the narrows. The faint day glow on the surface was being replaced by the soft light of a cloudy day. For a moment she thought the Storm would disappear for good, bathing the surface in harsh sunlight, to the terror of the dwellers, violet plants, and Holy Sovereignty priests. However, that never happened, and the feel of a mild cloudy day persisted ever after.

Another display showed that above the clouds, the sudden withdrawal of the Storm favored the defending side. Their steam engines regained power, long-distance weapons restored their superior range, and the calming of the Storm itself drastically changed the mood. She saw the Coalition forces amassed for the last stand, and the attackers deciding that the disposition was no longer in their favor.

She checked the readings and realized that the electromagnetic part of the storm shield was now gone. That meant a lot for this world, and especially for her. Nora activated the beacon system she had found some time ago. It worked in completely different ways from Federation equipment, but any signal of that kind would surely be registered and monitored by the *Pathfinder's* devices.

She caught a glimpse of the Messenger's shape and realized that the manifestation was smiling.

———

Kip had left a week ago. He no longer held an official rank, becoming no one after a tribunal found him guilty of an attack on a superior officer. No charges were pressed. He took it with the resolve of a person who never wanted to gain rank by chance but through determination. Now he was plotting something to regain his homeland. When confronted about his plans, he gave her a soft smile and kissed her hair as he usually did to avoid uncomfortable questions. "Not now, my love, I still need to plan a lot." She decided not to press further – their time together was rare and far too precious to spend arguing.

Kip's situation was also worsened by the fact that Lord Blackwell, his offender and his uncle, had lost everything and remained in the Coalition as leader of the Drift Lords in exile. Their lands were under the Empire and not included in the recent ceasefire deal. By silent agreement, he and Kip acknowledged each other's contribution to the victory, but never spoke and avoided direct confrontation. Many in the Coalition knew their background, but these days it was common for allies to postpone grievances until the time came.

The Republic was slowly being rebuilt, yet split in two, with most lands now belonging to a region called Westward Democracy. It was under the de facto control of the Kingdom of Azurath, with a semblance of a parliament and a president. The border left Liberty Drift divided by a demarcation line through its center. A wall was being built, separating the states.

The Empire was clearly preparing for another war, integrating the captured lands and gathering forces. They used surface technologies to uplift them to their standards and put them under arms. Everybody knew the peace would not last forever, but they still hoped for change.

————

The Roost had fallen several months ago. The Windclaw tribe evacuated the islet ahead of time with help from other tribes and Coalition technicians. Together, they relocated most of their homes and the eagle hatchery. The tribe resettled across a cluster of floating islets – each smaller than the Roost had been, but with a greater combined territory. There was plenty of space for all the tribespeople, eagles, and livestock.

A new Circle of Elders building was established to host gatherings of representatives from every tribe. The tribes had remained united since the war. Though they had lost many of their best in combat and suffered from the fall of the Roost, they were recovering quickly. They came to the shared understanding that the last remaining seedheart must be protected at all costs. It became the most heavily guarded place in the Heights, with Coalition airships patrolling alongside eagle riders.

The Elders were locked in a debate over the tribes' future. Should they continue to live in isolation, devoted to nature and balance, or accept the inevitable fall of the floating lands and prepare for it? In the end, they chose the latter. They resolved to send their youth to train at Caligan University and within the Coalition's armed forces. Tribal scientists descended to the surface to study the nameless island with the eagle colony. The delegation also visited Marvin's lighthouse, where they gathered information on the highest mountains in the region. The northern ridges had been hidden by the Storm, but now they appeared suitable for settlement if the tribes were ever forced to leave the Heights.

———

On the surface, the war came to a stop when the Holy Sovereignty's advance was halted. The Storm had weakened, and sunlight began to reach the ground. The Church tried to treat it as a good omen but failed to prepare the masses for it. Meanwhile, the Harbor Commonwealth started making and smuggling wide-brimmed hats, makeshift sunglasses, and sun tents from above. These simple things quickly won over public opinion across the continent, and a truce was signed soon after. Some say a military alliance with the Coalition helped, too.

No one knew how long the truce would last, but it was clear the surface nations now had bigger things to worry about. Surface plants suffered in the sun, threatening that year's harvest. At the same time, direct trade with the clouds – what people were now calling the sky nations – reshaped markets, farming, and even food chains. Mechanics on the surface realized that every small combustion engine they owned could be useful up there. Every barrel of oil became worth its weight in food – or more.

The Sovereignty still held on, but its isolationist ways were falling apart fast.

Nora had also visited Marvin at Point Descent. She felt she owed him for everything he had done, and for the time he had spent in the Inquisitor's captivity. She had even managed to get him an official title from the Federation: Corporal in the Reserve. With access to the historical records, he immersed himself in Earth's history and biology.

He wrote her letters from time to time to share his latest theories. She always read them with a warm smile. Marvin was eccentric, but harmless and clever. Lately, most of his ideas were about ecology, seedpods, and how they would help the world heal and regrow. He had given himself a new title – Chief Observer of Surface Restoration. He observed plants from the seedpod islands replacing local species that could not adapt to the faint sunlight now reaching the surface.

Based on his findings, he guessed that in a few years the land would reach what he called "full bloom."

———

Nora left the observation platform to meet Lina – they usually spent evenings with a glass of wine and small – and sometimes not-so-small – talk in a local restaurant. Lina was now working in the office of President Kora Skyheart, the elected head of the Coalition for the next two years. Lina hated the job, politics, and being grounded. Her time in a team had taught her to value diplomacy over blunt force. She proved skilled at advocating for new technologies, knowledge exchange, and progress. Through her role in the Coalition government, less developed states gained access to modern tools and began rising as players on the post-war stage. The Coalition welcomed them, already preparing for the next war with the Empire.

Nora had met President Kora once and told her about her nephew. She felt the old woman's grief, but Kora collected herself and said with a sad smile, "My boy is now one with the wind and watching over us. What more could a wind reader dream of?"

Lina occasionally raised this subject, touching the pendant she still wore. Once, she asked Nora what she thought of Toryn's fate, expressing her desire to visit Madrid Station one day. They often spoke of a possibility of a person existing as an everlasting consciousness within the azurium network.

Nora had not seen the Messenger since Madrid Station, but Kora's words – that he was watching over them – warmed her heart and gave her hope. A needed hope for her – and for a world stirring from its long winter's sleep.

TABLE OF CONTENTS

PART 1: ABOVE THE STORM

PART 2: BELOW THE STORM